Anonymous

The Lincoln Memorial

A record of the life, assassination, and obsequies of the martyred president

Anonymous

The Lincoln Memorial
A record of the life, assassination, and obsequies of the martyred president

ISBN/EAN: 9783337402754

Printed in Europe, USA, Canada, Australia, Japan

Cover: Foto ©Raphael Reischuk / pixelio.de

More available books at **www.hansebooks.com**

LINCOLN MEMORIAL.

The Early Home of Abraham Lincoln as it now stands in Elizabethtown, Hardin County, Kentucky

NEW YORK:
BUNCE & HUNTINGTON, PUBLISHERS,

THE

LINCOLN MEMORIAL:

A RECORD

OF

THE LIFE, ASSASSINATION,

AND

OBSEQUIES

OF THE

MARTYRED PRESIDENT.

NEW YORK:
BUNCE & HUNTINGTON,
540 BROADWAY.
1865

PREFACE.

THE death of President Lincoln and the terrible circumstances attending it, his funeral rites, solemn beyond example in history, and the passage of his honored remains from city to city for thousands of miles, created too deep an impression not to make the scenes and the words spoken by the great and eloquent in that season matters to be preserved as a record for after time and thought.

To meet this feeling, the present Memorial has been compiled. Original matter has been furnished, and the full reports of the press, in all parts of the country, freely used.

Giving a sketch of the late President's life, an account of his death and obsequies, the effect here and in Europe, it may be said to include all that is worthy of preservation, and, as such, is submitted to the public.

CONTENTS.

I.

LIFE OF ABRAHAM LINCOLN.

I.

LIFE OF ABRAHAM LINCOLN.

THERE is perhaps no point in which all human history, and the records of inspiration, are more clearly illustrative of each other than this—that Providence, in working out the great and mighty revolutions in the civil and social, no less than in the religious order, chooses the unknown, the lowly, the apparently unfit. But though drawn from obscurity, these instruments in the Mighty Hand are always intrinsically great—great in clearness of thought, great in calm deliberation, great in earnestness, in unaffectedness, in unselfish devotion to duty.

Thus viewed, Abraham Lincoln was truly great. Raised suddenly to the station which Washington was the first to fill, his sudden elevation sent a pang to the hearts of many, as though a sad degeneracy had fallen on our times; while others shuddered at the unequalness of the man for the most critical position which had yet arisen in American affairs.

Four years have so changed all this, that his name is universally revered; the great qualities which he really possessed, his knowledge of men, his uprightness and honesty, his kindliness of heart, his extreme caution in the unnumbered difficulties that daily arose in the constant civil and military emergencies, with a firmness that was never swerved by flattery or fear—all these, and the great results effected under his administration, have given him in the heart of the people a place second only to that of the Father of his Country. The sudden and terrible assassination which so suddenly cut short his second administrative term, has embalmed his memory, and in its very suddenness convinced men of all opinions and all parties of the extent and greatness of the national loss.

Sprung from the people, with no ancestral renown or services, with none of the auxiliaries which wealth, social position, or academic honors afford the mass of aspirants to great public honors, Abraham Lincoln rose step by step to the highest station in the gift of his fellow-countrymen. And although party virulence, which in our press has no check, persistently coupled his name with odious epithets, there has never been the slightest charge of any thing to detract from a high moral character. He was too great to stoop to vile means to accomplish his ends.

No Cæsar he, whom we lament,
A Man without a precedent,
    Sent, it would seem, to do
    His work, and perish too!

The study of the life of the unpretending, homely Abraham Lincoln is, then, a study for the American people and the world. He is a man possible only under our form of government, and in life and death a proof of its excellence. He is no common man whose loss is so deplored; he is no common man whose loss a ruler-choosing-nation sees no one to fill in its confidence and affection.

Some industrious genealogist, tracing out the Lincoln family in America, will hereafter tell us of the original ancestor of the President in this country. He was, from all that family tradition preserves, one of the clear-headed honest Friends who came to settle the colony granted to William Penn, and made his new home in Berks county, Pennsylvania. Some of his descendants pushing southward became citizens of Virginia, and here in Rockingham county was born Abraham Lincoln, the grandfather of the President, and the eldest of five brothers. The influence of affairs had transformed the staid Quakers into hardy backwoodsmen, and when Boone laid open to the adventurous the rich lands of Kentucky, then an outlying wilderness forming the western part of Virginia, Abraham Lincoln was one of the host of stalwart pioneers who, unheralded and unsung, pushed westward to found on the southern shore of the Ohio the high-toned State of Kentucky.

The young pioneer settled, it is generally supposed, on Floyd's Creek, and rearing there the log-cabin of a pioneer, cleared the forest to begin the necessary cultivation. But before he could see his labors crowned with success, or a home for himself and his children blooming in the wilderness, the torrent of Indian war, so cruelly kept alive by the English authorities against us in the Revolution, swept that exposed frontier, and Abraham Lincoln was killed and scalped by the savages in one of their forays.

The widow, with her little family, was left thus bereft of all, far from the aid of civilized society; but her boys struggled manfully, and Thomas, the youngest, with the clear hereditary head and self-reliance, stood the buffets of fortune till he reached manhood. He married, in 1806, Lucy Hankes, and settled in Hardin county. Here, on a knoll that rises from the banks of Nolen Creek, and about a mile above Hodgensville, Abraham Lincoln was born, on the 12th of February, 1809, and here he remained until his sixth year, when his father removed a few miles further on to a new location.

At seven years of age he was sent to school to a Mr. Hazel, carrying with him an old copy of Dilworth's spelling-book, one of the three volumes that constituted the family library. He was also for a time under another teacher, of the name of Riney; but the whole period during which he was enabled to enjoy any of the advantages of a school was extremely limited, not exceeding at most a few months.

The family, as will readily be seen, were poor, and in a poor part of the country. Mr. U. F. Linder, a leading Democratic lawyer of Illinois, a friend of Mr. Lincoln from boyhood, says: —"I knew his father and his relatives in Kentucky. They were a good family. They were poor, and the very poorest people, I might say, of the middle classes; but they were true." In a slave State, the position of the poor white was one utterly disheartening and crushing; and Thomas Lincoln, after battling wearily with his disadvantages, resolved to strike forward to a field opening greater prospects of success for himself and his children. When Abraham was in his eighth year, his father sold his clearing, and, placing all his household goods on a raft, sought a new home in the wilds of Spencer county, Indiana. After seven days' journey through an almost uninhabited country, and, for part of the way, actually hewing a road through the woods, the pioneers reached their new home.

A log hut soon rose in the clearing, Abraham giving such

assistance as his age and strength permitted, for he was never in life an idler. His life here during the next twelve years furnishes few incidents. For education, his opportunities were even less than in his native State; but he was ambitious, and sought to improve. Books were not more plenty in the cabins of the neighbors than in the humble domicil of the Lincolns; but Abraham sought out all that he could find, and, aided by his mother, he read them with avidity. A copy of Weems's Life of Washington, which he read, impressed him deeply, and the poor boy, little dreaming that he was ever to succeed the Father of his Country as the head of the Government, paid in toil for the pleasure which the perusal of the life afforded him. The rain at night, penetrating through the chinks of the cabin, spoiled the book, and some days' hard labor for the owner was the boy's only means of compensation, and this, with his proverbial honesty, he insisted on performing.

The arrival of a young man in the neighborhood who could write, and who kindly offered to teach young Lincoln, was indeed an epoch. Already filled with the idea that he needed but education to rise, and that he had good sound sense enough to fight his way, he allowed no occasion of improvement to escape.

He was now to lose his mother—his almost only teacher— a good, simple, pious woman, who sought to instil into her son the principles of virtue and religion, and give him such education as her ability afforded. Abraham deeply deplored her loss, and his first letter was one addressed to the Rev. Mr. Elkins, a travelling preacher and an old friend of his mother's, requesting him to come and perform funeral exercises over her grave. Three months after, the clergyman and the friends assembled to pay a last tribute to one universally beloved and respected.

A brief term at a school established near them, and we find Abraham, at the age of eighteen, seeking employment and preparing to relieve his father by doing for himself. A neighbor starting with a boat-load of stores for New Orleans invited him to join him, and the young man readily accepted the opportunity. In March, 1830, his father, who had married again, removed to a spot on the north side of the Sangamon river, ten miles west of Decatur, in Macon county, Illinois; and Abraham, after assisting him in the removal, as well as in erecting a new house, split the rails for a fence—an incident which was taken up in the canvass for the Presidency, and made his rails as famous as Harrison's log cabin.

Working around by day, studying and improving himself by night, the young man pushed ahead, and, in the spring of 1831, was taken into the employ of a speculating trader named Denton Offutt, who had noticed his good qualities. With him, he took a boat again to New Orleans, but, on its return, the boat got aground near New Salem, in Illinois, near a mill and store. Offutt, deeming it a place for an opening, got possession of the place and opened the store, Lincoln being his clerk and manager. He soon made his mark: an attempt of a gang of the bullies of the place to give him a beating resulted in the defeat of their champion by the tall, sinewy stranger, who at once became a favorite with those who guaged men by their physical endurance and courage, while his affable manners, his unfailing cheerfulness, his ready wit, and his stories, made him a favorite with all. A store was soon his own; but he was too honest and too kind-hearted to drive sharp bargains, and soon found himself in difficulties which it required years of subsequent struggle to clear away, but which he allowed to stand no longer than his ability to discharge them. Honest Abraham Lincoln knew no bankrupt's discharge, but a receipt in full on payment in full.

The office of postmaster of New Salem, a petty office indeed, was his first public position, and one which gave him intense pleasure from the opportunity of reading it afforded him; and it is not a little remarkable that he began life, we may say, by serving the General Government in a civil, and, soon after, in a military capacity.

While still a clerk, the Black Hawk war broke out, and a company of volunteers was raised which elected him captain. He marched his force to Beardstown, but they were not called into active service during their term of thirty days; yet, with persistence characteristic of him, he enlisted in another company, and remained in service till the war was ended.

This early choice of one who was at most a clerk and hand in a country store, shows how clearly his fellow-citizens had recognized him as one born to be a ruler of men. At the next election for members of the Legislature, he was taken up as the candidate of his district, and so completely united the votes of all parties in his precinct that he received every vote but seven out of 284; and though he was defeated in the district at large, it was the only occasion in which he failed in a popular election.

About this time, by the advice and aid of John Calhoun, afterwards prominent in the troubles in Kansas, as president of the Lecompton Constitutional Convention, Mr. Lincoln studied surveying, and soon met with sufficient employment; but difficulties weighed so heavily on him, that his instruments were actually at one time seized for debt.

He still took an active part in politics, and in August, 1834, was elected to the Legislature by a large majority. In this new field he learned much. He was a persistent student, and had already, by close application, made up for much of the deficiency of his early education. He analyzed all he read, and gave up nothing till he had thoroughly mastered it. This gave him a correctness and precision of thought which never failed him. Naturally modest, he discharged his legislative duties without any of the parade or elation which makes some inexperienced members mere tools of the wily politician or personally ridiculous. His clearness and eloquence struck the Hon. John T. Stuart, one of his fellow-members, and he urged the young member to study law.

Acting on this advice, he set himself to Blackstone with ardor, his favorite retreat being a wooded knoll near New Salem, where, stretched under an oak, he would pore over the doctrines of the Common Law, utterly unconscious of all passing around him, and impressing some, at least, of his neighbors with doubts of his entire sanity. In 1836, he was admitted to the bar, and was the same year again elected to the Legislature —an honor conferred on him by his fellow-citizens successively in 1838 and 1840.

This closed for a time his political career. During the eight years of his service in the assembly, a great rage prevailed for public improvements; but we find Mr. Lincoln's name recorded in favor of none of those extravagant projects which were subsequently so disastrous. He always favored improvements which his practical sound sense commended as judicious. During his first term of service, he was a member of the Committee on Public Accounts and Expenditures. Every act in favor of education, agricultural improvements, the relief of the struggling poor man, met his warm support. Questions of a national character seldom came up; but pro-slavery resolutions having been presented to the House, in 1837, Mr. Lincoln, in the following protest, recorded views, which show how early he formed his opinion and how little he ever swerved from it:—

MARCH, 3, 1837.

The following protest was presented to the House, which was read and ordered to be spread on the journals, to wit:—

"Resolutions upon the subject of domestic slavery having passed both branches of the General Assembly, at its present session, the undersigned hereby protest against the passage of the same.

"They believe that the institution of slavery is founded on both injustice and bad policy; but that the promulgation of abolition doctrines tends rather to increase than abate its evils.

"They believe that the Congress of the United States has no power, under the Constitution, to interfere with the institution of slavery in the different States.

"They believe that the Congress of the United States has the power, under the Constitution, to abolish slavery in the District of Columbia; but that the power ought not to be exercised, unless at the request of the people of said District.

"The difference between these opinions and those contained in the said resolutions, is their reason for entering this protest.

"(Signed)

"DAN. STONE,
"A. LINCOLN,
"*Representatives from the County of Sangamon.*"

In 1837, he moved to Springfield, and became a partner of his friend, Mr. Stuart, the connection thus formed continuing till the election of Mr. Stuart to Congress, when Mr. Lincoln became the partner of Judge Logan, one of the leaders of the bar.

Mr. Lincoln's characteristics as an advocate were an earnestness and sincerity of manner, and a directness, conciseness, and strength of style; he appealed, at other times, to the weapons of good-humored ridicule as ably as to the heavier arms of forensic combat. He was strongest in civil cases, but in a criminal cause that enlisted his sympathy he was also great. It was then that the advocate's convictions, presented to the jury in terse and forcible yet eloquent language, sometimes outweighed the charge of the judge. Juries listened to him and concurred in his arguments; for his known truth had preceded his arguments, and he triumphed. There might be law and evidence against him, but the belief that Lincoln was *right*, nothing could shake in the minds of those who knew the man.

He prepared his cases with infinite care, when he had nothing but technical work before him. No detail of the affair escaped him. All the parts were perfectly fitted together, and the peculiar powers of his keen analytic mind were brought into full play.

Lincoln did not grow rich at the law, though possessing a decent competence and owing no man any thing. No early friend of Lincoln ever appealed to him in vain; and his biographers relate his defence of young Armstrong, the son of an early benefactor, for whom he secured an acquittal when every thing seemed to render his conviction certain.

Another old friend, U. F. Linder, Esq., a member of the Illinois bar, at a meeting of the profession called when the sad tidings of Mr. Lincoln's death arrived, alluding to a case in which his own son was involved in a similar difficulty, said :—

"On that occasion, many seemed to avail themselves of the opportunity to wreak vengeance upon me in the death of my son. I wrote to Mr. Lincoln. I was in a quarter of the country where I knew he was a tower of strength, where his name raised up friends, where his arguments at law had more power than the instructions of the court. I feared—many of his political friends being united against my son—that his services and his talents might be enlisted against him. I wrote to him, giving him all the circumstances, telling him of my wife's grief and my own, and soliciting that he would come and assist me to defend my son ; that I thought he had been employed against him. I preserved his letter for a long time. I wish I had it now ; I should rejoice in its possession. The sum of it was this : he condoled with me and my wife in our misfortune, and assured us that no matter what business he might be engaged in, he would come ; and he was truly sorry that I supposed that he would take part in the prosecution of the son of a friend of his. I had offered him a fee, and in that letter he also said that he knew of no act of his life that would justify me in supposing that he would take money from me or any dear friend for assisting in the defence of the life of a child. I give this as a proof of his friendship; and that friendship has been cherished by me through all mutations of life. In politics we have ever been opposed; but I thank God to-day that he always was my friend."

Meantime, in the year 1842, Lincoln married a woman worthy to be the companion of his progress towards honor and distinction. Miss Mary Todd, who became his wife, is the daughter of Robert Todd, of Lexington, Kentucky, a man well known in that State, and at one period the clerk of the lower house of Congress. At the time of her marriage, Miss Todd was the belle of Springfield society—accomplished and intellectual, and possessing all the social graces native in the women of Kentucky.

The fruit of their Union were four sons—Robert Lincoln, now a captain on General Grant's staff, born in 1843; a second son, born in 1846, and William, born in 1850, both of whom are dead; and Thaddeus, born in 1853, who stands beside his illustrious father in the last photograph taken of the President.

It gives some idea of the prominence of Mr. Lincoln in Illinois, that, though elected to the Legislature only in 1834, he was a Whig candidate for Presidential electors at every election from 1836 to 1852. An early and warm admirer of Henry Clay, he came forward, in 1844, and stumped the entire State of Illinois in his favor, and then crossed into Indiana, attracting attention by the homely force, humor, energy, and eloquence of his addresses. Thus thrown again into active politics, he was elected to Congress in 1846, from the Central District of Illinois, by a majority of 1,500, being the only Whig member from the State.

Called now into the great council of the nation, Mr. Lincoln took his seat among great men. In the Senate, Clay, Calhoun, Webster, Benton, still shaped the destinies and restrained the passions of men; and men of great ability stood forth in the lower House. Mr. Lincoln was opposed to the annexation of Texas and to the Mexican war. Deeming unfounded the assertion of President Polk, that American blood had been shed on American soil, he offered, on the 22d of December, the following resolutions:—

"*Whereas*, the President of the United States, in his Message of May 11, 1846, has declared that 'the Mexican government refused to receive him [the envoy of the United States], or listen to his propositions, but, after a long-continued series of menaces, have at last invaded *our territory*, and shed the blood of our fellow-citizens on *our own soil.*'

"And again, in his Message of December 8, 1846, that 'we had ample cause of war against Mexico long before the breaking out of hostilities; but even then we forbore to take redress into our own hands, until Mexico basely became the aggressor, by invading *our soil* in hostile array, and shedding the blood of our citizens.'

"And yet again, in his Message of December 7, 1847, 'The Mexican government refused even to hear the terms of adjustment which he (our minister of peace) was authorized to propose, and finally, under wholly unjustifiable pretexts, involved the two countries in war, by invading the Territory of the State of Texas, striking the first blow, and shedding the blood of our citizens on *our own soil.*'

"And whereas this House is desirous to obtain a full knowledge of all the facts which go to establish whether the particular spot on which the blood of our citizens was so shed, was, or was not, at that time, *our own soil.* Therefore,

"*Resolved, by the House of Representatives,* That the President of the United States be respectfully requested to inform this House—

"1st. Whether the spot on which the blood of our citizens was shed, as in his memorial declared, was, or was not, within the territory of Spain, at least, after the treaty of 1819, until the Mexican revolution.

"2d. Whether that spot is, or is not, within the territory which was wrested from Spain by the revolutionary government of Mexico.

"3d. Whether that spot is, or is not, within a settlement of people, which settlement has existed ever since long before the Texas revolution, and until its inhabitants fled before the approach of the United States Army.

"4th. Whether that settlement is, or is not, isolated from any and all other settlements of the Gulf and Rio Grande on the south and west, and of wide uninhabited regions on the north and east.

"5th. Whether the people of that settlement, or a majority of them, have ever submitted themselves to the government or laws of Texas, or of the United States, of consent or of compulsion, either of accepting office or voting at elections, or paying taxes, or serving on juries, or having process served on them, or in any other way.

"6th. Whether the people of that settlement did, or did not, flee at the approaching of the United States Army, leaving unprotected their homes and their growing crops *before* the blood was shed, as in the message stated; and whether the first blood so shed was, o:

was not, shed within the inclosure of one of the people who had thus fled from it.

"7th. Whether our *citizens* whose blood was shed, as in his message declared, were, or were not, at that time, armed officers and soldiers sent into that settlement by the military order of the President, through the Secretary of War.

"8th. Whether the military force of the United States was, or was not, so sent into that settlement after General Taylor had more than once intimated to the War Department that, in his opinion, no such movement was necessary to the defence or protection of Texas."

These resolutions sufficiently evince Mr. Lincoln's sense of justice. He was accused afterwards of siding with the enemy in the war. He opposed the war as unjust; but it was a war of the country, and it was equally just that the country should pay the soldiers called to the field; and Mr. Lincoln never voted against, or avoided voting for, any bill for army pay or supplies or the relief of the soldiers.

When, in 1848, Mr. Gott, of New York, introduced a resolution instructing the Committee on the District of Columbia to report a bill for the abolition of the slave-trade in the District, Mr. Lincoln, after consulting Mayor Seaton, of Washington, proposed, on the 10th of January, that the committee should be instructed to report a bill forbidding the sale, beyond the District of Columbia, of any slave born within its limits, or the removal of slaves from the District, except such servants as were in attendance upon their masters temporarily residing at Washington; establishing an apprenticeship of twenty-one years for all slaves born within the District subsequent to the year 1850; providing for their emancipation at the expiration of the apprenticeship; authorizing the United States to buy and emancipate all slaves within the District, whose owners should desire to set them free in that manner; finally, submitting the bill to a vote of the citizens of the District for approval.

The Wilmot proviso had made its appearance in August, 1847, during the previous session, but frequently came up in that on which Mr. Lincoln served. He steadily supported it, and, as he said in one of his debates with Judge Douglas, "had the pleasure of voting for it, in one way or another, about forty times."

Mr. Lincoln was a member of the Philadelphia convention

which nominated General Taylor for President, in 1848, and, during the campaign, visited the East, speaking at New Bedford and elsewhere. Illinois gave her vote, however, to General Cass. In 1849, Mr. Lincoln retired from Congress, where he had always maintained a dignified and respectable position. He was the unsuccessful candidate for United States Senator, General Shields having been elected.

After his retirement from Congress, Mr. Lincoln devoted himself, with greater earnestness than ever before, to the duties of his profession, and extended his business and repute. He did not reappear in the political arena until 1852, when his name was placed on the Scott electoral ticket.

In the canvass of that year, so disastrous to the Whig party throughout the country, Lincoln appeared several times before the people of his State as the advocate of Scott's claims for the Presidency. But the prospect was everywhere so disheartening, and in Illinois the cause was so utterly desperate, that the energies of the Whigs were paralyzed, and Lincoln did less in this Presidential struggle than in any in which he had ever engaged.

During that lethargy which preceded the dissolution of his party, he had almost relinquished political aspirations. Successful in his profession, happy in his home, secure in the affection of his neighbors, with books, competence, and leisure, ambition could not tempt him.

When the term of General Shields as Senator from Illinois expired in 1854, a close contest ensued in the State legislature on the choice of his successor. The Whig party was fast melting away, and the new Republican party had not yet assumed form. Mr. Lincoln was again a candidate for the Senate, but as some anti-Nebraska Democrats adhered to Mr. Trumbull, Mr. Lincoln gave way in his usual unselfish spirit, viewing the choice of Mr. Trumbull more safe than that of some less decided man.

It was in the same spirit that he declined the nomination for Governor, when tendered by the anti-Nebraska Democrats: he felt that as an old Whig campaigner he was necessarily still an object of antagonism, and till the old party lines disappeared, some men who had mingled less prominently in the arena of political strife, would be more certain of success. Governor Bissell was then nominated and elected.

When the Republican party finally took shape, and met in convention to nominate its candidates for the Presidency and Vice-Presidency, Abraham Lincoln stood so high that he was one of those at once proposed, and received one hundred and two votes for the second office. He stood at the head of the Fremont electoral ticket of Illinois, and labored for the success of that candidate, although the country was not yet prepared to adopt the Republican doctrines.

In 1858 it was determined in Illinois to give the senatorial question the form of a contest by electing a Legislature pledged either to Douglas or Lincoln. A most extraordinary canvass then ensued. The two candidates stumped the State, and at last came into the presence of each other, giving the contest all the interest of direct personal debate.

Mr. Lincoln's first speech was made at Springfield on the 17th of June, before the State convention which nominated him.

The reply made by Douglas to this speech was on the occasion of his reception at Chicago in the July following. Lincoln was present, and spoke in the same city on the next day. Two more great speeches by Douglas, and one more speech by Lincoln were made before they entered the lists in debate.

In one of those speeches, Douglas found occasion—for he was then addressing Lincoln's old friends at Springfield—to pay his tribute to the worth and greatness of his opponent:

"You all know that I am an amiable, good-natured man, and I take great pleasure in bearing testimony to the fact that Mr. Lincoln is a kind-hearted, amiable, good-natured gentleman, with whom no man has a right to pick a quarrel, even if he wanted one. He is a worthy gentleman. I have known him for twenty-five years, and there is no better citizen, and no kinder-hearted man. He is a fine lawyer, possesses high ability, and there is no objection to him, except the monstrous revolutionary doctrines with which he is identified."

On the 24th of July, Lincoln wrote to Douglas proposing debates.

The challenge was accepted, and seven debates followed, at Ottawa, Freeport, Jonesboro', Charleston, Galesburg, Quincy, and Alton. These are unsurpassed in our campaign annals for eloquence, ability, adroitness, or comprehensiveness. Mr. Doughas represented the moderate Democracy, and Mr. Lincoln the new Republicanism. The standing of the two men, antagonists well matched, and soon to be rival candidates on a wider field,—the one more polished, courtier-like, adroit; the other solid, earnest, clear-headed and persuasive,—gave their words no ordinary effect on the minds of men.

Mr. Lincoln was now fully roused, and during the canvass made more than fifty speeches in other parts of Illinois, till the State fairly shook with excitement. The result, while it showed the great influence of Mr. Lincoln, proved that many still hesitated. Mr. Douglas was elected to the Senate by a small majority, effected, his opponents claimed, by the unfair districting of the State. Mr. Lincoln thought more of the cause than of personal success. Being now in the field he extended his tour to other States, following Judge Douglas to Ohio, and in Kansas exciting hearty applause. A speech on National Policy at the Cooper Institute, New York, brought him before the Republicans of that city.

The National Convention of 1860, called by the party whose interests he considered those of right and justice, was convened on the 16th of May, in the Wigwam, an immense structure erected at Chicago. Governor Morgan, of New York, called to order, and George Ashmun, of Massachusetts, was chosen permanent president. It soon became evident that the delegates of the Republican party from all parts of the Union, came prepared to select for the nomination to the Presidency, one of two men, the experienced and polished William H. Seward, of New York, or the homely, clear-headed pioneer of the West, Abraham Lincoln, of Illinois. On the first ballot Seward received 173 votes and Lincoln 102; on the second Seward received 184 and Lincoln 181, but a third ballot showed that Mr. Seward's friends yielded the contest. Mr. Lincoln received 231 votes, and on motion of W. M. Evarts, of New York, the nomination was made unanimous.

Mr. Lincoln was at Springfield at the time, and when the message was brought from the telegraph office, showed little exultation, but simply remarking that there was a little woman at his house who would be glad to hear the news, went to the quiet residence, which was soon to be made familiar to all throughout the land.

The next day the excursion train arrived in Chicago with a large number of delegates, and the Committee appointed by the Convention to make Lincoln officially acquainted with his nomination.

The deputation was received at Mr. Lincoln's house, and when the guests had assembled in the parlor, Mr. Ashmun, the President of the Convention, said:

"I have, sir, the honor in behalf of the gentlemen who are present, a Committee appointed by the Republican Convention, recently assembled at Chicago, to discharge a most pleasant duty. We have come, sir, under a vote of instructions to that Committee, to notify you that you have been selected by the Convention of the Republicans at Chicago, for President of the United States. They instruct us, sir, to notify you of that selection, and that Committee deem it not only respectful to yourself, but appropriate to the important matter which they have in hand, that they should come in person, and present to you the authentic evidence of the action of the Convention; and, sir, without any phrase which shall either be considered personally plauditory to yourself, or which shall have any reference to the principles involved in the questions which are connected with your nomination, I desire to present to you the letter which has been prepared, and which informs you of the nomination, and with it the platform, resolutions, and sentiments which the Convention adopted. Sir, at your convenience we shall be glad to receive from you such a response as it may be your pleasure to give us."

To this address Mr. Lincoln listened with grave attention, and replied:

"MR. CHAIRMAN AND GENTLEMEN OF THE COMMITTEE:

"I tender to you, and through you to the Republican National Convention, and all the people represented in it, my profoundest thanks for the high honor done me, which you now formally announce. Deeply, and even painfully sensible of the great responsibility which is inseparable from this high honor—a responsibility which I could almost wish had fallen upon some one of the far more eminent men and experienced statesmen whose distinguished names were before the Convention—I shall, by your leave, consider more fully the resolutions of the Convention denominated the platform, and without unnecessary or unreasonable delay, respond to you, Mr. Chairman, in writing, not doubting that the platform will be found satisfactory, and the nomination gratefully accepted.

" And now I will not longer defer the pleasure of taking you, and each of you, by the hand."

Mr. Lincoln subsequently accepted the nomination in this formal letter:

"SPRINGFIELD, ILLINOIS, May 23, 1860.

" HON. GEORGE ASHMUN,
      ' President of the Republican National Convention :

" Sir : I accept the nomination tendered me by the Convention over which you presided, of which I am formally apprized in the letter of yourself and others acting as a Committee of the Convention for that purpose. The declaration of principles and sentiments which accompanies your letter meets my approval, and it shall be my care not to violate it, or disregard it in any part.

" Imploring the assistance of Divine Providence, and with due regard to the views and feelings of all who were represented in the Convention, to the rights of all the states and territories and people of the nation, to the inviolability of the Constitution, and the perpetual union, harmony, and prosperity of all, I am most happy to co-operate for the practical success of the principles declared by the Convention.

" Your obliged friend and fellow-citizen,

"ABRAHAM LINCOLN."

Emerson in his eloquent remarks, given in full in this volume, expresses well the despondency felt in the East on the announcement of Mr. Lincoln's nomination. To them he was an almost unknown, an unprepossessing man, apparently ill-fitted for the gravest crisis of American history. There was little in him to excite enthusiasm, but the party took up the ticket with zeal, and Mr. Lincoln stood before the people as a candidate for the Presidency. His party selected as their nominee for the Vice-Presidency, Hannibal Hamlin, a Senator from Maine. The Democratic party was rent in twain. The violence of Southern leaders, the imperiousness of their demands, and the manifest determination on their part to drive matters to a point where no solution but civil war was possible, had alarmed many life-long Democrats. A strong party rallied round Judge Douglas, of Illinois, believing that a moderate policy might yet secure under a Democratic President that return to calmness and reason, which was necessary for a compromise between the extreme elements agitating the country. But the action of the extreme Southern men broke up the Democratic convention at Charleston, and the delegates forming two different bodies, severally adopted platforms and nominated candidates. Stephen A. Douglas was the nominee of the moderate, with Herschell V. Johnson as candidate for Vice-President, while John C. Breckenridge, actually Vice-President of the United States, was the extreme Southern candidate for the Presidency, with Mr. Lane, of Oregon. As though this were not sufficient diversity, a fourth ticket was presented in the vain hope of healing dissensions, and under the name of the Union ticket offered to the votes of the people the names of John Bell, of Tennessee, for President, and Edward Everett, of Massachusetts, for Vice-President.

Never had the country seen an election which excited more general interest or deeper feeling. The result, however, was not doubtful. The Republicans were enthusiastic, organized, hopeful; the Democratic party rent in twain, was of course dispirited, and the Southern section seemed to court the defeat, whose certainty they had contrived, as a pretext for a movement already planned.

The Republicans, forming a body of nearly two millions of voters, carried for Mr. Lincoln the States of Maine, New Hampshire, Vermont, Massachusetts, Rhode Island, Connecticut, New York, Pennsylvania, Ohio, Indiana, Illinois, Michigan, Iowa, Wisconsin, Minnesota, and California, comprising all the free States, except New Jersey, which gave four votes to Mr. Lincoln and three to Mr. Douglas. Mr. Breckenridge received the electoral vote of all the slave States, except Kentucky, Tennessee, and Virginia, which voted for Bell. Douglas, once so popular, received only the vote of Missouri, and, as we have seen, part of that of New Jersey, although his popular vote was nearly half a million more than that of Mr. Breckenridge.

Thus was Mr. Lincoln chosen on the 6th of November, 1860, President of the United States, receiving in the electoral college 180 votes, representing sixteen States and 1,857,610 votes. To his election there existed no constitutional objection. His antagonist, Mr. Breckenridge, since a rebel general and Secretary of War, declared officially, as Vice-President of the United States, that Abraham Lincoln was lawfully elected President of the United States.

Here, in a manner, the history of his Administration begins.

The State of South Carolina, the very day after choosing electors, passed an act calling a Convention, and openly announced its determination not to submit to the election. How rapidly they followed up their determination by action, we need not detail here. While Mr. Lincoln awaited at Springfield the moment when he should proceed to Washington to enter on the duties of his office, the Southern States, unchecked, unimpeded, were seizing the arsenals, forts, custom-houses, navy yards, mints, and other property of the General Government, forming a Confederacy, adopting a Constitution, and proceeding to the choice of a President and Vice-President.

On the 11th of February, Mr. Lincoln left his home in Springfield. He could not conceal from himself the terrible task before him. To him the office of President was not to be one of quiet routine. In a few days, States that took part in the late election, would have chosen a President who would claim authority over nearly half the land, prepared to uphold that claim by force of arms. Impressed with the solemnity of the occasion, he bade farewell to his friends and neighbors in these words, which, read at the present time, have indeed a mournful interest:

"My Friends: No one not in my position can appreciate the sadness I feel at this parting. To this people I owe all that I am. Here I have lived more than a quarter of a century; here my children were born, and here one of them lies buried. I know not how soon I shall see you again. A duty devolves upon me which is, perhaps, greater than that which has devolved upon any other man since the days of Washington. He never would have succeeded except for the aid of Divine Providence, upon which he at all times relied. I feel that I cannot succeed without the same Divine aid which sustained him, and on the same Almighty Being I place my reliance for support; and I hope you, my friends, will all pray that I may receive that Divine assistance, without which I cannot succeed, but with which success is certain. Again I bid you all an affectionate farewell."

On the 13th, he reached Columbus, where he was formally welcomed in the Hall of the Assembly, at the State Capitol, by Lieutenant-Governor Kirk, on behalf of the Legislature. At this imposing reception he justified the silence which he had observed as to his policy, and again expressed his sense of the importance of the moment.

He was received enthusiastically at the different large cities on his route, and spoke freely on the various points of public policy likely to arise, impressing all with a sense of his uprightness, fairness, and desire to administer the Government with firmness. Of the South he spoke in terms of conciliation, believing, and wishing all to believe, that the Southern movement would soon die of itself.

At Philadelphia, the President elect visited Independence Hall, and in those walls, still echoing with the voices of the great patriot founders of the Republic, he was escorted to a platform prepared for the purpose, and after a few words of patriotic devotion to the flag, affirming that to his deliberate convictions of principle he must adhere, even if assassination were his fate, he raised the Stars and Stripes, amid the plaudits of thousands and the thunder of artillery.

At Harrisburg, information was brought to him that his life was to be attempted, as he passed through Baltimore, and he took an earlier train to baffle the plot. Many at the time treated this as an idle fear; but the evidence is beyond all dispute. Threats had been current that he would never live to be inaugurated, and during his journey an attempt was made to throw the train off the track, on the Toledo and Western Railroad, and a hand-grenade was found concealed in the train in which he left Cincinnati.

In Washington, preparations, such as were possible, were made, to prevent any act of violence on the day of inauguration. A large military force was in attendance, under the immediate command of General Scott, but nothing occurred to interrupt the harmony of the occasion. Mr. Lincoln proceeded to the Capitol with Mr. Buchanan, whose term of office expired, and the ceremony of inauguration took place, March 4th, 1861, in front of the Capitol, in presence of an immense multitude.

His inaugural address, delivered before taking the oath of office administered by Chief-Justice Taney, who thus lived to swear into their high position ten successive Presidents, was in these words:—

" FELLOW-CITIZENS OF THE UNITED STATES:

"In compliance with a custom as old as the Government itself, I appear before you to address you briefly, and to take, in your presence, the oath prescribed by the Constitution of the United States to be taken by the President, before he enters on the execution of his office.

"I do not consider it necessary, at present, for me to discuss those matters of administration about which there is no special anxiety or excitement. Apprehension seems to exist among the people of the Southern States, that, by the accession of a Republican Administration, their property and their peace and personal security are to be endangered. There has never been any reasonable cause for such apprehension. Indeed the most ample evidence to the contrary has all the while existed, and been open to their inspection. It is found in nearly all the published speeches of him who now addresses you. I do but quote from one of those speeches when I declare that 'I have no purpose, directly or indirectly, to interfere with the institution of slavery in the States where it exists.' I believe I have no lawful right to do so; and I have no inclination to do so. Those who nominated and elected me, did so with the full knowledge that I had made this, and made many similar declarations, and had never recanted them. And more than this, they placed in the platform, for my acceptance, and as a law to themselves and to me, the clear and emphatic resolution which I now read:—

"'*Resolved*, That the maintenance inviolate of the rights of the States, and especially the right of each State to order and control its own domestic institutions according to its own judgment exclusively, is essential to that balance of power on which the perfection and endurance of our political fabric depend; and we denounce the lawless invasion by armed force of the soil of any State or Territory, no matter under what pretext, as among the gravest of crimes.'

"I now reiterate these sentiments; and in doing so I only press upon the public attention the most conclusive evidence of which the case is susceptible, that the property, peace, and security of no section are to be in anywise endangered by the now incoming Administration.

"I add, too, that all the protection which, consistently with the Constitution and the laws, can be given, will be cheerfully given to all the States when lawfully demanded, for whatever cause, as cheerfully to one section as to another.

"There is much controversy about the delivering up of fugitives from service or labor. The clause I now read is as plainly written in the Constitution as any other of its provisions:—

"'No person held to service or labor in one State, under the laws thereof, escaping into another, shall, in consequence of any law or regulation therein, be discharged from such service or labor, but shall be delivered up on claim of the party to whom such service or labor may be due.'

" It is scarcely questioned that this provision was intended by those who made it for the reclaiming of what we call fugitive slaves; and the intention of the lawgiver is the law.

" All members of Congress swear their support to the whole Constitution—to this provision as well as any other. To the proposition, then, that slaves whose cases come within the terms of this clause, ' shall be delivered up,' their oaths are unanimous. Now, if they would make the effort in good temper, could they not, with nearly equal unanimity, frame and pass a law by means of which to keep good that unanimous oath?

" There is some difference of opinion whether this clause should be enforced by national or by State authority; but surely that difference is not a very material one. If the slave is to be surrendered, it can be of but little consequence to him or to others by which authority it is done; and should any one, in any case, be content that this oath shall go unkept on a merely unsubstantial controversy as to how it shall be kept?

" Again, in any law upon this subject, ought not all the safeguards of liberty known in the civilized and humane jurisprudence to be introduced, so that a free man be not, in any case, surrendered as a slave? And might it not be well, at the same time, to provide by law for the enforcement of that clause in the Constitution, which guarantees that ' the citizens of each State shall be entitled to all the privileges and immunities of citizens in the several States?'

" I take the official oath to-day with no mental reservations, and with no purpose to construe the Constitution or laws by any hypercritical rules; and while I do not choose now to specify particular acts of Congress as proper to be enforced, I do suggest that it will be much safer for all, both in official and private stations, to conform to and abide by all those acts which stand unrepealed, than to violate any of them, trusting to find impunity in having them held to be unconstitutional.

" It is seventy-two years since the first inauguration of a President under our national Constitution. During that period, fifteen different and very distinguished citizens have, in succession, administered the executive branch of the Government. They have conducted it through many perils, and generally with great success. Yet, with all this scope for precedent, I now enter upon the same task, for the brief constitutional term of four years, under great and peculiar difficulties.

" A disruption of the Federal Union, heretofore only menaced, is now formidably attempted. I hold that in the contemplation of universal law and of the Constitution, the Union of these States is perpetual. Perpetuity is implied, if not expressed, in the fundamental law of all national governments. It is safe to assert that no government proper ever had a provision in its organic law for its own termination. Continue to execute all the express provisions of our national Constitution, and the Union will endure forever, it being impossible to destroy it except by some action not provided for in the instrument itself.

" Again, if the United States be not a Government proper, but an association of States in the nature of a contract merely, can it, as a contract, be peaceably unmade by less than all the parties who made it ? One party to a contract may violate it—break it, so to speak; but does it not require all to lawfully rescind it ? Descending from these general principles, we find the proposition that, in legal contemplation, the Union is perpetual, confirmed by the history of the Union itself.

" The Union is much older than the Constitution. It was formed, in fact, by the Articles of Association, in 1774. It was matured and continued in the Declaration of Independence, in 1776. It was further matured, and the faith of all the then thirteen States expressly plighted and engaged that it should be perpetual, by the Articles of Confederation, in 1778; and, finally, in 1787, one of the declared objects for ordaining and establishing the Constitution was to form a more perfect Union. But if the destruction of the Union by one or by a part only of the States be lawfully possible, the Union is less than before, the Constitution having lost the vital element of perpetuity.

" It follows, from these views, that no State, upon its own mere motion, can lawfully get out of the Union; that resolves and ordinances to that effect are legally void; and that acts of violence within any State or States against the authority of the United States are insurrectionary or revolutionary, according to circumstances.

" I therefore consider that, in view of the Constitution and the laws, the Union is unbroken, and to the extent of my ability, I shall take care, as the Constitution itself expressly enjoins upon me, that the laws of the Union shall be faithfully executed in all the States. Doing this, which I deem to be only a simple duty on my part, I shall perfectly perform it, so far as is practicable, unless my rightful masters, the American people, shall withhold the requisition, or, in some authoritative manner, direct the contrary.

" I trust this will not be regarded as a menace, but only as the declared purpose of the Union that it will constitutionally defend and maintain itself.

"In doing this there need be no bloodshed or violence; and there shall be none, unless it is forced upon the national authority.

"The power confided to me *will be used to hold, occupy, and possess the property and places belonging to the Government,* and collect the duties and imposts; but, beyond what may be necessary for these objects, there will be no invasion, no using of force against or among the people anywhere.

"Where hostility to the United States shall be so great and so universal as to prevent competent resident citizens from holding the Federal offices, there will be no attempt to force obnoxious strangers among the people that object. While strict legal right may exist of the Government to enforce the exercise of these offices, the attempt to do so would be so irritating, and so nearly impracticable withal, that I deem it better to forego for the time the uses of such offices.

"The mails, unless repelled, will continue to be furnished to all parts of the Union.

"So far as possible, the people everywhere shall have that sense of perfect security which is most favorable to calm thought and reflection.

"The course here indicated will be followed, unless current events and experience shall show a modification or change to be proper; and in every case and exigency my best discretion will be exercised according to the circumstances actually existing, and with a view and hope of a peaceful solution of the national troubles, and the restoration of fraternal sympathies and affections.

"That there are persons, in one section or another, who seek to destroy the Union at all events, and are glad of any pretext to do it, I will neither affirm nor deny. But if there be such, I need address no word to them.

"To those, however, who really love the Union, may I not speak, before entering upon so grave a matter as the destruction of our national fabric, with all its benefits, its memories, and its hopes? Would it not be well to ascertain why we do it? Will you hazard so desperate a step, while any portion of the ills you fly from have no real existence? Will you, while the certain ills you fly to, are greater than all the real ones you fly from? Will you risk the commission of so feeble a mistake? All profess to be content in the Union if all constitutional rights can be maintained. Is it true, then, that any right, plainly written in the Constitution, has been denied? I think not. Happily the human mind is so constituted, that no party can reach to the audacity of doing this.

Think, if you can, of a single instance in which a plainly-written provision of the Constitution has ever been denied. If, by the mere force of numbers, a majority should deprive a minority of any clearly-written constitutional right, it might, in a moral point of view, justify revolution; it certainly would, if such right were a vital one. But such is not our case.

"All the vital rights of minorities and of individuals are so plainly assured to them by affirmations and negations, guarantees and prohibitions in the Constitution, that controversies never rise concerning them. But no organic law can ever be framed with a provision specifically applicable to every question which may occur in practical administration. No foresight can anticipate, nor any document of reasonable length contain, express provisions for all possible questions. Shall fugitives from labor be surrendered by national or by State authorities? The Constitution does not expressly say. Must Congress protect slavery in the Territories? The Constitution does not expressly say. From questions of this class spring all our constitutional controversies, and we divide upon them into majorities and minorities.

"If the minority will not acquiesce, the majority must, or the Government must cease. There is no alternative for continuing the Government but acquiescence on the one side or the other. If a minority in such a case will secede rather than acquiesce, they make a precedent which, in turn, will ruin and divide them; for a minority of their own will secede from them whenever a majority refuses to be controlled by such a minority. For instance, why not any portion of a new confederacy, a year or two hence, arbitrarily secede again, precisely as portions of the present Union now claim to secede from it? All who cherish disunion sentiments are now being educated to the exact temper of doing this. Is there such perfect identity of interests among the States to compose a new Union as to produce harmony only, and prevent renewed secession? Plainly, the central idea of secession is the essence of anarchy.

"A majority, held in restraint by constitutional check and limitations, and always changing easily with deliberate changes of popular opinions and sentiments, is the only true sovereign of a free people. Whoever rejects it, does, of necessity, fly to anarchy or to despotism. Unanimity is impossible; the rule of a majority, as a permanent arrangement, is wholly inadmissible. So that, rejecting the majority principle, anarchy or despotism in some form is all that is left.

"I do not forget the position assumed by some, that constitutional questions are to be decided by the Supreme Court, nor do I deny that such decisions must be binding in any case upon the parties to a suit, as to the object of that suit, while they are also entitled to very high respect and consideration in all parallel cases by all other departments of the government : and while it is obviously possible that such decision may be erroneous in any given case, still the evil effect following it, being limited to that particular case, with the chance that it may be overruled and never become a precedent for other cases, can better be borne than could the evils of a different practice.

"At the same time, the candid citizen must confess that, if the policy of the government upon the vital questions affecting the whole people is to be irrevocably fixed by the decisions of the Supreme Court, the instant they are made, as in ordinary litigation, between parties in personal actions, the people will have ceased to be their own masters, unless having to that extent practically resigned their government into the hands of that eminent tribunal.

"Nor is there in this view any assault upon the court or the judges. It is a duty from which they may not shrink, to decide cases properly brought before them ; and it is no fault of theirs if others seek to turn their decisions to political purposes. One section of our country believes slavery is right, and ought to be extended; while the other believes it is wrong, and ought not to be extended; and this is the only substantial dispute ; and the fugitive slave clause of the Constitution, and the law for the suppression of the foreign slave-trade, are each as well enforced, perhaps, as any law can ever be in a community where the moral sense of the people imperfectly supports the law itself. The great body of the people abide by the dry legal obligation in both cases, and a few break over in each. This, I think, cannot be perfectly cured, and it would be worse, in both cases, after the separation of the sections, than before. The foreign slave-trade, now imperfectly suppressed, would be ultimately revived, without restriction in one section ; while fugitive slaves, now only partially surrendered, would not be surrendered at all by the other.

" Physically speaking, we cannot separate—we cannot remove our respective sections from each other, nor build an impassable wall between them. A husband and wife may be divorced, and go out of the presence and beyond the reach of the other, but the different parts of our country cannot do that. They cannot but remain face to face ; an intercourse, either amicable or hostile, must continue between them. Is it possible, then, to make that intercourse more advantageous or more satisfactory after separation than before ? Can aliens make treaties easier than friends can make laws ? Can treaties be more faithfully enforced between aliens than laws can among friends ? Suppose you go to war, you cannot

3

fight always ; and when, after much loss on both sides, and no gain
on either, you cease fighting, the identical questions as to terms of
intercourse are again upon you.

" This country, with its institutions, belongs to the people who
inhabit it. Whenever they shall grow weary of the existing government, they can exercise their constitutional right of amending,
or their revolutionary right to dismember or overthrow it. I cannot
be ignorant of the fact that many worthy and patriotic citizens are
desirous of having the national Constitution amended. While I
make no recommendation of amendment, I fully recognize the full
authority of the people over the whole subject, to be exercised in
either of the modes prescribed in the instrument itself, and I should,
under existing circumstances, favor, rather than oppose, a fair opportunity being afforded the people to act upon it.

" I will venture to add that to me the convention mode seems
preferable, in that it allows amendments to originate with the people themselves, instead of only permitting them to take or reject
propositions originated by others not especially chosen for the purpose, and which might not be precisely such as they would wish
either to accept or refuse. I understand that a proposed amendment to the Constitution (which amendment, however, I have not
seen) has passed Congress, to the effect that the Federal Government shall never interfere with the domestic institutions of States,
including that of persons held to service. To avoid misconstruction
of what I have said, I depart from my purpose not to speak of particular amendments, so far as to say that, holding such a provision
to now be implied constitutional law, I have no objection to its being
made express and irrevocable.

" The chief magistrate derives all his authority from the people,
and they have conferred none upon him to fix the terms for the separation of the States. The people themselves, also, can do this if
they choose, but the Executive, as such, has nothing to do with it.
His duty is to administer the present government as it came to his
hands, and to transmit it, unimpaired by him, to his successor.
Why should there not be a patient confidence in the ultimate justice
of the people ? Is there any better or equal hope in the world ? In
our present differences, is either party without faith of being in the
right ? If the Almighty Ruler of nations, with his eternal truth and
justice be on your side of the North, or on yours of the South, that truth
and that justice will surely prevail by the judgment of this great
tribunal, the American people. By the frame of the government
under which we live, this same people have wisely given their public servants but little power for mischief, and have, with equal wis-

dom, provided for the return of that little to their own hands at very short intervals. While the people retain their virtue and vigilance, no Administration, by any extreme wickedness or folly, can very seriously injure the Government in the short space of four years.

"My countrymen, one and all, think calmly and well upon this whole subject. Nothing valuable can be lost by taking time.

"If there be an object to hurry any of you, in hot haste, to a step which you would never take deliberately, that object will be frustrated by taking time ; but no good object can be frustrated by it.

"Such of you as are now dissatisfied, still have the old Constitution unimpaired, and, on the sensitive point, the laws of your own framing under it ; while the new Administration will have no immediate power, if it would, to change either.

"If it were admitted that you who are dissatisfied hold the right side in the dispute, there is still no single reason for precipitate action. Intelligence, patriotism, Christianity, and a firm reliance on Him who has never yet forsaken this favored land, are still competent to adjust, in the best way, all our present difficulties.

"In your hands, my dissatisfied fellow-countrymen, and not in mine, is the momentous issue of civil war. The government will not assail you.

"You can have no conflict without being yourselves the aggressors. You have no oath registered in heaven to destroy the government ; while I shall have the most solemn one to 'preserve, protect, and defend it.'

"I am loth to close. We are not enemies, but friends. We must not be enemies. Though passion may have strained, it must not break our bonds of affection.

"The mystic cords of memory, stretching from every battlefield and patriot grave to every living heart and hearthstone all over this broad land, will yet swell the chorus of the Union, when again touched, as surely they will be, by the better angels of our nature."

Mr. Lincoln on assuming the reins of government found the North immersed in the affairs of peace ; the national government almost destitute of arms and means, and the South busy preparing for war, manufacturing powder, shell, balls, and other munitions of war, and already in possession of most of the arms belonging to the United States, which had been, during the administration of his predecessor, sent from the Northern to the Southern States ; and while the United States government had but its petty regular army, the congress of the revolted

States, only two days after his accession, on the 6th of March passed an act to raise an army of 100,000 men.

Such was his position. The South not only defied the General Government, but menaced the North. The President could not, with the barons of old England, say merely, *Nolumus mutare leges angliæ:* like the pontiffs, his word could but be, *Non Possumus.* With the inauguration oath still sounding from his lips, he could not consent to see half the land he was chosen to rule severed from the estate he received from the line of his predecessors. Mr. Stephens, actually Vice-President of that pseudo-republic to which the crowned heads of Europe were to do reverence, was of Mr. Lincoln's opinion : "Shall the people of the South secede from the Union in consequence of the election of Mr. Lincoln to the Presidency of the United States? My countrymen, I tell you candidly, frankly, and earnestly, that I do not think that they ought. In my judgment, the election of no man constitutionally chosen to that high office, is sufficient cause for any State to separate from the Union. It ought to stand by and aid still in maintaining the Constitution of the country."

If Mr. Stephens thought that Georgia should aid still in maintaining the Constitution of the country, much more did Mr. Lincoln deem it his duty to maintain it, so far as the people would support him. To him the path of duty was clear. He would do it, as long as the people gave him the power: when they prevented him, the responsibility shifted from his shoulders.

Mr. Lincoln's first act was to select his Cabinet. For the important position of Secretary of State he selected his late competitor, William H. Seward, of New York, whose death was plotted and nearly effected with his own ; Salmon P. Chase, now Chief-Justice of the United States, called upon to administer the oath of office to Mr. Lincoln's successor, took the portfolio of the Treasury ; Simon Cameron, of Pennsylvania, became Secretary of War ; Gideon Welles, of Connecticut, Secretary of the Navy ; Caleb B. Smith, of Indiana, Secretary of the Interior ; the direction of the Post-office Department was confided to Montgomery Blair, of Maryland ; and Edward Bates, of Missouri, became Attorney-General. These nominations were all confirmed by the Senate, and his Cabinet at once began their arduous duties.

On the 12th of March, John Forsyth, of Alabama, and Crawford of Georgia, requested an unofficial interview with the Secretary of State, which was declined. On the 13th they sent a communication stating that they were commissioners from a government composed of seven States which had withdrawn from the United States, and desired to open negotiations. After due deliberation Mr. Seward, on the 8th of April, informed them that it " would not be admitted that the States referred to had, in law or fact, withdrawn from the Federal Union ; or that they could do so, in any other manner than with the consent and concert of the people of the United States, to be given through a National Convention to be assembled in conformity with the provisions of the Constitution of the United States."

This reply telegraphed to the South made them resolve to begin the hostilities which they so long covertly and at last openly prepared. General Beauregard, at Charleston, was ordered to reduce Fort Sumter. On the 12th he opened on the fort from the numerous batteries planted around the fort, and Major Anderson, after holding it under heavy fire for thirty-three hours with only sixty men, finding it impossible to save the fort or be relieved, agreed to evacuate, and did so on Sunday, April 14th, 1861.

This blow decided the hesitating Southern States, which now saw that war was inevitable. To the incredulous North it was a thunder-clap. The South really meant war ; and forgetting all party distinctions, the North rose as a man, its dogged persistence roused to fire.

President Lincoln regarding it as an armed attack on a government fort by a combination, issued a proclamation in these words :—

" *Whereas*, The laws of the United States have been for some time past, and now are opposed, and the execution thereof obstructed, in the States of South Carolina, Georgia, Alabama, Florida, Mississippi, Lousiana, and Texas, by combinations too powerful to be suppressed by the ordinary course of judicial proceedings, or by the powers vested in the marshals by law; now, therefore, I, ABRAHAM LINCOLN, President of the United States, in virtue of the power in me vested by the Constitution and the laws, have thought fit to call forth, and hereby do call forth, the militia of the several

States of the Union to the aggregate number of 75,000, in order to suppress said combinations and to cause the laws to be duly executed.

"The details for this object will be immediately communicated to the State authorities through the War Department. I appeal to all loyal citizens to favor, facilitate, and aid this effort to maintain the honor, the integrity, and existence of our national Union, and the perpetuity of popular government, and to redress wrongs already long enough endured. I deem it proper to say that the first service assigned to the forces hereby called forth, will probably be to repossess the forts, places, and property which have been seized from the Union; and in every event the utmost care will be observed, consistently with the objects aforesaid, to avoid any devastation, any destruction of, or interference with property, or any disturbance of peaceful citizens of any part of the country; and I hereby command the persons composing the combinations aforesaid, to disperse and retire peaceably to their respective abodes, within twenty days from this date.

"Deeming that the present condition of public affairs presents an extraordinary occasion, I do hereby, in virtue of the power in me vested by the Constitution, convene both Houses of Congress. The Senators and Representatives are, therefore, summoned to assemble at their respective chambers at twelve o'clock, noon, on Thursday, the fourth day of July next, then and there to consider and determine such measures as, in their wisdom, the public safety and interest may seem to demand.

"In witness whereof, I have hereunto set my hand, and caused the seal of the United States to be affixed.

"Done at the City of Washington, this fifteenth day of April, in the year of our Lord one thousand eight hundred and sixty-one, and of the independence of the United States the eighty-fifth.

"By the President: ABRAHAM LINCOLN.
"WILLIAM H. SEWARD, Secretary of State."

To this proclamation the Northern States responded heartily. Maryland attacked Northern troops on their way to Washington; and the border States showed that they were likely to be soon all arrayed against the Union. Southern army officers had already resigned and joined the rebels, and many from the border States were ready to follow the example. On the 17th of April Virginia formally seceded, having first admitted Confederate troops into her limits, and Robert E. Lee, a trusted officer, left Washington to command the troops of that State and eventually of the whole Confederacy, followed by all who deemed an obligation to take part in a State crime a higher virtue than fidelity to oaths or patriotic devotion to their country.

One of the earliest duties of Mr. Lincoln was to assume a proper ground with regard to foreign powers. He took the broad ground that it was a domestic rebellion, which the United States government was competent to put down. To our minister at London this explicit instruction was sent: "You may assure them promptly that, if they are determined to recognize the seceded States, they may at the same time prepare to enter into alliance with the enemies of this republic. You alone will represent your country at London, and you will represent the whole of it there. When you are asked to divide the duty with others, diplomatic relations will be suspended."

This declaration was not made too soon; for England and France had precipitately, and before the arrival of Mr. Adams, recognized the rebels as a belligerent power; and when Mr. Lincoln gave his adhesion to the principles of the Paris Convention of 1859, agreeing, among other things, to suppress privateering, the two great European allies required that they should not apply to the rebellion in the United States, but this Mr. Lincoln declared inadmissible. England and France thus, in violation of all good faith, set aside the treaties with this country, and put the national government merely on a par with its rebellious subjects, giving the latter every advantage conceded to our national vessels.

This unwise and malignant policy made it also a matter of importance with Mr. Lincoln how best to act with regard to Southern ports. To close them, presented difficulties not to be disguised. The President, therefore, by proclamation, on the 19th and 27th of April, declared the blockade of all the Southern ports; and announced that privateers should be treated as pirates. This position was at first ridiculed. The rebels and their foreign friends declared a blockade impossible, and the jealous European powers required it to be made effective. But Mr. Lincoln, while rapidly and thoroughly collecting and equipping the land forces necessary, pushed also the increase of the navy, and soon had means to establish such a blockade as had never before been witnessed. Blockade runners constantly contrived, indeed, to run from the pestilent little English islands off our Southern coast into Southern harbors; but their losses were heavy, and in some cases overwhelming.

Mr. Lincoln convened his first Congress on the 4th of July, 1861. After sitting about a month, it adjourned, clothing the President with ample power for suppressing the rebellion, and avoiding all topics likely to mar the harmony or cool the ardent patriotism of the Northern States.

Meanwhile, important military operations had taken place. Long standing on the defensive, the armies at last moved forward to repel the menacing hosts of rebellion, but the popular hopes were sadly dashed by the terrible overthrow sustained by the national arms at Bull Run, Va., in June. Still the plans of the government were steadily pushed. Fort Hatteras, Port Royal, and Ship Island, were taken on the coast, and the rebels checked in Western Virginia, Kentucky, and Missouri. General Scott having resigned, Mr. Lincoln appointed to command the armies Major-General George B. McClellan, whose success in Western Virginia justified the choice, but whose management of affairs did not answer the favorable anticipations formed.

In the delicate matter of the seizure, by Commodore Wilkes, of Mason and Slidell, rebel envoys, on the English steamer Trent, Mr. Lincoln, with great sagacity, restored them to the English authority, on the ground that Commodore Wilkes should have taken them before a legal tribunal, instead of himself assuming to decide their liability to capture.

The abolition of slavery was a great topic for consideration. That the rebels brought their slave property within the operation of the confiscation laws, was unquestionable, and the main difficulty seemed to be with the border States. Here Mr. Lincoln urged those States to act, and Congress offered pecuniary aid to States wishing to abolish it. But no State accepted the offer. Rather than take a single step, they preferred to wait till slavery should fall. Mr. Lincoln was strongly in favor of sending the liberated slaves to some foreign country, Central America or some other, but his plan met with difficulties which led to its total abandonment.

As the war progressed, new questions arose. As territory

was regained, government, courts, and other institutions were to be established. Much had to be left to the discretion of military commanders; and in the exercise of this discretion, they required the constant watchfulness of the calm, far-seeing President.

Congress had given him full power under the Confiscation Act to liberate slaves. Many urged him to do so; but he declined to use the power. The saving of the Union was his great object, to which the question of emancipation was absolutely subordinate. Whenever and so far as emancipation would help to save the Union, then and that far he would adopt it. Till then he restrained the ardent and impetuous.

At last, on the 22d of September, 1862, Mr. Lincoln issued this proclamation, which will stand as one of the greatest State papers in American history.

"I, Abraham Lincoln, President of the United States of America, and Commander-in-Chief. of the Army and Navy thereof, do hereby proclaim and declare that hereafter as heretofore the war will be prosecuted for the object of practically restoring the constitutional relation between the United States and the people thereof in those States in which that relation is, or may be, suspended or disturbed ; that it is my purpose upon the next meeting of Congress to again recommend the adoption of a practical measure tendering pecuniary aid to the free acceptance or rejection of all the slave States, so called, the people whereof may not then be in rebellion against the United States, and which States may then have voluntarily adopted, or thereafter may voluntarily adopt, the immediate or gradual abolishment of slavery within their respective limits, and that the effort to colonize persons of African descent, with their consent, upon the continent or elsewhere, with the previously obtained consent of the government existing there, will be continued ; that on the first day of January, in the year of our Lord one thousand eight hundred and sixty-three, all persons held as slaves within any State, or any designated part of a State, the people whereof shall then be in rebellion against the United States, shall be then, thenceforward and forever, free, and the executive government of the United States, including the military and naval authority thereof, will recognize and maintain the freedom of such persons, and will do no act or acts to depress such persons, or any of them, in any efforts they may make for their actual freedom ; that the Executive will, on the first day of January aforesaid, by proclamation, designate the States and parts of States, if any, in which the people thereof respectively shall then be in rebellion against the United States; and the fact that any State, or the people thereof, shall on that day be in good faith represented in the Congress of the United States by members chosen thereto, at elections wherein a majority of the qualified voters of such State shall have participated, shall, in the absence of strong countervailing testimony, be deemed conclusive evidence that such State and the people thereof have not been in rebellion against the United States.

"That attention is hereby called to an act of Congress entitled, 'An act to make an additional article of war,' approved March 13, 1862, and which act is in the words and figures following:

"'*Be it enacted by the Senate and House of Representatives of the United States of America, in Congress assembled*, That hereafter the following shall be promulgated as an additional article of war for the government of the army of the United States, and shall be observed and obeyed as such.

"'*Article* —. All officers or persons of the military or naval service of the United States are prohibited from employing any of the forces under their respective commands for the purpose of returning fugitives from service or labor who may have escaped from any persons to whom such service or labor is claimed to be due; and any officer who shall be found guilty by a court-martial of violating this article, shall be dismissed from the service.

"'*Sec*. 2. And be it further enacted, That this act shall take effect from and after its passage.'

"Also to the ninth and tenth sections of an act entitled, 'An act to suppress insurrection, to punish treason and rebellion, to seize and confiscate property of rebels, and for other purposes,' approved July 17, 1862, and which sections are in the words and figures following:

"'*Sec*. 9. And be it further enacted, That all slaves of persons who shall hereafter be engaged in rebellion against the government of the United States, or who shall in any way give aid or comfort thereto, escaping from such persons and taking refuge within the lines of the army; and all slaves captured from such persons or deserted by them, and coming under the control of the Government of the United States, and all slaves of such persons found on (or being within) any place occupied by rebel forces and afterwards occupied by the forces of the United States, shall be deemed captives of war, and shall be forever free of their servitude, and not again held as slaves.

"'*Sec*. 10. And be it further enacted, That no slave escaping into any State, Territory, or the District of Columbia, from any of the States, shall be delivered up, or in any way impeded or hindered of his liberty, except for crime, or some offence against the laws, unless the person claiming said fugitive shall first make oath that the person to whom the labor or service of such fugitive is alleged to be due, is his lawful owner, and has not been in arms against the United States in the present rebellion, nor in any way given aid and comfort thereto ; and no person engaged in the military or naval service of the United States shall, under any pretence whatever, assume to decide on the validity of the claim of any person to the service or labor of any other person, or surrender up any such person to the claimant, on pain of being dismissed from the service.'

" And I do hereby enjoin upon, and order all persons engaged in the military and naval service of the United States to observe, obey, and enforce within their respective spheres of service the act and sections above recited.

" And the executive will in due time recommend that all citizens of the United States who shall have remained loyal thereto throughout the rebellion, shall (upon the restoration of the constitutional relation between the United States and their respective States and people, if the relation shall have been suspended or disturbed) be compensated for all losses by acts of the United States, including the loss of slaves.

" In witness whereof, I have hereunto set my hand and caused the seal of the United States to be affixed.

"Done at the city of Washington, this twenty-second day of September, in the year of our Lord one thousand eight hundred and sixty-two, and of the Independence of the United States the eighty-seventh.

" By the President: " ABRAHAM LINCOLN.

" WILLIAM H. SEWARD, *Secretary of State.*"

This was followed by another, issued on the first of January, 1863, and worded as follows :

" *Whereas*, on the twenty-second day of September, in the year of our Lord one thousand eight hundred and sixty-two, a proclamation was issued by the President of the United States containing among other things the following, to wit:

" That on the first day of January, in the year of our Lord one thousand eight hundred and sixty-three, all persons held as slaves within any State, or designated part of a State, the people whereof shall then be in rebellion against the United States, shall be then, thenceforth and forever free, and the Executive Government of the

United States, including the military and naval authorities thereof, will recognize and maintain the freedom of such persons, and will do no act or acts to repress such persons, or any of them, in any efforts they may make for their actual freedom.

"That the Executive will, on the first day of January aforesaid, by proclamation, designate the States and parts of States, if any, in which the people therein respectively shall then be in rebellion against the United States, and the fact that any State, or the people thereof, shall on that day be in good faith represented in the Congress of the United States by members chosen thereto, at elections wherein a majority of the qualified voters of such States shall have participated, shall, in the absence of strong countervailing testimony, be deemed conclusive evidence that such State and the people thereof are not then in rebellion against the United States.

" Now, therefore, I, Abraham Lincoln, President of the United States, by virtue of the power in me vested as Commander-in-Chief of the Army and Navy of the United States in time of actual armed rebellion against the authority and Government of the United States, and as a fit and necessary war measure for suppressing said rebellion, do, on this first day of January, in the year of our Lord one thousand eight hundred and sixty-three, and in accordance with my purpose so to do, publicly proclaimed for the full period of one hundred days from the day of the first above-mentioned order, and designate, as the States and parts of States wherein the people thereof respectively are this day in rebellion against the United States, the following, to wit: Arkansas, Texas, Louisiana, except the parishes of St. Bernard, Plaquemines, Jefferson, St. John, St. Charles, St. James, Ascension, Assumption, Terre Bonne, Lafourche, St. Mary, St. Martin, and Orleans, including the City of New Orleans ; Mississippi, Alabama, Florida, Georgia, South Carolina, North Carolina, and Virginia, except the forty-eight counties designated as West Virginia, and also the counties of Berkeley, Accomac, Northampton, Elizabeth City, York, Princess Anne, and Norfolk, including the cities of Norfolk and Portsmouth, and which excepted parts are, for the present, left precisely as if this proclamation were not issued.

" And by virtue of the power and for the purpose aforesaid, I do order and declare that all persons held as slaves within said designated States and parts of States are, and henceforward shall be free; and that the Executive Government of the United States, including the military and naval authorities thereof, will recognize and maintain the freedom of said persons.

" And I hereby enjoin upon the people so declared to be free, to abstain from all violence, unless in necessary self-defence, and I recommend to them, that in all cases, when allowed, they labor faithfully for reasonable wages.

"And I further declare and make known, that such persons of suitable condition will be received into the armed service of the United States, to garrison forts, positions, stations, and other places, and to man vessels of all sorts in said service.

"And upon this, sincerely believed to be an act of justice, warranted by the Constitution, upon military necessity, I invoke the considerate judgment of mankind, and the gracious favor of Almighty God.

"In witness whereof, I have hereunto set my hand, and caused the seal of the United States to be affixed.

"Done at the city of Washington, this first day of January, in the year of our Lord one thousand eight hundred and sixty-
[L. s.] three, and of the Independence of the United States of America the eighty-seventh.

"By the President : "Abraham Lincoln.

"William H. Seward, *Secretary of State.*"

The proclamation excited various opinions. To some it was unconstitutional, to others unwise, as unable to reach the class in question; but its effect was immense, as we now see. It would be impossible, in the space we can here give to the administration of Mr. Lincoln, to enter into his various acts of office, his calls for troops, his various appointments, or the various steps that he adopted, from time to time, in the well-grounded hope that they would bring peace to the land. On the 8th of December, 1863, he issued his important amnesty proclamation, in which, after reciting the existence of the rebellion, he proceeds :

"Therefore, I, Abraham Lincoln, President of the United States, do proclaim, declare, and make known to all persons who have, directly or by implication, participated in the existing rebellion, except as hereinafter excepted, that a FULL PARDON is hereby granted to them and each of them, with restoration of all rights of property, except as to slaves, and in property cases where rights of third parties shall have intervened, and upon the condition that every such person shall take and subscribe an oath, and thenceforward keep and maintain said oath inviolate; and which oath shall be registered for permanent preservation, and shall be of the tenor and effect following, to wit :

"'I, ———, do solemnly swear, in presence of Almighty God, that I will henceforth faithfully support, protect, and defend the Constitution of the United States, and the union of the States thereunder; and that I will, in like manner, abide by and faithfully support all acts of Congress, passed during the existing rebellion, with reference to slaves, so long and so far as not repealed, modified, or held void by Congress, or by decision of the Supreme Court; and that I will, in like manner, abide by and faithfully support all proclamations of the President, made during the existing rebellion, having reference to slaves, so long and so far as not modified or declared void by decision of the Supreme Court. So help me God.'

"The persons exempted from the benefits of the foregoing provisions are all who are or shall have been civil or diplomatic officers or agents of the so-called Confederate Government; all who have left judicial stations under the United States to aid the rebellion; all who are or shall have been military or naval officers of said Confederate Government above the rank of Colonel in the army, or of Lieutenant in the navy; all who left seats in the United States Congress to aid the rebellion; all who resigned their commissions in the army or navy of the United States, and afterwards aided the rebellion, and all who have engaged in any way, in treating colored persons or white persons, in charge of such, otherwise than lawfully, as prisoners of war, and which persons may be found in the United States service, as soldiers, seamen, or in any other capacity.

"And I do further proclaim, declare, and make known, that whenever, in any of the States of Arkansas, Texas, Louisiana, Mississippi, Tennessee, Alabama, Georgia, Florida, South Carolina, and North Carolina, a number of persons, not less than one-tenth in number of the votes cast in such State at the Presidential election of the year of our Lord 1860, each having taken the oath aforesaid, and not having since violated it, and being a qualified voter by the election law of the State existing immediately before the so-called act of secession, and excluding all others, shall re-establish a State government which shall be Republican, and in nowise contravening said oath, such shall be recognized as the true government of the State, and the State shall receive thereunder the benefits of the Constitutional provision, which declares that 'the United States shall guarantee to every State in this Union a Republican form of government, and shall protect each of them against invasion; and, on application of the Legislature, or the executive (when the Legislature cannot be convened), against domestic violence.'

"And I do further proclaim, declare, and make known, that any provision which may be adopted by such State government, in relation to the freed people of such State, which shall recognize and declare their permanent freedom, provide for their education, and which may yet be consistent, as a temporary arrangement, with their present condition as a laboring, landless, and homeless class, will not be objected to by the National Executive. And it is suggested as not improper, that, in constructing a loyal State government in any State, the name of the State, the boundary, the subdivisions, the Constitution, and the general code of laws, as before the rebellion, be maintained, subject only to the modifications made necessary by the conditions hereinbefore stated, and such others, if any, not contravening said conditions, and which may be deemed expedient by those framing the new State government.

"To avoid misunderstanding, it may be proper to say, that this proclamation, so far as it relates to State governments, has no reference to States wherein loyal State governments have all the while been maintained. And for the same reason, it may be proper to further say, that whether members sent to Congress from any State shall be admitted to seats constitutionally, rests exclusively with the respective Houses, and not to any extent with the Executive. And still further, that this proclamation is intended to present the people of the States wherein the national authority has been suspended, and loyal State governments have been subverted, a mode in and by which the national authority and loyal State governments may be re-established within said States, or in any of them; and, while the mode presented is the best the Executive can suggest, with his present impressions, it must not be understood that no other possible mode would be acceptable.

"Given under my hand at the city of Washington, the eighth day of December, A. D. one thousand eight hundred and sixty-three, and of the Independence of the United States of America the eighty-eighth.

"By the President :   "ABRAHAM LINCOLN.

"WILLIAM H. SEWARD, *Secretary of State.*"

As the term of Mr. Lincoln's administration drew towards a close, other prominent men of the party were spoken of in political circles, as possible candidates; but it was soon evident that the sound common sense of the people demanded his continuance. There was no longer contemptuous scorn or abuse. The man had risen far above that. If in that complicity of character, springing from the inartificial society in which he was reared, he used the apologue to enforce his opinions, the people felt that what would have made him a sage in antiquity could not make his real wisdom less now. He had made a hard-working, earnest, true, patient, cautious, kind-hearted, yet most firm President. Men felt loosened from party shackles, and many inwardly resolved, against all former political bias, to cast their votes for Mr. Lincoln.

The National Union Convention assembled at Baltimore, June 7, 1864, nominated him for President, and Andrew Johnson, another self-made Southern man, for Vice-President.

On the 29th of August, in the same year, a Democratic Convention at Chicago nominated General George B. McClellan for the Presidency, and George H. Pendleton, of Ohio, for Vice-President, with a platform which General McClellan virtually repudiated.

Meanwhile Grant, after reducing Vicksburg and opening the Mississippi by the fall of Port Hudson, had proceeded to Tennessee, and taking in hand the army there, driven the rebels from before Chattanooga. Appointed Lieutenant-General, he forced Lee back to Richmond, while his able lieutenant, Sherman, forced Bragg back to Atlanta. The rebellion began to totter. A few Southern leaders in Canada endeavored to open negotiations for terms. Their advances elicited this characteristic reply:

" EXECUTIVE MANSION, WASHINGTON, July 18, 1864.

" *To whom it may concern:* Any proposition which embraces the restoration of peace, the integrity of the Union, and the abandonment of slavery, and which comes by and with authority that can control the armies now at war against the United States, will be received and considered by the Executive Government of the United States, and will be met by liberal terms on other substantial and collateral points, and the bearers thereof shall have safe conduct both ways.

" ABRAHAM LINCOLN."

The Presidential election took place upon the eighth of November, 1864, and it resulted in the triumph of Mr. Lincoln in every loyal State except Kentucky, New Jersey, and Delaware. The official returns for the entire vote polled summed up 4,034,789.

Of these Mr. Lincoln received 2,223,035, and McClellan received 1,811,754, leaving a majority of 411,281 on the popular vote. Mr. Lincoln was elected by a plurality in 1860. In 1864 his majority was decided and unmistakable.

The covert attempt to negotiate having failed, the rebels in February, 1865, applied directly for permission to send their Vice-President, Stephens of Georgia, R. M. T. Hunter of Virginia, and J. A. Campbell of Alabama, through the lines as quasi Commissioners to treat for peace. It had been distinctly stated that no recognition of the Southern Confederacy by the general Government must be expected; still the envoys wished to come, and President Lincoln proceeded to Fortress Monroe then, on the steamer River Queen. The conference led to no results. The envoys made the recognition indispensable, while Mr. Lincoln, in his friendly and genial conversation with them, as firmly insisted that he could not for a moment entertain it.

On the 4th of March Mr. Lincoln was inaugurated for a second term of four years, to which he had been chosen by so preponderating a vote of confidence. The day was rainy, and the ceremonies began in the Senate Chamber. A few moments before twelve o'clock, the official procession entered the chamber. First, came the members of the Supreme Court, who took seats on the right of the Vice-President's chair. Soon after Mr. Lincoln entered, escorted by Vice-President Hamlin, and followed by the members of the cabinet, the chiefs of the diplomatic corps, officers of the army and navy who have received the thanks of Congress, Governors, &c.

Vice-President Hamlin briefly took leave of the Senate, and his successor, with the Senators elect to the Thirty-Ninth Congress, were then sworn in. After this the official procession was formed and moved to the platform in front of the portico of the eastern front of the Capitol, where the ceremony of inauguration was concluded. After being welcomed with enthusiastic cheers, Mr. Lincoln pronounced the following inaugural:

"*Fellow Countrymen:* At this second appearing to take the oath of the Presidential office, there is less occasion for an extended address than there was at the first. Then a statement somewhat in detail of a course to be pursued seemed fitting and proper. Now, at the expiration of four years, during which public declarations

4

have been constantly called forth on every point and phase of the great contest which still absorbs the attention and engrosses the energies of the Nation, little that is new could be presented.

"The progress of our arms, upon which all else chiefly depends, is as well known to the public as to myself, and it is, I trust, reasonably satisfactory and encouraging to all. With high hope for the future, no prediction in regard to it is ventured.

"On the occasion corresponding to this four years ago, all thoughts were anxiously directed to an impending civil war. All dreaded it; all sought to avoid it. While the Inaugural Address was being delivered from this place, devoted altogether to *saving* the Union without war, insurgent agents were in this city seeking to *destroy* it without war—seeking to dissolve the Union and destroy its effects by negotiation. Both parties deprecated war, but one of them would *make* war rather than let the nation survive, and the other would *accept* war rather than let it perish; and the war came.

"One-eighth of the whole population were colored slaves, not distributed generally over the Union, but localized in the Southern part of it. These slaves constituted a peculiar and powerful interest. All knew that this interest was somehow the cause of the war. To strengthen, perpetuate and extend this interest was the object for which the insurgents would rend the Union even by war, while the Government claimed no right to do more than to restrict the territorial enlargement of it.

"Neither party expected for the war the magnitude or the duration which it has already attained. Neither anticipated that the *cause* might cease with or even before the conflict should cease. Each looked for an easier triumph and a result less fundamental and astounding.

"Both read the same Bible and pray to the same God, and each invokes his aid against the other. It may seem strange that any men should dare to ask a just God's assistance in wringing their bread from the sweat of other men's faces; but let us judge not, that we be not judged. The prayers of both could not be answered—that of neither has been answered fully. The Almighty has His own purposes. 'Woe unto the world because of offences, for it must needs be that offences come; but woe to the man by whom the offence cometh.' If we shall suppose that American slavery is one of these offences, which in the providence of God must needs come, but which having continued through His appointed time, He now wills to remove, and that He gives to both North and South this terrible war as the woe due to those by whom the offences came, shall we discern therein any departure from these Divine attributes which the believers in a living God always ascribe to Him?

"Fondly do we hope, fervently do we pray, that this mighty scourge of war may speedily pass away. Yet, if God wills that it continue until all the wealth piled by the bondman's two hundred and fifty years of unrequited toil shall be sunk, and till every drop of blood drawn with the lash shall be paid by another drawn with the sword, as was said three thousand years ago, so, still it must be said, that the judgments of the Lord are true and righteous altogether.

"With malice towards none, with charity for all, with firmness in the right, as God gives us to see the right, let us strive on to finish the work we are in; to bind up the nation's wounds, to care for him who shall have borne the battle, and for his widow and his orphans; to do all that may achieve and cherish a just and a lasting peace among ourselves and with all nations."

The oath of office was then administered by Chief-Justice Chase and the re-inaugurated President escorted back to the White House.

On the 24th of March Mr. Lincoln went again to the peninsula to see the close of Grant's campaign. Petersburg was assaulted before his eyes, and while at City Point, April 2d, Richmond, the Rebel capital fell into our hands. The President immediately proceeded to the city, entering it in triumph, and in the evening held a levee in the late residence of Jefferson Davis. This was his hour of joy unmingled. His anxious hours of care seemed now to be fast closing and brighter days arising. His return to Washington had nothing to dampen this joy. The news of Lee's surrender followed soon after, and on the eventful 14th of April, 1865, the day appointed for raising once more the old flag at Sumter, while awaiting the tidings of Johnson's capture his life was brought to a sudden and startling close.

II.

ASSASSINATION
AND LAST MOMENTS.

II.

THE ASSASSINATION AND LAST MOMENTS OF THE PRESIDENT.

Friday, the fourteenth day of April, will ever stand a memorable day in the American annals. Without reflecting on its being a day set apart in many Christian denominations to commemorate in prayer and recollection the death of the Saviour, it had been at first announced as a day for public rejoicing, for it was the anniversary of the evacuation of Fort Sumter by Major Anderson, that opening scene of the terrible civil war, which now seemed closed. Grant's generalship had driven Lee from Richmond and forced him to surrender, while Sherman, who had succeeded to his Western army, had driven Johnson back, scattered his army when under Hood, and swept around through Georgia and South Carolina into North Carolina, near enough to visit Grant. The war was over, and General Anderson on this eventful day, amid the thunder of cannon and the thundering cheers of loyal hearts, had again raised his flag over the ruins of Sumter.

President Lincoln was already planning ways of peace. The pseudo Confederacy, as an organization, was gone. Its last great army was at bay. The reduction of the national army, the diminution of the heavy expenditures, the restoration of the Southern States, the healing up of the wounds of the terrible strife, such were the thoughts and cares of the great and good man when he was suddenly cut down by the hand of a cowardly assassin, who struck from behind, for it has been well said, that no one could have looked Abraham Lincoln in the face and done the deed.

For success in the accomplishment of the deadly purpose, for the ease with which the crime was perpetrated and the murderer's escape effected, the act is almost without a parallel. In the presence of hundreds, the chief of a great nation was murdered in an instant, and for a long time no trace of the recognized assassin could be found, although he must have galloped in the dead hour of night past officers and sentries apparently unquestioned and unchecked.

A plot, the whole extent and ramifications of which are not yet made known, had long been formed to assassinate the President and the prominent members of the Cabinet. Originating apparently in the Confederate government, this act, with others, such as the attempt to fire New York, the St. Alban's raid, the seizure of vessels on the lakes and at sea, was confided to an association of army officers, who when sent on these errands were said to be on detached service. There is direct proof of Booth's actual consultation with officers known to belong to this organization, during Lee's retreat from Gettysburg. The assassination of the President was a thing so commonly talked of in the South that it excited at last no surprise, and one of the Southern papers actually offered a reward for the assassination of the President, Vice-President, and Secretary of State.

The documents already come to light show that a previous attempt to take the life of Mr. Lincoln, by poison, was made, but failed. Then parties were sent and employed to do the work surely. To John Wilkes Booth, lured apparently by a high reward, the great act was committed.

The threats of assassination had at first induced care on the part of the authorities. At the time of the first inauguration steps were taken to prevent the consummation of any such nefarious design. Gradually, however, these threats were treated lightly, and less precautions were taken. Warning had been conveyed to Mr. Seward on the day that an accident laid him a sufferer on his bed of pain, but without inducing any unusual caution or watchfulness.

The visit of the President to Richmond, where he walked unattended, had seemed to some too rash, and friends remonstrated against his thus imperilling a life on which all America had a claim. On the very day of his death he wrote to General Van Alen : "I intend to adopt the advice of my friends and use due precaution."

But the time and place of the terrible crime were at last decided upon by the band of hired assassins. One of the chief theatres of Washington was directed by John T. Ford, who had placed the State Box, as it was called, at the disposal of President Lincoln. Mr. Ford seems to have been no party to the plot, although from his former association with the riotous class of Baltimore suspicion may have been at first excited.

The 14th was to be the benefit of Miss Laura Keene, and the President with General Grant and other prominent men had been invited and were expected to be present. Whether this invitation was part of the plot or merely furnished the opportunity remains to be seen. Be that as it may, the theatre was prepared for the fearful deed.

The private box adjoined the dress circle, and had two doors, as it was at times by a partition converted into two boxes: these doors opened into a dark passage, closed by a door at the end of the dress circle. During the day, or previously, John Wilkes Booth, or his accomplice, Spangler, the stage carpenter, had bored gimlet holes in the box doors, enlarged by a pen-knife on the inside sufficiently to enable him to survey the position of the parties within at the moment of action. The hasps of the locks, which were on the inside of the box doors had been weakened by partly withdrawing the screws, so that a man could easily press them open, if locked.

These were not the only preparations. The very arrangement of the chairs and sofa in the box was evidently part of the plan, and the work of Booth or a confederate among those employed in the theatre. It gave an unobstructed passage from the door to the President, throwing the others at a considerable distance from him, and in positions not to observe an entrance. Mr. Lincoln's chair was placed in the front corner of the box, furthest from the stage; that of Mrs. Lincoln was more remote from the front, and just by the column in the centre. The other chair and a sofa were placed at the side nearest the stage, leaving the centre of the box clear for the assassin's operations, and enabling him to enter unseen. They had also provided a board to prevent the passage door from being opened from the outside in case any attempt was to follow him, and they had made a secret niche in the opposite wall to receive the end of the board not braced against the

door. For the criminal act Booth selected a small silver
mounted Derringer pistol and a bowie knife. He had
long shown a nicked bullet with which he declared that he intended to kill the President, and during a recent visit to Boston
spent much of his time at the pistol gallery of Floyd and Edwards, on Chapman Place, practising firing behind his neck,
between his legs, and in many strange and awkward positions.
For his escape he had no less carefully provided. He took a
stable in the alley in the rear of the theatre, and on the afternoon of Friday hired of James Pumphrey a fine bay mare,
and taking it to the stable employed Spangler, the stage carpenter, to watch it. It was saddled and ready to mount, as
he had ordered the bridle not to be taken off; he put his
horse in charge of Spangler, who promised to give him all aid
in his power, and who prepared the scenes so that he could
readily reach the back door. Of this door Spangler took
charge, relieving the boy who was sent to hold Booth's horse
during the performance.

An illegitimate son of the celebrated English actor Booth,
John Wilkes had inherited a small share of his father's talent
and more than his madness. His wild and dissipated life, his
unsteadiness and low associations, had lost him the countenance of most of his friends, but no importance was attached
to his boasts and threats. In Washington, however, from his
dress and manners he was received into social circles from
which his life should have excluded him for ever. He was,
therefore, a man as little likely to excite suspicion as anyone
that could have been selected.

The assassin spent most of Friday in a very excited manner,
drinking frequently at the bar of a saloon next-door to the
theatre. During the afternoon, he called at the Kirkwood
House, where Vice-President Johnson resided, and sent up a
card, with these words:

"I don't wish to disturb you, but would be glad to have an
interview.

"J. WILKES BOOTH."

Mr. Johnson was fortunately not within, and to this, probably, owes his life. It seems strange that Booth should have

attempted this crime while arranging for the other, but the one deputed to kill the Vice-President seems to have become alarmed, and Booth, after failing to reach Mr. Johnson, returned to his hotel about four o'clock, and wrote a letter to his mother, apparently under great excitement. He took his tea at the hotel at the usual hour, and then proceeded to the theatre. Colored people living on the alley saw him in conference with Spangler, and placing his horse in position after the hour when the performance commenced. Others saw him around the entrance soon after. An officer, as we shall see, saw him enter the passage leading to the State Box, but neither the police in front, the soldier who overheard his language full of menace against the President, nor the officer whom his apparent rudeness shocked, nor the President's own attendant, seemed to have had the slightest suspicion of the coming tragedy. No angel whispered a word of warning. Providence permitted the lull of security to surround all.

But we will now follow President Lincoln in the events of the day which closed his mortal career with such appalling suddenness.

His son, Captain Robert Lincoln, who is on General Grant's staff, breakfasted with him on Friday morning, having just returned from the capitulation of Lee, and the President passed a happy hour listening to all the details. While at breakfast, he heard that Speaker Colfax was in the house, and sent word that he wished to see him immediately in the reception-room. He conversed with him nearly an hour about his future policy as to the rebellion, which he was about to submit to the cabinet. Afterward, he had an interview with Mr. Hale, minister to Spain, and several senators and representatives.

At eleven o'clock, the cabinet and General Grant met with him; and, in one of the most satisfactory and important cabinet meetings held since his first inauguration, the future policy of the administration in the great work of reconstruction, and restoring the Southern States to their ancient place beside their sister States, was harmoniously and unanimously agreed on. When it adjourned, Secretary Stanton said he felt that the government was stronger than at any previous period since the rebellion commenced; and the President is said, in his characteristic way, to have told them that some important news would soon come, as he had had a dream of a ship sailing very rapidly, and had invariably had that same dream before great events in the war, Bull Run, Antietam, Gettysburg, &c.

In the afternoon, the President had a long and pleasant interview with Governor Oglesby, Senator Yates, and other leading citizens of his State. In the evening, Mr. Colfax called again at his request, and Mr. Ashmun, of Massachusetts, who presided over the Chicago Convention of 1860, was present. To them he spoke of his visit to Richmond, and when they stated that there was much uneasiness at the North while he was at the rebel capital, for fear that some traitor might shoot him, he replied jocularly that he would have been alarmed himself if any other person had been President, and gone there, but that he did not feel any danger whatever. Conversing on a matter of business with Mr. Ashmun, he made a remark that he saw Mr. Ashmun was surprised at; and immediately, with his well-known kindness of heart, said, "You did not understand me, Ashmun; I did not mean what you inferred, and I will take it all back, and apologize for it." He afterwards gave Mr. Ashmun a card, written on his knee, to admit himself and friend early the next morning to converse further about it.

Turning to Mr. Colfax, he said, "You are going with Mrs. Lincoln and me to the theatre, I hope." But Mr. Colfax had other engagements, expecting to leave the city the next morning.

He then said to Mr. Colfax, "Mr. Sumner has the gavel of the Confederate Congress, which he got at Richmond to hand to the Secretary of War, but I insisted then that he must give it to you; and you tell him for me to hand it over." Mr. Ashmun alluded to the gavel which he still had, and which he had used at the Chicago Convention, and the President and Mrs. Lincoln, who was also in the parlor, rose to go to the theatre. It was half an hour after the time they had intended to start, and they spoke about waiting half an hour longer, for the President went with reluctance, as General Grant had gone north, and he did not wish the people to be disappointed, as they had both been advertised to be there.

Mr. Lincoln finally stated that he must go to the theatre, and warmly pressed Speaker Colfax and Mr. Ashmun to accompany him ; but they excused themselves on the score of previous engagements. At about 8 p. m., Mr. and Mrs. Lincoln started for the carriage, the latter taking the arm of Mr. Ashmun, and the President and Mr. Colfax walking together. As soon as the President and Mrs. Lincoln were seated in the carriage, the latter gave orders to the coachman to drive around to Senator Harris' residence for Miss Harris. As the carriage rolled away they both said " good-by, good-by," to Messrs. Ashmun and Colfax, and the carriage had in a moment more disappeared from the grounds in front of the White House.

As they proceeded at once to the residence of Senator Harris, we cannot give an account more detailed or authentic than that delivered under oath by Major Rathbone, the step-son of the Hon. Mr. Harris, and which Miss Harris confirms in every particular.

"Henry R. Rathbone, Brevet Major in the Army of the United States, being duly sworn, says, that on the 14th day of April, instant, at about twenty-minutes past eight o'clock in the evening, he, with Miss Clara H. Harris, left his residence at the corner of Fifteenth and H streets, and joined the President and Mrs. Lincoln and went with them in their carriage to Ford's Theatre in Tenth street. The box assigned to the President is in the second tier on the right-hand side of the audience, and was occupied by the President and Mrs. Lincoln, Miss Harris, and this deponent, and by no other person. The box is entered by passing from the front of the building in the rear of the dress circle to a small entry or passageway, about eight feet in length and four feet in width. This passageway is entered by a door which opens on the inner side. The door is so placed as to make an acute angle between it and the wall behind it on the inner side. At the inner end of this passageway is another door, standing squarely across, and opening into the box. On the left-hand side of the passageway, and being near the inner end, is a third door, which also opens into the box. This latter door was closed. The party entered the box through the door at the end of the passageway. The box is so constructed that it may be divided into two by a movable partition, one of the doors described opening into each. The front of the box is about ten or twelve feet in length, and in the centre of the railing is a small pillar overhung with a curtain. The depth of the box from front to rear is about nine feet. The elevation of the box above the stage, including the railing, is about ten or twelve feet.

"When the party entered the box, a cushioned arm chair was standing at the end of the box furthest from the stage and nearest the audience. This was also the nearest point to the door by which the box is entered. The President seated himself in this chair, and, except that he once left the chair for the purpose of putting on his overcoat, remained so seated until he was shot. Mrs. Lincoln was seated in a chair between the President and the pillar in the centre above described. At the opposite end of the box, that nearest the stage, were two chairs, in one of these, standing in the corner, Miss Harris was seated. At her left hand, and along the wall running from that end of the box to the rear, stood a small sofa. At the end of this sofa, next to Miss Harris, this deponent was seated. The distance between this deponent and the President, as they were sitting, was about seven or eight feet, and the distance between this deponent and the door was about the same. The distance between the President, as he sat, and the door was about four or five feet. The door, according to the recollection of this deponent, was not closed during the evening.

"When the second scene of the third act was being performed, and this deponent was intently observing the proceedings upon the stage, with his back towards the door, he heard the discharge of a pistol behind him, and looking around, saw through the smoke a man between the door and the President. At the same time deponent heard him shout some word which deponent thinks was 'Freedom.' This deponent instantly sprang towards him and seized him. He wrested himself from the grasp and made a violent thrust at the breast of deponent with a large knife. Deponent parried the blow by striking it up, and received a wound several inches deep in his left arm between the elbow and the shoulder. The orifice of the wound is about an inch and a half in length, and extends upwards towards the shoulder several inches. The man rushed to the front of the box and deponent endeavored to seize him again, but only caught his clothes as he was leaping over the railing of the box. The clothes, as deponent believes, were torn in this attempt to seize him. As he went over upon the stage, deponent cried out with a loud voice, 'Stop that man.' Deponent then turned to the President. His position was not changed. His head was slightly bent forward and his eyes were closed. Deponent saw that he was unconscious, and, supposing him mortally wounded, rushed to the door for the purpose of calling medical aid. On reaching the outer door of the passageway as above described, deponent found it barred by a heavy piece of plank, one end of which was secured in the wall and the other rested against the door. It had been so securely fastened that it required considerable force to remove it. This wedge or bar was about four feet from the floor. Persons upon the outside were beating against the door for the purpose of entering. Deponent removed the bar and the door was opened. Several persons who represented themselves to be surgeons were allowed to enter. Deponent saw there Colonel Crawford, and requested him to prevent other persons from entering the box. Deponent then returned to the box and found the surgeons examining the President's person. They had not yet discovered the wound. As soon as it was discovered it was determined to remove him from the theatre. He was carried out, and this deponent then proceeded to assist Mrs. Lincoln, who was intensely excited, to leave the theatre. On reaching the head of the stairs deponent requested Major Potter to aid him in assisting Mrs. Lincoln across the street to the house to which the President was being conveyed. The wound which deponent had received had been bleeding very profusely, and, on reaching the house, feeling very faint from the loss of blood, he seated himself in the hall, and soon after fainted away and was laid upon the floor. Upon the return of consciousness deponent was taken in a carriage to his residence.

" In the review of the transaction, it is the confident belief of the deponent that the time which elapsed between the discharge of the pistol and the time when the assassin leaped from the box, did not exceed thirty seconds. Neither Mrs. Lincoln nor Miss Harris had left their seats."

H. R. RATHBONE.

Subscribed and sworn before me }
  this 17th day of April, 1865, }

A. B. OLIN,

Justice of the Supreme Court of the
District of Columbia.

District of Columbia, City of Washington, ss:
" Clara H. Harris, being duly sworn, says, that she has read the foregoing affidavit of Major Rathbone, and knows the contents thereof; that she was present at Ford's Theatre with the President and Mrs. Lincoln, and Major Rathbone, on the evening of the 14th. of April, instant; that at the time she heard the discharge of the pistol she was attentively engaged in observing what was transpiring upon the stage, and looking around she saw Major Rathbone spring from his seat and advance to the opposite side of the box; that she saw him engaged as if in a struggle with another man, but

the smoke with which he was enveloped prevented this deponent from seeing distinctly the other man; that the first time she saw him distinctly was when he leaped from the box upon the stage ; that she then heard Major Rathbone cry out, 'Stop that man,' and this deponent then immediately repeated the cry, 'Stop that man,' 'Won't somebody stop that man?' A moment after, some one from the stage asked, 'What is it?' or 'What is the matter?' and deponent replied, 'The President is shot.' Very soon after two persons, one wearing the uniform of a naval surgeon and the other that of a soldier of the Veteran Reserve Corps, came upon the stage, and the deponent assisted them in climbing up to the box.

"And this deponent further says, that the facts stated in the foregoing affidavit, so far as the same came to the knowledge or notice of the deponent, are accurately stated therein.

"CLARA H. HARRIS."

Subscribed and sworn before me, }
   this 17th day of April, 1865, }
        A. B. OLIN,
    Justice of the Supreme Court of the
       District of Columbia.

Such is the account of the brief but tragic act given by one within the box. One of the actors at the moment on the stage, makes the following statement, showing what was seen from his position, and he was the only one of the company on the stage, at the time, Miss Laura Keane being about to enter:

"I was," says Mr. Hawke, "playing 'Asa Trenchard,' in the American Cousin.' The 'old lady' of the theatre had just gone off the stage, and I was answering her exit speech when I heard the shot fired. I turned, looked up at the President's box, heard the man exclaim 'Sic semper tyrannis,' saw him jump from the box, seize the flag on the staff, and drop to the stage ; he slipped when he gained the stage, but got upon his feet in a moment, brandished a large knife, saying 'The South shall be free!' turned his face in the direction I stood, and I recognized him as John Wilkes Booth. He ran towards me, and I, seeing the knife, thought I was the one he was after, ran off the stage and up a flight of stairs. He made his escape out of a door, directly in the rear of the theatre, mounted a horse and rode off.

"The above all occurred in the space of a quarter of a minute, and, at the time, I did not know that the President was shot; although if I had tried to stop him, he would have stabbed me."

Few of the audience had any idea of what was occurring, but Captain Theodore McGowan, A.A.G. to General Augur, makes this statement:

"On the night of Friday, April 14, 1865, in company with a friend I went to Ford's theatre. Arriving there just after the entrance of President Lincoln and the party accompanying him, my friend Lieutenant Crawford, and I, after viewing the Presidential party from the opposite side of the dress circle, went to the right side, and took seats in the passage above the seats of the dress circle, and about five feet from the door of the box occupied by President Lincoln. During the performance, the attendant of the President came out and took the chair nearest the door. I sat, and had been sitting, about four feet to his left and rear, for some time.

"I remember that a man, whose face I do not distinctly recollect, passed me, and inquired of one sitting near who the President's messenger was, and learning, exhibited to him an envelope, apparently official, having a printed heading, and superscribed in a bold hand. I could not read the address, and did not try. *I think now it was meant for Lieutenant-General Grant.* That man went away.

"Some time after I was disturbed in my seat by the approach of a man who desired to pass up on the aisle in which I was sitting. Giving him room by bending my chair forward, he passed me, and stepped one step down on the level below me. Standing there, he was almost in my line of sight, and I saw him, while watching the play. He stood, as I remember, one step above the messenger, and remained perhaps one minute apparently looking at the stage and orchestra below. Then he drew a number of visiting cards from his pocket, from which, with some attention, he drew or selected one. These things I saw distinctly. I saw him stoop, and I think, descend to the level of the messenger, and by his right side. He showed the card to the messenger, and as my attention was then more closely fixed upon the play, I do not know whether the card was carried in by the messenger, or his consent given to the entrance of the man who presented it. I saw, a few moments after, the same man entering the door of the lobby leading to the box and the door closing behind him. This was seen because I could not fail from my position to observe it; the door side of the proscenium box and the stage were all within the direct and oblique lines of my sight. How long I watched the play after entering I do not know. It was, perhaps, two or three minutes, possibly four. The house was perfectly still, the large audience listening to the dialogue between 'Florence Trenchard' and 'May Meredith,' when the sharp report of a pistol rang through the house. It was apparently fired behind the scenes, on the right of the stage. Looking towards it and behind the Presidential box, while it startled all, it was evidently accepted by every one in the theatre as an introduction to some new passage, several of which had been interpolated in the early part of the play. A moment after a man leaped from the front of the box, directly down nine feet on the stage, and ran rapidly across it, bare-headed, holding an unsheathed dagger in his right hand, the blade of which flashed brightly in the gaslight as he came within ten feet of the opposite rear exit. I did not see his face as he leaped or ran, but I am convinced he was the man I saw enter. As he leaped he cried distinctly the motto of Virginia, '*Sic Semper Tyrannis.*' The hearing of this and the sight of the dagger explained fully to me the nature of the deed he had committed. In an instant he had disappeared behind the side scene. Consternation seemed for a moment to rivet every one to his seat, the next moment confusion reigned supreme. I saw the features of the man distinctly before he entered the box, having surveyed him contemptuously before he entered, supposing him to be an ill-bred fellow who was pressing a selfish matter on the President in his hours of leisure. The assassin of the President is about five feet nine and a half inches high, black hair, and I think eyes of the same color. He did not turn his face more than quarter front, as artists term it. His face was smooth, as I remember, with the exception of a moustache of moderate size, but of this I am not positive. He was dressed in a black coat, approximating to a dress frock, dark pants, and wore a stiff-rimmed, flat-topped round crowned black hat of felt, I think. He was a gentlemanly looking person, having no decided or obtruding mark. He seemed for a moment or two to survey the house with the deliberation of an habitue of the theatre."

Several had observed Booth around the entrance of the theatre and the boxes, but neither this nor his leaving his horse in the rear, from his profession and actual occasional appearance on the boards of the theatre, could or did excite the slightest suspicion. A soldier, however, states that he heard him and another man in front of the theatre, speaking as though they intended to attack the President as he came out: he states too that men stationed apparently at intervals, kept calling out the time every few minutes, evidently to notify confederates in the rear. All the preparations however, show that the box was the place appointed in the councils of the conspirators.

At the moment of the fearful deed the President was seated in a large and comfortable crimson velvet patent rocking-chair, his right elbow upon the arm of the chair, and his head resting upon his hand. The left hand was extended to pull aside the flag (belonging to the Treasury Guard), which draped the side of the box nearest him. His eyes were directed towards the orchestra, a kindly smile upon his face. At this instant the assassin burst open the door immediately behind the President, and deliberately shot him, as already stated. It was all the work of a moment! The flash of the pistol, the curling of the smoke, were scarce noticed, when the murderer was seen to spring from the box on the stage beneath, some twelve feet distant. As the intruder struck the stage, he fell forward, but soon gathered himself up and turned, erect, in full view of the audience. With singular audacity the assassin stood there long enough to photograph himself forever even in the minds of those among the throng who had never seen him before. They saw a slim, graceful figure, elegantly clad, waving a dagger with a gesture that none but a tragedian by profession would have made; a classic face, pale as marble, lighted up by two gleaming eyes—which had made crowds shudder often in past days when *Gloster* struggled with death in mimic phrensy—and surmounted by waves of curling, jet black hair. The assassin, with calmness which only could come of careful premeditation, uttered the words, " *Sic Semper Tyrannis*" in tones so sharp and clear that every person in the theatre heard them. He said something more, but in that second of time Mrs. Lincoln had screamed in horror, the unusual occurrences had created an excitement, the audience begun to rise, and no one heard the words distinctly. Booth, who already heard his name pronounced by a score of lips, waited for no further bravado, but rushed across the stage, by *Dundreary*, by *Florence Trenchard*, at the wing, rudely pushing Miss Keane out of his way, as she stood ready to come upon the stage, down the long passage behind the scenes, thrusting his knife at a man who seemed to interrupt his flight, and out by the stage door into the darkness. Only one man, Mr. J. B. Stewart, of the Washington bar, had presence of mind to pursue him; but unfamiliar with the theatre, Booth reached the back door before him, and closing it, was enabled to thrust aside the boy and spring to his saddle, before Mr. Stewart could open it. All was instantly confusion in front. Both before and behind the scenes every one knew that the President had been shot. Actors rushed upon the stage, and the audience into the orchestra. Mr. Lincoln had sunk down without a groan or a struggle. Mrs. Lincoln had fainted after her first shriek—Major Rathbone was disabled by a stab which Booth's knife had given him in the struggle—Miss Harris was bewildered by the sudden and fearful occurrence. The audience surged to and fro in frantic excitement. Some attempted to climb up the supports and into the box. Then came those clear and distinct tones of Laura Keene, first in the theatre to understand and appreciate the emergency :—" Keep quiet in your seats—give him air." In another moment certain gentlemen found presence of mind to order the throng to leave the theatre. The gas was turned down. The crowd at last animated by an impulse pushed for the outer doors.

As the news spread through the city, another horror fell upon all. It was announced that, simultaneously with the tragic events at Ford's theatre, and, as near as can be ascertained, at the precise moment, another fiend entered the house of Secretary Seward, after some parleying with the servants, and, it seems, there dealt out his blows in all directions. Some six or seven persons who were in attendance upon the family during the night have made their positive statements of the manner in which the assault was made here. It is well established that Payne, the assassin, applied at Seward's residence as the pretended bearer of a prescription of medicine. Having succeeded in evading the servant at the door, he rushed to Seward's chamber, but was confronted by Frederick Seward, when he had quite a parley for a moment about the medicine which he had been directed to deliver in person. Finding that he could not succeed in that way, he made an attack upon Frederick Seward. The desperado was a large and powerful man. He was determined to enter the bedchamber, and drew his pistol and snapped it twice, but did not succeed in discharging it. He struck Seward twice upon the head with such force that it not only felled him to the floor, and crushed the skull in two or three places, but also breaking the pistol, separating the chamber from the barrel. He then immediately rushed into the room, and applied his knife to Secretary Seward, who was lying prostrate in bed. It is evident, from the wounds, that he tried to cut the Secretary's throat. He succeeded in inflicting severe gashes upon his face, laying open both cheeks; but his blows were partially warded off by the bedclothes about the Secretary's neck, and by the additional fact that Mr. Seward rolled out upon the floor. A soldier, acting as nurse, meanwhile sprung upon the assassin. He stabbed the soldier in the side, and succeeded in breaking away, and, after wounding Major Seward, another son of the Secretary, and an attendant, succeeded in making his escape from the house, mounted his horse and rode away, shouting, like Booth, "*Sic Semper Tyrannis!*" as he sprang into the saddle.

The surgeons who entered found Mr. Lincoln insensible, and were satisfied the wound was mortal. They immediately prepared to carry the body from the box, and it was with difficulty borne out of the theatre and across the street to the house of a Mr. Petersen. The Hon. M. B. Field, Assistant-Secretary of the Treasury, in a letter, thus describes the place and sad scene enacted there :—

I proceeded at once to the room in which the President was lying, which was a bedroom in an extension, on the first or parlor floor of the house. The room is small, and is ornamented with prints, a very familiar one of Landseer's, a white horse, being prominent, directly over the bed. The bed was a double one, and I found the President lying diagonally across it, with his head at the outside. The pillows were saturated with blood, and there was considerable blood upon the floor immediately under him. There was a patchwork coverlet thrown over the President, which was only so far removed, from time to time, as to enable the physicians in attendance to feel the arteries of the neck or the heart, and he appeared to have been divested of all clothing. His eyes were closed and injected with blood, both the lids and the portion surrounding the eyes being as black as if they had been bruised by violence. He was breathing regularly, but with effort, and did not seem to be struggling or suffering. . . .

For several hours, the breathing above described continued regularly, and apparently without pain or consciousness. But about 7 o'clock a change occurred, and the breathing, which had been continuous, was interrupted at intervals. These intervals became more frequent and of longer duration, and the breathing more feeble. Several times the interval was so long, that we thought him dead, and the surgeon applied his finger to the pulse, evidently to ascertain if such was the fact. But it was not till 22 minutes past 7 o'clock in the morning that the flame flickered out. There was no apparent suffering, no convulsive action, no rattling of the throat, none of the ordinary premonitory symptoms of death. Death in this case was a mere cessation of breathing.

The fact had not been ascertained one minute, when Dr. Gurley offered up a prayer. The few persons in the room were all profoundly affected. The President's eyes, after death, were not, particularly the right one, entirely closed. I closed them myself, with my fingers. The expression immediately after death was purely negative; but in fifteen minutes there came over the mouth, the nostrils, and the chin, a smile that seemed almost an effort of life. I had never seen upon the President's face an expression more genial and pleasing.

About fifteen minutes before the decease, Mrs. Lincoln came into the room, and threw herself upon her dying husband's body. She was allowed to remain there only a few minutes, when she was removed in a sobbing condition, in which, indeed, she had been during all the time she was present.

After completing his prayer in the chamber of death, Dr. Gurley went into the front parlor, where Mrs. Lincoln was, with Mrs. and Miss Kinney, and her son Robert, Gen. Todd, of Dacotah (a cousin of hers), and Gen. Farnsworth, of Illinois. Here another prayer was offered up, during which I remained in the hall. The prayer was continually interrupted by Mrs. Lincoln's sobs. Soon after its conclusion, I went into the parlor, and found her in a chair, supported by her son Robert. Presently her carriage came up, and she was removed to it. She was in a state of tolerable composure at that time, until she reached the door, when, glancing at the theatre opposite, she repeated three or four times : "That dreadful house !—that dreadful house !"

The following minutes, taken by Dr. Abbott, show the condition of the late President throughout the night:

Eleven o'clock—Pulse 44.
Five minutes past eleven—Pulse 45, and growing weaker.
Ten minutes past eleven—Pulse 45.
Quarter past eleven—Pulse 42.
Twenty minutes past eleven—Pulse 45, respiration 27 to 29.
Twenty-five minutes past eleven—Pulse 42.
Thirty-two minutes past eleven—Pulse 48, and full.

Forty minutes past eleven—Pulse 45.

Quarter to twelve—Pulse 45, respiration 22.

Twelve o'clock—Pulse 48, respiration 22.

Quarter past twelve—Pulse 48, respiration 21.   Ecchymosis both eyes.

Half-past twelve—Pulse 45.

Thirty-two minutes past twelve—Pulse 60.

Thirty-five minutes past twelve—Pulse 66.

Forty minutes past twelve—Pulse 69, right eye much swollen, and ecchymosis.

Forty-five minutes past twelve—Pulse 70.

Fifty-five minutes past twelve—Pulse 80, struggling motion of arms.

One o'clock—Pulse 86, respiration 30.

Half-past one—Pulse 95, appearing easier.

Forty-five minutes past one—Pulse 86; very quiet; respiration irregular.   Mrs. Lincoln present.

Ten minutes past two—Mrs. Lincoln retired with Robert Lincoln to an adjoining room.

Half-past two—President very quiet; pulse 54; respiration 28.

Fifty-two minutes past two—Pulse 48; respiration 30.

Three o'clock visited again by Mrs. Lincoln.

Twenty-five minutes past three—Respiration 24, and regular.

Thirty-five minutes past three—Prayer by the Rev. Dr. Gurley.

Four o'clock—Respiration hard; regular.

Quarter past four—Pulse 60; respiration 25.

Fifty minutes past five—Respiration 28, regular; sleeping.

Six o'clock—Pulse failing; respiration 28.

Half-past six—Still failing, and labored breathing.

Seven o'clock—Symptoms of immediate dissolution.

Twenty-two minutes past seven—Death.

Shortly after 9 o'clock the remains were removed in a coffin to the White House, attended by a dense crowd, and escorted by a squadron of cavalry and several distinguished officers. At a later hour a *post-mortem* examination was made of the remains, by Surgeon-General Barnes, Dr. Stone, the late President's family physician, Drs. Crane, Curtis, Woodward, Taft, and other eminent medical men.

The external appearance of the face was that of a deep black stain about both eyes.   Otherwise the face was very natural.

The wound was on the left side of the head behind, on a line with and three inches from the left ear.

The course of the ball was obliquely forward, towards the right eye, crossing the brain obliquely a few inches behind the eye, where the ball lodged.

In the track of the wound were found fragments of bone, which had been driven forward by the ball.

The ball was found imbedded in the anterior lobe of the west hemisphere of the brain.

The orbit plates of both eyes were the seat of comminuted fracture, and the orbits of the eyes were filled with extravasated blood.

The serious injury to the orbit plates was due to the centre coup, the result of the intense shock of so large a projectile fired so closely to to the head.

The ball was evidently a derringer, hand cast, and from which the neck had been clipped.

A shaving of lead had been removed from the ball in its passage of the bones of the skull, and was found in the orifice of the wound. The first fragment of bone was found two and a-half inches within the brain : the second and larger fragment about four inches from the orifice. The ball lay still further in advance. The wound was half an inch in diameter.

III.

EFFECT ON THE COUNTRY.

III.

THE EFFECT ON THE COUNTRY.

NEVER in our national history did a blow fall with more terrible earnestness than the news of the assassination of Mr. Lincoln, as it flashed along the telegraph through the land, and penetrated from stations to more distant points. A general gloom pervaded all men. Every face wore a look of deepest sorrow at the loss of one who, wise and beyond reproach, had just carried the country through its terrible struggle.

In the greatest cities of the land, men streamed down from their homes to the centres of business and labor; but as with one accord, when the certainty of the President's death was announced, all places of business began to close. At the earliest tidings, the flags and streamers which, in exultation over Sumter's restoration, had, the day before, been fluttering so victoriously in the breeze, had been silently lowered. When Mr. Lincoln breathed his last, the flags hung draped at half-mast, and the fronts of public buildings and of stores were draped in black. Before sunset, almost every dwelling showed the same habiliments of woe.

Meanwhile the heads of departments, the commanders of our armies, governors of States, mayors of cities, issued their orders expressing their sense of the loss, and calling on those under their direction to join in the universal sorrow. Except where a few madmen exulted, to be cut down with an indignation that acted swiftly and sure, all party feeling was forgotten. The papers everywhere paid their tribute to the worth of Mr. Lincoln.

Most appreciative perhaps of all was the editorial in the New York World, ever opposed to the course and policy of the murdered President.

THE LATE PRESIDENT LINCOLN.

Never before in history has there been an occasion so fraught
with public consequence that was, at the same time, so like an overwhelming domestic affliction. This portentous national calamity,
conscious as we all are of its weighty and inscrutable significance
in the future politics of the country, is also so full of affecting pathos
and tragic horror that a smitten people are overborne by a flood of
sensibility, like a bereaved family who have no heart to think on
their estate and prospects when the tide of sudden affliction has
swept away the supporting prop of the household. By no other
single achievement could Death have carried such a feeling of deso-
lation into every dwelling, and have caused this whole land to
mourn as over the sundering of some dear domestic tie.

The terrible deed which has filled the national heart with grief
and consternation, lacks no conceivable accessory of tragic horror.
When the storm which has gone over us seemed to have spent its
force, there is suddenly shot from an unexpected quarter, without
warning or preparation, a swift thunderbolt which strikes away the
chief pillar of the state and shakes the whole edifice to its foundations. Death, always affecting, becomes horrible when dealt by the
hand of an assassin; even though the victim be but a private individual, the deed of violence spreads a feeling of uneasiness and
alarm through an excited community. The demise of the chief magistrate of a great nation, even though he die calmly in his bed, in
the most tranquil times, is an awful and affecting event; when an
assassin deals the blow, the surcharge of horror is naturally as great
in proportion as in the case of a murdered individual; but if the
calamity comes in a crisis when that particular life is unusually felt
to be of supreme value to a nation's hopes and prospects, the awful-
ness of the tragedy is heightened by all the considerations that can
give overwhelming poignancy to a nation's grief. Even the unimportant circumstances and surroundings of this foul deed have a
tragic complexion. Perpetrated on the anniversary of the opening
of the war; in a place of public amusement; in the presence of a
paralyzed multitude who had come clustering together to witness a
spectacle; the murderer an actor by profession, trained to an exag-
gerated admiration of certain historic characters, whose suggestive
names had become prefixes in his family; his escape from a crowded
assembly by leaping upon the stage and disappearing behind the
scenes with a Latin motto in his mouth, while the consort of his
illustrious victim was swooning in an agony of which no imagination can measure the depth;—and then the cry that arose at mid-

night in all the cities of this afflicted land, and the horror and consternation that fell upon all hearts as the sun heaved up his orb into
the morning sky—all this together completes a spectacle for the
horror-struck imagination such as history, even with the trappings
of the tragic muse to set it off, has seldom or never approached.
What has the Eternal Mind, that presides over and shapes out the
course of human history, in store for us, that He has thus permitted
to be spread upon the canvas allotted to this country and this century a scene so affecting and awful that none of its colors can fade
till both continents are ingulfed in the all-effacing ocean?

Whatever a wise and unsearchable Providence may bring out
of this appalling visitation, we can, as yet, see nothing in it but
calamity. It is a terrible proof of the depth, intensity, and danger
of those passions which have been awakened into such fearful vigor
by the events of the war. An ardent young man, not personally
predisposed to crime; brought up to an art which stands aloof from
political associations; accustomed to view the events of history only
on their pathetic or their scenic side; trained to regulate every gesture and mold every lineament of his face to court public admiration;
this young man, with this imaginative training, is not transformed
into an assassin by the vulgar impulses of an ordinary murderer.
In this terrible deed, as in the ordinary exercise of his profession,
he has been a candidate for sympathy and approbation. It was his
instinctive and sympathetic knowledge of what lurks in the hearts
of the baffled secessionists, which made him see that this unavailing
act of vengeance would enshrine him in their affections, and make
his a dear and canonized name. His dreadful act is an awful commentary on the consequences of party passions when they are fanned
into such rage that they strip the most odious crimes of their horror
and clothe them in the seductive drapery of public virtue. While
the disabled half of the country is yet a caldron of unsubdued and
seething passions, it is lamentable that there should be taken from
us a mild and paternal chief magistrate who was preparing to pour
over these agitated passions the soothing influence of his natural
clemency. As soon as the war-cloud visibly lifted, he set himself
to the performance of acts which commanded the approval even of
his former opponents; and the day which preceded his death was
passed in employments more full of promise than any other in the
calendar of this momentous era. There will fall into his opening
and honored grave no warmer or more plentiful tribute of honest
sensibility than is shed by those of his loyal fellow-citizens who did
not contribute to his re-election.

Of the career brought thus suddenly to this tragic close it is yet too early to make any estimate that will not require revision. It is probable that the judgment of history will differ in many respects from that of Mr. Lincoln's contemporaries; and in no respect, perhaps, more than in reversing the current tenor of the public thinking on what has been considered the vacillation of his character. It must never be overlooked that Mr. Lincoln was elevated to the presidency without previous training; that he was a novice in the discharge of high executive functions. Confronted at the very threshold with problems of a novelty, magnitude, and difficulty which would have caused the most experienced statesman to quail, beset on all sides by the most conflicting advice, it would not have been wisdom, but shallow and foolhardy presumption, indicating unseemly levity of character, if he had affected a display of the same kind of confident decision with which an old sailor manages a cock-boat in fair weather. If, under such circumstances, he had played the *role* of a man of decision, he would have forfeited all title to be considered a man of sense. When the most experienced and reputable statesmen of the country came to opposite conclusions, it is creditable to the strength, solidity, and modesty of Mr. Lincoln's mind, that he acted with a cautious and hesitating deliberation, proportioned rather to a sense of his great responsibilities, than to a theatrical notion of political stage effect.

Had the country, previous to Mr. Lincoln's first election, foreseen what was coming it would not have chosen for President a man of Mr. Lincoln's inexperience and peculiar type of character. But if his party was to succeed, we doubt whether foresight and deliberation would have made so good a choice. With the Republican party in power, this terrible struggle was inevitable; and, with a man of fixed views and inflexible purpose at the head of the Government, it would probably have resulted either in a dissolution of the Union or civil war in the North. In either event, we should have lost our institutions. The stability of a republican government, and, indeed, of any form of free government, depends upon its possessing that kind of flexibility which yields easily to the control of public opinion. In this respect, the English Government is more pliable than our own, the administration being at all times subject to immediate change by losing the confidence of the representatives of the people; whereas, under our Constitution, an iron inflexibility can maintain itself in office for the full period of four years, without any possibilty of displacing it except by revolution.

In ordinary times, this works well enough; for the growth of opinion in any ordinary four years, could not be so rapid as to indispose the people to await the presidential election. But when there was let loose upon us, at the beginning of the last administration, the wild outbreakings of turbulence and treason, the development of opinion went forward with gigantic strides, corresponding in some degree to the violence and magnitude of the contest. *Any* policy which a Republican President might have adopted with decision in the spring of 1861, and adhered to with steadiness during the four years, would have exposed the government to be shivered into fragments by the shocks of changing opinion. What was wanting in the flexibility of our political system was made up in the character of Mr. Lincoln. Whatever may be thought of the absolute merits of the late President's administration—on which it would not be decorous to express our views on this occasion—it cannot well be denied that it has been, throughout, a tolerably faithful reflex of the predominant public opinion of the country. Whether that opinion was, at any particular stage, right and wise, is a different question; but it cannot be doubtful that the predominant opinion carries with it the predominance of physical strength. A government against which this is arrayed in gathering force, must yield to it or go to pieces. Had Mr. Lincoln started with his emancipation policy in the spring of 1861, his administration would have been wrecked by the moral aid which would have been given the South by the northern conservatives, including a large part of the Republican party. Had he refused to adopt the emancipation policy much beyond the autumn of 1862, the Republican party would have refused public support to the war, and the South would have gained its independence by their aid. With a stiff Republican Senate, the government would have been at a dead-lock, and the violence of opinion would have wrenched its conflicting parts asunder. Regarding the growth of opinion simply in the light of a *fact*, we must concede that Mr. Lincoln's slowness, indecision, and reluctant changes of policy have been in skillful, or at least fortunate, adaptation to the prevailing public sentiment of the country. Some have changed more rapidly, some more slowly than he; but there are few of his countrymen who have not changed at all.

If we look for the elements of character which have contributed to the extraordinary and constantly growing popularity of Mr. Lincoln, they are not far to seek. The kindly, companionable, jovial turn of his disposition, free from every taint of affectation, puerile vanity, or *parvenu* insolence, conveyed a strong impression of worth, sense, and solidity, as well as goodness of heart. He never disclosed the slightest symptom that he was dazzled or elated by his great position, or that it was incumbent upon him to be any body but plain Abraham Lincoln. This was in infinitely better taste than would have been any attempt to put on manners that did not sit easily upon training and habits, under the false notion that he would be supporting the dignity of his office. No offense in manners is so intolerable as affectation; nor any thing so vulgar as a soul haunted by an uneasy consciousness of vulgarity. Mr. Lincoln's freedom from any such upstart affectations was one of the good points of his character; it betokened his genuineness and sincerity.

The conspicuous weakness of Mr. Lincoln's mind on the side of imagination, taste, and refined sensibility, has rather helped him in the estimation of the multitude. Except so far as they contribute something to dignity of character, these qualities have little scope in the pursuits of a statesman; and their misplaced obtrusion is always offensive. They are a great aid, to be sure, in electric appeals to the passions; but in times like these through which we have been living, the passions have needed sedatives, not incentives; and the cool mastery of emotion has deserved to rank among the chief virtues. Mr. Lincoln had no need of this virtue, because the sluggishness of his emotional nature shielded him against the corresponding temptation; but this defect has served him as well as the virtue amid the more inflammable natures with which he has been in contact. His character was entirely relieved from repulsive matter-of-fact hardness by the unaffected kindliness of his disposition and the flow of his homely and somewhat grotesque mother-wit — the most popular of all the minor mental endowments.

The total absence from Mr. Lincoln's sentiments and bearing of anything lofty or chivalric, and the hesitating slowness of his decisions, did not denote any feebleness of character. He has given a signal proof of a strong and manly nature in the fact that although he surrounded himself with the most considerable and experienced statesmen of his party, none of them were able to take advantage of his inexperience and gain any conspicuous ascendency over him. All his chief designs have been his own; formed indeed, after much anxious and brooding consultation, but, in the final result, the fruit of his own independent volition. He has changed or retained particular members of his cabinet, and indorsed or rejected particular dogmas of his party, with the same ultimate reliance on the decisions of his own judgment. It is this feature of his character, which was gradually disclosed to the public view, together with the cautious and paternal cast of his disposition, that gave his strong and increasing hold on the confidence of the masses.

Among the sources of Mr. Lincoln's influence, we must not omit to mention the quaint and peculiar character of his written and spoken eloquence. It was as completely his own, as much the natural outgrowth of his character, as his personal manners. Formed on no model, and aiming only at the most convincing statement of what he wished to say, it was terse, shrewd, clear, with a peculiar twist in the phraseology which more than made up in point what it sometimes lost by its uncouthness. On the multitude, who do not appreciate literary refinement, and despise literary affectation, its effect was as great as the same ideas and arguments could have produced by any form of presentation. His style had the great redeeming excellence of that air of straightforward sincerity which is worth all the arts of the rhetorician.

The loss of such a man, in such a crisis; of a man who possessed so large and growing a share of the public confidence, and whose administration had recently borrowed new lustre from the crowning achievements of our armies; of a ruler whom victory was inspiring with the wise and paternal magnanimity which sought to make the conciliation as cordial as the strife has been deadly; the loss of such a President, at such a conjuncture, is an afflicting dispensation which bows a disappointed and stricken nation in sorrow more deep, sincere, and universal than ever before supplicated the compassion of pitying Heaven.

In New York City, Wall street became a public meeting, in which resolutions were passed, and among other addresses the following were delivered :

Speech of Gen. Butler.

Fellow Citizens: But a day or two since we assembled throughout the nation in joy, gladness, and triumph, at the success of the armies of the republic, which opened to us the promise of a glorious peace and a happy country in the future. These flags, now the token of mourning, were then raised in gladness. To-day, in a short hour, Abraham Lincoln has been struck down by the hand of an assassin, and we assemble to mingle our grief with that of the loved ones at home, who mourn the honest man, the incorruptible patriot, the great statesman, the saviour of his country in its crisis. And while we reverently pray to God to overrule this dispensation for our good, we mingle our tears together as a nation for the loss, and we find the hearts of those around him melted in sadness. Yet, to us there are higher, sterner duties, and that is to

6

see that his death is not lost to the country. Other rebellions in
other countries have heretofore almost ever been inaugurated by
the assassin's knife. It is left for us to exhibit the spectacle of a
rebellion crushed in its body, crushed in its strength, crushed
in its blood, crushed in its bones, revivifying its soul by assassination and death. And, with a blind hate which has ever
characterized its purpose, it has struck down in cold silence the
most forgiving, the most lenient, the most gracious friend that
the misguided rebel ever had in this country. If rebellion
can do this to the good, the wise, the kind, the beneficent,
what does it teach us we ought to do to those who, from high
places, incite the assassin's mind and guide the assassin's knife.
Shall we content ourselves with merely crushing out the strength,
the power, the material resources of the rebellion? Shall we
leave its spirit and soul unsubdued, to light the torch in this
city, and fire the pistol in the capital at all the good and great?
Are we to have peace in fact or only in name? Is this nation
hereafter to be peaceable? Are the avocations of life to go
on, each man going about without fear and without dread, or
are we to rival hereafter the tales we have heard of the old
world, where every man feared his neighbor, and no man went
about except armed to the teeth or in panoply of steel? This
is the question that is to be decided this day, ay, this hour,
by the American people. And perhaps I may say, reverently,
that this dispensation of God's good providence is sent to teach
us that the spirit of the rebellion has not been broken by the
surrender of its armies. And, my friends, echoing the words
of the last speaker, I would say, be of good heart. There is
no occasion of despondency. A great, a good man has gone,
in the fullness of his fame, in the height of his glory, to join
the sages and patriots of the revolutionary days. His life was
saved four years ago when it was needed, and he went through
Baltimore, and the waves of the rebellion were beating around him.
But now his work was done; and it remains for us to do that which
is left for us to do in the same direction. He has driven out
the life and the spirit, and it is for us to take care of the soul
of the rebellion. And I am glad to speak here, to assure you,
what I know to be the sentiment of the present President of the
United States, who has succeeded by this great dispensation of
Providence to the highest place on earth, that he feels as you and I
do, I know it, on the subject, that the rebellion is to be put down.
He has had a nearer view of it than we have had. It has been at
his hearth-stone, and he has had almost his roof-tree blazing over

him. And every one ought to know that he is not only able but willing and desirous that it should be dealt with as we would have it dealt with. And therefore, let every man be of cheer. It may be said, I hear it has been said, that those who recommend condign punishment for treason and other wrongs are blood-thirsty —that we desire to shed blood for the shedding of blood. But, fellow-citizens, could he who has gone before us have foreseen what would have been the end of his policy—of his clemency and forgiveness—it might have soured his heart, but it might have informed his judgment, and we had him spared to us this hour. If he could have seen that forgiveness meant assassination—that clemency meant death, that even the sick man whom the providence of God had spared for a season, was to be murdered on his sick-bed as a result of the rebellion—perhaps he would have nerved his heart against these men, and forgot the goodness of his nature. But he has gone before us, the first victim of this clemency ; with words of forgiveness upon his tongue, even, has he died, and it is left for us to review the course, and see whether or not we are to be instructed by his death. And therefore I say it to you my friends—not in the spirit of revenge, not in the spirit of vengeance, not, I trust, in any spirit of destruction, God forbid ! but in the spirit of mercy for thousands I ask that punishment should be visited upon those who have caused this great wrong. The nation demands it. The widowed wives of those of our fallen soldiers sleeping in southern soil cry out for it. The insulted majesty of the nation has determined upon it, and woe be to him that gets in the path of justice and of the execution of the law.

SPEECH OF HON. DANIEL S. DICKINSON.

The spirit of the rebellion, my friends and fellow-citizens, has finally culminated in the assassination of the President of the United States. The spirit of rebellion and of slavery has finally whet its knife, and finding it could not accomplish the death of this nation, has wreaked its vengeance in the heart's blood of the Chief Magistrate. In all the history of men, savage and civilized; in the history of nations, ancient and modern; you can find nothing in the annals of the French Revolution, or elsewhere, equal to this in atrocity and abomination. The only criticisms that were ever passed upon that great and good man were that he had been too lenient, too forgiving in his spirit, too moderate against rebellion. The assassin, not at midnight, but in the midst of a public assembly,

has drawn his weapon against the life of the President; and what
is more cowardly, more ferocious, more abominable, if there is a
grade of crime in assassination, was the attempt on the life of the
Secretary of State, who was lying almost upon his dying bed. It
required the spirit of the rebellion; it required slavery in its last
struggling death throes, to do this. This thing—I but repeat what
I said long ago—is to be hunted out like a savage beast. And if
there is any one thing in my human experience that I thank God
more devoutly for than any other, it is that I have not anywhere
winked at any thing, but have been in favor of hewing them down
from beginning to end. It is not merely the death of Abraham
Lincoln—great, good, patient, faithful, sincere as he was—but
it is this great nation that has been wounded in her Chief Magistrate, that she had, with great and unusual *eclat*, continued in the
position, and said, 'Well done, good and faithful servant.' Let
our humanity extend to the humbler misguided men of the rebellion; but let us march on together to take out the roots and
pull up the seed of it. I tell you that I will never slumber or
sleep till every thing belonging to the rebellion, in number, person, and case, is abolished. I spent the best years of my life in
endeavoring to reconcile differences between North and South. I
saw in this rebellion a determination on the part of the rebel murderers, thieves, and conspirators, not to be conciliated. I say now
that they must be hunted from the abodes of men. I care not
whether this was the act of one man or the act of a hundred; it results from a sentiment which has been inculcated to destroy this
great nation. It is acting practically upon the sentiment; and
whether one conspirator's arm were nerved or whether a million
had been brought forward, that is not the question—it was a determination to destroy this nation in the person of the President of the
United States, and of the Secretary of State, whose prudent policy
has prevented them from embarrassing us with a war with foreign
nations. They come forward now and then and whet their knives
for the destruction of individuals. Like the sending of Joseph into
Egypt, they meant it for evil, but God means it for our good. He
has torn the veil from the face of this infernal rebellion, and it is
perfectly revealed in all its hideousness. Who will follow it now
except to slay it between the porch and the altar? I had hoped
that its dying days would be calm and tranquil; that it would go
down to the grave unhonored and unsung, but in peace. I am for
calling upon every man with a loyal heart, be he north or south,
east or west, be he old or young, be he of one political organization
or another, to now say, whatever his previous opinions have been,

that there has come a time when the people must take this thing into their own hand, in all their power, in all their majesty, until the last of the rebellion shall be numbered with the things that were.

At Nashville processions postponed from the previous day were just forming when the news was received. Instantly joy gave place to sorrow, the strains of exultation changed to funeral marches, and the military, with arms reversed, returned to their camps.

At Cincinnati, Columbus, Wheeling, Louisville, St. Louis, and even at San Francisco and the cities of California, the same scenes were repeated. Everywhere, spontaneous cessation of business, the closing of courts, the draping of the towns in mourning.

Even in the British Provinces marks of respect were shown. In Nova Scotia, the Governor was about to visit the Legislative Council, to give assent to the laws with the usual ceremonies, but on hearing of the sad news sent the following message to the Council :

"GOVERNMENT HOUSE, HALIFAX, N. S.,
" Saturday, April 15, 1865.

" MY DEAR SIR—Very shocking intelligence which has just reached me of the murder of President Lincoln by the hand of an assassin, and my sense of the loss which the cause of order has sustained by the death of a man whom I have always regarded as eminently upright in his intentions, indisposes me to make any public ceremony such as I had contemplated in my intended visit to the Legislative Council to-day. I beg, therefore, to notify to you the postponement of that visit, and, perhaps, under the circumstances, men of all parties may feel that the suspension of further public business for the day would be a mark of sympathy not unbecoming the Legislature to offer, one which none could misconstrue. Believe me to be, very dear sir, your obedient servant,

" RICHARD GROVES McDOWELL.

" To EDWARD KINNEY,
" President of the Legislative Council."

At Toronto, the flags on the Custom House, and the shipping were displayed at half-mast, and Canadians shared in the expressions manifested by resident Americans.

At Concord, N. H., on the evening after the reception of the news of the President's death a very large crowd of people called at the house of ex-President Franklin Pierce, and they were addressed by him as follows.

Speech of Ex-President Pierce.

Fellow-Townsmen—I come to ascertain the motives of this call. What is your desire?

[Some person in the crowd replied, "We wish to hear some words from you on this sad occasion." General Pierce proceeded.]

I wish I could address you words of solace. But that can hardly be done. The magnitude of the calamity, in all aspects, is over-whelming. If your hearts are oppressed by events more calculated to awaken profound sorrow and regret than any which have hitherto occurred in our history, mine mingles its deepest regrets and sorrows with yours.

It is to be hoped that the great wickedness and atrocity was confined, morally and actually, to the heads and hearts of but two individuals of all those who still survive on this continent ; and that they may speedily, and in obedience to law, meet the punishment due to their unparalleled crimes. It is well that you—it is well that I—well that all men worthy to be called citizens of the United States, make manifest in all suitable forms the emotions incident to the bereavement and distress which have been brought to the hearths and homes of the two most conspicuous families of the Republic. I give them my warm, outgushing sympathy, as I am sure all persons within the hearing of my voice must do.

But beyond personal grief and loss, there will abide with us inevitably the most painful memories. Because, as citizens obedient to law, revering the Constitution, holding fast to the Union, thankful for the period of history which succeeded the Revolution in so many years of peaceful growth and prosperity, and loving with the devotion of true and faithful children all that belongs to the advancement and glory of the nation, we can never forget or cease to deplore the great crime and deep stain.

[A voice from the crowd—"Where is your flag?"]

It is not necessary for me to show my devotion for the stars and stripes by any special exhibition, or upon the demand of any man or body of men. My ancestors followed it through the Revolution—one of them, at least, never having seen his mother's roof from the beginning to the close of that protracted struggle. My brothers followed it in the war of 1812, and I left my family in the spring of

1847, among you, to follow its fortunes and maintain it upon a foreign soil.

But this you all know. If the period during which I have served our State and country in various situations, commencing more than thirty-five years ago, have left the question of my devotion to the flag, the Constitution and Union, in doubt, it is too late now to remove it by any such exhibition as the inquiry suggests. Besides, to remove such doubts from minds where they may have been cultivated by a spirit of domination and partisan rancor, if such a thing were possible, would be of no consequence to you, and it is certainly of none to me. The malicious questionings would return to re-assert their supremacy and pursue the work of injustice.

Conscious of the infirmities of temperament which, to a greater or less extent, beset us all, I have never felt or found that violence or passion was ultimately productive of beneficent results. It is gratifying to perceive that your observation, briefer than mine, has led your minds to the same conclusion. What a priceless commentary upon this general thought is the final reported conversation between the late President and his Cabinet ! and with that dispatch comes news to warrant the cheering hope, that in spite of the knife of the assassin, the life and intellect of the Secretary of State may, through Providence, be spared to us in this appalling emergency.

I thank you for the silent attention with which you have listened to me, and for the manifestations of your approval as my neighbors, and will not detain you in this storm longer than to add my best wishes for you all, and for what, individually and collectively, we ought to hold most dear—our country—our whole country. Good night.

The bishops of the Catholic and Episcopal Churches, the heads of other denominations, all came forward to join in the public grief, and appoint services for Wednesday, which was set apart for the funeral.

In many of the synagogues, on the day of his death, prayers were offered for Mr. Lincoln, according to Jewish usage.

Among the discourses pronounced on the following day, Sunday, we select that delivered at the New York Avenue Presbyterian Church, by the Rev. Dr. Gurley. This church, which was the one attended by Mr. Lincoln, his chosen place of worship, was well filled by a congregation among which were many high officials of the Government. Treasurer Spinner,

Governor Oglesby, General Eaton, and many other gentlemen no less eminent, were present.

The church was hung with crape, and the mute, heart-rending eloquence of the empty pew was not decreased by the black drapery that told the reason of the absence of its august owner.

After the singing of the 103d Hymn, which was preceded by the reading of the 103d Psalm, Dr. Gurley remarked that it was with his congregation a sacramental Sabbath, and that the services of the morning would have reference to that fact; but he added that, before uniting in prayer, he would say a few words regarding the great bereavement which had so suddenly come upon us as a nation.

He then said :—

"This is such a Sabbath as our nation never saw before. It is a day of mourning, of great and bitter lamentation. *Our beloved Chief Magistrate is dead!* The man whom the people had learned to trust with a confiding and a loving confidence, and upon whom, more than upon any other, were centred, under God, our best hopes for the true and speedy pacification of the country, the restoration of the Union, and the return of harmony and love—that great and honored man has passed away. Just as the prospect of peace was brightly opening upon us, and he was hoping to enjoy with the people the blessed fruit and reward of his and their toil, and care, and patience, and self-sacrificing devotion to the interests of liberty and the Union—just then he fell and passed away. That such a life should be sacrificed at such a time by such an agency! Oh it is a dark, a mysterious, a most afflicting visitation. But, while we mourn we must not murmur; while we weep we must not complain. Above the foul, and cruel, and bloody hand of the assassin—far, far above it—we must see *another hand*—the chastening hand of a wise and faithful God. We know that his judgments are right, and that in faithfulness he has afflicted us. In the midst of our rejoicings we needed this stroke, this dealing, this discipline, and therefore he has sent it. Let us remember our affliction has not come forth of the dust, and our trouble has not sprung out of the ground. Through and beyond all second causes we must look, and see the sovereign, permissive agency of the great First Cause. And while we bow and worship, let us also be still and know that He is God. "Clouds and darkness are round about Him; righteousness and judgment are the habitation of his throne." It is his prerogative to bring light out of darkness, and good out of evil. Surely the wrath of man shall praise Him, and the remainder of wrath He will restrain.   In the light of a clearer day we may yet see that the wrath which planned and perpetrated the death of the President was overruled by Him whose judgments are unsearchable and his ways past finding out, for the highest welfare of all those interests which are so clear to the Christian patriot and philanthropist, and for which a loyal people have made such an unexampled sacrifice of treasure and blood.   Let us not be faithless, but believing.

> ' Blind unbelief is prone to err,
> And scan his work in vain ;
> God is his own interpreter,
> And He will make it plain.'

"We will wait for his interpretation, and we will wait in faith, nothing doubting. He who has led us so well, and defended and prospered us so wonderfully during the last four years of civil strife, *will not forsake us now.* He may chasten, but he will not destroy. He may purify us more and more in the furnace of trial, but He will not consume us. No, no. He has chosen us, as He did his people of old, in the furnace of affliction, and he has said of us as he said of them, 'This people have I formed for myself; they shall show forth my praise.' Let our principal anxiety now be that this new sorrow may be a *sanctified* sorrow; that it may lead us to deeper repentance, to a more humbling sense of our dependence upon God, and to the more unreserved consecration of ourselves and all that we have to the cause of truth and justice, of law and order, of liberty and good government, of pure and undefiled religion. Then, though weeping may endure for a night, joy will come in the morning. Blessed be God ! despite of this great and sudden and temporary darkness, the morning has begun to dawn—the morning of a bright and glorious day, such as our country has never seen. That day will come, and not tarry, and the death of a hundred Presidents and their Cabinets can never, never prevent it. While we are thus hopeful, however, let us also be humble. Oh, that all our rulers and all our people may lie low in the dust to-day beneath the chastening hand of God ! and may their voices go up to Him as one voice, and their hearts go up to Him as one heart, pleading with Him for mercy, for grace to sanctify our great and sore bereavement, and for wisdom to guide us in this our time of need. Such a united cry and pleading will not be in vain. It will enter into the ear and heart of Him who sits upon the throne, and He will say to us, as to ancient Israel, ' In a little wrath I hid my face from thee for a moment; but with everlasting kindness will I have mercy upon thee, saith the Lord, thy Redeemer.' "

SERMON BY REV. HENRY W. BELLOWS,

Delivered at All Souls' Church, New York, on Easter Morning.

"Sorrow hath filled your heart. Nevertheless I tell you the truth. It is expedient for you that I go away, for if I go not away, the Comforter will not come unto you ; but if I depart, I will send him unto you."—*St. John*, xvi. 7.

So Jesus, in view of his own approaching death, comforted his disciples ! He was to leave them, robbed by violence of their accustomed leader; he whom they had believed should redeem Israel snatched wickedly and ignominiously from their side; all their hopes of prosperity and power in this world utterly destroyed. He was to leave them a dismayed and broken-hearted band, terror-stricken and scattered abroad, the enemies of their beloved Lord triumphant over Him; His words and teachings as yet involved in obscurity and mystery; their souls ungrown in his likeness; the nature of their Master's errand in this world not yet understood—nay, misunderstood almost as sadly by his disciples as by the Jews who murdered him. Knowing, as our Saviour did, just how they were to be affected by his death, how utterly appalled and bewildered, he still tells them, " It is expedient for you that I go away, for if I go not away the Comforter (who should abide with them forever) will not come unto you ; but if I depart I will send him unto you."

We understand now, looking back nineteen centuries, how truly Jesus spake. We see that without that death there could not have been that resurrection from the dead; that Jesus Christ was revealed to his disciples as a spiritual prince and deliverer, as Lord over the grave and king of saints immortal, in the defeat of all ambitions having their seat in this world ; that he died to prove that death was not the end of being, but the real beginning of a true life ; rose again to show that it was " appointed unto all men once to die," it was not because fate and matter were stronger than spirit, or because death was inevitable, but simply because thus man broke out of fleshly garments into a higher mode of existence. We see now that He finally left his disciples, and ascended into heaven, to show them that absence in the flesh is often only a greater nearness of the spirit—that His power to enlighten, guide, animate, and bless them—yes, to comfort and cheer them, was greater as an unseen Saviour, sitting at the right hand of God, than as a present incarnate martyr, in whose bosom John could lie, and into whose side and into the prints of whose hands Thomas could thrust his doubting fingers. And what He promised He fully performed ! The crucifixion which darkened the heavens with its gloom, gave way to the resurrection, which not only broke Christ's own tomb and the tombs of many saints, but slew the Angel of Death himself, leaving him only the mock dignity of a name without reality; which let into the apostles' minds, and through them into the world, their first conception of the utter spirituality of Christ's kingdom; converted them from Jews into Christians indeed; began the new era, and from ordinary fishermen created those glorious, sublime apostles whose teachings, character, deeds, and sufferings built up the Church on the chief corner-stone, and established our holy religion in the world.

And it was not only expedient for Jesus Christ to die, that he might rise again clothed with his conquest over the grave, his victory over the doubts and fears of his disciples, and the bold predictions and short triumph of his murderers—but expedient for him, in his ascension, to go away utterly from all bodily presence with his disciples and followers, drawing their thoughts and affections after him into the unseen world. Thus alone could Jesus keep the minds and hearts of his disciples wide open and stretched to the full compass of his spiritual religion—keep them from closing in again with their narrow earthly horizon—keep them from falling back into schemes of worldly hope—from substituting fondness for and devotion to his visible person, for that elevated, spiritual consecration to his spirit and his commandments, on which their future high and holy influence depended. Jesus went away that the Christ might return to be the anointing, and illumination, and Comforter of his disciples. His nearest friends never knew him till he had wholly gone away. They never loved him till he was beyond their embraces. John lying in his bosom was not as near his heart as thousands of his humblest disciples have been who have had Christ formed within them by communion with his Holy Spirit. That going away created and inspired the apostles, who, under God and Christ, created and inspired the Church. Jesus shook off his Judaic, his local and his merely human character, and became the universal Son of Man, the native of all countries, the contemporary of all times and eras, the ubiquitous companion and common Saviour. His death, his resurrection, his ascension, rehearsed and symbolized the common and sublime destiny of Humanity. Man is mortal, and must die ; man is immortal, and must rise again ; man is a spirit, and must quit the limitations of earth and sense, to dwell with God in a world of spiritual realities !

Thus Jesus honored the flesh he took upon himself, and the world he lived in; honored by accepting the universal lot of life and death.   But at the same time that he honored our visible conditions and circumstances, he discrowned them of their assumed sovereignty over us by triumphing over the grave, and returning in the flesh to life and to its duties and necessities; and then, finally, he lifted man above not only the grave, but above time and sense, matter and affairs, by ascending into the unseen world, as into a more real state of existence, and promising from that invisible seat to conduct the triumph of his Church, to visit and cheer the hearts of his disciples, and to be with them until the end of the world, when His kingdom should come fully, and God's will be done in earth as in heaven.   Then he would deliver the Kingdom up unto the Father, that God might be all in all.

And has it not indeed been so?   The Comforter has come!   He came to the Apostles, and wiped away their doubts and fears, their personal ambitions, their Jewish prejudices, their self-seeking and self-saving thoughts!   For tongues that spake only the dialects of their local experience, it gives them tongues of fire, burning with an eloquence intelligible in all lands and all ages.

And what but a Holy Spirit, a descending Saviour, taking of the things of God and showing them unto men, has been the strength and salvation of human hearts from that hour to this?   How has the Master's influence grown, how mighty his consolations, how irresistible the inspirations of his grace and truth!   Buried in catacombs, overwhelmed with the wrath of mighty kings and princes, resisted and withstood by all the pride of philosophers and sages, protested by the vulgar senses and denied by the coarse appetites of man—the holy faith, planted in Christ's broken tomb, has withstood the rigors of every climate, outlived the swords and axes that have turned their edge against it, the hoofs of horses and the iron heels of mailed hosts that have trampled it in the dust, been nourished by the blood of the martyrs that died for its glory and defence, and has overrun the very cities that slew its apostles, crossed oceans unknown to the empires that defied or despised it, become the glory and hope of a civilization known only by its name!   The Comforter indeed!   What visible bodily master could visit every day the millions of homes that the ascended Christ now takes in the daily circuit of His divine walk?   And what lips could articulate the unspeakable wisdom he distils into lowly hearts that feel, but can never tell, the joy and trust and truth he imparts?   Ah! the best part of the gospel is that word which cannot be uttered, but which comes and abides with the believing soul—that tender experience of a life hidden with Christ in God, which it is no more given to reveal in language, than it is to describe the things which God hath prepared for them that love him ! Yes ! on this holy Easter morning, when the mild spring air is full of God's quickening love, and the breeze goes whispering in the ear of every dry root and quivering stalk, the promise of a new life, a glorious resurrection, is there not a winged but viewless Comforter, noiselessly fluttering in at the windows of all Christian homes, and gently stirring in the hearts that have inherited their fathers' faith the blessed assurance of God's eternal love; of the soul's superiority to time and sense, to death and hell, of the supporting presence of a Saviour's love and care, with all the pageant invitations, encouragements and comforts that breathe from the Gospels, vital with the spirit of life, the death and resurrection of him whose history they record ? Can we read the New Testament to-day and feel that it is only common print we peruse ? Are Christ's living words only remembered phrases ? or do we seem to hear them spoken from heaven by Him who is the Word of God, and with a music and a meaning that all " the harpers, harping with their harps" could not intensify or sweeten, making our souls burn within us as when of old he walked and talked by the way, at Emmaus, with his disciples.

It is, dear brethren, the faith and hope and trust of those inspired by the Comforter Jesus sent, that enables us to confront without utter dismay the appalling visitation that has just fallen with such terrible suddenness upon the country and the national cause! With a heart almost withered, a brain almost paralyzed by the shock, I turn in vain for consolation to any other than the Comforter! Just as we were wreathing the laurels of our victories and the chaplets of our peace in with the Easter flowers that bloom around the empty sepulchre of our ascended Lord ; just as we were preparing the fit and luminous celebration of a nation's joy in its providential deliverance from a most bloody and costly war, and feeling that the Resurrection of Christ was freshly and gloriously interpreted by the rising of our smitten, humiliated, reviled, and crucified country, buried in the distrust of foreign nations and the intentions of rebel hearts; a country rising from the tomb, where she had left as discarded grave-clothes, the accursed vestments of slavery that had poisoned, enfeebled, and nearly destroyed her first life ; a country rising to a higher, purer existence under the guidance of a chief whom it fondly thought sent from above to lead it cautiously, wisely, conscientiously, successfully, like another Moses, through the Red Sea into the promised land ; just then, at the proud moment when the nation, its four years of conflict fully sounded, had announced its ability to diminish its armaments, withdraw its call for troops and its restrictions on intercourse, comes as out of a clear heaven the thunderbolt that pierces the tender, sacred head that we were ready to crown with a nation's blessings, while trusting to its wisdom and gentleness, its faithfulness and prudence, the closing up of the country's wounds, and the apparelling of the nation, her armor laid aside, in the white robes of peace.

Our beloved President, who had enshrined himself not merely in the confidence, the respect, and the gratitude of the people, but in their very hearts, as their true friend, adviser, representative, and brother ; whom the nation loved as much as it revered ; who had soothed our angry impatience in this fearful struggle with his gentle moderation and passionless calm; who had been the head of the nation, and not the chief of a successful party ; and had treated our enemies like rebellious children, and not as foreign foes, providing even in their chastisement for mercy and penitent restoration ; our prudent, firm, humble, reverential, God-fearing President is dead !

The assassin's hand has reached him who was belted round with a nation's devotion, and whom a million soldiers have hitherto encircled with their watchful guardianship.   Panoplied in honesty and simplicity of purpose, too universally well-disposed to believe in danger to himself, free from ambition, self-consequence, and show, he has always shown a fearless heart, gone often to the front, made himself accessible to all at home, trusted the people, joined their amusements, answered their summons, and laid himself open every day to the malice and murderous chances of domestic foes.   It seemed as if no man could raise his hand against that meek ruler, or confront with purpose of injury that loving eye, that sorrow-stricken face, ploughed with care, and watchings, and tears!   So marked with upright patient purposes of good to all, of justice and mercy, of sagacious roundabout wisdom, was his homely paternal countenance, that I do not wonder that his murderer killed him from behind, and could not face the look that would have disarmed him in the very moment of his criminal madness.

But he has gone !   Abraham Lincoln, President of the United States during the most difficult, trying, and important period of the nation's history; safe conductor of our policy through a crisis such as no other people ever had to pass; successful summoner of a million and a quarter of American citizens to arms in behalf of their flag and their Union ; author of the Proclamation of Emancipation ; the people's President; the heir of Washington's place at the hearths and altars of the land ; legitimate idol of the negro race—the perfect type of American democracy—the astute adviser of our generals in the field ; the careful student of their strategy, and their personal friend and inspirer ; the head of his Cabinet, prevailing by the passionless simplicity of his integrity and unselfish patriotism over the larger experience, the more brilliant gifts, the more vigorous purposes of his constitutional advisers ; a President indeed ; not the mere figure-head of the State, but its helmsman and pilot; shrinking from no perplexity, magnanimous in self-accusation and in readiness to gather into his own bosom the spears of rebuke aimed at his counsellors and agents; the tireless servant of his place ; no duty so small and wearisome that he shirked it, none so great and persistent that he sought to fling it upon others ; the man who, fully tried (not without fitful vacillations of public sentiment which visited on him the difficulties of the times and situation), tried through four years in which every quality of the man, the statesman, the Christian, was tested ; in the face of a jeering enemy and foreign sneers and domestic ribaldry, elected again by overwhelming majorities to be their chief and their representative during another term of office, in which it was supposed even superior qualities and services would be required to meet the nation's exigencies. This tried, this honored, this beloved head of the government and country is, alas ! suddenly snatched from us at the moment of our greatest need and our greatest joy, and taken up higher to his heavenly reward ! Thank God, he knew how the nation loved and reverenced him ! His re-election was the most solid proof of that which could possibly have been given.   He has tasted, too, the negro's pious gratitude and tearful, glorious affection !   He had lived to give the order for ceasing our preparations for war—an act almost equivalent to proclaiming peace !   He had seen of the travail of his soul, and was satisfied.   He had done the work of a life in his first term of service ; almost every day of his second term, not forty days old, had been marked with victories, until no good news could have been received that would have much swelled his joy and honest pride ! And now, as the typical figure, the historic name of this great era, its glory rounded and full, the Almighty Wisdom has seen fit to close the record, and isolate the special work he has done, lest by any possible mischance the flawless beauty and symmetric oneness of the President's career should be impaired, its unique glory compromised by after issues, or its special lustre mixed with rays of another color, though it might be of an equal splendor !

The Past, at least, is secure !   Nothing can touch him further. Standing the central form in the field of this mighty, providential struggle, he fitly represents the purity, calmness, justice, and mercy of the loyal American people ; their unconquered resolution to conquer secession and break slavery in pieces ; their sober, mild sense; their religious confidence that God is on their side, and their cause the cause of universal humanity ! Let us be reconciled to the appointment which has released that weighty and patient head, that pathetic tender heart, that worn and weary hand from the perplexing details of national rehabilitation. Let the lesser, meaner cares and anxieties of the country fall on other shoulders than those which have borne up the pillars of the nation when shaken with the earthquake.

And seeing it is God who has afflicted us, who doeth all things well, let us believe that it is expedient for us that our beloved chief should go away. He goes to consecrate his work by flinging his life as well as his labors and his conscience into the nation's cause. He that has cheered so many on to bloody sacrifice, found unexpected, surprising opportunity to give also his own blood! He died, as truly as any warrior dies on the battle-field, in the nation's service, and shed his blood for her sake ! It was the nation that was aimed at by the bullet that stilled his aching brain. As the representative of a cause, the type of a victory, he was singled out and slain ! His life and career now have the martyr's palm added to the statesman's, philanthropist's, and patriot's crowns. His place is sure in the innermost shrine of his country's gratitude. His name will match with Washington's, and go with it laden with blessings down to the remotest posterity !

And may we not have needed this loss, in which we gain a national martyr and an ascended leader, to inspire us from his heavenly seat, where with the other father of his country he sits in glory, while they send united benedictions and lessons of comfort and of guidance down upon their common children—may we not have needed this loss to sober our hearts in the midst of our national triumph, lest in the excess of our joy and our pride we should overstep the bounds of that prudence and the limits of that earnest seriousness which our affairs demand ? We have stern and solemn duties yet to perform, great and anxious tasks to achieve. We must not, after ploughing the fields with the burning share of civil war, and fertilizing them with the blood and bones of a half million noble youth, lose the great harvest by wasting the short season of ingathering in festive joy at its promise and its fulness ! We have, perhaps, been prematurely glad. In the joy of seeing our haven in view we have been disposed to slacken the cordage and let the sails flap idly, and the hands go below, when the storm was not fairly over nor all the breakers out of sight ! God has startled us, to apprize us of our peril; to warn us of possible mischances, and to caution us how we abuse our confidence and overtrust our enemy. I hope and pray that the nation may feel itself, by the dreadful calamity that has befallen it, summoned to its knees ; called to a still more pious sense of its dependence, toned up to its duties, and compelled to watch with the most eager patience the course of its generals, its statesmen, and its press. It cannot be for nothing vast and important that the venerated and beloved head of this people and his chief counsellor and companion have thus been brought low in an hour, one to his very grave, the other to the gates of death !

It would seem as if every element of tragic power and pathos were fated to enter this rebellion and mark it out forever as a warning to the world. It really began in the Senate House, when the bludgeon of South Carolina felled the State of Massachussetts and the honor of the Union in the person of a brave and eloquent Senator. The shot at Fort Sumter was not so truly the fatal beginning of the war as the blow in the Senate Chamber. That blow proclaimed the barbarism, the cruelty, the stealthiness, the treachery, the recklessness of reason and justice, the contempt of prudence and foresight which a hundred years of legalized oppression and inhumanity had bred in the South ! And now, that blow, deepening into thunder, echoes from the head of the Chief Magistrate, as if slavery could not be dismissed forever, until her barbaric cruelty, her reckless violence, her political blasphemy, had illustrated itself upon the most conspicuous arena, under the most damning light and the most memorable and unforgetable circumstances in which crime was ever yet committed !

And in the same hour that the thoughtful, meek, and care-worn head of the President was smitten to death—a head that had sunk to its pillow for so many months full of unembittered, gentle, conciliatory, yet anxious and watchful thoughts—the neck on which that President had leaned with an affectionate confidence that was half womanly, during all his administration, was assailed with the bowie-knife, which stands for Southern vengeance, and slavery's natural weapon ! The voice of the free North, the tongue and throat of liberty, was fitly assailed, when slavery and secession would exhibit her dying feat of malignant revenge. Through the channels of that neck had flowed for thirty years, the temperate, persistent, strong, steady currents of this nation's resistance to the encroachments of the slave-power, of this people's aspirations for release from the curse and the peril of a growing race of slaves. That throat had voiced the nation's great argument in the Senate Chamber. The arm that had written the great series of letters

7

which defended the nation from the schemes of foreign diplomatists, was already accidentally broken ; the jaw that had so eloquently moved was dislocated too ; but slavery remembered the neck that bowed not when most others were bent to her power; remembered the throat that was vocal in her condemnation when most others in public life were silent from policy or fear ; remembered the words of him, who more than any man, slew her with his tongue ; and so her last assault was upon the jugular veins of the Secretary of State. Her bloodhounds sprang at the throat of him who had denied their right and broken their power to spring at the neck of the slave himself !

But thus far, thank God, slavery is baffled in her last effort. Mr. Seward lives to tell us what no man knows so well, the terrible perils through which we have passed at home and abroad ; lives to tell us the goodness, the wisdom, the piety of the President he was never weary of praising. "He is the best man I ever knew," he said to me a year ago. What a eulogy from one so experienced, so acute, so wise, so gentle! Ah, brethren, the head of the government is gone ; but he who knew his counsels, and was his other self, still lives, and may God hear to-day a nation's prayer for his life.

Meanwhile heaven rejoices this Easter morning in the resurrection of our lost leader, honored in the day of his death ; dying on the anniversary of our Lord's great sacrifice, a mighty sacrifice himself for the sins of a whole people.

We will not grudge him his release, or selfishly recall him from his rest and his reward ! The only unpitied object in this national tragedy, he treads to-day the courts of light, radiant with the joy that even in heaven celebrates our Saviour's resurrection from the dead ! The sables we hang in our sanctuaries and streets have no place where he is ! His hearse is plumed with a nation's grief ; his resurrection is hailed with the songs of revolutionary patriots, of soldiers that have died for their country. He, the commander-in-chief, has gone to his army of the dead ! The patriot President has gone to our Washington ! The meek and lowly Christian is to-day with him who said on earth, "Come unto me, all ye that labor and are heavily laden, and I will give you rest," and who, rising to-day, fulfils his glorious words, "I am the resurrection and the life; he that believeth in me, though he were dead, yet shall he live: and whoso liveth and believeth in me shall never die."

At St. Patrick's Cathedral, New York, after the Pontifical Mass was finished, Archbishop McCloskey, from the steps of the altar, spoke as follows:

"You will, I trust, beloved brethren, pardon me if, notwithstanding the length of the services at which you have been assisting, I should ask the privilege of trespassing for a few moments more upon your patience. The privilege I ask is, indeed, a sad and mournful one, a privilege that I have reserved for myself alone, for the reason that I could not, and that I cannot, without injustice to my own feelings, and, I am sure, to your feelings also, allow myself to forego it; and that privilege, as you doubtless already anticipate, is of addressing to you at least a few brief and imperfect words in regard to the great, and, I may say, the awful calamity which has so unexpectedly and so suddenly fallen upon our beloved and now still more than ever afflicted country. But two days ago we beheld the rejoicings of an exultant people, mingling even with the sorrowful memory of our Saviour's crucifixion. To-day we behold that same people's sorrow mingling with the grand rejoicings of our Saviour's resurrection. It is, indeed, a sad and a sudden transformation. It is a mournful—it is even a startling contrast. The Church could not divest herself of her habiliments of woe in Good Friday, neither can she now lay aside her festive robes, nor hush her notes of joy, gladness, and thanksgiving on this, her glorious Easter Sunday. Still, although as children of the Church we must and do participate in all her sentiments of joy, yet, at the same time, as children of the nation, as children of this Republic, we do not less sincerely, or less feelingly, or less largely, share in that nation's grief and sorrow. Oh, no! There is but one feeling that pervades all hearts, without distinction of party or of creed, without distinction of race or of color ; one universal sentiment of a great and a fearful bereavement, of the heavy, and I had almost said, crushing suffering, that has just befallen us. All feel, all acknowledge, that in that death which has so recently come to pass, in that sudden and awful death of the Chief Magistrate of this country, the entire nation, North and South, has sustained a great, a very great loss; and if we took counsel of our fears, we might say an almost irreparable loss. But, no! Our hopes are stronger, far stronger, than our fears; our trust and confidence in a good, gracious, and merciful God is stronger than the foreshadowings of what may be awaiting us in the future; and it is to Him to-day, in our trials and adversities, we raise our voices in supplication. Him we beseech to give light to those who are and who are to be the rulers of the destinies of our nation, that He may give life and safety and peace to our beloved country. We pray that those sentiments of mercy, of clemency, and of conciliation, that filled the heart of the beloved President we have just lost, may animate the breast and guide the actions of him who in this most trying hour is called to fill his place. And we may take comfort, beloved brethren, in the thought that in the latest intelligence which has reached us, the honored Secretary of State (a man full of years and of honors), who was, like his superior, stricken down by the hand of a ruthless assassin, still lives, and well-founded hopes are entertained of his final recovery. Let us pray, then, that a life always valuable, but in this critical state of affairs dear to every one of us, may be long preserved, and that the new President may have the advantage of the wisdom, the experience, and the prudence of this honored Secretary of State. I need not tell you, my beloved brethren, children of the Catholic Church, to leave nothing undone to show your devotion, your attachment, and your fidelity to the institutions of your country in this great crisis, this trying hour. I need not ask you to omit nothing in joining in every testimonial of respect and honor to the memory of that President, now, alas! no more. On whatever day may be appointed for his obsequies, although the solemn dirge of requiem cannot resound within these walls, yet the dirge of sorrow, of grief, and of be-wailing, can echo and re-echo within your hearts. And, on that day, whenever it may be, the doors of this Cathedral shall be thrown open, that you, beloved brethren, may bow down before this altar, adoring the inscrutable decrees of a just and all-wise Providence, beseeching His mercy on us all, and imploring Him, that now at least His anger may be appeased, and that the cruel scourge of war cease, and that those rivers and torrents of human blood, of fratricidal blood, that have been saturating for so long a time the soil of our beloved country may no longer flow over our unhappy land. Yes, let us pray, while almost even in sight of that deed of horror, which, like an electric shock, has come upon and appalled our fellow-citizens in every section of the land—let us pray to Him that we may now forget our enmities, and that we may be enabled to restore that peace which has so long been broken. Let us take care, beloved brethren, that no spirit of retribution or of wicked spite, or of malice, or of resentment, shall, at this moment, take possession of our hearts. The hand of God is upon us; let us take care that we do not provoke Him to bow us down with misery and woe. Even over the grave of the illustrious departed who has been taken from us, over the graves of so many enemies and friends, in every section of the land, fallen in the deadly conflict, let us hope that those who are spared, who are still living, may come and join their hands together in sweet forgiveness; and let us pledge ourselves, one to the other, that we will move and act together in unity and in perpetual and Divine peace."

The Rev. Henry Ward Beecher not arriving in season to pronounce a discourse on that day, delivered at Plymouth Church, Brooklyn, on the ensuing Sunday, this sermon.

DISCOURSE OF REV. HENRY WARD BEECHER.

" And Moses went up from the plains of Moab, unto the mountain of Nebo, to the top of Pisgah, that is over against Jericho : and the Lord showed him the land of Gilead, unto Dan.

" And all Naphtali, and the land of Ephraim and Manasseh, and all the land of Judah, unto the utmost sea.

" And the South, and the plain of the valley of Jericho, the city of palm-trees, unto Zoar.

" And the Lord said unto him, This is the land which I sware unto Abraham, unto Isaac, and unto Jacob, saying, I will give it unto thy seed : I have caused thee to see it with thine eyes, but thou shalt not go over thither.

" So Moses, the servant of the Lord, died there in the land of Moab, according to the word of the Lord."

There is no historic figure more noble than that of the Jewish lawgiver. After many thousand years the figure of Moses is not diminished, but stands up against the background of early days, distinct and individual as if he lived but yesterday. There is scarcely another event in history more touching than his death. He had borne the great burdens of state for forty years, shaped the Jews to a nation, filled out their civil and religious polity, administered their laws, and guided their steps, or dwelt with them in all their sojourning in the wilderness, had mourned in their punishment, kept step with their marches, and led them in wars, until the end of their labors drew nigh, the last stages were reached, and Jordan only lay between them and the promised land. The Promised Land ! Oh what yearnings had heaved his breast for that Divinely promised place! He had dreamed of it by night, and mused by day; it was holy, and endeared as God's favored spot; it was to be the cradle of an illustrious history. All his long, laborious, and now weary life, he had aimed at this as the consummation of every desire, the reward of every toil and pain. Then came the word of the Lord to him, "Thou must not go over. Get thee up into the mountain, look upon it, and die." From that silent summit the hoary leader gazed to the north, to the south, to the west, with hungry eyes. The dim outlines rose up, the hazy recesses spoke of quiet valleys. With eager longing, with sad resignation, he looked upon the promised land, that was now the forbidden land. It was a moment of anguish. He forgot all his personal wants and drank in the vision of his people's home. His work was done. There lay God's promise fulfilled. There was the seat of coming Jerusalem— there the city of Jehovah's King, the sphere of judges and prophets, the mount of sorrow and salvation, the country whence were to fly blessings to all mankind. Joy chased sadness from every feature, and the prophet laid him down and died. Again a great leader of the people has passed through toil, sorrow, battle, and war, and came near to the promised land of peace, into which he might not pass over. Who shall recount our martyr's sufferings for this people? Since the November of 1860, his horizon has been black with storms. By day and by night he trod a way of danger and darkness. On his shoulders rested a government, dearer to him than his own life. At its life millions were striking at home; upon it foreign eyes were lowered, and it stood like a lone island in a sea full of storms, and every tide and wave seemed eager to devour it. Upon thousands of hearts great sorrows and anxieties have rested, but upon not one such, and in such measure, as upon that simple, truthful, noble soul, our faithful and sainted Lincoln. Never rising to the enthusiasm of more impassioned natures in hours of hope, and never sinking with the mercurial in hours of defeat to the depths of despondency, he held on with unmovable patience and fortitude, putting caution against hope, that it might not be premature, and hope against caution that it might not yield to dread and danger. He wrestled ceaselessly through four black and dreadful purgatorial years, when God was cleansing the sins of this people as by fire. At last the watchman beheld the gray dawn. The mountains began to give forth their forms from out of the darkness, and the East came rushing towards us with arms full of joy for all our sorrows. Then it was for him to be glad exceedingly that had sorrowed immeasurably. Peace could bring to no other heart such joy, such rest, such honor, such trust, such gratitude. He but looked upon it as Moses looked upon the promised land. Then the wail of a nation proclaimed that he had gone from among us. Not thine the sorrow, but ours.

Sainted soul, thou hast indeed entered the promised rest, while we are yet on the march. To us remains the rocking of the deep, the storm upon the land, days of duty and nights of watching; but thou art sphered above all darkness and fear, beyond all sorrow or weariness. Rest, O weary heart! Rejoice exceedingly, thou that hast enough suffered. Thou hast beheld Him who invariably led thee in this great wilderness. Thou standest among the elect; around thee are the royal men that have ennobled human life in every age; kingly art thou, with glory on thy brow as a diadem, and joy is upon thee for evermore! Over all this land, over all the little cloud of years that now, from thine infinite horizon, waver back from thee as a spark, thou art lifted up as high as the star is above the clouds that hide *us*, but never reach *it*. In the goodly company of Mount Zion thou shalt find that rest which so many have sought in vain, and thy name, an everlasting name in heaven, shall flourish in fragrance and beauty as long as men shall last upon the earth, or hearts remain to revere truth, fidelity, and goodness. Never did two such orbs of experience meet in the same hemisphere as the joy and sorrow of the same week in this land. The joy was as sudden as if no man had expected it, and as entrancing as if it had fallen from heaven. It rose up over sobriety, and swept business from its moorings, and down through the land in irresistible course. Men wept and embraced each other; they sang or prayed, or deeper yet, could only think thanksgiving and weep gladness. That peace was sure—that government was firmer than ever—the land was cleansed of plague—that ages were opening to our footsteps, and we were to begin a march of blessings—that blood was stanched, and scowling enmities sinking like spent storms beneath the horizon—that the dear fatherland, nothing lost but much gained, was to rise up in unexampled honor among the nations of the earth—these thoughts, and that undistinguishable throng of fancies, and hopes, and desires, and yearnings, that filled the soul with tremblings like the heated air of midsummer days—all these kindled up such a surge of joy as no words may describe. In an hour, joy lay without a pulse, without a gleam or breath. A sorrow came that swept through the land, as huge storms swept through the forest and field, rolling thunder along the skies, dishevelling the flames and daunting every singer in the thicket or forest, and pouring blackness and darkness across the land and up the mountains.

Did ever so many hearts in so brief a time touch two such boundless feelings? It was the uttermost joy and the uttermost of sorrow—noon and midnight without space between. The blow brought not a sharp pang. It was so terrible that at first it stunned sensibility. Citizens were like men awakened at midnight by an earthquake, and bewildered to find every thing that they were accustomed to trust wavering and falling. The very earth was no longer solid. The first feeling was the least. Men waited to get strength to feel. They wandered in the streets as if groping after some impending dread, or undeveloped sorrow. They met each other as if each would ask the other, "Am I awake, or do I dream?" There was a piteous helplessness. Strong men bowed down and wept. Other and common griefs belong to some one in chief, they are private property ; but this was each man's and every man's. Every virtuous household in the land felt as if its first-born were gone. Men took it home. They were bereaved, and walked for days as if a corpse lay unburied in their dwellings. There was nothing else to think of. They could speak of nothing but that, and yet of that they could speak only falteringly. All business was laid aside, pleasure forgot to smile. The city for nearly a week ceased to roar, and great Leviathan laid down and was still. Even Avarice stood still, and Greed was strangely moved to generous sympathy with universal sorrow. Rear to his name monuments, found charitable institutions, and with his name above their heights, but no monument will ever equal the universal, spontaneous, and sublime sorrow that in a moment swept down lines and parties, and covered up animosities, and in an hour brought a divided people with unity of grief and indivisible fellowship of anguish! For myself, I cannot yet command that quietness of spirit needed for a just and temperate delineation of a man whom Goodness has made great. I pass, then, to some considerations aside from the martyr President's character, reserving that for a future occasion, which are appropriate to this time and place. And, first, let us not mourn that his departure was so sudden, nor fill our imagination with horror at its method. When good men pray for deliverance from hidden death, it is only that they may not be plunged, without preparation and all disrobed, into the presence of the Judge. Men long eluding and evading sorrow, when suddenly overtaken, seem enchanted to make it great to the uttermost—a habit which is not Christian, although it is doubtless natural. When one is ready to depart, suddenness is a blessing. It is a painful sight to see a tree overthrown by a tornado, wrenched from its foundation and broken down like a reed; but it is yet more painful to see a vast and venerable tree lingering with vain strife, when age and infirmity have marked it for destruction. The process of decay is a spectacle humiliating and painful; but it seems good and grand for one to go from duty done with pulse high, with strength full and nerve strong, terminating a noble life in a fitting manner. Nor are we without Scripture warrant for these thoughts : "Let your loins be girded about . . . . . . Blessed are those servants whom the Lord, when He cometh, shall find watching."   . . . Not those who die in stupor are blessed,

but they who go with all their powers about them, and wide awake
as to a wedding. He died watching. He died with armor on. In
the midst of hours of labor, in the very heart of patriotic consulta-
tions, just returned from camps and council, he was stricken down.
No fever dried his blood—no slow waste consumed him. All at
once, in full strength and manhood, with his girdle tight about him,
he departed, and walks with God. Nor was the manner of his
death more shocking, if we will surround it with higher associations. Have not thousands of soldiers fallen on the field of battle
by the bullets of an enemy, and did not he? All soldiers that fall
ask to depart in the hour of victory, and at such an hour he fell.
There was not a poor drummer-boy in all this war that has fallen
for whom the great heart of Lincoln would not have bled; there is
not one private soldier without note of name, slain among thousands, and hid in the pit among hundreds, without even the memorial of a separate burial, for whom the President would not have
wept. He was a man from and of the people, and now that he who
might not bear the march, the toil and battle, with these humble citizens, has been called to die by the bullet, as they were, do you
not feel that there is a peculiar fitness to his nature and life, that he
should in death be joined with them in a final common experience?
For myself, when any event is susceptible of a nobler garnishing,
I cannot understand the nature or character of those who seek
rather to drag it down, degrading and debasing, rather than en-
nobling and sanctifying it.

Secondly. This blow was but the expiring rebellion; and as a
miniature gives all the form and feature of its subject, so, epito-
mized in this foul act, we find the whole nature and disposition of
slavery. It begins in a wanton destruction of all human rights, and
in the desecration of all the sanctities of heart and home. It can
be maintained only at the sacrifice of every right moral feeling in
its abettors and upholders. It is a two-edged sword, cutting both
ways, desolating alike the oppressed and the oppressor, and vio-
lently destroying manhood in the victim, it insidiously destroys manhood in the master. No man born and bred under the influence of
the accursed thing can possibly maintain his manhood, and I would
as soon look for a saint in the darkness of perdition as for a man of
honor in this hot-bed of iniquity. The problem is solved, its demonstration is complete. Slavery wastes its victims, it wastes estates.
It destroys public morality, it corrupts manhood in its centre. Communities in which it exists are not to be trusted. Its products are
rotten. No timber grown in its cursed soil is fit for the ribs of our
ship of State or for our household homes. The people are selfish in

their patriotism, and brittle, and whoever leans on them for support is pierced in his hand. Their honor is not honor, but a bastard quality which disgraces the name of honor, and for all time the honor of the supporters of slavery will be throughout the earth a by-word and a hissing. Their whole moral nature is death-smitten. The needless rebellion, the treachery of its leaders to oaths and trusts, their violations of the commonest principles of fidelity, sitting in the senate, councils, and places of trust only to betray them —the long, general, and unparalleled cruelty to prisoners, without provocation or excuse—their unreasoning malignity and fierceness— all mark the symptoms of the disease of slavery, that is a deadly poison to soul and body. There may be exceptions, of course, but as a rule malignity is the nature and the essence. Slavery is itself barbarous, and the nation which upholds and protects it is likewise barbarous. It is fit that its expiring blow should be made to take away from men the last forbearance, the last pity, and fire the soul with invincible determination that the breeding-ground of such mischiefs and monsters shall be utterly and forever destroyed. It needed not that the assassin should put on paper his belief in slavery. He was but the sting of the monster Slavery which has struck this blow, and as long as this nation lasts, it will not be forgotten that we have had our " Martyr President," nor while heaven holds high court or hell rots beneath, will it be forgotten that slavery murdered him.

Third. This blow was aimed at the life of government and of the nation. Lincoln was slain, but America was meant. The man was cast down, but the government was smitten at. The President was killed, but national life-breathing freedom and benignity was sought. He of Illinois, as a private man, might have been detested, but it was because he represented the cause of just government, liberty, and kindness he was slain. It was a crime against universal government, and was aimed at all. Not more was it at us than at England or France, or any well-compacted government. It was aimed at mankind. The whole world will repudiate it and stigmatize it as a deed without a redeeming feature. It was not the deed of the oppressed stung to madness by the cruelty of the oppressor ; it was not the avenging hand against the heart of a despot ; it was the exponent of a venomous hatred of liberty, and the avowed advocacy of slavery.

[Mr. Beecher illustrated the point by a report of the interview between Governor Pickens and Lieutenant Talbot, a few days prior to the attack on Fort Sumter, wherein Pickens admitted that the South really had no cause of complaint ; but that the leaders, hoping to deceive the people, had manufactured the necessary indignation at Northern insults, and were determined to separate, even though confessedly without good grounds.]

Fourth. But the blow has signally failed. The cause is not stricken, but strengthened: men hate slavery the more and love liberty better. The nation is dissolved, but only in tears, and stands more square and solid to-day than any pyramid in Egypt. The government is not weakened, it is strengthened. How readily and easily the ranks closed up! We shall be more true to every instinct of liberty, to the Constitution, and to the principles of universal freedom. Where, in any other community, the crowned head being stricken by the hand of an assassin, would the funds have stood so firm as did ours, not wavering the half of one per cent.? After four years of drastic war, of heavy drafts upon the people, on top of all, the very head of the nation is stricken down, and the funds never quivered, but stand as firm as the granite ribs in the mountains. Republican institutions have been vindicated in this very experience. God has said by the voice of his providence that republican liberty, based upon universal freedom, shall be as firm as the foundations of the globe.

Fifth. Even he who now sleeps has, by this event, been clothed with new influence. Dead, he speaks to men who now willingly hear what before they shut their ears to. Like the words of Washington will his simple, mighty words be pondered on by your children and children's children. Men will receive a new accession to their love of patriotism, and will for his sake guard with more zeal the welfare of the whole country. On the altar of this martyred patriot I swear you to be more faithful to your country. They will, as they follow his hearse, swear a new hatred to that slavery which has made him a martyr. By this solemn spectacle I swear you to renewed hostility to slavery, and to a never-ending pursuit of it to its grave. They will admire and imitate his firmness in justice, his inflexible conscience for the right, his gentleness and moderation of spirit, and I swear you to a faithful copy of his justice, his mercy, and his gentleness. You I can comfort, but how can I speak to the twilight millions who revere his name as the name of God? Oh, there will be wailing for him in hamlet and cottage, in woods and wilds, and the fields of the South. Her dusky children looked on him as on a Moses come to lead them out from the land of bondage. To whom can we direct them but to the Shepherd of Israel, and to His care commit them for help, for comfort, and protection? And now the martyr is moving in triumphal march, mightier than when alive. The nation rises up at his coming. Cities and States are his pall-bearers, and cannon beat the hours with solemn procession. Dead ! dead ! dead ! he yet speaketh ! Is Washington dead? Is Hampden dead ? Is David dead? Now, disenthralled of flesh, and risen to the unobstructed sphere where passion never comes, he begins his illimitable work. His life is grafted upon the Infinite, and will be fruitful now as no earthly life can be. Pass on, thou that hast overcome ! Your sorrows, O people, are his pœan ! Your bells, and bands, and muffled drum sound in his ear a triumph. You wail and weep here. God makes it triumph there. Four years ago, O Illinois, we took him from your midst, an untried man from among the people. Behold, we return him a mighty conqueror. Not thine, but the nation's ; not ours, but the world's ! Give him place, ye prairies ! In the midst of this great continent, his dust shall rest a sacred treasure to millions who shall pilgrim to that shrine, to kindle anew their zeal and patriotism. Ye winds that move over the mighty spaces of the West, chant his requiem ! Ye people, behold a martyr, whose blood as articulate words pleads for fidelity, for law, for liberty !

IV.

FUNERAL AT WASHINGTON.

IV.

THE FUNERAL AT WASHINGTON.

WHEN Mr. Lincoln's body had been removed to the President's House, the embalmers proceeded to prepare it for the grave. Mr. Harry P. Cattell, in the employ of Doctors Brown and Alexander, who, three years before, had prepared so beautifully the body of little Willie Lincoln, now made as perpetual as art could effect the peculiar features of the late beloved President. The embalming was performed in the President's own room, in the west wing, in the presence of President Johnson, Generals Augur and Rucker, and the attending physicians of the late President. The body was drained of its blood, and the parts necessary to remove to prevent decay were carefully withdrawn, and a chemical preparation injected, which soon hardened to the consistence of stone, giving the body the firmness and solid immobility of a statue.

The solemn sadness of every thing around the Executive Mansion, during the morning of Wednesday, was one of the characteristics of the day. No person was admitted except those who had charge of the arrangements for the funeral, or such as had some labor to perform in completing the preparations, and the invited guests. It was in reality the house of mourning, and those very rooms which the public have seen on State occasions filled with life, animation, and joy, were dressed in the habiliments of woe. Entering the front door, this stillness seemed almost deathlike. Every person moved along on tiptoe, as if fearful of disturbing the long and deep sleep of the great and good man whose body lay within those walls.

The Green Room, in which the body had been placed, was darkened, and a shade of night seemed to hang over it. The blinds were nearly closed, allowing but a faint streak of light to enter the windows. The doors, windows, cornices, and chandelier were richly hung with the weeds of grief and mourning, through which could be faintly seen the rich damask and lace curtains which adorned the room on all other occasions. The numerous large mirrors were also heavily draped, with a panel of white crape covering the face of the glass. In fact, everywhere were the marks of sorrow, which spoke of the bereavement of hearts, of household ties severed, and of a nation weeping and mourning over a chief that has fallen.

Near the centre of the room stood the grand catafalque, upon which rested the mortal remains of the illustrious dead, inclosed in a beautiful mahogany coffin lined with lead, and with a white satin covering over the metal. It was finished in the most elaborate style, with four silver handles on each side, stars glistening between the handles, and a vein of silver winding around the whole case in a serpentine form. To the edges of the lid hung a rich silver tassel, making a chaste and elaborate fringe to the whole case. The silver plate bore the simple inscription:

ABRAHAM LINCOLN,
SIXTEENTH PRESIDENT OF THE UNITED STATES,
Born February 12, 1809.
Died April 15, 1865.

The catafalque stood lengthwise to the room, or north and south, and immediately in front of the double doors which lead to the wide hall. The floor of the catafalque was about four feet in height, and approached by one step on all sides, making it easy to view the face of the honored dead. Above this was a canopy, in an arched form, lined on the under side with white fluted satin, covered otherwise with black velvet and crape. This was supported by four posts, heavily encased with the emblem of mourning. The canopy, the posts, and the main body of the catafalque were festooned with crape and fastened at each fold with rosettes of black satin.

On the top of the coffin lay three wreaths of moss and evergreen, with white flowers and lilies intermingled. At the head of the coffin, standing upon the floor of the catafalque, and leaning against the metallic case, stood a beautiful cross, made of japonicas, lilies, and other white flowers, as bright and blooming as though they were still on their parent stem, and had not been plucked to adorn the house of the dead, its pure and immaculate white furnishing a strong contrast with the deep black on all sides. On the foot of the coffin lay an anchor of flowers. Encircling the coffin, in a serpentine form, was a vein of evergreens, studded with pure white flowers, and within its meandering folds were deposited several wreaths of the same material. These had all been brought by some friendly hands, the tokens of love and affection, and deposited around and near the case that contained the mortal remains of the man who had been near and dear to them. Here, then, were the emblems of the dead, the marks of rank, the tokens of grief, deep and sorrowful, the signs of love and affection, and the living emblems of purity and happiness hereafter, as well as hope and immortality in the future. Surely the scene in honor to the illustrious dead was a worthy exhibition of the love, esteem, and pride of a free people in their fallen chief—fallen, too, in the midst of his usefulness, and just when his greatness and goodness were being recognized by all.

Steps were arranged rising to the back wall, to enable those behind to witness the ceremony as well as those in front.

The guard of honor which had been watching over the body of the illustrious dead were still there:—General Hunter, General Dyer, of the Ordnance Bureau; General Thomas, of the Quartermaster's Department, assisted by Captain C. E. Nesmith, of New York, and Captain E. Dawes, of Massachusetts. There they stood, guarding with a jealous and anxious eye the earthly casket of their late Commander-in-chief. Hunter, compact and dark and reticent, walks about the empty chamber in full uniform, his bright buttons and sash and sword contrasting with his dark blue uniform, gauntlets upon his hands, crape on his arm and blade, his corded hat in his hands, a paper collar just apparent above his velvet tips; and now and then he speaks to Captain Nesmith or Captain Dawes, of General Harding's staff, rather as one who wishes company than one who has any thing to say. His two silver stars upon his shoulder shine dimly in the draped apartment. He was one of the first in the war to urge the measure which Mr. Lincoln afterwards adopted. The aids walked to and fro, selected without reference to any association with the late President. Their clothes are rich, their

8

swords wear mourning; they go in silence; every thing is funereal.

"Close by the corpse sit the relatives of the deceased, plain, honest, hardy people, typical as much of the simplicity of our institutions as of Mr. Lincoln's self-made eminence. No blood relatives of Mr. Lincoln were to be found. It is a singular evidence of the poverty of his origin, and therefore of his exceeding good report, that, excepting his immediate family, none answering to his name could be discovered. Mrs. Lincoln's relatives were present, however, in some force. Dr. Lyman Beecher Todd, General John B. S. Todd, C. M. Smith, Esq., and Mr. N. W. Edwards, the late President's brother-in-law. Plain, self-made people were here, and were sincerely affected. Captain Robert Lincoln sat during the services with his face in his handkerchief, weeping quietly, and little Tad, his face red and heated, cried as if his heart would break. Mrs. Lincoln, weak, worn, and nervous, did not enter the East Room nor follow the remains. She was the Chief Magistrate's lady yesterday; to-day, a widow bearing only an immortal name."

A few minutes after eleven A. M., a large number of clergymen, representing various sections of the country, came marching in from the reception-room, and took their positions near the centre of the south end of the room, directly in range with the feet of the corpse. A few minutes later, the delegates from New York city, headed by William Orton, marched in, and, passing along the east side of the catafalque, took their places on the north side of the room, directly opposite the clergy. They had but just stationed themselves, when the heads of bureaus in the several departments made their appearance, and took their places in the northeast corner of the room; among whom were Kennedy, of the Census Bureau; Newton, of the Agricultural Bureau; the several auditors of the Treasury Department, and the chiefs of most of the bureaus in the War and Navy Departments. Next in order came the city authorities of Washington, with several members of the New York and Philadelphia common councils as invited guests. They took their places by the side of the clergy, and filled the space between the latter and the west side of the room.

The representatives of the Christian and Sanitary Commissions here were the next to enter the room, and passing over the same route of the New York delegation, took their station next to the heads of bureaus, on the north side of the room, near the northeast corner.

Following close behind these came the Governors of States and their attendants. There were but few Governors of States present. Among the party were Governors Fenton, of New York; Andrew, of Massachusetts; Parker, of New Jersey; Stone, of Iowa; Oglesby, of Illinois; Buckingham, of Connecticut; Brough, of Ohio; and Lieutenant-Governor Cox, of Maryland, and ex-Governor Farwell, of Wisconsin. They marched around the east side of the body, and took their places on the east side of the room, just east of the heads of bureaus.

The Assistant Secretaries followed immediately and took their position just east of the Governors of States. Among these were Charles A. Dana, of the War Department, Captain Fox, of the Navy Department, M. B. Field, of the Treasury, A. W. Randall, Assistant Postmaster, Judge Otto, of the Interior Department, and T. J. Coffin, Assistant Attorney General.

The Assistant Secretaries had but just taken their positions when the members of the Senate were ushered in and took their position on the east side of the room, and east of the space set apart for the Cabinet. In this party were Senators Dixon, Ramsay, Harris, Chandler, Cowan, Sumner, McDougal, Creswell, Wilkinson, Stewart, Nye, Collamer and Sprague. In the same connection were the members of the last House of Representatives who were in town, headed by the Sergeant at Arms and the Clerk of the House, Mr. McPherson.

The following are the names of the members present:— Messrs. Darling, Radford, Herrick, A. W. Clarke, Steele, and T. Clarke, of New York; Schenck, of Ohio; Davis, Webster, and Phelps, of Maryland; O'Neill, Myers, Covode, and Calver, of Pennsylvania; Higby and Shannon, of California; Hooper, Dawes, and Gooch, of Massachusetts; Marston and Rollins, of New Hampshire; Pike and Rice, of Maine; Latham, Bradford and Whaley, of West Virginia; Farnsworth and Arnold, of Illinois; Donnelly and Winder of Minnesota; F. W. Kellogg and Tracy, of Michigan.

Immediately after these followed four members of the Supreme Court—Chief-Justice Chase, Associate Justices Swayne,

Wayne and Davies—escorted by Marshal Lamon and the Clerk of the Court. They stationed themselves on the right, and next west of the space left for the Cabinet.

Then came the diplomatic corps and the members of their legations. Every foreign minister and their *attachés* now in the country were in the procession. The position assigned to them was next west of the Supreme Court and on the east side of the room.

The Judges of the local courts, and such other judicial officers of the country who were present in the city were next in turn ushered in, and were assigned a position on the north end of the room, near the members of the Sanitary Commission.

Then came the pall-bearers, who were stationed on the north side of the room, near the west side. Speaker Colfax and Senator Foster took their position in front, and the others in double file, extending to the rear of the room. The representatives of the army and navy among the pall-bearers went over to a space set apart for those two arms of the public service, and were soon after joined by several officers of the army and navy of more or less note. Among the number was Commodore Goldsborough, General Burnside, and others.

The following ladies of the families of the Cabinet and Senators then were ushered in, and were stationed immediately in the rear of the Cabinet ministers: Mrs. Stanton, Mrs. Usher, Mrs. and Miss Dennison, Mrs. Welles, Mrs. Sprague, Miss Nettie Chase.

Next in order were forty representatives from Illinois and twenty from Kentucky, who had been given in the programme the position of chief mourners. They were assigned a position in the southeast corner of the room, just in the rear of the seats set apart for the family of the President.

At precisely twelve o'clock President Johnson was ushered in, supported by Preston King on one side, and ex-Vice-President Hamlin on the other, followed by the several members of the Cabinet, with the exception of Secretary Seward.

Immediately in front of the Kentucky and Illinois delegations was the family of the deceased. Mrs. Lincoln, however, was not able to be present, and the multitude gathered there were not permitted to see the weeping widow as she came to pay the last respects to the body of her honored husband.

Captain Robert Lincoln was the only member of the late President's immediate family who was present during the ceremony. The other chief mourners were N. W. Edwards and C. M. Smith, of Illinois, brothers-in-law of Mrs. Lincoln. General J. B. S. Todd, of Dacotah, and Dr. L. B. Todd, of Kentucky, cousins of Mrs. Lincoln, were all the blood relatives of the family who participated in the solemn rites. They were seated on the southeast corner of the space in front of the raised platforms, Robert resting his head upon his hands, and seemed bowed down with grief at the great loss which he had sustained in the tragic death of his father.

A moment before the services commenced President Johnson and Preston King stepped forward and took the last long gaze at the features of him who but a few days since occupied the chair of the Chief Magistrate of the nation.

Rev. Dr. Hall, of the Episcopal church in Washington, opened the services by reading the Episcopal Service of the Dead.

Bishop Simpson, of the Methodist Church, then pronounced this prayer :

Almighty God, our Heavenly Father, as with smitten and suffering hearts we come into thy presence, we pray, in the name of our blessed Redeemer, that Thou wouldst pour upon us Thy Holy Spirit, that all our thoughts and acts may be acceptable in Thy sight. We adore Thee for all Thy glorious perfections. We praise Thee for the revelation which Thou hast given us in Thy works and in Thy Word. By Thee all worlds exist. All beings live through Thee. Thou raisest up kingdoms and empires, and castest them down. By Thee kings reign and princes decree righteousness. In Thy hand are the issues of life and death. We confess before Thee the magnitude of our sins and transgressions, both as individuals and as a nation. We implore Thy mercy for the sake of our Redeemer. Forgive us all our iniquities. If it please Thee, remove Thy chastening hand from us ; and, though we be unworthy, turn away from us Thine anger, and let the light of Thy countenance again shine upon us.

At this solemn hour, as we mourn for the death of our President, who was stricken down by the hand of an assassin, grant us also the grace to bow in submission to Thy holy will. May we recognize Thy hand high above all human agencies, and Thy power as controlling all events, so that the wrath of man shall praise Thee, and that the remainder of wrath Thou wilt restrain. Humbled under the suffering we have endured and the great afflictions through

which we have passed, may we not be called upon to offer other
sacrifices. May the lives of all our officers, both civil and military,
be guarded by Thee; and let no violent hand fall upon any of them,
Mourning as we do for the mighty dead by whose remains we
stand, we would yet lift our hearts unto Thee in grateful acknowl-
edgment for Thy kindness in giving us so great and noble a commander. Thou art glorified in good men, and we praise Thee that
Thou didst give him unto us so pure, so honest, so sincere, and so
transparent in character. We praise Thee for that kind, affectionate heart, which always swelled with feelings of enlarged benevolence. We bless Thee for what Thou didst enable him to do; that
Thou didst give him wisdom to select for his advisers and for his
officers, military and naval, those men through whom our country
has been carried through an unprecedented conflict.

We bless Thee for the success which has attended all their efforts, and victories which have crowned our armies; and that Thou
didst spare Thy servant until he could behold the dawning of that
glorious morning of peace and prosperity which is about to shine
upon our land; that he was enabled to go up as Thy servant of old
upon Mount Pisgah, and catch a glimpse of the promised land.
Though his lips are silent and his arm is powerless, we thank Thee
that Thou didst strengthen him to speak words that cheer the
hearts of the suffering and the oppressed, and to write that declaration of emancipation which has given him an immortal reward;
that though the hand of the assassin has struck him to the ground,
it could not destroy the work which he has done, nor forge again
the chains which he has broken. And while we mourn that he has
passed away, we are grateful that his work was so fully accomplished, and that the acts which he has performed will forever remain.

We implore Thy blessing upon his bereaved family, Thou husband of the widow. Bless her who, broken-hearted and sorrowing,
feels oppressed with unutterable anguish. Cheer the loneliness of
the pathway which lies before her, and grant to her such consolations of Thy Spirit, and such hopes, through the resurrection, that
she shall feel that "Earth hath no sorrows which Heaven cannot
heal."

Let Thy blessing rest upon his sons; pour upon them the spirit
of wisdom, be Thou the guide of their youth, prepare them for usefulness in society, for happiness in all their relations. May the re-
membrance of their father's counsels, and their father's noble acts,
ever stimulate them to glorious deeds, and at last may they be heirs
of everlasting life.

Command thy rich blessings to descend upon the successor of our lamented President. Grant unto him wisdom, energy, and firmness for the responsible duties to which he has been called; and may he, his cabinet, officers, and generals who shall lead his armies, and the brave soldiers in the field, be so guided by Thy counsels that they shall speedily complete the great work which he had so successfully carried forward.

Let Thy blessing rest upon our country. Grant unto us all a fixed and strong determination never to cease our efforts until our glorious Union shall be fully re-established.

Around the remains of our loved President may we covenant together by every possible means to give ourselves to our country's service until every vestige of this rebellion shall have been wiped out, and until slavery, its cause, shall be forever eradicated.

Preserve us, we pray Thee, from all complications with foreign nations. Give us hearts to act justly towards all nations, and grant unto them hearts to act justly towards us, that universal peace and happiness may fill our earth. We rejoice, then, in this inflicting dispensation Thou hast given, as additional evidence of the strength of our nation. We bless Thee that no tumult has arisen, and in peace and harmony our Government moves onward; and that Thou hast shown that our Republican Government is the strongest upon the face of the earth. In this solemn presence, may we feel that we too are immortal! May the sense of our responsibility to God rest upon us; may we repent of every sin; and may we consecrate anew unto Thee all the time and all the talents which Thou hast given us; and may we so fulfil our allotted duties that finally we may have a resting-place with the good, and wise, and the great, who now surround that glorious throne! Hear us while we unite in praying with Thy Church in all lands and in all ages, even as Thou hast taught us, saying—Our Father, &c.

The funeral oration was delivered by Rev. P. D. Gurley, D. D., pastor of the New York Avenue Presbyterian Church, which Mr. Lincoln and his family were in the habit of attending.

FAITH IN GOD:

A SERMON ON THE DEATH OF THE PRESIDENT,

Preached in the East Room of the Executive Mansion, April 19th, 1865, by the Rev.
P. D. Gurley, D.D., Pastor of the New York Avenue Presbyterian Church, Washington, D. C.

MARK xi. 22.—"Have faith in God."

As we stand here to-day, mourners around this coffin and around
the lifeless remains of our beloved Chief Magistrate, we recognize
and we adore the sovereignty of God. His throne is in the heavens, and His kingdom ruleth over all. He hath done, and He hath
permitted to be done, whatsoever he pleased. "Clouds and darkness are round about him ; righteousness and judgment are the habitation of His throne." "His way is in the sea, and his path in the
great waters, and His footsteps are not known." "Canst thou by
searching find out God? Canst thou find out the Almighty unto
perfection? It is as high as heaven: what canst thou do? deeper
than hell: what canst thou know? The measure thereof is longer
than the earth, and broader than the sea. If he cut off, and shut
up, or gather together, then who can hinder Him? For He
knoweth vain men ; He seeth wickedness also ; will He not then
consider it?" We bow before his infinite majesty. We bow, we
weep, we worship—

> "Where reason fails, with all her powers,
>   There faith prevails, and love adores."

It was a cruel, cruel hand, that dark hand of the assassin, which
smote our honored, wise, and noble President, and filled the land
with sorrow. But above and beyond that hand, there is another
which we must see and acknowledge. It is the chastening hand of
a wise and a faithful Father. He gives us this bitter cup. And
the cup that our Father hath given us, shall we not drink it?

> "God of the just, thou gavest us the cup :
>   We yield to thy behest, and drink it up."

"Whom the Lord loveth he chasteneth." Oh, how these blessed
words have cheered, and strengthened, and sustained us through
all these long and weary years of civil strife, while our friends and
brothers on so many ensanguined fields were falling and dying for
the cause of Liberty and Union! Let them cheer, and strengthen,
and sustain us to-day. True, this new sorrow and chastening has
come in such an hour and in such a way as we thought not, and it
bears the impress of a rod that is very heavy, and of a mystery
that is very deep. That such a life should be sacrificed, at such a

time, by such a foul and diabolical agency; that the man at the head of the nation, whom the people had learned to trust with a confiding and a loving confidence, and upon whom, more than upon any other, were centred, under God, our best hopes for the true and speedy pacification of the country, the restoration of the Union, and the return of harmony and love ; that he should be taken from us, and taken just as the prospect of peace was brightly opening upon our torn and bleeding country, and just as he was beginning to be animated and gladdened with the hope of ere long enjoying with the people the blessed fruit and reward of his and their toil, and care, and patience, and self-sacrificing devotion to the interests of Liberty and the Union;—oh, it is a mysterious and a most afflicting visitation !   But it is our Father in heaven, the God of our fathers and our God, who permits us to be so suddenly and sorely smitten; and we know that His judgments are right, and that in faithfulness He has afflicted us.   In the midst of our rejoicings we needed this stroke, this dealing, this discipline, and therefore he has sent it.   Let us remember, our affliction has not come forth of the dust, and our trouble has not sprung out of the ground.   Through and beyond all second causes, let us look, and see the sovereign permissive agency of the great First Cause.   It is His prerogative to bring light out of darkness, and good out of evil.   Surely the wrath of man shall praise Him, and the remainder of wrath He will restrain.   In the light of a clearer day we may yet see that the wrath which planned and perpetrated the death of the President, was overruled, by Him whose judgments are unsearchable and His ways past finding out, for the highest welfare of all those interests which are so dear to the Christian patriot and philanthropist, and for which a loyal people have made such an unexampled sacrifice of treasure and of blood. Let us not be faithless, but believing.

> "Blind unbelief is prone to err,
>   And scan His work in vain ;
>   God is His own interpreter,
>   And He will make them plain."

We will wait for His interpretation, and we will wait in faith, nothing doubting.   He who has led us so well, and defended and prospered us so wonderfully during the last four years of toil, and struggle, and sorrow, *will not forsake us now.* He may chasten, but He will not destroy.   He may purify us more and more in the furnace of trial, but He will not consume us.   No, no.   He has chosen us as He did His people of old in the furnace of affliction, and He has said of us as He said of them, " This people have I formed for

myself ; they shall show forth My praise."   Let our principal anxiety now be that this new sorrow may be a *sanctified* sorrow ; that
it may lead us to deeper repentance, to a more humbling sense of
our dependence upon God, and to the more unreserved consecration
of ourselves and all that we have to the cause of truth and justice,
of law and order, of liberty and good government, of pure and undefiled religion.   Then, though weeping may endure for a night, joy
will come in the morning.

Blessed be God! despite of this great, and sudden, and temporary darkness, the morning has begun to dawn—the morning of a
bright and glorious day, such as our country has never seen.   That
day will come and not tarry, and the death of a hundred Presidents
and their Cabinets can never, never prevent it.   While we are thus
hopeful, however, let us also be humble.   The occasion calls us to
prayerful and tearful humiliation.   It demands of us that we lie
low, very low, before Him who has smitten us for our sins.   Oh
that all our rulers and all our people may bow in the dust to-day,
beneath the chastening hand of God! and may their voices go up
to Him as one voice, and their hearts go up to Him as one heart,
pleading with Him for mercy, for grace to sanctify our great and
sore bereavement; and for wisdom to guide us in this our time of
need.   Such a united cry and pleading will not be in vain.   It will
enter into the ear and heart of Him who sits upon the throne, and
He will say to us, as to His ancient Israel, "In a little wrath I hid
My face from thee for a moment; but with everlasting kindness will
I have mercy upon thee, saith the Lord, thy Redeemer."

I have said that the people confided in the late lamented President with a full and a loving confidence.   Probably no man, since
the days of Washington, was ever so deeply and firmly imbedded
and inshrined in the very hearts of the people as Abraham Lincoln.
Nor was it a mistaken confidence and love.   He deserved it, deserved it well, deserved it all.   He merited it by his character, by
his acts, and by the whole tenor, and tone, and spirit of his life.
He was simple and sincere, plain and honest, truthful and just,
benevolent and kind.   His perceptions were quick and clear, his
judgments were calm and accurate, and his purposes were good
and pure beyond a question.   Always and everywhere he aimed
and endeavored to *be* right and to *do* right.   His integrity was
thorough, all-pervading, all-controlling, and incorruptible.   It was
the same in every place and relation, in the consideration and the
control of matters great or small,—the same firm and steady principle of power and beauty, that shed a clear and crowning lustre
upon all his other excellencies of mind and heart, and recommended

him to his fellow-citizens as *the* man, who, in a time of unexampled peril, when the very life of the nation was at stake, should be chosen to occupy, in the country and for the country, its highest post of power and responsibility. How wisely and well, how purely and faithfully, how firmly and steadily, how justly and successfully he did occupy that post and meet its grave demands, in circumstances of surpassing trial and difficulty, is known to you all, known to the country and the world. He comprehended from the first the perils to which treason had exposed the freest and best government on the earth—the vast interests of liberty and humanity that were to be saved or lost forever in the urgent impending conflict; he rose to the dignity and momentousness of the occasion, saw his duty as the Chief Magistrate of a great and imperilled people; and he determined to *do* his duty, and his whole duty, seeking the guidance and leaning upon the arm of Him of whom it is written, "He giveth power to the faint; and to them that have no might He increaseth strength." Yes; he leaned upon *His* arm. He recognized and received the truth, that "the kingdom is the Lord's; and He is the governor among the nations." He remembered that "God is in history," and he felt that nowhere had His hand and His mercy been so marvellously conspicuous as in the history of this nation. He hoped and he prayed that that same hand would continue to guide us, and that same mercy continue to abound to us in the time of our greatest need. I speak what I know, and testify what I have often heard him say, when I affirm, that that guidance and mercy were the prop on which he humbly and habitually leaned; they were the best hope he had for himself and for his country. Hence, when he was leaving his home in Illinois and coming to this city to take his seat in the executive chair of a disturbed and troubled nation, he said to the old and tried friends who gathered tearfully around him and bade him farewell, "I leave you with this request—*pray for me.*" They did pray for him; and millions of others prayed for him; nor did they pray in vain. Their prayer was heard, and the answer appears in all his subsequent history; it shines forth, with a heavenly radiance, in the whole course and tenor of his administration from its commencement to its close. God raised him up for a great and glorious mission, furnished him for his work, and aided him in its accomplishment. Nor was it merely by strength of mind, and honesty of heart, and purity and pertinacity of purpose, that He furnished him ; in addition to these things, He gave him a calm and abiding confidence in the overruling providence of God, and in the ultimate triumph of truth and righteousness through the power and the blessing of God. This confidence strengthened him in all his hours of anxiety and toil, and inspired him with calm and cheering hope when others were inclining to despondency and gloom. Never shall I forget the emphasis and the deep emotion with which he said, in this very room, to a company of clergymen and others who called to pay him their respects in the darkest days of our civil conflict, "Gentlemen, my hope of success in this great and terrible struggle rests on that immutable foundation, the justice and goodness of God. And when events are very threatening and prospects very dark, I still hope that, in some way which man cannot see, all will be well in the end, because our cause is just and God is on our side."

Such was his sublime and holy faith, and it was an anchor to his soul both sure and steadfast. It made him firm and strong. It emboldened him in the pathway of duty, however rugged and perilous it might be. It made him valiant for the right—for the cause of God and humanity; and it held him in steady, patient, and unswerving adherence to a policy of administration which he thought, and which we all now think, both God and humanity required him to adopt. We admired and loved him on many accounts—for strong and various reasons: we admired his childlike simplicity; his freedom from guile and deceit; his staunch and sterling integrity; his kind and forgiving temper; his industry and patience; his persistent self-sacrificing devotion to all the duties of his eminent position, from the least to the greatest; his readiness to hear and consider the cause of the poor and humble, the suffering and the oppressed; his charity towards those who questioned the correctness of his opinions and the wisdom of his policy; his wonderful skill in reconciling differences among the friends of the Union, leading them away from abstractions, and inducing them to work together and harmoniously for the common weal; his true and enlarged philanthropy, that knew no distinction of color or race, but regarded all men as brethren and endowed alike by their Creator with certain inalienable rights, among which are "life, liberty, and the pursuit of happiness;" his inflexible purpose that what freedom had gained in our terrible civil strife should never be lost, and that the end of the war should be the end of slavery, and, as a consequence, of rebellion; his readiness to spend and be spent for the attainment of such a triumph, a triumph the blessed fruits of which should be as wide-spreading as the earth and as enduring as the sun;—all these things commanded and fixed our admiration and the admiration of the world, and stamped upon his character and life the unmistakable impress of *greatness*. But more sublime than any or all of these, more holy and influential, more beautiful, and strong, and sustaining, *was his abid-*

*ing confidence in God, and in the final triumph of truth and right-
eousness through Him and for His sake.* This was his noblest virtue, his grandest principle, the secret alike of his strength, his patience, and his success. And this, it seems to me, after being near
him steadily and with him often for more than four years, is the
principle by which, more than by any other, "he, being dead, yet
speaketh." Yes; by his steady enduring confidence in God, and in
the complete ultimate success of the cause of God, which is the
cause of humanity, more than in any other way, does he now speak
to us and to the nation he loved and served so well. By this he
speaks to his successor in office, and charges him to have faith in
God. By this he speaks to the members of his Cabinet, the men
with whom he counselled so often and was associated so long, and
he charges them to have faith in God. By this he speaks to all
who occupy positions of influence and authority in these sad and
troublous times, and he charges them all to have faith in God. By
this he speaks to this great people as they sit in sackcloth to-day,
and weep for him with a bitter wailing, and refuse to be comforted,
and he charges them to have faith in God. And by this he *will*
speak through the ages and to all rulers and peoples in every land,
and his message to them will be, "Cling to liberty and right; battle
for them; bleed for them; die for them, if need be; and have confidence in God.' Oh that the voice of this testimony may sink down
into our hearts to-day and every day, and into the heart of the nation, and exert its appropriate influence upon our feelings, our faith,
our patience, and our devotion to the cause now dearer to us than ever
before, because consecrated by the blood of its most conspicuous
defender, its wisest and most fondly-trusted friend !

He is dead ; but the God in whom he trusted lives, and He can
guide and strengthen his successor as He guided and strengthened
him. He is dead ; but the memory of his virtues, of his wise and
patriotic counsels and labors, of his calm and steady faith in God,
lives, is precious, and will be a power for good in the country quite
down to the end of time. He is dead ; but the cause he so ardently
loved, so ably, patiently, faithfully represented and defended, not
for himself only, not for us only, but for all people in all their coming generations till time shall be no more—that cause survives his
fall, and will survive it. The light of its brightening prospects
flashes cheeringly to-day athwart the gloom occasioned by his death,
and the language of God's *united* providences is telling us, that
though the friends of liberty die, liberty itself is immortal. There
is no assassin strong enough and no weapon deadly enough to
quench its inextinguishable life, or arrest its onward march to the

conquest and empire of the world. This is our confidence and this is our consolation as we weep and mourn to day. Though our beloved President is slain, our beloved country is saved. And so we sing of mercy as well as of judgment. Tears of gratitude mingle with those of sorrow. While there is darkness, there is also the dawning of a brighter, happier day upon our stricken and weary land. God be praised, that our fallen Chief lived long enough to see the day dawn, and the day-star of joy and peace rise upon the nation. He saw it, and he was glad. Alas! alas! he only saw the *dawn*. When the *sun* has risen full-orbed and glorious, and a happy re-united people are rejoicing in its light, it will shine upon his grave. But that grave will be a precious and a consecrated spot. The friends of Liberty and of the Union will repair to it in years and ages to come, to pronounce the memory of its occupant blessed, and gathering from his very ashes and from the rehearsal of his deeds and virtues fresh incentives to patriotism, they will there renew their vows of fidelity to their country and their God.

And now I know not that I can more appropriately conclude this discourse, which is but a sincere and simple utterance of the heart, than by addressing to our departed President, with some slight modification, the language which Tacitus, in his Life of Agricola. addresses to his venerable and departed father-in-law:—" With you we may now congratulate: you are blessed, not only because your life was a career of glory, but because you were released when, your country safe, it was happiness to die. We have lost a parent, and, in our distress, it is now an addition to our heartfelt sorrow that we had it not in our power to commune with you on the bed of languishing, and receive your last embrace. Your dying words would have been ever dear to us: your commands we should have treasured up, and graved them on our hearts. This sad comfort we have lost, and the wound, for that reason, pierces deeper. From the world of spirits behold your disconsolate family and people: exalt our minds from fond regret and unavailing grief to the contemplation of your virtues. Those we must not lament; it were impiety to sully them with a tear. To cherish their memory, to embalm them with our praises, and, so far as we can, to emulate your bright example, will be the truest mark of our respect, the best tribute we can. offer. Your wife will thus preserve the memory of the best of husbands, and thus your children will prove their filial piety. By dwelling constantly on your words and actions, they will have an illustrious character before their eyes, and, not content with one bare image of your mortal frame, they will have, what is more valuable, the form and features of your mind. Busts and statues, like their originals, are frail and perishable. The soul is formed of finer elements, and its inward form is not to be expressed by the hand of an artist with unconscious matter : our manners and our morals may in some degree trace the resemblance. All of you that gained our love, and raised our admiration, still subsists, and will ever subsist, preserved in the minds of men, the register of ages and the records of fame. Others, who figured on the stage of life, and were the worthies of a former day, will sink, for want of a faithful historian, into the common lot of oblivion, inglorious and unremembered ; but you, our lamented friend and head, delineated with truth, and fairly consigned to posterity, will survive yourself, and triumph over the injuries of time."

At the conclusion of the sermon, after a brief silence, Dr. Gray, chaplain of the United States Senate, offered the following prayer.

O Lord God of Hosts, behold a nation prostrate before Thy throne, clothed in sackcloth, who stand around all that now remains of our illustrious and beloved chief. We thank Thee that Thou hast given to us such a patriot, and the country such valor, and to the world such a noble specimen of manhood. We bless Thee that Thou hast raised him to the highest position of trust and power in the nation, and that Thou hast spared him so long to guide and direct the affairs of government in its hour of peril and conflict. We trusted it would be he who should deliver Israel, that he would have been retained to us while the nation was passing through its baptism of blood; but in an evil hour, in an unexpected moment, when joy and rejoicing filled our souls and was thrilling the hearts of the nation, he fell. O God, give grace to sustain us under this dark and mysterious providence; help us to look up unto Thee and say, Not our will, but Thine, O God, be done. We commend to Thy merciful regard and tender compassion the afflicted family of the deceased. Thou seest how their hearts are stricken with sorrow and wrung with agony. Oh help them as they are now passing through a dark valley and shadow of death, to fear no evil, but to lean upon Thy staff for support. Oh help them to cast their burden upon the great Burden-bearer and find relief. Help them to look beyond human agencies and human means, and recognize Thy hand, O God, in this providence, and say, It is the Lord, let Him do what seemeth good in His sight; and as they proceed slowly and sadly on their way with the remains of a husband and father, to consign them to their last resting-place, may they look beyond the grave to the morning of resurrection, when that which they now sow in weakness shall be raised in strength; what they now sow a mortal body, shall be raised a spiritual body; what they now sow in corruption shall be raised in incorruption, and shall be fashioned like unto Christ's most glorious body. O God of the bereaved, comfort and sustain this mourning family.

Bless the new Chief Magistrate. Let the mantle of his predecessor fall upon him. Bless the Secretary of State in his family. O God, if possible according to Thy will, spare their lives, that they may render still important service to the country. Bless all the members of the Cabinet; endow them with wisdom from above. Bless the commanders of our army and navy and all the brave defenders of the country, and give them continued success. Bless the ambassadors from foreign countries, and give us peace with the nations of the earth. O God, let treason that has deluged our land with blood, and devastated our country, and bereaved our homes, and filled them with widows and orphans, and has at length culminated in the assassination of the nation's great ruler, God of justice and avenger of the nation's wrong! let the work of treason cease, and let the guilty author of this horrible crime be arrested and brought to justice. Oh hear the cry and prayer, and see the tears now arising from a nation's crushed and smitten heart; and deliver us from the power of all our enemies, and send speedy peace unto all of our borders : through Jesus Christ our Lord. Amen.

The hearse arrived shortly before the conclusion of the services in the White House. It was built expressly by G. R. Hall. The lower base of the hearse is fourteen feet long and seven feet wide, and eight feet from the ground. The upper base, upon which the coffin rests, is eleven feet long, and is five feet below the top of the canopy. The canopy is surmounted by a gilt eagle, covered with crape. The whole hearse is covered with cloth, velvet, crape, and alpaca. The seat is covered with hammer-cloth, and on each side is a splendid black lamp. The hearse is fifteen feet high, and the coffin is so placed as to afford a full view to all spectators. It was drawn by six gray horses.

The funeral cortege started with military precision at two o'clock. The avenue was cleared the whole length from the Presidential mansion to the Capitol. Every window, housetop, balcony, and every inch of the sidewalks on either side was densely crowded with a living throng to witness the procession. In all this dense crowd hardly a sound was heard. People conversed with each other in suppressed tones. Presently the monotonous thump of the funeral drum sounded upon the street, and the military escort of the funeral car began to march past with solemn tread, muffled drums, and arms reversed.

A scene so solemn, imposing, and impressive as that which the national metropolis presented, and upon which myriad eyes of saddened faces were gazing, was never witnessed, under circumstances so appalling, in any portion of our beloved country. Around us is the capital city, clad in the habiliments of mourning; above us, the cloudless sky, so bright, so tranquil, so cheerful, as if Heaven would, on this solemn occasion, specially invite us, by the striking contrast, to turn our thoughts from the darkness and the miseries of this life to the light and the joy that shine, with endless lustre, beyond it. The mournful strains of the funeral dirge, borne on the gentle zephyrs of this summer-like day, touch a responsive chord in every human heart of the countless thousands that, with solemn demeanor and measured step, follow to their temporary resting-place in the nation's capitol the cold, inanimate form of one who, living, was the honored Chief Magistrate of the American people, and, dead, will ever be endeared in their fondest memories. Never did a generous and grateful people pay, in anguish and tears, a tribute more sincere or merited to a kind, humane, and patriotic chieftain; never were the dark and bloody deeds of crime brought out in relief so bold, and in horror and detestation so universal, as in the sublime and imposing honors this day tendered to the corpse of Abraham Lincoln. Such a scene is the epoch of a lifetime. Strong men are deeply affected; gentle women weep; children are awe-stricken; none will ever forget it. Memory has consecrated it on her brightest tablet; and it will ever be thought, spoken, and written of as the sublime homage of a sorrowing nation at the shrine of the martyred patriot.

The following was in the main the order of procession:

Tenth Regiment, Veteran Reserve Corps, Major George Bowers commanding.

The Ninth Regiment, Veteran Reserve Corps, Lieut. Colonel R. E. Johnson, the band playing a dirge.

Colonel George W. Gile was in command of the brigade, whose flags were draped in mourning. The men marched with reversed arms and muffled drums.

14

Battalion of Marines, Major Graham.

The Marine Band played the funeral march, composed by Brevet Major-General J. G. Barnard, dedicated to the occasion.

A detachment of artillery from Camp Barry, consisting of eight brass pieces draped in mourning, the whole under the command of Brigadier General Hall.

Sixteenth New York cavalry; two battalions of the Sixteenth Illinois cavalry; and one battalion of the Eighteenth Illinois cavalry, under the command of Colonel M. B. Sweitzer.

Band of the Sixteenth New York cavalry.

Commander of escort, Major-General Augur and Staff.

General Hardee and Staff.

General Gamble and Staff.

Dismounted Officers of the Marine Corps, Navy, and Army, nearly three hundred in number.

Mounted Officers of Marine Corps, Navy, and Army, in very large numbers.

Several hundred paroled officers of the army.

Medical Staff of the army, &c., in and about Washington.

Paymasters of the United States army, under the command of Brevet Brigadier-General B. W. Brice, Paymaster General.

CIVIC PROCESSION.

Marshal Ward H. Lamon, supported by his aids.

The clergy in attendance, the Rev. P. D. Gurley, D.D., Rev. Charles H. Hall, D.D.

Right Rev. Bishop Simpson, D.D., and Rev. E. H. Gray, D.D., Surgeon-General Barnes, of the United States army, and Dr. Stone, physicians of the deceased.

PALL-BEARERS:

On the part of the Senate:
  Mr. Foster, of Conn.,
  Mr. Morgan, of New York,
  Mr. Johnson, of Md.,
  Mr. Yates, of Illinois,
  Mr. Wade, of Ohio,
  Mr. Conness, of California.

On the part of the House:
  Mr. Dawes, of Mass.,
  Mr. Coffroth, of Penn.,
  Mr. Smith, of Kentucky,
  Mr. Colfax, of Indiana,
  Mr. Worthington, of Nevada,
  Mr. Washburne, of Ill.

ARMY.
Lieut. General U. S. Grant,
Major-General H. W. Halleck,
Bt. Brigadier-General Nichols.

NAVY.
Vice-Admiral Farragut,
Rear-Admiral Shubrick,
Colonel Jacob Zeilen, M. C'ps.

CIVILIANS.
O. H. Browning,   Thomas Corwin,
George Ashmun.   Simeon Cameron.

The Hearse, drawn by six gray horses, each led by a groom.

The horse of the deceased, led by two grooms, caparisoned.

The family of the deceased, relatives, private secretaries, and friends.

Delegations of the States of Illinois and Kentucky as mourners.

The President of the United States, accompanied by Hon. Preston King.

Members of the Cabinet.

The Diplomatic Corps in full Court Dress.

Ex Vice-President Hamlin.

Chief-Justice S. P. Chase and the Associate Justices of the Supreme Court of the United States.

The Senate of the United States, with their officers.

Members of the late and the next House of Representatives, with the officers of the last House.

Governors of the several States and Territories.

Members of the State and Territorial Legislatures.

Judges of the Court of Claims.

The Federal Judiciary and the Judiciary of the several States and Territories.

Assistant Secretaries of the several Departments.

Officers of the Smithsonian Institution.

Members and officers of the Sanitary and Christian Commissions.

The Judges of the several Courts, and members of the Bar of the city of Washington.   .

Band.

Washington Commandary of Knights Templar, S. P. Bell, Marshal, preceded by the band of the Campbell Hospital, with the banners of their order.

The Councils and other members of the Corporation of the city of Baltimore.

Members of the Corporation of Alexandria.

Members of the Councils of the city of New York.

The Select and Common Councils of the city of Philadelphia.   Also, delegations from the civic authorities of Boston, and Brooklyn, N. Y.

Committee of the Union League of Philadelphia, headed by Horace Binney, Jr., Esq., and Morton McMichael, Esq.

Members of the Christian Commission of the city of Philadelphia.

Band.

The Perseverance Hose Company of the city of Philadelphia, of which President Lincoln was an honorary member, in black suits, with badges on their hats designating their organization.

The Corporate Authorities of Washington and Georgetown, headed by Mayors of five cities, Washington, Georgetown, Alexandria, Baltimore, and Boston.

Ministers of various religious denominations, white and colored.

Delegations from the various States in the following order:

Massachusetts, about seventy-five in number, besides the band, which they brought from Boston. The State flag which they bore was draped in mourning. Major-General B. F. Butler, in citizen's dress, occupied a position in this portion of the line; Marshal Gardiner Tufts. New Hampshire, numbering about twenty men; Marshal Matthew G. Emery.

Ohio had eighty men in line, under the marshalship of H. M. Slade, Esq.

New York numbered three hundred.

New Jersey was represented by one hundred of her sons, and led by Mr. Prevost, acting marshal.

California, Oregon, and Nevada united and had one hundred representatives of the Far West, under the marshalship of Mr. Wray.

Maine sent a large delegation, led by Mr. S. P. Brown.

Band.

The heads and chiefs of Bureaus of the Treasury Department, under the marshalship of Messrs. A. E. Edwards, assisted by Capt. Jones and Col. Willett, preceded by the band of the Treasury Regiment. They carried with them the flag torn by Booth, as he leaped to the stage of Ford's Theatre on the night of the assassination.

The Journeymen Bookbinders and Printers of the Government establishment, marshalled by Mr. George W. Francis.

The War Department employees turned out in large force, and were marshalled by Mr. Potts.

The Pension Office had one hundred employees in line, marshalled by Commissioner Barrett and Mr. Pearson, chief clerk.

The clerks and employees of the Post-office Department were marshalled by Dr. McDonald and Major Scott.

The clerks of the Ordnance Office.

The clerks of the Agricultural Bureau.

Quartermaster's Band.

Major-General M. C. Meigs, and the heads of divisions of the Quartermaster's Department.

A brigade, composed of the employees of the Quartermaster's Department.

Office battalion Quartermaster's regiment, Major Wagner commanding.

First regiment Quartermaster's Volunteers, Col. C. H. Tompkins commanding.

Second regiment, Col. J. M. Moore commanding.

Brig.-General Rucker commanded the brigade, and Brig.-General J. A. Ekin and Col. J. J. Dana were the marshals.

Clerks of the Quartermaster's Department, in citizens' dress.

Eight survivors of the war of 1812—viz., Chapman Lee, Fielder R. Dorsett, Smith Minor, Thomas Foster, R. M. Harrison, Isaac Burch, Joseph P. Wolf, and Capt. John Moore.

The clerks and employees of the Baltimore Custom-house and Post-office, marshalled by Dr. E. C. Gaskill, one hundred and eighty in number, with band of the Eighth Regiment, U. S. Infantry.

Society of the Brotherhood of the Union, Capitol Circle No. 1. Thomas H. Robinson marshal.

Band.

The Fenian Brotherhood, Marshal P. H. Donegan, State Centre, D. C., three hundred men, their flag draped.

A detachment of the guard stationed at Seminary Hospital, Georgetown, marshalled by Sergeant Conway.

Band.

Employees of the United States Military Railroad, under the command of General McCullum.

The National Republican Association of the Seventh Ward, marshalled by Captain McConnell.

A delegation of citizens of Alexandria, headed by the band attached to Gen. Slough's headquarters.

Firemen of Alexandria: Friendship and Sun Fire Companies.

Civic societies of Alexandria; Andrew Jackson Lodge A. Y. M. Delegation from the Christian Commission of Alexandria.

Two German Glee Clubs.

The Mount Vernon Association.

The Potomac Hose Company, of Georgetown, Samuel R. Swain, marshal.

About four hundred convalescents from the Lincoln Hospital, preceded by their band.

Workingmen and mechanics of the Mount Clair Works, Baltimore, to the number of seven hundred, were marshalled by Wm. H. Shepley.

Convalescents from Finley Hospital to the number of nearly three hundred, under charge of Steward Hill.

Operatives employed at the Arsenal, under the marshalship of William H. Godron.

Two hundred and fifty pupils of Gonzaga College, under the charge of Father Wiget, with whom were a number of Catholic clergymen and teachers. Band.

Union Leagues of East Baltimore, Washington, Georgetown, and New York, marshalled by James D. McKean.

German societies and citizens: Relief Association of Washington, mounted; Relief Association, on foot; Turners, of Washington; Washington Sangerbund; Germania Lodge, No. 1, Order of Odd Fellows; Franklin Lodge of Independent Brothers, No. 1; and the Swiss Association. Marshal, Col. Joseph Gerhardt, assisted by Messrs. Charles Walter, F. Stosch, M. Rosenberg, F. Martin, Andrew Lutz, and Franz Buehler. The delegation was headed by Lebnartz's Baltimore band.

The Sons of Temperance, preceded by the band of Carver Hospital, and was marshalled by G. W. P., F. M. Bradley; divisions No. 1 and 10, Good Samaritan and Meridian, marshalled by P. W. Summy; Excelsior Division, No. 6, Federal City Division, No. 2, and Equal Division, No, 3, marshalled by S. C. Spurgeon and S. S. Bond, and preceded by a band; Aurora Division, No. 9 (Finley Hospital), marshalled by H. D. Maynard; Lincoln Division, marshalled by M. F. Kelley; Mount Pleasant Division, Sergeant O. G. Lane marshal; Cliffburne Division, J. M. Roney marshal; Mount Vernon and McKee Divisions, Alexandria, T. A. Dolan marshal; Everett Division, No. 25 (Camp Barry), W. H. Perkins marshal.

The Columbia Typographical Society, marshalled by Mr. L. F. Clements.

The Hebrew Congregation, one hundred and twenty-five men, marshalled by B. Kaufman.

A delegation of two or three hundred Italians, under the marshalship of ex Lieutenant Maggi. They carried the national flags of Italy and the United States.

Convalescents from Emory Hospital, under Hospital Steward W. C. Branhill.

Colored people to the number of several thousand, among whom were the following:

The Annual Conference of the African Methodist Episcopal Church, headed by Right Revs. Bishops Payne and Wayman.

Clergy of the various denominations.

G. U. O. O. Nazarites, marshal Noah Butler.

Delegation of the First Colored Christian Commission of Baltimore.

D. A. Payne Lodge of Good Samaritans.

The G. U. O. O. Fellows, preceded by the Grand Council.

Blue Lodge of Ancient York Masons.

Masonic Grand Lodge of the United States and Canadas.

Colored citizens of Baltimore, George A. Hackett chief marshal.

Washington United Benevolent Association, who carried with them a banner on which was inscribed the words, " We mourn our loss."

Band.
Colored men of Washington Sons of Levi.
Eastern Star Lodge, No. 1,028, I. O. O. F.
John F. Cook Lodge, No. 1,185.
Union Friendship Lodge, No. 891.
Potomac Union Lodge, of Georgetown, No. 892
Olive Lodge, No. 967, A. Y. M.
The Catholic Benevolent Association, carrying a banner bearing the motto, "In God we trust."
Harmony Lodge of Odd Fellows.
Union Grand Lodge of Maryland

A colored regiment from the front arrived at precisely two o'clock, and not being able to proceed any further than the corner of Seventh street, halted in front of the Metropolitan Hotel, wheeled about, and became by that manœuvre the very head and front of the procession. They appeared to be under the very best discipline, and displayed admirable skill in their various exercises.

Long before the solemnities began at the White House, crowds of people flocked to the Capitol. The magnificent edifice was handsomely draped with black. All the pillars and windows wore the solemn emblems of mourning, and high upon the splendid dome the same sad symbols drooped despondingly. It was arranged that the funeral procession should pass up by the north side of the Capitol, and enter the building at the central door of the east front. There stood the black platform by means of which the coffin was to be lifted down from the car, and over the central door there was a small black canopy.

The people gathered in groups, picnicked on the grass or covered the marble steps. Inside there reigned a solemn silence, broken only by the thunders of artillery just beyond the Capitol grounds. On the west balcony sat Simon Cameron, who was to have been one of the pall-bearers, but who was unable to get into the White House, and so awaited the arrival of the procession.

The tolling of bells and the minute-guns from the forts announced that the *cortége* was forming, and made the solemnity of the deserted Capitol almost oppressive. Then the mournful pageant could be discerned moving slowly down the grand avenue—moving, and yet it did not seem to move, so gradual was its advance. It was after three o'clock before the President's remains reached the rotunda.

All the pictures on the rotunda walls were covered with black, and the statues were completely draped, except the statue of Washington, which wore a black scarf. In the centre of the marble floor stood the catafalque, covered with black. It was about nine feet long, three feet high, and four feet broad. The black cloth was ornamented with silver fringe and looped with silver stars. At each corner of the structure was the fasces, and on either side were muskets, rifles, carbines, bayonets, sabres, and cutlasses, arranged as trophies. No flag was displayed in the rotunda. On every hand were the black hangings and the black crape, and the effect was inexpressibly gloomy.

Just after three o'clock the head of the *cortége* wheeled into the open space in front of the eastern entrance. The soldiers filed past in the order already given, and when the infantry extended quite across the open space they halted and faced inward, thus inclosing the entrance in a military square. The artillery passed behind the infantry, and took a position on the hill opposite the entrance. The cavalry remained without in the street. Then the officers of the army and navy gathered in great groups in front of the infantry. Finally, the carriages rolled slowly up to deposit the pall-bearers, mourners, and Committee of Arrangements, who formed in double line up the steps leading to the east door. On either hand, and behind the soldiery, throngs of spectators looked silently on, the colored men and women being especially conspicuous, since they had secured the best posts of observation. A burst of sad melodies filled the air, and the funeral car stopped to allow Abraham Lincoln to enter the Capitol for the last time.

Six weeks and a half ago President Lincoln stood upon a platform built over the very steps up which he was now being carried, and delivered his second inaugural address. With few exceptions the same faces surrounded him then as now. Then the same crowd was assembled to do him honor, and long lines of soldiers presented arms at his approach—just as they do to-day. Though the Lieutenant-General was not present then, Vice-Admiral Farragut stood by the President's side, and the glittering galaxies of brave officers of the army and navy were there, and the Cabinet ministers were at his left hand, and Andrew Johnson was quite as conspicuous, and Senators and Congressmen and diplomatists were as numerous. Then the sun broke through the storm-clouds as if blessing him, and now it beamed as brightly upon his upturned face. There was the same scene, the same actors, the same spectators; but over all there was a terrible change. Then the President lived, and now he lay in his coffin, murdered by his assassin. Then he spoke pious words of peace, of good-will, and of his steadfast determination to preserve the Union. Now he spoke still more powerfully in his death, and every man felt the force of the lesson taught by that cold still form, and said amen to its moral.

The troops presenting arms, the bands playing a requiem, the assemblage standing uncovered, and the artillery thundering solemnly, the coffin was carefully removed from the funeral car, carried into the rotunda by a detail from the President's bodyguard, and placed upon the catafalque. Preceding the little procession came Major French, whose officers stood in line with heads bared. Then followed the pall-bearers, who parted on either side of the catafalque. The coffin came next, and the moment it was placed in position, Dr. Gurley, standing at the head of the coffin, uttered a few brief and most impressive remarks, chiefly in solemn words of Scripture, consigning the dead ashes once animated by the soul of Abraham Lincoln to their original dust. The deep tones of his voice reverberated from the vast walls and ceiling of the rotunda, now first used for such a solemn occasion, and during the impressive scene many were affected to tears :—

"It is appointed unto men once to die. The dust returns to the earth as it was, and the spirit to God who gave it. All flesh is but as grass, and the glory of man as the flower of grass; the grass withereth, and the flower thereof fadeth away. We know that we must die and go to the house appointed for all living. For what is our life? It is even as a vapor that appeareth for a little time and then vanishes away. Therefore, be ye also ready; for in such an hour as ye think not the Son of Man cometh. Let us pray—

"Lord, so teach us to number our days that we may apply our hearts unto wisdom. Wean us from this transitory world. Turn away our eyes from beholding vanity. Lift our affections to the things which are above, where Christ sitteth on the right hand of God. There may our treasure be, and there may our hearts be also. Wash us in the blood of Christ. Clothe us in the righteousness of Christ. Renew and sanctify us by his word and spirit. Lead us in the paths of piety for his name's sake. Gently, Lord, oh gently guide us through all the duties and changes and trials of our earthly pilgrimage. Dispose us to pass the time of our sojourning here in fear, denying ungodliness and worldly lusts, and living soberly, righteously, and godly in this present world; and when, at the last, our time shall come to die, may we be gathered to our fathers, leaving the testimony of a good conscience in the communion of the Christian Church, in the confidence of a certain faith, in the comfort of a reasonable, religious, and holy hope, in favor with Thee, our God, and in perfect charity with the world; all which we ask through Jesus Christ, our blessed Lord and Redeemer. Amen.

"Forasmuch as it hath pleased Almighty God, in his wise providence, to take out of this clay tabernacle the soul that inhabited it, we commit its decaying remains to their kindred element—earth to earth, ashes to ashes, dust to dust—looking for the general resurrection, through our Lord Jesus Christ, at whose coming to judge the world, the earth and sea shall give up their dead, and the corruptible bodies of them that sleep in Him shall be fashioned like unto his glorious body, according to the working whereby He is able to subdue all things unto himself. Wherefore, let us comfort one another with these words. And now may the God of Peace, that brought again from the dead our Lord Jesus, that great Shepherd of the sheep, through the blood of the everlasting covenant, make you perfect in every good work, to do his will, working in you that which is well-pleasing in his sight, through Jesus Christ, the resurrection and the life, our Redeemer and our hope, to whose care we now commit these precious remains, and to whose name be glory forever and ever. Amen."

As the prayer closed, President Johnson entered the rotunda, attended by several senators. Lieutenant-General Grant, who had hitherto stood modestly but conspicuously among the pall-bearers, next to General Halleck, now fell back out of sight. Captain Robert Lincoln and the family relatives appeared more prominently. Then the President's bodyguard and the cavalry escort filed in and formed in double column to the west of the catafalque. The only persons in the rotunda were the relatives, the clergymen, the officers in charge of the body, the pall-bearers, the President and his Cabinet, four representatives of the press, the Illinois and Kentucky delegations, Marshal Lamon and a few of his committee, the soldiers already mentioned, Commissioner French, and the Capitol police. There was no delay in Dr. Gurley's remarks, and the shuffling of feet as the distinguished persons outside tried to steal in before the conclusion of the ceremonies was the only interruption. The prayer followed close upon the burial service, and the benediction as closely followed the prayer.

The rotunda was then cleared, and President Lincoln lay almost alone. A detail of soldiers was then made. Guards were stationed at all the doors leading from the rotunda. Instructions were issued to admit no one. Secretary Stanton remained behind for a while, apparently to give these orders and see them executed. General Augur and his officers took charge of the corpse. Commissioner French stationed his officers around the building. The attendant carefully brushed every spot of dust from the coffin and catafalque. The undertaker then arrived, and all those not on duty retired. The simple ceremonies in the rotunda were over by four o'clock.

The corpse of the President was placed beneath the right concave, now streaked with mournful trappings, and left in state, watched by guards of officers with drawn swords. This was a wonderful spectacle—the man most beloved and honored, in the ark of the Republic. The storied paintings representing eras in its history were draped in sable, through which they seemed to cast reverential glances upon the lamented bier. The thrilling scenes depicted by Trumbull, the commemorative canvases of Leutze, the wilderness vegetation of Powell, glared from their separate pedestals upon the central spot where lay the fallen majesty of the country. At night the jets of gas concealed in the spring of the dome were lighted up, so that their bright reflection upon the frescoed walls hurled masses of burning light, like marvellous haloes, upon the little box where so much that was loved and honored rested on its way to the grave. And so through the starry night, in the fane of the great Union he had strengthened and recovered, the ashes of Abraham Lincoln, zealously guarded, lay in calm repose.

V.

OBSERVANCES IN OTHER CITIES.

V.

FUNERAL SERVICES IN OTHER CITIES.

THE FAST DAY.

On the death of the President, and in the condition to which the Secretary of State was reduced, Mr. Hunter, the Acting Secretary, issued the following official document.

DEPARTMENT OF STATE,
WASHINGTON, April 17, 1865.

To the People of the United States:

The undersigned is directed to announce that the funeral ceremonies of the lamented Chief Magistrate will take place at the Executive Mansion in this city at twelve o'clock, noon, on Wednesday, the 19th instant. The various religious denominations throughout the country are invited to meet in their respective places of worship at that hour for the purpose of solemnizing the occasion with appropriate ceremonies.

W. HUNTER, Acting Secretary of State.

The invitation which it contained was cordially responded to ; as the following, from those denominations whose organizations made the pastoral direction of a Bishop necessary, testify.

To the Clergy and Laity of the Diocese of New York:

DEAR BRETHREN—The authorities at Washington have announced that the funeral solemnities of the late President of the United States will take place in that city at twelve o'clock on Wednesday of this week ; and they have expressed the hope that each Christian congregation in the country will assemble at that hour in its place of worship and unite in services of an appropriate character. In this suggestion I most heartily concur, as I am sure you will. I do therefore most affectionately recommend to the clergy and congregations of this diocese to appear before God in their holy places, on Wednesday, the 19th, at noon, and while the last offices are being performed over the mortal remains of their late venerated Chief Magistrate, to bow down in humble recognition of the Almighty hand, to adore His Majesty, to revere His justice, to magnify His mercies, to implore Him to sanctify to us His dealings with us as a people, and at the same time to testify respect for the memory of the wise, upright, and benignant ruler who has been so mysteriously removed from this mortal scene. The following order of services is hereby appointed for the occasion :

1. The Lesser Litany—"O Christ, hear us," &c., and including the Prayer— "We humbly beseech thee," &c.
2. The Anthem, in the Burial Office—"Lord, let me know my end," &c.
3. The Lesson—1st Corinthians, xv. 20.
4. A Hymn.
5. The Prayer for the Nation in Affliction, as recently set forth.
6. The prayer, " In time of war and tumult."
7. The two prayers at the end of the burial service.
8. " The grace of our Lord Jesus Christ," &c.

Again commending you, very dear brethren, to the divine protection and blessing, I remain, most affectionately, your brother in Christ,

HORATIO POTTER, Bishop of New York.
New York, Easter Monday, April 17, 1865.

To the Reverend Clergy of the Diocese of Western New York :

REVEREND BRETHREN—The death of the President of the United States, by the hand of an assassin, is a calamity which it needs no words to impress on the heart of the nation.

The crime is not regicide, but it is parricide.

That such an unnatural sin should have been committed against the Divine Majesty and against the ruler of a free people, is cause for profound humiliation not less than unfeigned sorrow.

In obedience to the new order of his Excellency the Governor, the service for the 20th instant is changed as follows :

Instead of the *Venite,* shall be used (Psalm 51st), the *Miserere.* The first lesson, followed by the *Benedicite,* shall be Deuteronomy xxxii., to verse 42; and the second lesson, St. Matthew xi., from verse 15th. The Litany shall be said entire.

Other appropriate devotions from the prayer-book may be used at the discretion of the minister, and also those for the nation and rulers, as set forth by my Reverend predecessor.

On Wednesday, the day of the President's funeral, the burial service may be said at twelve o'clock, omitting the committal.

The Lord be with you, and with all our afflicted countrymen.

Your affectionate Bishop,

A. CLEVELAND COXE.

Easter Monday, New York, April 17, 1865.

Fellow-Citizens—A deed of blood has been perpetrated which has caused every heart to shudder, and which calls for the execration of every citizen. On Good Friday, the hallowed anniversary of our blessed Lord's crucifixion, when all Christendom was bowed down in penitence and sorrow at His tomb, the President of these United States was foully assassinated, and a wicked attempt was made on the life of the Secretary of State ! Words fail us in expressing detestation for a deed so atrocious—hitherto, happily, unparalleled in our history. Silence is, perhaps, the best and most appropriate expression for a sorrow too great for utterance.

We are quite sure that we need not remind our Catholic brethren in the Archdiocese of the duty—which we are confident they will willingly perform—of uniting with their fellow-citizens in whatever may be deemed most suitable for indicating their horror of the crime, and their feeling of sympathy for the bereaved. We also invite them to join together in humble and earnest supplication to God for our beloved but afflicted country; and we enjoin that the bells of all our churches be solemnly tolled on the occasion of the President's funeral.

Given from our residence in Baltimore on Holy Saturday, the 15th day of April, 1865.

MARTIN JOHN SPALDING,
Archbishop of Baltimore.

Rev. Dear Sir—We hereby request that to-morrow you will announce to your people in words expressive of your common sorrow the melancholy tidings which have come so suddenly amid the first rejoicings of the Easter festival to shock the heart of the nation, and plunge it into deepest distress and mourning. A life most precious to all, the life of the honored President of these United States, has been brought to a sad and startling close by the violent hand of an assassin ; the life of the Secretary of State and that of his son have been assailed by a similar act of wickedness, and both are now lying in a critical condition. While bowing down in humble fear and in tearful submission to this inscrutable dispensation of Divine Providence, let us all unite in pouring forth our prayers and supplications with renewed earnestness for our beloved country in this mournful and perilous crisis.

Given at New York, this 15th day of April, 1865.

✝ JOHN, Archbishop of New York.

SECRETARY'S OFFICE, No. 198 MADISON-AVE.
New York, April 17, 1865.

REVEREND AND DEAR SIR—As the funeral obsequies of the late lamented President of the United States will take place in Washington City on Wednesday next, the 19th inst., the Most Reverend Archbishop directs that, in sympathy with the national sorrow, the various churches of the city and Diocese be open on that day for public service at 10½ o'clock, A. M., and that at the several Masses the collect, "*Pro quacumque tribulatione*," be recited in addition to the usual collects of the day.

It is likewise recommended that at the end of Mass the psalm *Miserere* should be read or chanted, supplicating God's mercy for ourselves and all the people.

By order of the Most Reverend Archbishop.

FRS. McNEIRNY, Secretary.

To the Reverend Clergy and Faithful of the Diocese of Philadelphia :

REVEREND BRETHREN AND BELOVED CHILDREN—It is not necessary for us to announce to you the sad calamity which has befallen the nation. It is already known in every city, village, and hamlet of our widely extended country. Everywhere it has sent a thrill of horror through the hearts of all true and law-abiding citizens. We desire thus publicly to declare both for ourselves and you our utter abhorrence and execration of the atrocious deed, and at the same time, our sympathy and condolence with all our fellow-citizens, and especially with those most nearly interested in this sad and afflicting bereavement. We desire to enter fully and cordially into the universal expression of the national grief and into the public demonstrations by which it is appropriately manifested. In times of peril and danger, it is the duty of all to recur by most earnest prayer to the Divine Disposer of all events, and with due resignation to our existing afflictions and calamities, to pour forth our supplications to God that we may be saved from future and impending evils. We prescribe to the clergy the recitation, in the Holy Sacrifice of the Mass, of the prayer "*Pro quacumque tribulatione*," for the space of one month, and enjoin on the faithful the sacred duty of imploring in their daily prayers and devotions the aid of Almighty God to our afflicted nation in its necessities.

Dominus sit semper vobiscum.

JAMES FREDERIC, Bishop of Philadelphia.

Easter Monday, 1865.

The prayers prescribed by the Rt. Rev. Bishop, and which may with great propriety be used by the faithful, are as follows :

COLLECT.

Turn not away Thine eyes, O most merciful God, from Thy people crying out to Thee in their affliction; but for the glory of Thine own name relieve us in our necessities, through Christ our Lord.

SECRET.

Mercifully receive, O Lord, the offerings by which Thou vouch-safest to be appeased ; and by Thy great goodness restore us to safety, through Christ our Lord.

POST-COMMUNION.

Look down mercifully, we beseech Thee, O Lord, in our tribulation, and turn away the wrath of Thy indignation, which we justly deserve, through Christ our Lord.   Amen.

Our Father.   Hail Mary.

Wednesday was accordingly, by common consent, devoted to mourning.   Public authorities, the heads of religious denominations, all as by a common instinct called upon the nation to unite in prayer before their several altars ; while at the capital of the nation the last solemn rites were offered in the home of the lost Ruler ere he was borne from the residence of American Presidents to that greater than Rome's capitol, where he was to lie in state till the convoy began its march of miles to be told by hundreds before the body reached the city of the West identified with his career in manhood.

Throughout the loyal States there was a universal suspension of ordinary avocations and a closing of places of business, out of respect to the departed.   In nearly every city, town, and village the streets were hung in black, while the solemn tolling of the bells and the booming of the minute-guns added to the general solemnity.   The stores and offices being closed and the noise of traffic and amusement hushed, a Sabbath repose rested on the land.   The churches were crowded with worshippers, and the clergy in fitting discourses paid their

10

homage to departed greatness, their testimony of affection to a bereaved country, their words of sympathy to her who felt more keenly even than the nation her sudden loss.

Never before was such a general sadness; never again, we trust, will there be such a cause. It was no lip service; the grief was deep and heartfelt. The people were bereaved, and they knew it. They felt the blow that slew their President, and saw that it was not aimed at him individually, but that it was the concentration of that hate which made his election a pretext for rebellion.

In New England, where the funeral procession would not pass on its way to Springfield, this day contained the highest expression of civic grief. At Roxbury, a procession, the largest and most imposing seen for many years, moved from the City Hall to Dr. Putnam's church, where appropriate services were held. At Chelsea, the city government in a body attended the services at the Chestnut Street Congregational Church. In Pepperell also a procession moved to the church, where impressive services were held. At Providence a procession escorted the Governor to the Public Hall, where a eulogy was pronounced. At Concord, Ralph W. Emerson delivered the following address:

We meet under the gloom of a calamity which darkens down over the minds of good men in all civilized society, as the fearful tidings travel over sea, over land, from country to country, like the shadow of an uncalculated eclipse over the planet. Old as history is, and manifold as are its tragedies, I doubt if any death has caused so much pain to mankind as this has caused, or will cause, on its announcement; and this not so much because nations are, by modern arts, brought so closely together, as because of the mysterious hopes and fears which, in the present day, are connected with the name and institutions of America.

In this country, on Saturday, every one was struck dumb, and saw, at first, only deep below deep, as he meditated on the ghastly blow. And, perhaps, at this hour, when the coffin which contains the dust of the President sets forward on its long march through mourning States, on its way to its home in Illinois, we might well be silent, and suffer the awful voices of the time to thunder to us. Yes, but that first despair was brief; the man was not so to be mourned. He was the most active and hopeful of men, and his work had not perished; but acclamations of praise for the task he had accomplished burst out into a song of triumph, which even tears for his death cannot keep down.

The President stood before us a man of the people. He was thoroughly American, had never crossed the sea, had never been spoiled by English insularity or French dissipation; a quiet native, aboriginal man, as an acorn from the oak; no aping of foreigners, no frivolous accomplishments, Kentuckian born, working on a farm, a flatboatman, a captain in the Blackhawk war, a country lawyer, a representative in the rural Legislature of Illinois—on such modest foundations the broad structure of his fame was laid. How slowly, and yet by happily prepared steps, he came to his place !

All of us remember—it is only a history of five or six years—the surprise and disappointment of the country at his first nomination at Chicago. Mr. Seward, then in the culmination of his good fame, was the favorite of the Eastern States. And when the new and comparatively unknown name of Lincoln was announced (notwithstanding the report of the acclamations of that Convention) we heard the result coldly and sadly.

It seemed too rash, on a purely local reputation, to build so grave a trust, in such anxious times; and men naturally talked of the chances in politics as incalculable. But it turned out not to be chance. The profound good opinion which the people of Illinois and of the West had conceived of him, and which they had imparted to their colleagues, that they also might justify themselves to their constituents at home, was not rash, though they did not begin to know the richness of his worth.

A plain man of the people, an extraordinary fortune attended him. Lord Bacon says : "Manifest virtues procure reputation; occult ones, fortune." He offered no shining qualities at the first encounter: he did not offend by superiority. He had a face and manner which disarmed suspicion, which inspired confidence, which confirmed good-will. He was a man without vices. He had a strong sense of duty, which it was very easy for him to obey. Then he had what farmers call a long head; was excellent in working out the sum for himself, in arguing his case, and convincing you fairly and firmly.

Then it turned out that he was a great worker; had prodigious faculty of performance; worked easily. A good worker is so rare; everybody has some disabling quality. In a host of young men that start together, and promise so many brilliant leaders for the next age, each fails on trial: one by bad health, one by conceit or by love of pleasure, or by lethargy, or by a hasty temper—each has some disqualifying fault that throws him out of the career. But this man was sound to the core, cheerful, persistent, all right for labor, and liked nothing so well.

Then he had a vast good-nature, which made him tolerant and accessible to all; fair-minded, leaning to the claim of the petitioner; affable, and not sensible to the affliction which the innumerable visits paid to him, when President, would have brought to any one else. And how this good-nature became a noble humanity, in many a tragic case which the events of the war brought to him, every one will remember; and with what increasing tenderness he dealt, when a whole race was thrown on his compassion. The poor negro said of him, on an impressive occasion, "Massa Linkum am eberywhere."

Then his broad good-humor, running easily into jocular talk, in which he delighted and in which he excelled, was a rich gift to this wise man. It enabled him to keep his secret; to meet every kind of man, and every rank in society; to take off the edge of the severest decisions; to mask his own purpose and sound his companion, and to catch with true instinct the temper of every company he addressed. And, more than all, it is to a man of severe labor, in anxious and exhausting crises, the natural restorative, good as sleep, and is the protection of the overdriven brain against rancor and insanity.

He is the author of a multitude of good sayings, so disguised as pleasantries that it is certain they had no reputation at first but as jests; and only later, by the very acceptance and adoption they find in the mouths of millions, turn out to be the wisdom of the hour. I am sure if this man had ruled in a period of less facility of printing, he would have become mythological in a very few years, like Æsop or Pilpay, or one of the Seven Wise Masters, by his fables and proverbs.

But the weight and penetration of many passages in his letters, messages, and speeches, hidden now by the very closeness of their application to the moment, are destined hereafter to a wide fame. What pregnant definitions; what unerring common sense; what foresight; and, on great occasions, what lofty, and more than national, what humane tone! His brief speech at Gettysburg will not easily be surpassed by words on any recorded occasion. This, and one other American speech, that of John Brown to the court that tried him, and a part of Kossuth's speech at Birmingham, can only be compared with each other, and with no fourth.

His occupying the chair of State was a triumph of the good sense of mankind, and of the public conscience. This middle-class country had got a middle-class President at last. Yes, in manners, sympathics, but not in powers, for his powers were superior. His mind mastered the problem of the day; and, as the problem grew, so did his comprehension of it. Rarely was man so fitted to the event. In the midst of fears and jealousies, in the Babel of counsels and parties, this man wrought incessantly with all his might and all his honesty, laboring to find what the people wanted, and how to obtain that.

It cannot be said there is any exaggeration of his worth. If ever a man was fairly tested he was. There was no lack of resistance, nor of slander, nor of ridicule. The times have allowed no State secrets; the nation has been in such a ferment, such multitudes had to be trusted, that no secret could be kept. Every door was ajar, and we know all that befell.

Then what an occasion was the whirlwind of the war! Here was place for no holiday magistrate, no fair-weather sailor; the new pilot was hurried to the helm in a tornado. In four years—the four years of battle-days—his endurance, his fertility of resources, his magnanimity, were sorely tried and never found wanting.

There, by his courage, his justice, his even temper, his fertile counsel, his humanity, he stood an heroic figure in the centre of an heroic epoch. He is the true history of the American people in his time. Step by step he walked before them; slow with their slowness, quickening his march by theirs; the true representative of this continent; an entirely public man; father of his country, the pulse of twenty millions throbbing in his heart, the thought of their minds articulated by his tongue.

Adam Smith remarks that the axe, which, in Honbraken's portraits of British kings and worthies, is engraved under those who have suffered at the block, adds a certain lofty charm to the picture. And who does not see, even in this tragedy so recent, how fast the terror and ruin of the massacre are already burning into glory around the victim? Far happier this fate than to have lived to be wished away; to have watched the decay of his own faculties; to have seen—perhaps, even he—the proverbial ingratitude of statesmen; to have seen mean men preferred.

Had he not lived long enough to keep the greatest promise that ever man made to his fellow-men—the practical abolition of slavery? He had seen Tennessee, Missouri, and Maryland emancipate their slaves. He had seen Savannah, Charleston, and Richmond surrendered; had seen the main army of the rebellion lay down its arms. He had conquered the public opinion of Canada, England, and France. Only Washington can compare with him in fortune.

And what if it should turn out, in the unfolding of the web, that he had reached the term; that this heroic deliverer could no longer serve us; that the rebellion had touched its natural conclusion, and what remained to be done required new and uncommitted hands— a new spirit born out of the ashes of the war; and that Heaven, wishing to show the world a completed benefactor, shall make him serve his country even more by death than by his life. Nations, like kings, are not good by facility and complaisance. "The kindness of kings consists in justice and strength." Easy good-nature has been the dangerous foible of the Republic, and it was necessary that its enemies should outrage it, and drive us to unwonted firmness, to secure the salvation of this country in the next ages.

The ancients believed in a serene and beautiful Genius which ruled in the affairs of nations; which, with a slow but stern justice, carried forward the fortunes of certain chosen houses, weeding out single offenders or offending families, and securing at last the firm prosperity of the favorites of Heaven. It was too narrow a view of the Eternal Nemesis. There is a serene Providence which rules the fate of nations, which makes little account of time, little of one generation or race, makes no account of disasters, conquers alike by what is called defeat or by what is called victory, thrusts aside enemy and obstructions, crushes every thing immoral as inhuman, and obtains the ultimate triumph of the best race by the sacrifice of every thing which resists the moral laws of the world. It makes its own instruments, creates the man for the time, trains him in poverty, inspires his genius, and arms him for his task. It has given every race its own talent, and ordains that only that race which combines perfectly with the virtues of all shall endure.

In New York, fitting remarks and discourses were delivered at the service by Bishop Coxe, at Calvary Church; Rev. Dr. Dix, at Trinity Church, in the presence of General Dix and Governor Fenton; Archbishop McCloskey at the Cathedral; by Dr. Cheever, at the Church of the Puritans; Rev. Dr. Osgood, at the Church of the Messiah; Rev. Dr. Chapin, Rev. M. R. Deleeuw, at the Synagogue Bnai Israel, and others in various parts.

The assemblies were not confined to the churches. Public bodies also met, and Parke Godwin, Esq., delivered at the Athenæum Club an address worthy of preservation.

"How grand and how glorious, yet how terrible, the times in which we are permitted to live! How profound and various the emotions that alternately depress and thrill our hearts, like these

April skies—now all smiles, and now all tears. Within a week—the Holy Week, as it is called in the rubrics of our churches—we have had our triumphal entries, amid the waving of the palms of Peace; we have had our dread Friday of crucifixion; we have had, too, in the recently renewed patriotism of the nation, a resurrection of a new and better life!

"It seems but a day or two since we listened to the music of the glad and festival parade; we saw the banners of our pride waving in beauty to every air, their stars brighter than the stars of the morning, and their rays of white and red, like the beams of the rainbow, telling that the tempest was passed ; we pressed hands and hurrahed, and grew almost delirious with the joy that Peace had come, that Unity was secured, that Liberty and Justice, like the cherubim of the ark, would stretch their wings over the altars of our Country and stand forever as the guardian angels of her sanctity and glory.

"But now those exultant strains are changed into the dull and heavy toll of bells ; those flags are folded and draped in the emblems of mourning; and our hearts, giving forth no more the cheering shouts of victory, are despondent and full of sadness.

"The great captain of our cause—the commander-in-chief of our armies and navies—the president of our civic councils—the centre and director of movement—this true son of the people—once the poor flatboatman—the village lawyer that was—the raw, uncouth, yet unsophisticated child of our American society and institutions, whom that society and those institutions had lifted out of his low estate to the foremost dignity of the world—Abraham Lincoln—smitten by the basest hand ever upraised against human innocence, is gone, gone, gone! He who had borne the heaviest of the brunt, in our four long years of war, whose pulse beat livelier, whose eyes danced brighter than any others, when

> ——" the storm drew off,
> In scattered thunders groaning round the hills,"

in the supreme hour of his joy and glory was struck down. That genial, kindly heart has ceased to beat; that noble brain has oozed from its mysterious beds; that manly form lies stiff in the icy fetters, and all of him that was mortal has sunk 'to the portion of weeds and outworn faces.'

"Our feelings are now too deep to ask or warrant any attempt at an analysis of the character or of the services of the man whose loss we deplore. Standing over his bier, looking down almost into the tomb to which he must shortly be consigned, we are conscious only of our grief. We know that one who was great in himself, as

well as by position, has suddenly departed. There is something
startling, ghastly, awful in the manner of his going off. But the
chief poignancy of our distress is not for the greatness fallen, but
for the goodness lost. Presidents have died before; during this
bloody war we have lost many eminent generals—Lyons, Baker,
Kearney, Sedgwick, Reno, and others; we have lost lately our
finest scholar, publicist, orator,

> ——'that when he spoke,
> The air, a chartered libertine, was still,
> To steal his sweet and honeyed sentences.'

Our hearts still bleed for the companions, friends, brothers, that
sleep the sleep 'that knows no waking,' but no loss has been com-
parable to his, who was our supremest leader—our safest counsellor—our wisest friend—our dear father. Would you know what
Lincoln was, look at this vast metropolis, covered with the habiliments of woe! Never in human history has there been so universal, so spontaneous, so profound an expression of a nation's bereavement. In all our churches, without distinction of sect; in all
our journals, without distinction of party; in all our workshops, in
all our counting-houses—from the stateliest mansion to the lowliest
hovel—you hear but the one utterance, you see but the one emblem
of sorrow. Why has the death of Abraham Lincoln taken such
deep hold of every class? Partly, no doubt, because of the awful
and atrocious method of his taking off; largely because he was our
Chief Magistrate; but mainly, I think, because through all his public functions there shone the fact that he was a wise and good man;
a kindly, honest, noble man; a man in whom the people recognized
their own better qualities; whom they, whatever their political convictions, trusted; whom they respected; whom they loved; a man
as pure of heart, as patriotic of impulse, as patient, gentle, sweet
and lovely of nature, as ever history lifted out of the sphere of the
domestic afflictions to enshrine forever in the affections of the
world.

"Yet, we sorrow not as those who are without hope. Our chief
is gone; but our cause remains; dearer to our hearts, because he is
now become its martyr; consecrated by his sacrifice; more widely
accepted by all parties; and fragrant and lovely forevermore in the
memories of all the good and the great, of all lands, and for all
time. The rebellion, which began in the blackest treachery, to be
ended in the foulest assassination—for as Shakspeare says,

> 'Treason and murder ever kept together,
> As two yoke-devils sworn to either's purpose'—

this rebellion, accursed in its motive, which was to rivet the shackles of slavery on a whole race for all the future; accursed in its means, which have been 'red ruin and the breaking up of laws,' the overthrow of the mildest and blessedest of governments, and the profuse shedding of brother's blood by brother's hands; accursed in its accompaniments of violence, cruelty, and barbarism, is now doubly accursed in its final act of cold-blooded murder.

"Cold-blooded, but impotent, and defeated in its own purposes! The frenzied hand which slew the head of the government, in the mad hope of paralyzing its functions, only drew the hearts of the people together more closely to strengthen and sustain its power. All the North once more, without party or division, clenches hands around the common altar; all the North swears a more earnest fidelity to Freedom; all the North again presents its breasts, as the living shield and bulwark of the nation's unity and life. Oh! foolish and wicked dream, oh! insanity of fanaticism! oh! blindness of black hate—to think that this majestic temple of human liberty, which is built upon the clustered columns of free and independent States, and whose base is as broad as the continent—could be shaken to pieces by striking off the ornaments of its capital! No! this nation lives, not in one man nor in a hundred men, however eminent, however able, however endeared to us; but in the affections, the virtues, the energies, and the will of the whole American people. It has perpetual succession, not like a dynasty, in the line of its rulers, but in the line of its masses. They are always alive; they are always present, to empower its acts, and to impart an unceasing vitality to its institutions. No maniac's blade, no traitor's bullet shall ever penetrate that heart, for it is immortal, like the substance of Milton's angels, and can only 'by annihilating die.'

"These sudden visitations of Providence; these mysterious and fearful vicissitudes in the destinies of nations and individuals, always seem to our shortsighted human wisdom as inscrutable. Nor would it be less than presumption in any one to attempt to interpret the meaning of the Divine Mind in this late and most appalling affliction. God, as he passes, the Scriptures tell us, can only be seen from behind, can only be seen when events have gone by. Until then we grope in the darkness, we guess at best but dimly, we more often muse in mere mute wonder and awe. Yet it is always permitted us to extract such good as we may from His seeming frowns and judgments. Thus I discern, in the removal of Mr. Lincoln—lamentable and horrible as it was in its circumstances—some reasons for a calm and hopeful submission to the Divine will.

I can see how our nation is cemented by its tears into a more universal and affectionate brotherhood ; I can see how the Proclamation of Freedom must become the eternal law of our hearts, if not of the land, through the martyrdom and canonization of its author; I can see how the atrocious crime of assassination must tear away from the rebellion every friend that it had left in the civilized world abroad; and I can see how the succession of Mr. Johnson—a Southern man, known to the Southern people by the fact of his origin and principles, not amenable to the prejudices knotted and gnarled about Mr. Lincoln—shall undermine the supremacy of the Southern leaders and reconcile the deluded masses more rapidly than any acts of amnesty or promises of forgiveness.

"But what impresses me most forcibly in all this business is the new demonstration that it has given of the inherent strength and elasticity of democratic government. We have conducted the most stupendous war ever undertaken—a war that involved the blockade of six thousand miles of sea-coast—the defence of two thousand miles of frontier—the clearing and holding of the second largest river of the globe and the occupation of a territory greater than all Europe (without Russia), not only energetically, but successfully. We have done it, without abandoning, or vitiating, or dislocating, any of our fundamental institutions. For, in the midst of this gigantic convulsion, we carried on a political canvass and a Presidential election as quietly as they choose a beadle or a church-warden elsewhere ; and now we have our principal men of office killed or disabled, and the government goes on without a jar, and society moves in its appointed ways without a ripple of outbreak or disorder. Oh yes, Americans, our goodly Ship of State, which the tempests assail with their wild fury, which the angry surges lift in their arms that they may drop her into the yawning gulf, which the treacherous hidden rocks below grind and torture, yet sails on securely to her destined port; and when the very Prince of the Power of the Air smites her captain at the helm and the first mate in his berth, she still sails on securely to her destined port; for her crew is still there; they know her bearings, and will steer right on by the compass of Eternal Justice, and under the celestial light of Liberty."

In Brooklyn, besides the services in the various churches of all denominations, a funeral procession of the German Turn-verein Saengerbund and other societies, proceeded from the Turn Hall through Grand-street, Montrose avenue, and other thoroughfares, to a square on Bushwick avenue, where a meeting was organized and addresses delivered, by Dr. Duai, Mr. Philip Wagner, and others.

In Montreal, C. E., where the Mayor, Mr. J. L. Beaudry had by proclamation invited the citizens to close their places of business, "as a tribute of respect to the memory of the late President of the United States, and of sympathy with the bereaved members of his family, and also as an expression of the deep sorrow and horror felt by the citizens of Montreal at the atrocious crime by which the President came to an untimely end," a large public meeting was held, in which addresses were delivered in French and English, by Hon. Messrs. Dorion and McGee.

At Quebec, a similar proclamation was issued by the Mayor, and no proclamation was ever so promptly and completely responded to. Toronto, Prescott, and other Canadian towns showed similar sympathy with the neighboring republic.

San Francisco honored the day by the grandest procession ever witnessed on the Pacific coast, which moved through streets, clad in the habiliments of woe.

In the South even, similar marks of respect were paid. A more universal demonstration of sorrow was not made in any city than in Memphis, where a solemn military and civic procession, numbering 20,000 persons, formed an imposing part of the ceremony, and at an impromptu meeting eloquent addresses were delivered by General Banks and General Washburn.

The procession at Nashville, which had a splendid funeral car drawn by six white and as many black horses, numbered upwards of 15,000 persons, among them Generals Thomas, Rousseau, Miller, Whipple, Fowler, and Donelson. Over ten thousand troops were in the procession; and besides Governor Brownlow, both Houses of the Legislature, the Quartermaster and Commissary Departments, and Fire Department, with their machines beautifully dressed. The various lodges of Masons, Odd Fellows, Eureka and Thalia clubs, the Fenian Brotherhood and Agnomen club, also swelled the list of societies. Subsequently appropriate ceremonies were held in a field in the suburbs. Addresses were made by his Excellency Governor Brownlow, Rev. Mr. Allen, and others.

At Little Rock, on the news, the Legislature adjourned and an impressive address was delivered by Senator Snow.

At Detroit, on the 25th of April, the obsequies of President Lincoln were performed with imposing ceremonies. The procession was more than four miles in length, headed by detachments of military, followed by a magnificent funeral car, officers of the army and navy, officers of the British army, the officers of the State and City Governments. The Canadian civil officers, the public schools, Masons, Odd Fellows, various benevolent societies, the trades unions, and German societies also participated. The ceremonies concluded with an oration by Senator Howard.

New Orleans received the tidings a little later, and the city was at once arrayed in mourning. A procession on the 22d moved to Lafayette Square, composed of the Fire Department, societies and citizens; and an immense mass of people moved with calm and sorrowful steps to the vast area. Here, after the organization of the meeting, and a prayer by Rev. Doctor Newman, with a few remarks from the Chairman, Judge Whitaker, addresses were delivered by General Banks and General Hurlbut. The following is that of General Banks.

MR. PRESIDENT AND FELLOW-CITIZENS—It is only since my arrival upon this platform that I have been informed of the part I am expected to take in the ceremonies of this occasion, and could wish for longer preparation, with the view of doing more perfect justice to the subject of the hour, but in accordance with the wishes of your committee I will proceed. God knows why it is, or how it is, or for what purpose it is, that we have been summoned here, but now, indeed, can we feel the nothingness of man, and that it is best for us to bow in supplication to God for His counsel and support. The language of the hour is that, not of comment, not of condolence, not of consolation, but of supplication, and we should stand before the throne of God to-day, in sackcloth and in ashes, in silent petition to Him for that counsel and support.

Human plans are failures; the ideas and purposes of God alone are successful. This very week was spontaneously and unanimously set apart by the American people as a season for thanksgiving and joy, for the great relief which the people had experienced from a terrible war, which had bereft nearly every family in the North and South of its dearest, and draped nearly every family altar as is now draped the national altar. Suddenly the skies were brightened, and universal peace was accepted by the nation as the reward of the terrible struggle in which we had been engaged. The opening of the Mississippi, the brilliant victories of the Army of the Cumberland in 1863, the fall of the rebel cities upon the Atlantic coast before the triumphant march of Sherman, the surrender of Lee to Grant, and the occupation of Mobile by the gallant chieftain who is here in our presence to-day, not waiting for the intelligence that the last army of the rebellion had surrendered to the glorious Sherman—all justified the assumption that God had given this nation permanent, lasting, honorable, and glorious peace! But while we were preparing for the announcement by the officers of the Government (always behind in instincts and purposes of power, the people of the government), unexpectedly, in the twinkling of an eye—as if with the suddenness, strength, and power of God—all of us lay low in sorrow, mourning, and despair. I believe that never before in human history were a people so horrified as by the announcement of the death of the President, and the fall of his great assistant in council and action—the Secretary of State. We know not why it is, but we have the great consolation to say that we believe it is for good to our nation. Aye, for good to the man that has fallen as our Representative. He had committed no crimes. There is not a man on the continent or globe that will, or can say, that Abraham Lincoln was his enemy, or that he deserved punishment or death for his individual acts. No, Mr. President, it was because he represented us that he died, and it is for our good and the glory of our nation that God, in his inscrutable Providence, has been pleased to do this, while for the late President it is the great crowning act and security of his career. To die is " to go home"—to go to our Father and be relieved from sorrow, care, suffering, labor, and from danger; but to live, aye, sir, to live is the great punishment inflicted upon man. All that we can ask is to go when all things are ready—when duty is discharged, strength exhausted, and the triumph effected; then it is our joy to go home to " Our Father," as has been beautifully said, sir :

"When faith is strong and conscience clear,
And words of peace the spirit cheer,
And visioned glories then appear,
'Tis joy—'tis triumph then to die."

God has given our great leader the privilege to go under circumstances like this. He had lived his time, fought his fight, and, God be thanked, had kept the faith. Let me say it reverently, that for Abraham Lincoln to live was for Abraham Lincoln to fall ! He had ascended to the highest point—the highest culmination of human destiny : to be better and greater and purer he must leave us and go to the bosom of God. He is enjoying the highest culmination of glory that God has given in his wise and mysterious dispensation for the human family.

Sir, I had seen him but little, but that which I had seen stamped upon my heart the indelible feeling that he was a rare man—not a great or a successful man ; many of both kinds have I seen, but he was a rare man, who believed in the power of ideas and knew that human agencies were unable to control or direct them.   In the dispensation of what men call power, I have seen Mr. Lincoln give it to the right and left as if of no consequence at all ; and when reproached for doing so, I have heard him say, "What harm did this generous confidence of men do me ?"   I have seen, amidst the hours of trial, his manifestations of patience and confidence, more almost than human, until I had come to believe that that which is designed to be done would be accomplished, if not by human power, at least by the concurrent action and support and will of God !

Though taken from us, his influence is still here, and there is not a man in this assembly to-day who is not more impressed with his spirit and purpose than he would be if Abraham Lincoln were living at this hour ; nor is there a man here to-day who is not a disciple of him and the agent of his works forevermore.   We may indeed be assured that his great purpose—the Union, first of all—will be carried out.   We might as well expect the Mississippi to turn back at its mouth and seek again the mountain rivulets and springs, as to believe that human power is to sunder the States of the Union. Abraham Lincoln's wisdom and patriotism have led us as far as human effort can bring us, and now his blood cements forever the holy Union of the States.

You know, fellow-citizens, how deeply he was interested in the destinies of Louisiana.   No friend in your midst ever thought so much about or wished so much for your good as the late President of the United States ; and it was among the first wishes of his heart that the prosperity of its people, the liberty of all its races, and their elevation, should be perfected during his administration, or, as he said in one of his letters to me, "My word is out for these things, and I don't intend to turn back from it."   It is not for me to act or speak in the spirit of prophecy, but I can say to you that I believe his wish will be consummated by the return of Louisiana to the Union, the honor, freedom, and elevation of all classes of its people.

To the colored people of this assembly and State, as well as of the Union, I can say that the work in which he was engaged will go on, and that the day is not far distant when they will enjoy the freedom that God and the people have given them, and also be advanced to all the privileges that under the Constitution of our country, or that of any other, God has deigned to bestow upon any class of people. But they must remember that they have a work to do, and that while God is just to all his people, he requires that they shall be just to Him. You shall be free, and invested with all the privileges of which men are capable of wise and proper exercise, for Abraham Lincoln's word is out!

It is not my right to suggest a word of counsel or advice for the future, but I have the right to say that there is one man who seeks your prayers and desires your counsel. It is he who has been recently inaugurated, unexpectedly—and distrustfully, as we are told—President of these United States. Though a President has gone, we must sustain the President that remains. I look upon the State of Tennessee, from which he comes, as being the centre of the great arch of the Union : midway between the South and North, with the climate of the one and the other, its soil susceptible of producing the products of both sections, it calls for all the consideration that either section of the country can demand for its people. Its political character and structure has the same variety and connection with the destinies of our country, and for thirty years has been more closely contested in political struggles than any other State of the Union. Its vote has decided many issues, and great men have represented its interests and destinies, and it has given us two Presidents, whose administrations have been identified closely, not only with the existence, but with the extension and interest of our country. Jackson, with his mailed arm, struck disunion down at its first appearance, and adapted the policy of the country to its need. Polk confirmed the policy of Jackson, and extended the boundaries of our happy land until it reached from the Atlantic to the Pacific coast. Among the great men of place we have had Benton, Houston, Bell, Foster, and hundreds of others whose names are known, and who have been and are connected indissolubly with the happiness and liberty of our people. From amid these men the new President has been called. Among them he has grown, and from their teachings has he been instructed. His life has been one of activity, energy, and integrity. Character is not made in a day; it will never be forfeited in an hour. Our lamented President, if he could advise us, would counsel us to sustain the Government and those left to take his place; and we are assured that the two great officers then at the head of the nation—a few days before the departure of the first and greatest —upon full consultation, found that they had perfectly concurrent views, and separated with the confidence that each wished the prosperity and success of the other. Let us then accept this day,

its grief, and the lesson which it imparts, and be more than ever determined, in the presence of God, and with the ability and power He
has given us, to do our duty to our country, by maintaining its institutions and perpetuating its principles and liberties.

VI.

WASHINGTON TO SPRINGFIELD.

FUNERAL CORTEGE FROM WASHINGTON TO SPRINGFIELD.

Departure from Washington, April 21st.

The body of President Lincoln was exposed to public view in the Capitol during the 20th, and so constant and numerous was the crowd which pressed forward all that dreary rainy day to gaze for the last time on the sad face so familiarized during the four years, that the Rotunda was kept open from six in the morning till nine o'clock at night.

Among the twenty-five thousand who passed before the coffin were thousands of soldiers, some of whom hobbled from the hospitals where they had long been confined, to look once more on their late Commander in-chief.

The hour of closing found some thousands who had waited for hours in vain.

The guard of honor, which had been on duty all day, was relieved by Brigadier-General James A. Ekin, and Major D. C. Welsh and Captain Joseph T. Powers, of his staff; and Brigadier-General James A. Hall, and Captain E. H. Nevin, Jr., and Lieutenant Terence Riley, of his staff, who stayed with the remains during the night. And at six o'clock in the morning, Hon. E. M. Stanton, Secretary of War; Hon. J. P. Usher, Secretary of the Interior; Hon. Gideon Welles, Secretary of the Navy; Hon. William Dennison, Postmaster-General; Hon. J. J. Speed, Attorney-General; Lieut.-Gen. Grant, and a portion of his staff, Major-General Meigs, Rev. Doctor Gurley, and several Senators, the Illinois delegation, and a number of officers of the army, arrived at the Capitol and took a last look at the face of the deceased. The coffin was then prepared for removal, and closed. It was at first determined not to open it till it reached Springfield, but subsequently entreaties induced the exposure once more of the face of the late ruler, and twelve orderly sergeants were called in to carry it to the hearse. Rev. Dr. Gurley, before the removal of the remains, made the following impressive prayer:

Lord, Thou hast been our dwelling place in all generations. Before the mountains were brought forth, or ever Thou hadst formed the earth and the world, even from everlasting to everlasting Thou art God. Thou turnest man to destruction, and sayest, Return, ye children of men. We acknowledge Thy hand in the great and sudden affliction that has befallen us as a nation, and we pray that in all these hours and scenes of sorrow through which we are passing we may have the guidance of Thy counsel and the consolations of Thy spirit. We commit to thy care and keeping this sleeping dust of our fallen Chief Magistrate, and pray Thee to watch over it as it passes from our view and is borne to its final resting-place in the soil of that State which was his abiding and chosen home. And grant, we beseech Thee, that, as the people in different cities and sections of the land shall gather around this coffin and look upon the fading remains of the man they loved so well, their love for the cause in which he fell may kindle into a brighter, intenser flame, and, while their tears are falling, may they renew their vows of eternal fidelity to the cause of justice, liberty, and truth. So may this great bereavement redound to Thy glory and to the highest welfare of our stricken and bleeding country; and all we ask is in the name and for the sake of Jesus Christ, our blessed Lord and Redeemer. Amen.

The remains were then removed by a detachment of the Quartermaster-General's volunteers, detailed by Brigadier-General Rucker, and escorted to the depot, without music, by the companies of Capts. Cromee, Bush, Hildebrand, and Dillon, of the 12th Veteran Reserve Corps, the whole under the command of Lieut.-Col. Bell. The remains were followed by Lieut.-Gen. Grant, Gen. Meigs, Gen. Hardie, the members of the Cabinet—Messrs. Stanton, Welles, McCulloch, Dennison, Usher, and Fields—and other distinguished personages.

At the depot they were received by President Johnson, Hon. W. T. Dole, Gen. Barnard, Gen. Rucker, Gen. Townsend, Gen. Howe, Gen. Ekin, and others, and placed in the hearse-car, to which the remains of his son Willie had been previously removed.

The 12th Veteran Reserve Corps, which had formed the escort to the depot, was ranged in line in front of the building, and guards were at once stationed at proper points to prevent outside parties from assembling within the building and blocking up the passage-ways. None were admitted except those who had tickets authorizing them to go with the remains, Senators and members of Congress, military officers, and passengers who intended going to Baltimore on the 7.30 train.

A large crowd was soon assembled, and all sorts of means were devised to gain access to the depot buildings, but they failed to succeed, and they were obliged to content themselves with a distant view of the passage of the funeral train, as it moved from the depot.

A few minutes before eight o'clock, Capt. Robert Lincoln, son of the President, accompanied by two relatives, arrived and took his seat in the cars.

Messrs. Nicolay and Hay, the late President's private secretaries, arrived a few moments later and also took their places.

Twenty-one first sergeants, of the 7th, 9th, 10th, 12th, 14th, 18th, and 24th Veteran Reserve Corps, accompanied the remains as a guard.

A few moments before eight o'clock, Rev. Dr. Gurley, standing upon the platform, made the following impressive prayer:

O Lord our God, strengthen us under the pressure of this great national sorrow as Thou only canst strengthen the weak, and comfort us as Thou only canst comfort the sorrowing, and sanctify us as Thou only canst sanctify people when they are passing through the fiery furnace of trial. May Thy grace abound to us according to our need, and in the end may the affliction that now fills our hearts with sadness and our eyes with tears, work for us a far more exceeding and eternal weight of glory.

And now may the God of Peace that brought again from the dead our Lord Jesus, that great Shepherd of the sheep, through the blood of the everlasting covenant, make you perfect in every good work to do His will, working in you that which is well-pleasing in his sight, through Jesus Christ, the Resurrection and the Life, our Redeemer and our hope, our fathers' God and our God, in whose care we now leave these precious remains, to whose blessing we renewedly commit our bereaved and beloved country, and to whose name be glory forever and ever. Amen.

The following is a list of the gentlemen specially invited to accompany the remains:

Relatives and family friends—Judge David Davis, Judge United States Supreme Court; N. W. Edwards; General J. B. S. Todd; Charles Alexander Smith. Guard of Honor—namely: General E. D. Townsend; Brigadier-General Charles Thomas; Brigadier-General A. D. Eaton; Brevet Major-General J. G. Barnard; Brigadier-General G. D. Ramsay; Brigadier-General A. P. Howe; Brigadier-General D. C. McCallum; Major-General David Hunter; Brigadier-General J. C. Caldwell; Rear-Admiral C. H. Davis, United States Navy; Captain William R. Taylor, United States Navy; Major T. Y. Field, United States Marine Corps. (The above constituted a guard of honor; Capt. Charles Penrose, quartermaster and commissary of subsistence for the entire party.) Dr. Charles B. Brown, embalmer; Frank T. Sands, undertaker. And on the part of the Senate and House of Representatives: Maine, Mr. Pike; New Hampshire, Mr. Rollins; Vermont, Mr. Baxter; Massachusetts, Mr. Hooper; Connecticut, Mr. Dixon; Rhode Island, Mr. Anthony; New York, Mr. Harris; Pennsylvania, Mr. Cowan; Ohio, Mr. Schenck; Kentucky, Mr. Smith; Indiana, Mr. Julian; Minnesota, Mr. Ramsay; Michigan, Mr. T. W. Ferry; Iowa, Mr. Harlan; Illinois, Mr. Yates, Mr. Washburne, Mr. Farnsworth, and Mr. Arnold; California, Mr. Shannon; Oregon, Mr. Williams; Kansas, Mr. Clarke; Western Virginia, Mr. Whaley; Nevada, Mr. Nye; Nebraska, Mr. Hitchcock; Colorado, Mr. Bradford; Idaho, Mr. Wallace; New Jersey, Mr. Newell; Maryland, Mr. Phelps; George T. Brown, sergeant-at-arms of the Senate; and N. G. Ordway, sergeant-at-arms of the House of Representatives.

Names of the delegates from Illinois appointed to accompany the remains of Abraham Lincoln, late President of the United States:—Governor Richard J. Oglesby; General Isham N. Haynie, Adjutant-General State of Illinois; Colonel James H. Bowen, A. D. C.; Colonel M. H. Hanna, A. D. C.; Colonel D. B. James, A. D. C.; Major S. Waite, A. D. C.; Colonel D. L. Phillips, United States Marshal Southern District of Illinois, A. D. C.; Hon. Jesse K. Dubois; Hon. J. T. Stuart; Colonel John Williams; Dr. S. H. Melvin; Hon. S. M. Cullum; General John A. McClernand; Hon. Lyman Trumbull; Hon. J. S. V. Reddenburg; Hon. Thomas J. Dennis; Lieutenant-Governor William Bross; Hon. Francis E. Sherman, Mayor of Chicago; Hon. Thomas A. Haine; Hon. John Wentworth; Hon. S. S. Hays; Colonel R. M. Hough; Hon. S. W. Fuller; Capt. J. B. Turner; Hon. I. Lawson; Hon. C. L. Woodman; Hon. G. W. Gage; G. H. Roberts, Esq.; Hon. J. Commisky; Hon. T. L. Talcott. Also, Governor Morton, of Indiana; Governor Brough, of Ohio; Governor Stone, of Iowa, together with their aids; Reporters for the press; L. A. Gobright, of Washington, and Cyrus R. Morgan, of Philadelphia, for the Associated Press; L. L. Crounz, New York *Times*; G. B. Woods, Boston *Daily Advertiser*; Dr. Adonis, Chicago *Tribune*.

When it was decided to remove the body of President Lincoln at once to Springfield, the War Department, to which the whole arrangement of the obsequies was assigned, immediately made preparations to have it conveyed by a train which should go directly through ; and all was arranged on the various roads to prevent any delay, and all connected with the transportation was placed under the care of General McCallum, whose practical knowledge would insure freedom from any error.

According to the schedule adopted, the train was to

> Leave Washington, Friday, April 21, 8 A. M.
> Arrive at Baltimore, Friday, April 21, 10 A. M.
> Leave Baltimore, Friday, April 21, 3 P. M.
> Arrive at Harrisburg, Friday, April 21, 8.20 P. M.
> Leave Harrisburg, Saturday, April 22, 12 M.
> Arrive at Philadelphia, Saturday, April 22, 6.30 P. M.
> Leave Philadelphia, Monday, April 24, 4 A. M.
> Arrive at New York, Monday, April 24, 10 A. M.
> Leave New York, Tuesday, April 25, 4 P. M.
> Arrive at Albany, Tuesday, April 25, 11 P. M.
> Leave Albany, Wednesday, April 26, 4 P. M.
> Arrive at Buffalo, Thursday, April 27, 7 A. M.
> Leave Buffalo, Thursday, April 27, 10.10 A. M.
> Arrive at Cleveland, Friday, April 28, 7 A. M.
> Leave Cleveland, Friday, April 28, midnight.
> Arrive at Columbus, Saturday, April 29, 7.30 A. M.
> Leave Columbus, Saturday, April 29, 8 P. M.
> Arrive at Indianapolis, Sunday, April 30, 7 A. M.
> Leave Indianapolis, Sunday, April 30, midnight.
> Arrive at Chicago, Monday, May 1, 11 A. M.
> Leave Chicago, Tuesday, May 2, 9.30 P. M.
> Arrive at Springfield, Wednesday, May 3, 8 A. M.

This route differs from that taken by Mr. Lincoln on his way to Washington in 1861 only by omitting Cincinnati and Pittsburg, and by making a detour by way of Chicago instead of going direct from Indianapolis to Springfield. Of the escort that accompanied Mr. Lincoln from Springfield to Washington, but three left Washington with the remains—Judge David Davis, of Illinois, Major-General David Hunter, and Ward H. Lamon.

The car assigned for the transportation of the remains is said to be the first railroad structure of the kind in this country. It was built by Mr. Jameson, of Alexandria, for the United

States Military Railroad, and was designed for the special use of the late President and other dignitaries when travelling over the military roads. It contains a parlor, sitting-room, and sleeping apartment fitted up with excellent taste, and has all the modern improvements. Small panels are arranged around the top of the car, on which are painted the coats of arms of each state. The car is completely robed in black, the mourning outside being festooned in two rows above and below the windows, while each window has a strip of mourning connecting the upper with the lower row. The coffin containing the remains of President Lincoln was placed upon a bier covered with black cloth, in the rear of the car. Six other cars accompany the train, all new, belonging to the Baltimore and Ohio road, and are all draped with mourning.

The engine (238) which drew the train was also new, and made at the Mount Clare works. It was draped with mourning, all the glittering portions covered and its flags draped. The engineer was Mr. Thomas Becket. To guard against accidents, a pilot-engine, similarly draped, was provided.

The train moved slowly from the Washington depot at eight o'clock, the engine bell tolling, and the immense assemblage reverently uncovering their heads. The guard and several thousand soldiers stationed near formed a long line at a present arms in sign of respect till the train passed.

To prevent accidents, the rate of speed was limited. No stoppage was made between Washington and Baltimore. In out-of-the-way places, little villages, or single farm-houses, people came out to the side of the track and watched, with heads reverently uncovered and faces full of genuine sadness, the passage of the car bearing the ashes of him who loved the people and whom the people loved. Every five rods along the whole line were seen these mourning groups, some on foot and some in carriages, wearing badges of sorrow, and many evidently having come a long distance to pay this little tribute of respect, the only one in their power, to the memory of the murdered President. At Annapolis Junction, General Tyler and his staff, who were stationed at the Relay House, joined the cortège.

OBSEQUIES IN BALTIMORE.

Baltimore prepared to receive the honored remains of the Chief Magistrate with every mark of reverence. A procession was arranged to meet them at the Camden Station of the Baltimore and Ohio Railroad; and this point, in spite of the inclemency of the weather, became a centre to which, from early dawn, people of all ages, sexes, and colors began to hasten. By eight o'clock, every thoroughfare near it, except those occupied and kept clear by the troops, was so densely crowded as to prevent all passage.

Shortly before ten o'clock, a pilot engine entered the depot, announcing the funeral train of the illustrious dead but a few moments behind. On the platform were assembled Governor Bradford; Lieutenant-Governor Cox; the Governor's staff; General Berry and staff; Hon. Wm. B. Hill, Secretary of State; Hon. Robert Fowler, State Treasurer, with other of the officials of the State government; Mayor Chapman; the City Council of Baltimore, with the heads of the departments of the city government; Major-General Wallace, Brigadier-General Tyler, Commodore Dornin, and many other officers of the army and navy.

At ten o'clock, the car bearing the body and escort reached the depot in charge of General McCallum and John W. Garrett, Esq., and in a brief time the coffin was removed by the guard —sergeants of the Invalid Corps—and, with uncovered heads and saddened hearts, it was escorted through the depot buildings by the State and city authorities to the hearse or funeral car awaiting its reception on Camden-street.

The hearse, furnished by Mr. John Cox, East Baltimore, was almost entirely of plate-glass, which enabled the vast crowd on the line of the procession to have a full view of the coffin. The supports of the top were draped with black cloth and white silk, and the top of the car itself was handsomely decorated with black plumes.

The escort from Washington was followed by an imposing military array, which excited admiration by their precision and soldierly appearance. The entire column, under the command of Brigadier-General H. H. Lockwood, attended by his staff and a number of aids, formed in line on Eutaw-street, right resting on Conway-street, and moved in reverse order. First came a detachment of cavalry, with their buglers on the right, who announced the approach of the line ; then followed the infantry troops of the First, Second, and Third Brigades, all of whom moved in platoons, with arms reversed, and accompanied by their fine bands, playing solemn dirges. An artillery battery, consisting of six three-inch parrots and caissons, each drawn by six horses. Included in the infantry were the Eleventh Indiana Volunteers, which are stationed at Fort McHenry, and commanded by Colonel Daniel McCauley. Following the battery was a detachment of United States marines, from the United States receiving ship Alleghany. A detachment of United States seamen followed the marines, Companies H and K of the Second United States Artillery, stationed at Fort McHenry, carrying the regimental flag, accompanied by the full band. These companies were posted on each side of the hearse containing the remains of the lamented President. The rear of the escort was brought up by a large number of officers of various departments, including medical and other branches, all mounted. Among these were Major-General Lew Wallace and staff, Surgeon Josiah Simpson, medical director, General E. B. Tyler, Brigadier-General J. R. Kenly, Colonel S. M. Bowman, and others.

The procession commenced to move precisely at 10.30 A. M., over the route previously designated. A few minutes before one o'clock, the head of the procession arrived at the southern point of the Exchange. As the head of the military escort reached Calvert-street the column halted, and the hearse, with its guard of honor, passed between the lines, the troops presenting arms, and bands of music wailing out the plaintive tune, " Peace, troubled soul."

The general officers dismounted, and formed with their staffs on either side of the approach from the gate to the main entrance to the Exchange. The remains were then removed from the funeral-car, and carried slowly and reverently into the building, and placed on a catafalque prepared for them. After they had been properly placed, and the covering removed, the officers present passed slowly forward on either side of the body.

The civic part of the procession, which was under John Q.

A. Herring, Esq., as Chief-marshal, and headed by Governor Bradford, Governor-elect Swan, and Lieutenant-Governor Cox, then followed.

The noble columns on the east and west sides of the Rotunda were draped with black cloth, whilst the base of the wall around the entire hall was covered with the same material. The galleries were likewise tastefully draped, and from the upper gallery, at the base of the dome, four large national flags, one starting from each cardinal point of the compass and meeting in the centre, draped in graceful folds over the catafalque, which was erected immediately beneath the dome. The ends of these flags were gathered in rich folds and united with festoons of black cloth, forming a circle of drapery over the catafalque. This structure was a model of good taste highly creditable to its designer, Charles T. Holloway, Esq. The catafalque consisted of a raised dais, eleven feet by four at the base, the sides sloping slightly to the height of about three feet; from the four corners rose graceful columns, supporting a canopy eight feet from the base, having a projecting cornice extending beyond the line of the base. The canopy rose to a point fourteen feet from the ground, terminating in clusters of rich black plumes. The whole structure was richly draped with exquisite taste. The floor and sides of the dais were covered with fine black cloth, and the canopy was formed of black *drap d'été*, rich folds drooping from the four corners and bordered with silver fringe. The cornice was adorned with silver braid and a row of silver stars, whilst the sides and ends of the dais were similarly ornamented. The interior of the canopy was of black cloth, gathered in fluted folds to a central point, where was a large star of black velvet, studded with thirty-six stars, one for each State of the Union.

The floor of the dais, on which the body of the illustrious martyred patriot rested, was bordered with evergreens, and a wreath of spiræa, azaleas, calla lilies, and other choice flowers, the whole presenting a most touching and beautiful and appropriate resting-place.

The crowd surrounding the building was immense, but owing to excellent police arrangements and a strong military guard, every thing passed off in an orderly and decorous manner. But a small portion of the throng in attendance were able to obtain a view of the President's remains. At about half-past two o'clock, to the regret of thousands of our citizens, the coffin was closed and the face that was so dear to the nation was hidden from view, and, escorted by the guards of honor, the body was removed to the hearse. The procession then reformed and took up its mournful march to the depot of the Northern Central Railroad Company. The coffin was placed in a car tastefully draped, and the escort on a train specially assigned to them, which was also draped, and started for Harrisburg at a few minutes past three o'clock.

OBSEQUIES AT HARRISBURG.

General Cadwallader, commanding the Department of Pennsylvania, accompanied Governor Curtin.

When the train reached York, at the request of the ladies of that town, a beautiful wreath was placed, with due solemnity, upon the coffin.

The remains arrived at Harrisburg at eight o'clock. Owing to the heavy rain, it was found impossible to proceed with the intended military and civic display. Throngs of people, however, lined the street and followed the remains to the State Capitol, where the body lay in state, in the House of Representatives. The coffin lay upon a catafalque, around which was a wreath of white flowering almonds. The coffin-lid was open from nine to twelve o'clock at night, during which the hall was crowded to excess with those wishing to get a view of the President's features. They passed in and out with order. At the appointed hour the doors were closed, and the remains locked up until seven o'clock next morning, when the lids were again thrown open and the vast assemblage commenced entering the hall. While citizens generally, especially ladies and children, were entering, the military escort, in column of march, formed in line of procession in the following order :—

Band of music, cavalry, artillery, 10th regiment Veteran Reserve Corps, Pennsylvania V. I.; officers of the army and navy, dismounted; officers of the army and navy mounted; commanding officers of the escort and staff; chief marshal and aids; clergy; pall-bearers and escort; the family relatives and the delegation of the State of Illinois as mourners; his Excellency A. G. Curtin, Governor of the Commonwealth of Pennsylvania, and Major-General George Cadwallader, commanding

Department of Pennsylvania, and staff; Diplomatic Corps; ex-Presidents; Chief-Justice and Associates of the Supreme Court of the U. States, Senate of the United States, House of Representatives of the United States; Federal Judiciary and Judges of other States and Territories; Secretary of the Commonwealth, and other State officers, including Justices of the Supreme Court and members of the Legislature; the authorities and judiciary of the county of Dauphin; Mayor of Harrisburg and City Council; Committee of Arrangements; delegations from other States; delegations from other places; soldiers of the war of 1812; honorably discharged soldiers of the present war; fire department and civic associations.

At nine o'clock, the hall of the House of Representatives was closed to all citizens and soldiers except those taking part in the military and civic procession. At the head of the catafalque sat Brigadier-General Eaten, who was assisted by Admiral Davis and another general officer. There were three general officers on duty every six hours. Just one hour was allowed for the various bodies comprising the procession to pass through, and this having expired, Mr. Sands, United States superintendent of burial, who had the body in charge, closed the coffin, after which all ingress to the Capitol was barred. During the procession and other demonstrations, guns were firing in memory of the honored dead. The hall was draped in the most artistic style, and in the centre, behind the Speaker's desk, was a portrait of President Lincoln, looking natural as life. The Speaker's desk was handsomely interworked with chaplets of flowers. Wherever one travelled in the city there was evidence of deep grief. The houses were draped in mourning, and the people everywhere manifested their reverence. The *Patriot* and *Telegraph* offices had suspended from them beautiful flags fringed with black. Eleven o'clock having been fixed for the departure, the special delegations were already at the depot. The military and civic processions escorted the *cortège*, followed by throngs of citizens.

An assemblage of the people of Elizabethtown, as well as from the country and villages, gathered around the car containing the remains, and vainly sought to gratify the longings of their hearts. At Mount Joy men and women stood with uncovered heads, and the latter wept.

Not less than 20,000 people gathered at Lancaster, every one seeming eager to know which car contained the President's remains. On being informed, all eyes turned eagerly to salute it. The carriage depot was wreathed with flags lined with black fringes and studded with rosettes of stars. As a work of art in honor of the honored dead, it was as exquisite as it was appropriate. On either side of the train, in line, were literary and religious societies, uncovered; and reaching out away beyond the suburbs, standing in the fields and on eminences close by the railroad, were a number of farmers, who, uncovered, with hats in left hand, held up their right to Heaven, as if vowing before God that they were now and ever ready to avenge their fallen chieftain. Near the little village of Gap passengers were out in fields adjacent, and stood uncovered until the train passed by, after which they resumed their seats in their own train and sped onward.

Through Parkersburg the people lined the houses, railroad cars, and fences, anxious mourning spectators. From poles erected on both sides the railroad lines floated drooping flags draped in mourning. In the suburbs of Philadelphia, tastefully draped private residences and drooping flags, and large assemblages, evidenced how truly the people felt their sorrow. As the train approached the heart of the city, the crowds of people increased—guns peal forth. At the depot, the Mayor and Council, and different societies, and an immense concourse of people awaited to convey the sacred treasure to Independence Hall. It may be said that the entire route from Baltimore to Philadelphia was amid crowds of sorrowing people, for between villages and towns, all the way, farmers and their families assembled in fields and about houses, seriously and reverently gazing at the fleeting funeral *cortège*.

AT PHILADELPHIA.

The funeral *cortège* reached Broad-street station in Philadelphia at half-past four o'clock. The procession did not move until six. The military, both white and black, made a fine display. The City Troop acted as bodyguard to the corpse. In the procession were the Mayor, the City Councils, and other municipal authorities, Federal officers, army and navy officers stationed in the city and neighborhood, the Judiciary members of the Legislature, Members of Congress, representatives of foreign courts, and numerous others of distinction. The firemen, and every society, institute, and organization, were well represented, especially the Knights Templars, the Odd Fellows, and the Fenians. Many colored men also appeared as members of charitable and other societies, with appropriate badges and regalia.

The procession occupied an hour and a half in passing the streets designated in the programme. It had been dark for more than an hour when the funeral car reached Independence Hall, and an hour after this, at half-past nine o'clock, the rear of the column had not started from the back streets in which the several divisions were formed. Notwithstanding the delay and the darkness, the immense numbers of people who had assembled from the city and surrounding country remained in the streets to witness the entire pageant. Extra trains had been running into the city all day from all directions, each bringing hundreds of visitors. Every inch of space along the route designated for the procession was contended for, and, doubtless, at least two hundred and fifty thousand people were out to see the spectacle. The hotels were overrun with guests, and many of the visitors from a distance passed the night shelterless and supperless in the streets, unable to obtain accommodations. The ashes of the nation's martyr found a fixed resting-place in Independence Hall, around which cluster so many historical memories, and over which, four years ago, the then President elect hoisted the American flag, with a declaration of his willingness to sacrifice his life rather than abandon the cause which he has at length fallen in defending, and where have since reposed the remains of the first prominent Union martyr, Colonel Ellsworth, and of General Lyon, Colonel Baker, Lieutenant Greble, and many others of our great army of dead heroes. The bier was close to the famous old Liberty Bell which first sounded forth in 1776 the tidings of Independence.

The interior of the Hall, as well as exterior, was heavily draped and most artistically illuminated. Around the remains were appropriate decorations, leaves of exquisite evergreens and flowers of an exquisite crimson bloom. At the head of the corpse were bouquets; beneath, the flaming tapers at the feet; from the elaborately hung walls the portraits of the great and good dead were eloquent in their silence, and seemed to say that not one of the great actors of other eras preserved in canvas, marble, and metal, looking down like living mourners on that honored catafalque, ever filled his space with more dignity than the dead Lincoln. Not Columbus, from his brazen door; not De Soto, planting his cross on the Mississippi; not Pocahontas; not Miles Standish, on the Mayflower; not William Penn, making peace with the Indians; not Benjamin Franklin, in his philosophy; not the fiery Patrick Henry, as he ejaculated his war-cry in the Virginia House of Delegates—nor John Adams, as he shouted it in Boston; not Washington, with his sword; nor Jefferson, with his pen; nor Hamilton, with his statesmanship; nor John Jay; nor John Marshall, the purest jurist of our earlier or later history; nor Perry, the Sea King of 1812, riding on billows of blood through a line of blazing ships; nor Jackson, with his triple triumph over savage, and Briton, and the spirit of incipient treason; not one was more worthy of the genius of the poet, the painter, the sculptor, and the orator, than the gentle and illustrious patriot whose virtues and whose genius the American people now mourn.

The next morning the body of President Lincoln was visited by thousands, on invitation tickets from the Select Council. Before daylight lines were formed east and west of Independence Hall, passing in by two stairways through the front windows and out by the rear into the Square. By ten o'clock these lines extended at least three miles, from the Delaware to the Schuylkill river, thousands occupying three or four hours before accomplishing their object—seeing the remains. A military guard and the police at Fifth and Sixth streets prevented the throng from accumulating in front of the Hall, none being allowed to pass except in line. Great numbers of females took position in line, and notwithstanding the fatigue of slow progress effected their object, many only giving up when they fainted and were carried off by their friends. Colored men and women were liberally sprinkled along the line.

The corpse was exposed at Independence Hall from nine o'clock at night until one o'clock next morning, at which hour thousands of persons were obliged to retire disappointed from the streets subsequently to renew their efforts. Although the doors were not opened until five o'clock in the morning, long before that hour an anxious crowd had assembled, and this comparatively small number was from minute to minute increased. By eight o'clock it was almost impossible to pass within two or three blocks of the Hall on the Chestnut-street side, while the cross-streets were pouring forth their myriads of human beings. A military and police force endeavored to restrain the pressure towards the door.   The long lines formed for miles were kept up until a late hour at night.   As they were diminished in the front, accessions were furnished in the rear.   Some had been waiting for six or eight hours before they gained admission to the Hall, while others became so weary as to be compelled to abandon their hope.

The scenes at the Hall were impressively solemn, and not a few persons were affected to tears.   An old colored woman, sixty-five or seventy years of age, thrilled the spectators with her open expressions of grief.   Gazing for a few moments on the face of the dead, she exclaimed, clasping her hands, while tears coursed down her withered cheeks : " Oh, Abraham Lincoln ; Oh ! he is dead, he is dead !"   The sympathy and love expressed by this poor woman found a response in every heart, and seemed to increase, if possible, the general grief.

The wounded soldiers hobbling in or borne to the spot in ambulances, formed a touching sight as they came to look on the great man who had fallen for the Union.

The funeral train left Philadelphia at 4 A. M., on the 24th of April.   The incidents of the journey were similar to those seen elsewhere. Sometimes the track was lined on both sides for miles with a continuous array of people.   The most impressive scene of the whole route thus far was furnished by the city of Newark, although no stop of any length was made there.   The track runs directly through the city, and the space on each side of the road is very broad and afforded ample room for spectators.   It seemed as if the inhabitants of Newark had resolved to turn out *en masse* to pay their brief tribute of respect to the memory of the departed as his coffin passed by.   For a distance of a mile, the observer on the train could perceive only one sea of human beings.   It was not a crowd surging with excitement or impatience like most great assemblages, but stood quiet and apparently subdued with grief unspeakable.

12

Every man, with hardly an exception, from one end of the town to the other, stood bareheaded while the train passed, half of the women were crying, and every face bore an expression of sincere sadness. Housetops, fences, and the very switches beside the track, were covered with men. Words can do no justice in the spectacle.

Of a grander character was the reception given to the remains at Jersey City. The depot, one of the largest halls in the country, was draped in the mourning garb assumed on the first news being received of the national loss. The balconies were hung with mourning, arranged in diagonal patterns of black and white, and at the eastern end of the building was the inscription—

"BE STILL, AND KNOW THAT I AM GOD."

At the other ends were the words:

"A NATION'S HEART WAS STRUCK,
APRIL 15, 1865."

On the ferry house was this motto:

"GEO. WASHINGTON, THE FATHER,
ABRAHAM LINCOLN, THE SAVIOUR,
OF HIS COUNTRY."

The long galleries were filled with ladies, and in the centre of the hall stood the choir of seventy singers.

The exterior of the depot was also draped, and the clock was stopped at twenty-two minutes past seven, the hour at which the President died. At the western end of the depot, close to the entrance through which it was arranged the funeral cortege should pass, one of the tracks was boarded over from platform to platform, so as to give abundant room for the removal of the body out of the funeral car.

Almost unheard, the nine cars of the funeral train, all draped with black, glided steadily in through the western gates of the station. The guards presented arms; a battery of the Hudson County Artillery, at a little distance, fired minute guns. As the richly decorated coffin, with its silver ornaments, was exposed to view, the choral societies began to chant the *Integer*

Vitæ. A body-guard of twenty-five sergeants and veterans of the reserve corps, under the command of Captain Campbell, surrounded the corpse.

Before the last sad notes of the funeral dirge were ended the coffin was raised on the shoulders of ten stalwart veterans, and the order of procession was formed. First walked General Dix and General Sandford; next, four undertakers, and Colonel McMahon and Captain Lord, of General Dix's staff. Then came the corpse, flanked by the remainder of the body-guard, with drawn swords, and followed, in irregular order, by Generals Thompson, Assistant Adjutant-General, representing the Secretary of War; General Eaton, Commissary-General of Subsistence; General McCallum, Superintendent of Military Roads; Generals Barnard, Hunter, Howe, Ramsay, Caldwell, and Townsend; Admirals Bell and Davis; Senators Anthony, Cowen, Ramsay, and Williams; Congressmen, preceded by their Sergeant-at-Arms; Captain Taylor, United States Navy; Major Fields, United States Marine Corps; Lieutenant John White; the remainder of the Washington guard of honor and delegation; Hon. Chauncey M. Depew, Secretary of State of New York; the Mayor and Common Council of Jersey City; the delegations from Hoboken, Hudson City, Bergen and Greenville, and other officials and mourners. Moving down the north platform, at which the train was drawn up, towards the eastern end of the building, the procession wound round and moved up the next platform, and so out at the western entrance of the depot, the choral societies meanwhile singing the *chorale*, "Rest in the Grave."

The hearse was neat; the sides and back were of plate glass, and on the top were eight large plumes of black and white feathers. Around the edge of the roof and the lower portion of the body of the hearse were American flags folded, draped in mourning, gracefully festooned, and fastened with knots of white and black ribbons. It was drawn by six gray horses covered with black cloth, each led by a groom dressed in mourning.

A strong line of guards kept clear a broad and ample space for the procession. Outside their line a great and dense but serious and silent crowd was gathered. All were quickly on board the ferry boat New Jersey, and moving at once out of the slip, she crossed without delay or accident to the foot of Desbrosses street.

Thus ended the reception at Jersey City, the most thrilling, as that at Newark was the most touching.

OBSEQUIES IN NEW YORK.

The scene there was most imposing, and could not fail to make a lasting impression upon the thousands who were congregated on the housetops and awnings for several blocks on each side of the ferry. The people commenced to collect at an early hour, and long before the police arrived every available spot was occupied along Desbrosses street, from West to Hudson streets. The window sashes of all the houses were removed, in order that the occupants might have an unobstructed view of the procession; and, as far as the eye could see, there was a dense mass of heads protruding from every window in the street. The fronts of the houses were tastefully draped with mourning, and the national ensign was displayed at half-mast from almost every housetop.

The Seventh Regiment, National Guard, Colonel Emmons Clark, which had been selected as the escort, arrived on the ground about half-past nine o'clock. The street, from its commencement at the ferry to its junction with Hudson street, was promptly cleared, and the space kept open until the arrival of the funeral party; three hundred policemen forming a double line from the ferry gate up to Hudson street.

A few minutes before eleven o'clock the firing of guns and the tolling of bells announced the near approach of the boat, and preparations were made for landing the remains of the honored dead amid a chant of the German Society. The anxiety of the people to obtain a view of the funeral was intense, and required the united exertions of the military and the police to preserve order.

Colonel Clark conferred with General Dix immediately upon the arrival of the boat, and arranged the order of the procession; and, on his return, formed his regiment into a hollow square, in the centre of which it was intended the funeral cortege should march. Every thing being in readiness, the procession started from the boat in the following order:

Police.
General Dix, General Sandford, Alderman Ryers, and other Military Officers
and Civilians.
Band.
Seventh Regiment.
Sergeants of the Invalid Corps.

Seventh	THE HEARSE.	Seventh
Regiment		Regiment.

Sergeants of the Invalid Corps.
Seventh Regiment.
Guard of Honor accompanying the Remains.

The procession passed up Hudson to Canal, thence through
it and Broadway to the Park, entering on the eastern side.

At precisely 11.30 o'clock the head of the procession entered
the east gate of the Park. The scene from the balcony at this
moment was one never to be forgotten. Far off and near
waved mournfully in the bright, balmy air, the draped colors
of a sorrow-stricken nation. From every possible point of exhibition were flung to the view of scores of thousands, clean
against the blue horizon, the red, white, and blue emblem of
liberty, sabled with the sombre tone of mourning. On the
right marched the Seventh. In front, reaching from the line
of the police to the further verge of the Park, resting literally
against the iron railings, stood an army of interested, anxious
men and women, whose uncovered heads and upturned coun-
tenances resembled a quiet sea of expectancy; the double force
of singers, bareheaded and ready for the dirge; the short line,
fifteen in all, of venerable men who fought and bled in their
country's cause half a century ago, lifted from their bald heads
their hats, banded with weeds; the strong sun in mid-heaven
sent down a summer heat; and the wind, which a few moments before whistled wildly along, burdened with clouds of

dust, hushed into a whisper, and breathed balmily on every spot. From distant batteries the cannon belched at each minute a thunder-tone of woe. From all the steeples came forth the wailing of bells, while from the spire of old Trinity floated upon the breeze the tuneful chimings of "Old Hundred."

Borne on the sturdy shoulders of the Veteran Reserve Corps, the coffin, with its sacred dust, was taken into the hall rotunda.

Meanwhile the eight hundred choristers without, chanted with fine effect and in perfect harmony the magnificent "Pilgrims' Chorus," from Tannhauser, and afterward as the solemn procession wound slowly along the spiral stairway, the singers gave the startling "Chorus of the Spirits," by Schubert. The interior of the rotunda presented at this moment a beautiful though mournful spectacle. The entire circle was covered up, representing a marque, the walls were formed of National, State, and city flags, extending from dome to level. Across these flags ran a winding chain of black paramatto, which formed a deep hem as it were, bordering the partitions made by the flags. At the rear of the rotunda, fronting the catafalque, was Carpenter's portrait of the late Mr. Lincoln, the frame studded with silver stars and edged around with black. The skylight was covered with black, causing a subdued light to pervade the interior, which was mellowed by the lights from two chandeliers on each side of an inclined plane at the head of the stairs, through which the light permeated by means of ground glass globes.

On this plane, which formed a portion of the catafalque, the coffin was placed; after which the troops retired, policemen were stationed at the head of either stairway, and sentries stood at all the doors.

The coffin resting on the plane formed a base line for the magnificent catafalque, which fronted on the rotunda, opening also into the Governor's Room. The front of the canopy presented the appearance of a dark square, on which rested an elliptical Gothic arch extending across the whole width of the square or parallelogram at the base of the arch. Its height from the peak of the arch to the base of the structure was twenty feet, the width ten feet, and the depth twelve feet. The exterior adornments were plain, elegant, and proper. The summit or peak of the arch was topped by an eagle, in silver, which slightly relieved the sombre aspect of all. The wings were folded, the head or beak slightly drooped. In the centre, under the eagle, was a bust of Mr. Lincoln, also in silver. The base of the arch of the canopy was fine cloth. The two sides of the canopy were adorned with urns covered with black cloth. The drapery in front of the arch, inside, was lined with white silk. Inside the catafalque the black was unrelieved, save by the dots of silver stars here and there through the surface, and underneath, standing at the four angles, were marble busts of Washington, Webster, Jackson, and Clay. The interior covering was black cloth and velvet, the canopy overhead being lined with fluted cloth, radiating in folds from the middle to the sides. The rest was all plain black cloth or black velvet. The two pillars of the City Hall, standing on each side of the catafalque, were wrapped in the national colors, heavily draped with crape and black silk.

So soon as all was ready, Mrs. Charles E. Strong, accompanied by General Burnside, entered the catafalque, and placed on the coffin a most beautiful arrangement of flowers. On a ground, shield-shaped, of scarlet azalias and double nasturtions, was a cross of pure white, made of japonicas and orange blossoms—an offering as rich and beautiful, as it was chaste and simple.

As soon as the moment arrived for the admission of the public, the immense mass who had been waiting patiently for hours began to pour in.

Guided by the sentries and the police, the crowd pushed on at the rate, now of fifty, now of thirty a minute, averaging, perhaps, during the first watch, thirty-five a minute. Few words were spoken, few tears shed, but over all and pervading all was a deep tone of sympathy, of regret, of respectful regard for the President who had gone. A noticeable feature was the preponderance, at first, of young girls—shop girls, apparently, between the ages of sixteen and twenty.

To many there seemed, indeed, less feeling in New York than elsewhere, less sorrow, but not less respect.

From this time till it left the City Hall five officers were on watch, relieved every two hours. Among these many are illustrious for services in the late war. Generals Hunter, Peck,

Anderson, Van Vliet, St. George Cook, Meagher, Admiral Paulding, Commodore Ringgold.

All night long the tide of people poured on in great masses; thinking that everybody else would avail themselves of the day-time, they had waited until night, and the consequence was that where there were thousands before, tens of thousands now stood helpless in the face of the impossible achievement before them. From the west gate of the Park twenty deep stood the crowd, three blocks long; down Murray street, twenty-abreast, stood a second crowd, two blocks long; across Print-ing-house-square in masses, away up Chatham street until Mul-berry street was touched, stood, not a crowd, but a deep dense mass.

At 12 o'clock precisely, the members of the Concordia, Ar-monia Quartette Club, and German Club, all of Hoboken, some eighty in number, including the President, Hugo Menzel, and the leader, F. A. Sorge, moved from the Astor House, and were conducted to the rotunda by Sergeant Robinson, of the Twenty-sixth Precinct. Ranging themselves on the left of the stairway they gave forth a mighty volume of sound, harmoni-ous in utterance, sublime in conception.

On the 25th of April, the metropolis took its final leave of the remains of Abraham Lincoln, and after a farewell more grand and imposing than any demonstration in the previous experience of this country, the sacred ashes started on their journey westward. New York may well feel proud of the display, and will never forget the great pageant, the magnitude and splendor of which no city in the world can ever excel. The formation of the procession began early, while yet a long line of people, some of whom had been attending on the pavement there all night, were steadily pushing their way forward tow-ards the entrance of the City Hall for a hurried glimpse of the remains. No business was done in any part of the city, and everybody seemed bent either on finding his place in the ranks of the procession, or on getting a place to see it pass. Every window on Broadway and the other streets of the route was of course occupied by a dozen or so of spectators, those at which seats were to be sold finding eager purchasers at any price de-manded. Every foot of sidewalk was lined along its edge with waiting men and women. Narrow cornices and ledges several

stories high furnished seats for some whose elevated and seem-
ingly dangerous positions made one dizzy even to look at.
Platforms were erected on the sidewalks at frequent intervals,
the seats on which were in great demand. Where the avenue
traversed by the procession was intersected by cross streets,
hacks, carts, and trucks were drawn up and afforded a large
number of excellent seats. The sidewalks were packed from
the curbstone to the wall with an assemblage which it required
all the efforts of the large police force in attendance to keep
from overflowing into the street, and all this long before the
hour designated for the starting of the procession.

Meanwhile the eight divisions of which the column was to
consist were assembling and forming in line in the different
streets assigned for them. The military formed chiefly on
Broadway, and before the procession moved the lines of soldiery extended from the City Hall the whole distance to Fourteenth street. In the narrow streets in the vicinity of the hall
were arranged the component parts of the civic procession, and
it seemed as if every court and alley was made the rallying
point of some organization with its banner and long line of men
in dark clothing. The omnibuses and coaches endeavoring to
make their way up or down town were forced to take some very
long detours on every trip, and sometimes found themselves
completely surrounded by such throngs that they were compelled to give up the journey altogether. Men and women
were still hurrying by the bier in the City Hall, where lay the
silent corpse, for the escort of which through the city so many
thousands were preparing.

The journeys, with the inevitable dust and frequent exposures
to the air, had their effect upon the 'remains which no embalmers could wholly provide against, and the view for which
many were so eager had none of those attractions which sometimes invest the remains of the lost and loved.

At twenty minutes to twelve o'clock the doors of admission
were closed, and, although at least one hundred and fifty thousand had been admitted, immense crowds were disappointed.
Preparations were now made to close the coffin, Archbishop
McCloskey being one of the last who gazed upon it. The appointed bearers took their places beside the coffin, and amid
the brilliant crowd of Generals, Admirals, Consuls, and distin-

guished men awaited the moment. When it was near one o'clock, six of them raised it on their shoulders, and to the tolling of the bell and the tap of the drum the body was borne out again into the open air in sight of the countless thousands, and through the double line formed by the Seventh Regiment, to the funeral car prepared for the occasion. This was fourteen feet long at its longest part, eight feet wide, and fifteen feet one inch in height. On the main platform which was five feet from the ground, was erected a dais six inches in height, at the corners of which were columns holding a canopy, which, curving inwards and upwards towards the centre, was surmounted by a miniature temple of liberty.

The platform was entirely covered with fine black cloth, drawn tightly over the body of the car, and reaching to within a few inches of the ground, edged with silver bullion fringe. Over this hung graceful festoons of the same material, spangled with silver stars, and edged also with silver bullion. At the base of each column were three American flags, slightly inclined, festooned, covered with crape. The columns were black, covered with vines of myrtle and camelias.

The canopy was of black cloth, drawn tightly, and from the base of the temple another draping of black cloth fell in graceful folds over the first; while from the lower edges of the canopy depended festoons, also of black cloth, caught under small shields. The folds and festoons were richly spangled and trimmed with bullion. At each corner of the canopy was a rich plume of black and white feathers.

The temple of liberty was represented as being deserted, having no emblems of any kind in or around it save a small flag on top, at half mast. The inside of the car was lined with white satin, fluted, and from the centre of the roof was suspended a large gilt eagle, with outspread wings, covered with crape, bearing in its talons a laurel wreath, and the platform around the coffin was strewn with laurel wreaths and flowers of various kinds.

The car was drawn by sixteen gray horses, with coverings of black cloth, trimmed with silver bullion, each led by a colored groom, dressed in the usual habiliments of mourning, with streamers of crape on their hats.

On this the body was now placed, all present reverently uncovering, and the band of the Seventh playing a funeral march. All seemed to feel the solemnity of the moment.

The procession then formed around the car; the Sergeants of the Reserve Corps surrounding the remains with drawn sabres, and the Seventh in a hollow square.

FIRST DIVISION.

Police in a solid phalanx cleared the way, and then a body of dragoons, in their gay attire, opened the march of the procession. Four generals and a number of staff officers followed: then came the Second Division N. Y. S. N. G., the Duncan Light Artillery of Brooklyn; the Fifty-second Regiment of infantry, Colonel Cole; the Forty-Seventh, Colonel Meserole; the Twenty-third Regiment, Colonel Pratt, all bearing crape on their arms, and their colors cased. These closed the Fifth Brigade. The Seventh-Regiment of Cavalry, the next in order, was followed by the Twenty-eighth and Fourteenth Regiments, the latter with its tattered colors proudly borne from Bull Run to Spottsylvania. The Thirteenth, another Brooklyn Regiment, succeeded.

The First Division N. Y. S. N. G., the New York City Regiments, followed, preceded by the garrison of Hart's Island, a fine body of veterans. The Seventy-ninth, with its record of gallant deeds in Virginia, Carolina, and Tennessee; the Sixty-ninth, Fifty-fifth, Seventy-first, Twenty-second and others, whose renown will now be undying, moved onward in solid columns, their tattered colors proclaiming them to be no longer mere carpet knights. The Fourth Artillery, Colonel Teller, closed the division.

The whole military pageant was grand. The eighteen city regiments in the parade, with their batteries and officers made a force of at least ten thousand men. Those from Brooklyn and the Regulars were nearly half that number, the whole in line of formation, or double line, extending from Barclay street to Twenty-fifth street, besides six blocks on Canal street, and around Union Square, a distance in all of four miles and a half.

The Seventh Regiment succeeded, followed by a battalion of marines, and other officers of the army and navy then in New York, including Major-General Palmer, Brigadier-Generals

Meagher, Este, Hunt, Kiernan, Admiral Paulding, Commodores Ringgold and Engle, with some French naval officers.

Then followed Major-General Dix and staff, preceding the guard of honor, which consisted of a detachment from the Seventh Regiment, formed two deep and in hollow square, inside of which marched the veteran guard surrounding the remains of the illustrious dead from Washington.

As the funeral-car passed on, a simultaneous hush seemed to come over the entire crowd; the men reverently lifted their hats, and all eyes, many of which were moist with tears, were fastened on the car and coffin from the time of its appearance till it passed out of sight; then there was a moment of death-like stillness, when the pent-up feelings of the immense throng seemed to relieve themselves with a simultaneous sigh.

Many waited to see no more of the procession as it passed on in its regular order, which was, the guard of honor, followed by a troop of cavalry as escort to Brigadier-General Hall, Grand Marshal, with his aids, after which came the Second Division.

THE SECOND DIVISION.

This division, which comprised the representatives of the State, county, and city governments of this and other cities and States, representatives of foreign nations, etc., formed a very prominent feature of the grand procession.

The order of arrangements agreed upon by the committee, owing to the immense number who turned out to do honor to the occasion, had to be temporarily abandoned, and the various sub-divisions were compelled to form in line in some of the adjoining streets.

The carriages provided for the foreign representatives, and delegations from the States and Territories of the United States, were formed in line in Chambers street, the right resting on Broadway, and the federal officers of the Custom House, Surveyors Office, Post Office, and the collectors, assessors, and deputies of the United States Internal Revenue, United States marshals, and the judges and officers of the United States courts, formed on Centre street, the head of the line resting on the corner of City Hall square and Tryon row.

The foreign representatives were dressed in full court costume, wearing on their persons the insignia of their rank. Some of their uniforms were of the most gorgeous description, and attracted particular attention. Many of them wore side-arms, and all wore the usual badge of mourning.

The whole division was in charge of N. B. Laban, assisted by William M. Tweed, Jr., as aid; the second in command being Colonel Van Brunt, W. R. Vermilyea, Jr., and S. R. Brunell acting as aids.

The following is the order in which this division took its place in the procession :—

The members of both Boards of the Common Council, twenty abreast, preceded by their Sergeant-at-Arms, all wearing the usual mourning badge on the left arm, and carrying in their hands their staves of office shrouded in crape, the *attachés* of both boards following in their proper places.

Next in order came the delegations that accompanied the remains from Washington, followed by delegations from the Common Councils of Washington, Baltimore, Philadelphia, Brooklyn, New Haven, Jersey City, and other cities.

Comptroller Brennan, City Inspector Boole, Commissioner Miller.
Board of Croton Commissioners, headed by President Stephens.
Counsel to Corporation.
City Chamberlain Devlin and clerks.
Board of Fire Commissioners.
Board of Appeals of Fire Department.
Chief Engineer Decker and assistants.
Supervisors, with their President and Sergeant-at-Arms.
Commissioners Bell, Nicholson, Bowen, and Brennan.
Board of Police Commissioners—Messrs. Acton, Berger, McMurray, and Bosworth, with their clerks.
Board of Education, headed by President McLean.
The Faculty of the Free Academy, with the venerable President Webster at their head.
The Central Park Commissioners.
Tax Commissioners and clerks.
Commissioners of Emigration.
Coroners and their deputies, Recorder Hoffman, and City Judge Russell.
Board of Police Magistrates, Judges Barnard, Sutherland, Ingraham, and clerks.
Judges, attended by their clerks and officers, wearing appropriate emblems of mourning.
District Attorney Hall and assistants, with clerks.

County Clerk Conner, and other county officials.

The Collector's office, in the absence of Mr. Draper, was represented by Deputy Collectors Clinch and Embury, accompanied by the Collector's private secretary and the officers of the department.

Surveyor Wakeman and his deputies.

Naval Officer Dennison, deputies, clerks, and other *attachés* of the office.

The Post Office Department, headed by Postmaster Kelly. A very handsome black banner, fringed with silver lace, and surmounted by a small gilt eagle, pendent from the beak of which was a small mourning wreath, was borne in front, with the name of the department in silver letters inscribed in the centre.

Collectors and Assessors of Internal Revenue, with their officers, clerks, and *attachés*.

The United States Marshal's office was represented by Joseph Thompson, first deputy. Captain Lansing and the officers of the old Independent Continental Guard, dressed in full uniform, formed the escort to the officers of the Marshal's office and the officers of the Federal courts and United States District Attorney's office.

Judge Benedict represented the United States Court for the Eastern District of New York.

The Sub-Treasurer, clerks, and employees of the Assay Office took their place in the line after the officers of the United States courts. All these civic Federal organizations marched twenty abreast, and formed a solid line extending from the front of the City Hall, through City Hall square, Centre and Chambers street, to the office of the United States Marshal.

The officers of the United States Navy-yard, of Brooklyn, headed by Capt. Case, and the ex-officers of the United States Army, and the officers and ex-officers of the United States Volunteers, brought up the rear of this division. The time occupied by the division in passing a given point was nearly an hour; and, at a moderate estimate, there must have been nearly, if not quite, twelve thousand persons comprised in this part of the procession.

THIRD DIVISION.

Closely following the Second Division came the Third Division.

This division was led by Colonel Frank E. Howe, Grand Marshal, and his aids, J. A. Stevens, Jr., and Major James R. Smith, mounted on splendid gray horses, and wearing mourning-scarfs of black silk over the shoulder. They were succeeded by the band and drum corps of the Twelfth United States infantry, from Fort Hamilton, who were immediately in front of a detachment of about forty of the Hawkins Zouaves, carrying old battle-flags draped in mourning, under Lieutenant Jackson. The medical faculty were next represented, and were succeeded by the clergy, on foot, among whom were the following:—Most Rev. Archbishop McCloskey, Very Rev. Dr. Starrs, V. G., Rev. Francis McNierny, Rev. J. P. Thompson, Rev. R. Hitchcock, Rev. Mr. Mooney, Rev. Mr. McMahon, Rev. Dr. Thompson, Rev. J. B. Dunne, Rev. U. H. Blair, Rev. H. S. Stevens, Rev. Mr. Loomis, Rev. O. Eastman, Rev. Wm. Binnet, Rev. J. H. Orter, Rev. Julius Hone, Rev. John T. Elmendorf, Rev. Mr. Huntington, Rev. Dr. Hedge, Rev. Dr. Weston, and Rev. C. Meheny.

The members of the Chamber of Commerce, wearing the mourning badges of the Chamber, followed, headed by General Strong as Grand Marshal. It is worthy of remark that one of the oldest members of the Chamber, Colonel Murray, who was present, and marched on foot the whole route, walked in the funeral procession of General Washington.

These were succeeded by the officers of the Associated Banks, and a delegation representing the New York Board of Fire Insurance Companies.

These were followed by the Athenæum Club, Wm. T. Blodget, President, numbering about three hundred persons, wearing appropriate mourning badges, and the Century Club, Mr. G. Bancroft, President, also numbering about three hundred persons, all wearing crape and badges, and headed by the banners of their respective clubs.

The Union League Club, Mr. Wm. P. Jones, Marshal, came next, headed by the band of the Fifth regiment United States Army, and numbered about five hundred persons, all of whom wore mourning badges. These were again succeeded by the Union General Committee, John H. White, Marshal; the Tammany General Committee, Noah Childs, Marshal; and the Mozart General Committee, preceded by their sergeants-at-arms, and wearing the usual mourning badges, and numbering in the aggregate about eight hundred men.

The delegation of the Union League of America, which followed next, headed by the Newark band, mustered in great numbers, reaching in the total nearly five thousand men, and were commanded by Charles H. Marshall. They marched in sub-divisions, each headed by a band and drum corps, and by flags heavily draped with black.

The German Central Committee, Mr. Conlopy, Marshal, wearing mourning emblems, and headed by their banner and band, and num-

bering about two hundred and fifty persons, followed, and were succeeded by the Historical Society of the city of New York, Richard
Warren, Chairman, with band and banner.

The Republican German Central Committee, G. F. Steinbruner,
Marshal, numbering about two hundred and fifty members with
banner and band, followed, and were again succeeded by the citizens of the Pacific coast, numbering about one hundred and fifty
persons, headed by the colossal figure of a California hunter, dressed
in a complete hunting suit, and bearing a heavy rifle draped in
mourning.

The rear of the division was brought up by the Cadets of Temperance, and the Grand Division of the Sons of Temperance, in full regalia, and numbering about four hundred men.

THE FOURTH DIVISION.

The fourth division was composed exclusively of the Masonic
fraternity and other orders. If the nearly total absence of the
usual regalia hindered the lodges from presenting the imposing
appearance which such a large body of men arrayed in the brilliant insignia of their order would undoubtedly exhibit, yet, at-
tired in uniform black habiliments, and aided only by simple,
unpretending mourning badges and sprigs of acacia—the emblem of immortality—worn by them, their appearance was
striking in the extreme, and appropriate to the mournful
occasion.

This division was headed by General Hobart Ward, Marshal, and
his aids, and a brass band, and were followed by the lodges of the
Free and Accepted Masons of New York, Brooklyn, Williamsburg,
Greenpoint, and Harlem.

These were succeeded by the Independent Order of Odd Fellows,
headed by their band and banner, and which consisted of the Grand
Lodge and nineteen subordinate lodges, numbering altogether one
thousand members. The next was the Independent Order of Red
Men, in front of whom was borne three massive links of a chain
draped with crape, followed by their banner also covered with black.
The eighteen lodges composing this sub-division numbered about
fifteen hundred men.

The fourteen lodges of the Bnai Bareth, or Sons of the Covenant,
came next, preceded by their band and banner, and numbered about
fifteen hundred members.

The Free Sons of Israel, consisting of nine lodges, with their band, succeeded them, and were headed by a very large white and black banner, with the word "Lincoln" in the centre, and around it the words, "The father of this country is dead; the nation mourns for him."

The next in order were Abraham Lodge, No. 1, O. B. A., numbering about forty-eight members; and the Sclavonic Union Society, A. B. Zaremba, Master, consisting of about three hundred members. These, again, were succeeded by the order of Bnai Morsch, which carried two beautiful colored banners, and numbered about four hundred persons. The Chebra Anshe Emuno, Martin Stark, President, numbering one hundred members, followed; after which the only order in the procession which wore the full regalia appeared—namely, the United Brother's Lodge, No. 1—with red scarfs, red aprons, and other insignia of their Order. This lodge was about one hundred strong.

THE FIFTH DIVISION.

This Division was composed of Irish societies. Green and gold, mingled unhappily with the solemn badges of the grave, were the devices which each man wore in the ranks.

The United Sons of Erin, with a banner heavily draped, numbered about one thousand men, each wearing the green collar tipped with gold, and, in some instances, draped.

The Ancient Order of Hibernians, in strong force—numbering, perhaps, two thousand men. They were headed by a splendid drum corps, and the melancholy notes of "The Blackbird"—which are familiar to every Irishman—played on the fife and drum, was their funeral dirge.

The Society of the Immaculate Conception.

St. Peter's Temperance Society.

Next the cadets of St. James's Temperance Society, followed by that body in large numbers. The cadets numbered one hundred and thirty-one boys, dressed neatly in green jackets and red capes, with green trimmings. On the left lapel of their jacket they wore the likeness of the lamented President, together with the following inscription:—"A nation mourns the departed patriot, statesman, and martyr."

St. Bridget's Mutual Benevolent and Burial Society next followed.

Then came the Father Mathew T. A. B. societies in the following order:—Young Men's Father Mathew T. A. B. Society of Brooklyn, No. 1, eight hundred strong. Father Mathew Union Benevolent

13

Total Abstinence Society of New York, headed by their cadets. Branch No. 1, of the same society; Father Mathew Society, No. 2, of Brooklyn; Assumption Society, of Brooklyn, headed by cadets; Father Mathew Society, No. 2, of New York, with cadets; Father Mathew Society, No. 3, of Brooklyn, E. D., with cadets; Father Mathew Society, No. 3, of New York; Father Mathew Society, No. 5, of Brooklyn; Father Mathew Society, No. 6, of Greenpoint, with cadets; Father Mathew Society, No. 4, of New York, with cadets; Father Mathew Society, No. 5, of New York, with cadets; Young Men's Father Mathew Total Abstinence Benevolent Society, of New York.

THE SIXTH DIVISION.

The New York Caulkers' Association numbered one thousand strong. In front they carried a handsome obelisk, elaborately draped in mourning, with a dial on either side, stopped at twenty-two minutes past seven, with suitable inscriptions.

'Longshoremen's Union Protective Association, No. 2. This organization was headed by their society banner, with inscriptions.

The New York and Brooklyn Sawyer's Associations, headed by a splendid banner draped in mourning, six hundred strong.

New York Steam Boiler Makers' Association, one thousand strong, headed by a magnificent banner, draped in the most elaborate manner.

Waiters' Protective Benevolent Association, which appeared in strong force.

The Cooper's Benevolent Society.

THE SEVENTH DIVISION.

This division consisted entirely of various trades and societies.

The American Protestant Association turned out in full numbers —three thousand.

The Workingmen's Union delegation from the different trades was very well represented. The total number of men was estimated at five thousand, the dry goods clerks alone being represented by over eight hundred. The house carpenters were also very well represented.

The New York Caledonian Club, numbering two hundred, presented a very fine appearance, the members all wearing black rosettes, with the badge of the association in the centre.

The Italian Society, Ceres Union, National Glee Club, Island, Rosedale Clubs, the Olympic, Friendly Sons and Knights of St. Patrick, followed.

The German Societies succeeded, taking their positions in the following order :

New York Sharpshooters, Captain Louis Geisler, forty men, in green uniform, and with badges of mourning.

The German Bakers (employers), about seven hundred men. These form two associations, of which Messrs. Jacob Eidt and John Dexheimer are the respective Presidents. They bore two banners, the United States flag and the bakers' banner, dressed in mourning.

The New York Turn Verein, President Metzner, in a body, numbering four hundred men.

The Turner Tambour Corps, twenty men.

Turner Sharpshooters, forty men.

The Turner Zoeglings Verein, forty members.

Turner delegates from Bloomingdale, Brooklyn, New Brooklyn, East New York, Strattonport, Jersey City, and Hudson City, numbering in all about two hundred men. The Turners appeared in their Turner dress, and wore white linen coats. They bore in the procession flags and banners dressed in mourning.

The veterans of the Turner regiment, President Strippel, fifty men. They bore the old regimental colors and battle flag dressed in mourning.

The veterans of the Twenty-ninth regiment, President Rudolph Carl; forty men.

Blenker's veterans, President Rosenberg; thirty-six men.

Veterans of the Garibaldi regiment, President Adam Urner; one hundred and fifty men, who bore the old battle-flag.

Veterans of the Steuben (volunteer) regiment, President Carl Kapf; thirty-six men.

Then followed the Social Reform Societies, which includes the Cabinetmakers' Association, numbering at least one thousand men. About a dozen flags and banners, all dressed in mourning, were borne by them.

Then followed the Arbeiter Bund (Working Men's Union), three hundred men; the German Carvers, two hundred men; the German Cigarmakers' Association, President August Koch, four hundred and fifty men; Normandie Aid Society, fifty men.

THE EIGHTH DIVISION

Comprised Brooklyn Societies and Citizens, Colonel E .J. Fowler, Marshal.

War Fund Committee, composed of the most prominent citizens of Brooklyn, under command of J. S. Stranahan, Esq., assisted by

Messrs. A. A. Low, Luther B. Wyman, G. T. Pierrepont, E. Griffith, and Mr. Fiske.

King's County Medical Society, headed by Dr. Bennet.

Hose Company, No. 17, Samuel Bouton, Foreman.

Temperance Cadets, No. 1 and 2, each numbering one hundred and fifty boys, carrying a huge banner draped in deep mourning.

They were succeeded by the Father Mathew and St. Ann's Total Abstinence Benevolent Society; the 'Longshoremen of Brooklyn; St. James's Roman Catholic Benevolent Society; Shamrock Benevolent Society.

The line was closed by about 1000 Brooklyn citizens, preceded by a banner borne by six men, inscribed as follows:

" CITIZENS OF THE FIFTH WARD OF BROOKLYN.

The hand of the Assassin has entwined the name of Abraham Lincoln in a wreath of immortality."

Following the Eighth division were the colored population of New York, who, though deprived of an invitation to join the grand pageant, nevertheless, when informed of the action taken by the military authorities, were only too glad to pay the last sad tributes of respect to their great benefactor. Having formed in Reade street, they patiently awaited the arrival of the left of the Eighth division, and then joined in the procession, numbering at least two thousand persons. They were preceded by a banner bearing the following inscription:

" ABRAHAM LINCOLN, OUR EMANCIPATOR."

On the reverse side of which were the following words:

" TO MILLIONS OF BONDSMEN HE LIBERTY GAVE."

All along the route, and particularly in Union Square, the colored people joining in the procession were vehemently applauded by the crowded assemblages.

This immense procession, almost every man wearing some emblem of mourning, pressed steadily on along the appointed route in solid lines, amid a multitude of spectators such as has seldom gathered together on earth. Every house and store was closed and draped in mourning. Inscriptions, pictures, monuments, attested the deep feeling of the people so suddenly and fiendishly deprived of its elected chief. The spectators numbered hundreds of thousands, the citizens of the great metropolis and the countless tides that had poured in by railway and steamboat.   For hours they awaited the coming of the procession ; and during the four hours its passage occupied, all was order and quiet: a feeling of sadness and bereavement had settled on all.   The procession passed up Broadway to Fourteenth street, thence through Fifth Avenue to Thirty-fourth, and across that wide street to Ninth Avenue, whence it passed into the Hudson River Railroad depot.

At three o'clock, the head having reached the depot, the column halted and formed in line facing to the west, to allow the funeral car and escort of mourners to pass.   At half-past three the approach of the car bearing the honored remains of the mortal body of the sixteenth President of the United States was made known by solemn refrains of bands and the muffled roll of martial drums.   As it passed fresh bands and other drums caught up the melancholy notes, regiments brought their arms to a present, officers saluted with their swords and colors draped in the badges of mourning dipped before the last of the mortal man who, as the head of the nation, devoted and sacrificed his life to that constitution which has given a deep significance to the colors of the American republic.   During the passing of the car the silence of the crowd was doubly profound.   Not a voice, not a whisper, not a sound was heard, save the tumultuous heaving of sorrowed hearts, often poured out in irrepressible tears, or deep inspirations of souls full of sadness, and prayers for the perpetuation of the nation and the protection of the widow and orphan children of the deceased.

The funeral escort rounded Ninth Avenue into Twenty-ninth street in the following order :

Mounted troop, Eighth regiment, New York.
Superintendent Kennedy.
Inspectors Carpenter and Leonard.
Broadway Squad.
Grand Marshal and Aids.
Grafulla's Band.
Seventh regiment.
General Dix and Guard of Honor, mounted.

Escort.   THE CATAFALQUE.   Escort.

Naval officers.

The Mayor and Governor Fenton.
Carriages containing foreign representatives.
Color guard, Irish brigade.
General Dix's bodyguard.
Police.

A stair case, with a top made so as to rest on the side of the catafalque, and reaching from the street, was then raised in position ; the sergeants of the Invalid corps ascended it, and, raising the coffin, descended with their burden to the sidewalk. At this moment the guard presented arms and all the spectators uncovered. The hearse-bearers, preceded by General Dix, then marched through the entrance into the depot, where they were met by the guard of honor who escorted the remains from Washington.

The word was given, and the parties who were to accompany the remains entered the cars assigned to them. At four o'clock precisely the pilot engine steamed out of the depot, and two minutes after, to the sound of a funeral dirge, the funeral train departed ; and thus New York paid the last homage of respect to all that was mortal of Abraham Lincoln.

SERVICES AT UNION SQUARE.

Meanwhile the appointed services began at Union square. The platform erected for the ceremonies was placed just opposite the Maison Dorée. Round the platform a reverent mass of people were congregated, filling up the square in front and for a considerable distance on either side. The mourning decorations of the platform were very appropriate. In front, before the stand of the orator of the evening, the circular railing was lowered, a small bench draped with black being provided for the occasion. On either side of this central space were the American flags, drawn close to the staff and heavily draped in black. On the left side was a broken pillar, festooned in mourning, on either side of which were marble figures of Hope and Justice.

Shortly after five o'clock the gentlemen of the committee entrusted with the closing ceremonies came upon the stand. Almost immediately afterwards,

Ex-Governor King opened the proceedings by introducing the Rev. Dr. Tyng, who offered up an appropriate prayer.

ORATION BY THE HON. GEO. BANCROFT.

A few words from the chairman introduced the orator of the occasion to the assemblage.

Our grief and horror at the crime which has clothed the continent in mourning find no adequate expression in words and no relief in tears. The President of the United States of America has fallen by the hands of an assassin. Neither the office with which he was invested by the approved choice of a mighty people, nor the most simple-hearted kindliness of nature, could save him from the fiendish passions of relentless fanaticism. The wailings of the millions attend his remains as they are borne in solemn procession over our great rivers, along the sea-side, beyond the mountains, across the prairie, to their final resting place in the valley of the Mississippi. The echoes of his funeral knell vibrate through the world, and the friends of freedom of every tongue and in every clime are his mourners. Too few days have passed away since Abraham Lincoln stood in the flush of vigorous manhood to permit any attempt at an analysis of his character or an exposition of his career. We find it hard to believe that his large eyes, which in their softness and beauty expressed nothing but benevolence and gentleness, are closed in death; we almost look for the pleasant smile that brought out more vividly the earnest cast of his features, which were serious even to sadness. A few years ago he was a village attorney, engaged in the support of a rising family, unknown to fame, scarcely named beyond his neighborhood ; his administration made him the most conspicuous man in his country, and drew on him first the astonished gaze, and then the respect and admiration of the world. Those who come after us will decide how much of the wonderful results of his public career is due to his own good common sense, his shrewd sagacity, readiness of wit, quick interpretation of the public mind ; his rare combination of fixedness and pliancy ; his steady tendency of purpose ; how much to the American people, who, as he walked with them side by side, inspired him with their wisdom and energy; and how much the overruling laws of the moral world, by which the selfishness of evil is made to defeat itself. But after every allowance, it will remain that members of the government which preceded his administration opened the gates to treason, and he closed them ; that when he went to Washington the ground on which he trod shook under his feet, and he left the republic on a solid foundation; that traitors had seized public forts and arsenals, and he recovered them for the United States, to whom they belonged ; that the capital which he found the abode of slaves, is now only the home of the free ; that the boundless public domain which was grasped at, and, in a great measure, held for the diffusion of slavery, is now irrevocably devoted to freedom; that then men talked a jargon of a balance of power in a republic between Slave States and Free States, and now the foolish words are blown away forever by the breath of Maryland, Missouri, and Tennessee ; that a terrible cloud of political heresy rose from the abyss threatening to hide the light of the sun, and under its darkness a rebellion was rising to undefinable proportions. Now the atmosphere is purer than ever before, and the insurrection is vanishing away ; the country is cast into another mould, and the gigantic system of wrong which had been the work of more than two centuries, is dashed down, we hope forever. And as to himself personally : he was then scoffed at by the proud as unfit for his station, and now against the usage of later years, and in spite of numerous competitors, he was the unbiassed and the undoubted choice of the American people for a second term of service. Through all the mad business of treason he retained the sweetness of a most placable disposition ; and the slaughter of myriads of the best on the battle-field and the more terrible destruction of our men in captivity by the slow torture of exposure and starvation, had never been able to provoke him into harboring one vengeful feeling or one purpose of cruelty.

How shall the nation most completely show its sorrow at Mr. Lincoln's death ? How shall it best honor his memory ? There can be but one answer. He was struck down when he was highest in its service, and in strict conformity of duty was engaged in carrying out principles affecting its life, its good name, and its relations to the cause of freedom and the progress of mankind. Grief must take the character of action, and breathe itself forth in the assertion of the policy to which he fell a sacrifice. The standard which he held in his hand must be uplifted again, higher and more firmly than before, and must be carried on to triumph. Above every thing else, his proclamation of the first day of January, 1863, declaring throughout the parts of the country in rebellion the freedom of all persons who had been held as slaves, must be affirmed and maintained. Events, as they rolled onward, have removed every doubt of the legality and binding force of that proclamation. The country and the rebel government have each laid claim to the public service of the slave, and yet but one of the two can have a rightful claim to such service. That rightful claim belongs to the United States, because every one born on their soil, with the few exceptions of the children of travelers and transcient residents, owes them a primary

allegiance. Every one so born has been counted among those represented in Congress ; every slave has ever been represented in
Congress—imperfectly and wrongly it may be—but still he has
been counted and represented. The slave born on our soil always
owed allegiance to the general government. It may in time past
have been a qualified allegiance, manifested through his master, as
the allegiance of a ward through its guardian, or of an infant through
its parent. But when the master became false to his allegiance the
slave stood face to face with his country, and his allegiance, which
may before have been a qualified one, became direct and immediate.
His chains fell off, and he stood at once in the presence of the nation, bound, like the rest of us, to its public defence. Mr. Lincoln's
proclamation did but take notice of the already existing right of the
bondman to freedom. The treason of the master made it a public
crime for the slave to continue his obedience; the treason of a State
set free the collective bondmen of that State. This doctrine is supported by the analogy of precedents. In the times of feudalism the
treason of the lord of the manor deprived him of his serfs ; the
spurious feudalism that existed among us differs in many respects
from the feudalism of the middle ages ; but so far the precedent
runs parallel with the present case ; for treason the master then,
for treason the master now, loses his slaves. In the middle ages the
sovereign appointed another lord over the serfs and the land which
they cultivated ; in our day the sovereign makes them masters of
their own persons, lords over themselves.

It has been said that we are at war, and that emancipation is not
a belligerent right. The objection disappears before analysis. In
a war between independent powers the invading foreigner invites
to his standard all who will give him aid, whether bond or free, and
he rewards them according to his ability and his pleasure with gifts
or freedom ; but when at peace he withdraws from the invaded
country he must take his aiders and comforters with him ; or if he
leaves them behind, where he has no court to enforce his decrees, he
can give them no security, unless it be by the stipulations of a
treaty. In a civil war it is altogether different. There, when rebellion is crushed, the old government is restored, and its courts re-
sume their jurisdiction. So it is with us ; the United States have
courts of their own that must punish the guilt of treason, and vin-
dicate the freedom of persons whom the fact of rebellion has set
free. Nor may it be said that because slavery existed in most of
the States when the Union was formed, it cannot rightfully be inter-
fered with now. A change has taken place, such as Madison fore-
saw, and for which he pointed out the remedy. The constitution of

States had been transformed before the plotters of treason carried them away into rebellion. When the Federal constitution was formed general emancipation was thought to be near, and everywhere the respective legislatures had authority, in the exercise of their ordinary functions, to do away with slavery; since that time the attempt has been made in what are called slave States to make the condition of slavery perpetual; and events have proved, with the clearness of demonstation, that a constitution which seeks to continue a caste of hereditary bondmen through endless generations is inconsistent with the existence of republican institutions. So, then, the new President and the people of the United States must insist that the proclamation of freedom shall stand as a reality; and, moreover, the people must never cease to insist that the constitution shall be so amended as utterly to prohibit slavery on any part of our soil forevermore.

Alas! that a State in our vicinity should withhold its assent to this last beneficent measure; its refusal was an encouragement to our enemies equal to the gain of a pitched battle, and delays the only hopeful method of pacification. The removal of the cause of the rebellion is not only demanded by justice; it is the policy of mercy, making room for a wider clemency; it is the part of order against a chaos of controversy; its success brings with it true reconcilement, a lasting peace, a continuous growth of confidence through an assimilation of the social condition. Here is the fitting expression of the mourning of to-day.

And let no lover of his country say that this warning is uncalled for. The cry is delusive, that slavery is dead. Even now it is nerving itself for a fresh struggle for continuance. The last winds from the South waft to us the sad intelligence that a man, who had surrounded himself with the glory of the most brilliant and most varied achievements, who but a week ago was named with affectionate pride among the greatest benefactors of his country and the ablest generals of all time, has usurped more than the whole power of the executive, and under the name of peace has revived slavery and given security and political power to traitors from the Chesapeake to the Rio Grande. Why could he not remember the dying advice of Washington—never to draw the sword but for self-defence or the rights of his country; and, when drawn, never to sheath it till its work should be accomplished? And yet from this bad act, which the people with one united voice condemn, no great evil will follow save the shadow on his own fame. The individual, even in the greatness of military glory, sinks into insignificance before the resistless movements in the history of man. No one can turn back or stay the march of Providence.

No sentiment of despair may mix with our sorrow. We owe it to the memory of the dead, we owe it to the cause of popular liberty throughout the world, that the sudden crime which has taken the life of the President of the United States shall not produce the least impediment in the smooth course of public affairs. This great city, in the midst of unexampled emblems of deeply seated grief, has sustained itself with composure and magnanimity. It has nobly done its part in guarding against the derangement of business or the slightest shock to public credit. The enemies of the Republic put it to the severest trial; but the voice of faction has not been heard; doubt and despondency have been unknown. In serene majesty the country rises in the beauty and strength and hope of youth, and proves to the world the quiet energy and the durability of institutions growing out of the reason and affections of the people. Heaven has willed it that the United States shall live. The nations of the earth cannot spare them. All the worn out aristocracies of Europe saw in the spurious feudalism of slaveholding their strongest outpost, and banded themselves together with the deadly enemies of our national life. If the Old World will discuss the respective advantages of oligarchy or equality; of the union of church and state, or the rightful freedom of religion; of land accessible to the many, or of land monopolized by an ever decreasing number of the few—the United States must live to control the decision by their quiet and unobtrusive example. It has often and truly been observed that the trust and affection of the masses gathers naturally round an individual; if the inquiry is made whether the man so trusted and beloved shall elicit from the reason of the people enduring institutions of their own, or shall sequester political power for a superintending dynasty, the United States must live to solve the problem. If a question is raised on the respective merits of Timoleon or Julius Cæsar, of Washington or Napoleon, the United States must be there to call to mind that there were twelve Cæsars, most of them the opprobrium of the human race, and to contrast with them the line of American Presidents.

The duty of the hour is incomplete, our mourning is insincere, if while we express unwavering trust in the great principles that underlie our government, we do not also give our support to the man to whom the people have entrusted its administration. Andrew Johnson is now, by the Constitution, the President of the United States, and he stands before the world as the most conspicuous representative of the industrial classes. Left an orphan at four years old, poverty and toil were his steps to honor. His youth was not passed in the halls of colleges; nevertheless he has received a thorough political education in statesmanship in the school of the people, and by long experience of public life. A village functionary; member successively of each branch of the Tennessee Legislature, hearing with a thrill of joy the words, "The Union, it must be preserved;" a representative in Congress for successive years; Governor of the great State of Tennessee, approved as its Governor by re-election; he was at the opening of the rebellion a senator from that State in Congress. Then at the Capitol, when senators, unrebuked by the government, sent word by telegram to seize forts and arsenals, he alone from that Southern region told them what the government did not dare to tell them—that they were traitors, and deserved the punishment of treason. Undismayed by a perpetual purpose of public enemies to take his life, bearing up against the still greater trial of the persecution of his wife and children, in due time he went back to his State, determined to restore it to the Union, or die with the American flag for his winding sheet. And now, at the call of the United States, he has returned to Washington as a conqueror, with Tennessee as a free State for his trophy. It remains for him to consummate the vindication of the Union.

To that Union Abraham Lincoln has fallen a martyr. His death, which was meant to sever it beyond repair, binds it more closely and more firmly than ever. The blow aimed at him was aimed, not at the native of Kentucky, not at the citizen of Illinois, but at the man who, as President, in the executive branch of the government, stood as the representative of every man in the United States. The object of the crime was the life of the whole people, and it wounds the affections of the whole people. From Maine to the southwest boundary on the Pacific it makes us one. The country may have needed an imperishable grief to touch its inmost feeling. The grave that receives the remains of Lincoln receives the martyr to the Union; the monument which will rise over his body will bear witness to the Union; his enduring memory will assist during countless ages to bind the States together, and to incite to the love of our one undivided, indivisible country. Peace to the ashes of our departed friend, the friend of his country and his race. Happy was his life, for he was the restorer of the Republic; he was happy in his death, for the manner of his end will plead forever for the Union of the States and the freedom of man.

As part of the proceedings laid down by the Committee of Arrangements, the last inaugural of the 4th of March was then read by the Rev. Dr. J. P. Thompson.

The Rev. W. H. Boole read the 94th Psalm, and the Rev. Dr. Rogers made an appropriate prayer.

Rabbi Isaacs, of the Broadway Tabernacle, then read selections from the Holy Scriptures and offered a prayer, after which Rev. Dr. Osgood recited the following:

ODE FOR THE FUNERAL OF ABRAHAM LINCOLN.

BY W. C. BRYANT.

O slow to smite and swift to spare,
    Gentle and merciful and just!
Who, in the fear of God, did'st bear,
    The sword of power – a nation's trust :

In sorrow by thy bier we stand,
    Amid the awe that hushes all,
And speak the anguish of a land
    That shook with horror at thy fall.

Thy task is done—the bond are free ;
    We bear thee to an honored grave,
Whose noblest monument shall be
    The broken fetters of the slave.

Pure was thy life ; its bloody close
    Hath placed thee with the sons of light,
Among the noble host of those
    Who perished in the cause of right.

Dr. Osgood also read the first three verses of a new national hymn, composed by Mr. Bryant at the request of the reader, and circulated among a few personal friends :—

"Thou hast put all things under his feet."

Oh, North, with all thy vales of green !
    Oh, South, with all thy palms !
From peopled towns and fields between
    Uplift the voice of psalms.
Raise, ancient East ! the anthem high,
And let the youthful West reply.

Lo, in the clouds of heaven appears
    God's well-beloved Son ;
He brings a train of brighter years ;
    His kingdom is begun ;
He comes a guilty world to bless
With mercy, truth, and righteousness.

O Father! haste the promised hour,
  When at His feet shall lie
All rule, authority, and power,
  Beneath the ample sky ;
When He shall reign from pole to pole,
  The Lord of every human soul.

The Chairman then announced that as the Most Reverend Archbishop McCloskey was so fatigued from his long attendance in the funeral *cortège* that he was unable to be present to pronounce the closing benediction, the venerable prelate's absence would be filled by Professor Hitchcock.

Professor Hitchcock then pronounced the benediction, and the ceremonies were closed, an excellent band on the platform playing a national air.

FROM NEW YORK TO ALBANY.

At Mount St. Vincent, near Yonkers, the Sisters of Charity, with their two hundred pupils, were drawn up on the sward in front of the Academy, with veiled heads, to pay their respects to the funeral train.

At Tarrytown, 5.20 P. M., the surface of one side of a frame structure was entirely covered with an American flag, trimmed in mourning and adorned with mottoes. Near it on a decorated platform were a number of young ladies, with clasped hands, dressed in pure white, with broad, black sashes, apparently immovable as statues. The houses bore the usual signs of grief, and one of the prominent mottoes read was "Bear him gently to his rest."

The crowd at Sing Sing was very large. The Cadets were in line, and a long row of men with heads uncovered, and a number of ladies dressed in white with black sashes, heightenened the effect of this interesting scene. Minute guns were fired. The most marked feature was an arch over the road. It was apparently twenty-five feet high, and eighteen wide. Its pillars were alternately striped with white and black. The verges were covered with black velvet, intertwined with evergreens, and prominent were the words, "We mourn our country's loss," and "He died for truth." On the keystone of the arch was a figure of Liberty, her cap covered with crape.

The people of Peekskill were evidently mournful spectators. The train halted for a short time. Minute guns were fired and companies of military and firemen filed past the funeral car with heads uncovered. Flags and mottoes were displayed, and a band of music performed a funeral march, greatly adding to the solemnity of the scene.

The station at Garrison's, opposite West Point, was adorned with national flags. A company of regulars and the West Point Cadets were drawn up in line, officers of the Academy standing with uncovered heads. The Cadet band performed funeral music in front of the train. A large number of people collected. Salutes were fired from the other side of the river at West Point.

At Cold Spring the testimonials of respect for the great departed were an arch with suitable emblems, under which on a raised pedestal was a young lady in crape personating Liberty ; two lads, one a soldier and the other a sailor, mourning, formed prominent features. The Union League formed a circle round the arch. The public authorities, private social organizations, and the whole population were out *en masse*. Minute guns were fired. The station building was handsomely decorated, displaying portraits of the illustrious dead.

The station at East Albany was elaborately and appropriately draped. Soldiers and firemen escorted the funeral party across the river. The bells of Albany tolled and minute guns fired, and the remains of Abraham Lincoln were conveyed to the Capitol.

It had been determined that the reception should be with the least possible ostentation, and the procession was therefore confined to a detail of three companies of the 10th and 25th Regiments of National Guards, three companies of firemen bearing torches, the State officers, members of the Legislature, and city authorities. The streets were densely crowded on the line. The hearse was drawn by four white horses.

At the Capitol the coffin was removed from the hearse to the Assembly Chamber and placed upon the catafalque directly under the chandelier. Guards of the State militia were immediately stationed in the chamber, halls and side-rooms, while companies from the 3d and 21st Reserve Corps were detailed for duty on the outside of the Capitol.

At half-past one next morning the coffin was opened and an immense throng of people about the park permitted to enter the chamber and view the remains. They passed by at the rate of sixty or seventy a minute.

A low estimate fixed the number of strangers in the city at 30,000. Never before had such multitudes gathered at the capital, and everybody seemed fully to participate in the solemnities. At noon State street was filled with a living mass and Broadway and many side streets were equally crowded. At one P. M. the military, fire department, and civic societies began to form and at two the coffin was closed. Fifty thousand men, women, and children visited the remains.

Soon after two o'clock the procession commenced to move over the prescribed route, Franklin Townsend, Esq., being Grand Marshal. It was composed of the 10th and 25th Regiments of Albany, the 24th and Light Horse Battery of Troy, State and city authorities, fire department, and a large number of civic societies. The military numbered 2000. The procession was thirty minutes in passing a given point, the length being over a mile.

State street, from the Capitol to Broadway, and Broadway from State to Lumber streets, altogether a distance exceeding a mile, was densely packed during the march. Such a mass of human beings (probably not less than 60,000) was never before seen in the streets of Albany. There were four bands, each with a full drum corps, in line; and as the procession moved down the hill, the bands playing mournful airs, grief was depicted in every face.

The hearse, with the coffin resting in an elegant and elaborately-finished catafalque, which was trimmed with white silk, adorned richly with silver mountings, and surmounted by the eagle, was drawn by eight horses.

At 3.45 the train of newly finished cars, furnished by the New York Central Railroad Company, each tastefully draped and trimmed with the emblems of sorrow, was reached at the Broadway crossing above Lumber street, and the coffin was transferred to the hearse car, in which it had been brought from Washington. At four o'clock the remains moved from Albany.

ALBANY TO CHICAGO.

At Herkimer, thirty-six ladies dressed in white, with black sashes, each holding in her hand a draped national flag, were ranged near the train. Music and minute-guns greeted the train on its arrival here. There were appropriate demonstrations of respect everywhere along the route.

The funeral *cortège* arrived at Syracuse at 11.50. At least 35,000 people witnessed the passage of the train. The firemen were drawn up in line, and their torches and the numerous bonfires lit up the scene solemnly. Bells were tolling and cannon booming.

At Utica the depot buildings were draped and flags at half-mast. There were minute-guns, dirges, and tolling of bells. At least 25,000 people were gathered here. The train moved on amidst the solemn music of the bands.

At Syracuse the depot was found elaborately and tastefully draped. In addition to gas lights, locomotive lamps illuminated the building. The bells were tolled and minute-guns fired. A band of music performed dirges and one hundred voices chanted appropriate hymns.

On entering Rochester minute-guns were fired and bells tolled. The 54th Regiment, together with the Reserves, hospital soldiers, and a battery, were in line. The band played dirges. The streets were filled and the houses draped.

At Batavia ex-President Fillmore joined the party in the train, besides other prominent citizens.

At Buffalo a procession formed between 7 and 8 o'clock and marched to St. James Hall. The coffin was deposited in the hall beneath a crape canopy. The Buffalo St. Cecilia Society, as the remains were brought into the hall, sang with deep pathos, "Rest, Spirit, Rest." The society then placed a beautiful heart composed of white flowers at the head of the coffin, after which the public were admitted.

The remains of President Lincoln were escorted to the cars, April 27th, at night, and left at 10 for Cleveland.

At Dunkirk the platform was elaborately decorated, and a group of young ladies representing the States formed a pleasing tableau. The train having reached it at midnight, the

14

scene with the glare of torch, the solemn music, the booming of cannon, was deeply impressive.

At Westfield, a party of ladies, led by one whose husband (Colonel Drake) fell at Cold Harbor, came to place a cross of flowers on the coffin.

At the other stations, crowds had gathered to show their respect.

On reaching the State line, Gen. Dix and his staff withdrew, and the Mayor of Erie joined the *cortège*.

By 3.48 on the 28th the train entered Ohio, and hurried on through Kingsville, Ashtabula, Saybrook, Geneva, Unionville, Madison, Perry, Paineville, Mentor and Willoughby. The depots at all points were draped, and surrounded by respectful crowds. As the train passed the bells tolled and minute-guns were fired.

Governor Brough and his staff joined the funeral party at Wickliffe.

The train reached Cleveland at seven o'clock. As the train passed the lake side of the city, thousands of persons gathered on the sloping green hillsides, all having a good view of the train. High up an arch bore the inscription, "Abraham Lincoln." It was draped in mourning, and the supports covered with alternate stripes of black and white. Immediately under the arch was a lady dressed in horizontal bars of the national colors, to represent the genius of Liberty. She held in her hand a flag, and this, together with her cap, was banded with mourning. All places of business were closed. Colors were displayed at half-mast. A national salute of thirty-six guns was fired, and half-hour guns were fired till sunset.

At Euclid Street station the coffin was placed in a hearse, the roofing of which was covered with the national flag, with black plumes, and otherwise tastefully and appropriately adorned. The military escort embraced Major-General Hooker and staff, and Governor Brough, of Ohio, and staff; and the guard of honor was followed in procession by the United States civil officers, veteran soldiers, members of the city council and city officers of Cleveland and other cities, members of the bar, the Board of Trade, Knights Templar, the orders of Masons and Oddfellows, temperance societies, the German Benevolent Society, Fenian Brotherhood, St. Vincent Society, the Equal Rights League, &c., and all the benevolent and other associations and citizens, on foot.

The procession embraced all conditions of the people, and presented a decidedly fine appearance as it moved through the streets of this truly beautiful city from Euclid street to Erie, down Erie to Superior, and thence to the park.

The sidewalks were densely crowded with mournful looking spectators, while thousands of persons beheld the *cortège* from the steps and windows of the beautiful residences which line the entire route. Emblems of mourning were everywhere prominent, together with expressive mottoes. In the park was erected a building especially for the reception of the remains, to which they were now conveyed. The building was twenty-four by thirty-six feet in dimensions, and fourteen feet high from the ground to the plate. The roof was of pagoda style, and the rafters were covered with white cloth over the centre of the main roof; and directly over the catafalque a second roof was raised about four feet, and covered in like manner. The catafalque consisted of a raised dais, four by twelve feet, on the ground. The coffin rested on this dais about two feet above the floor. On the four corners columns supported a canopy. The columns were draped and wreathed with evergreens and white flowers, in the most beautiful manner. Black cloth as curtains, and fringed with silver, was caught and looped back to these columns. From the centre of the canopy the floor and sides of the dais were covered with black cloth, dropping from the four corners, bordered with silver fringe, and the borders of the cornice, all brilliantly ornamented with white rosettes and stars of silver. The inside of the canopy was lined with black cloth, gathered in folds, and white and black crape served as plumage to the posts. At the corners of the catafalque, in the centre, was a large star of black velvet, with thirty-six stars, one for each State in the Union. The floor of the dais was covered with flowers, and a figure of the Goddess of Liberty was placed at the head of the coffin. The ceiling of the building was gracefully hung with beautiful festoons of evergreen and flowers. The four posts which sustain on either side the pagoda roof were hung with large rosettes of mingled evergreen and magnolias of two varieties. Appropriate drapery hung from the cornice of the building, and swung from pillar to pillar of the fairy structure. Glass lamps were attached to the pillars of the catafalque and to other points of the building, so that the remains could be easily seen at night and to good advantage.

The religious services, after the remains had been placed upon the dais, were performed by the Right Rev. Bishop McIlvaine, who, in the course of his prayer, asked the blessing of heaven on the immediate family of the deceased, and a sanctification of the event which had called the nation to mourn to the good of him who had succeeded to the chief magistracy. He then read a part of the funeral service of the Episcopal Church, slightly altering the text to suit the occasion. These services moved many of the listeners to tears.

The remains were then exposed to public view. The arrangements were so perfect that every one who desired to see them had no difficulty in being gratified.

The number who witnessed the remains of the President during the day was one hundred and eighty a minute. Two rows of spectators were constantly passing, one on each side of the coffin. The lid was freshly covered with flowers, in the form of harps, crosses, and bouquets, gathered at the hot-houses of Cleveland, and laid upon the coffin by ladies representing the Soldiers' Relief Association.

After leaving Cleveland, Columbia, Grafton, and Wilmington, Greenwich and Crestline showed the usual signs of mourning, and, even at that early hour, groups of citizens. At Cardington, the gathering near the handsomely draped depot was unusually large.

OBSEQUIES AT COLUMBUS.

The funeral train reached the capital of Ohio on the 29th of April, at half-past seven, and stopped so that the funeral car lay across High-street. Again the veterans removed the body to a hearse prepared for its reception, and the procession formed, Major John W. Skiles, Grand Marshal.

The 88th Ohio Volunteer Infantry, forming the escort, marched first with arms reversed.

The officiating clergyman and orator then proceeded to the hearse, a fine structure, seventeen feet long, eight and a half feet wide, and seventeen and a half feet from the ground to the apex of the canopy. The main platform was four feet from the ground, on which rested a dais for the reception of the coffin, twelve feet long by five feet wide, raised two and a half feet above the platform. The canopy resembled in shape a Chinese pagoda. The interior of the roof was lined with silk flags, and the outside covered with black broadcloth, as were the dais, the main platform, and the entire hearse. Black cloth, festooned, depended from the platform, within a few inches of the ground, fringed with silver lace, and ornamented with heavy tassels of black silk.

Surrounding the cornice of the canopy were thirty-six silver stars, and on the apex and the four corners were five heavy black plumes. The canopy was appropriately curtained with black cloth, lined with white merino. On each side of the dais was the word "Lincoln" in silver letters.

The hearse was drawn by six white horses, covered with black cloth, which was edged with silver fringe. The heads of the horses were surmounted with large black plumes.

Following the hearse came the escort from Washington, in open carriages, three abreast. Next came Major-General Hooker and staff, mounted; Brevet Brigadier-General W. P. Richardson and staff, mounted; Provost Marshal General Wilcox and staff, mounted; and Brigadier-General Wager Swayne and staff, in open carriages.

Officers of the army on duty, and temporarily at that post, on foot, commanded by Major Van Voosh, 18th U. S. Infantry, and soldiers at the post not on duty with escort, commanded by Captain L. T. Nichols, followed the carriage of General Swayne. The Committee of Arrangements, the Reverend Clergy, the Heads of Departments, the Mayors of Cincinnati and Columbus, the Presidents of City Councils of said cities, the City Councils of Cincinnati and Columbus, the Judges and officers of the United States Court, the Supreme Court of Ohio, and the Franklin County Courts, the Masonic order, and orders of Odd Fellows and Druids, the Fenian Brotherhood, the Mechanics, St. Martin's, St. John's, and Butcher's Associations, the Fire Department, the Colored Masonic Order, and Colored Benevolent Association, followed in regular order.

At about nine o'clock the head of the procession arrived at the west entrance of Capitol Square. The 88th O. V. I. acting as special escort, passed in immediately, forming lines in two

ranks on each side of the passway from the gate to the steps of
the Capitol. As the coffin passed toward the archway, the
bands struck up a dirge, the high officials in attendance assumed
their places as escort, and thousands of bowed heads said, as
plainly as the letters arching the entrance, " Ohio Mourns."

When the coffin was placed on its flowery bed, the Rev. Mr.
Felton offered an appropriate prayer. Amid a silence as of
death, the coffin was then opened, and Mrs. Hoffner, the only
lady present, stepped softly forward and placed at the foot of
the coffin an anchor composed of delicate white flowers and
evergreen boughs, a wreath of the same upon the breast of the
dead, and a cross at the head.

The entrance ways of the Rotunda and the corresponding
panels were uniformly draped with black cloth, falling in heavy
folds from the arches to the floor. In the panels the drapings
were gathered to the sides equidistant from arch to floor, and
then allowed to fall in full volume and closing at the bottom as
at the top. In three of these central spaces thus formed were
grouped the war-worn battle-flags of veteran Ohio regiments.
In the other panel, the one between the north and east en-
trances, tastefully mounted and appropriately draped was Mr.
Powell's painting, " Perry's Victory," the grouping of characters and the sublimity of the scene represented adding much to
the general and impressive beauty of the Rotunda. Above the
panels entirely round the dome were three rows of festoons,
with black and white pendants, the whole joining appropriately
the general draping below.

On a platform with a base of twenty-one and a half feet by
twenty-eight feet, rising by five steps until it presented a top
surface perhaps one half as large, was placed the dais for the
reception of the coffin. This platform, tastefully carpeted, the
rise of each step dressed in black, was ornamented with emblematical flowers and plants in vases so arranged as to present,
with their impression of beauty, the sorrow for the dead. At
the corners facing the west entrance, were large vases containing beautiful specimens of amaranth, and midway between them
a grand central vase glowing with the richness and beauty of
the choicest flowers of the season.

A similar disposition of vases faced the east entrance, from
the corner ones the flowers of the emblematical justitia reach-

ing to the height of the dais. Around these large vases were grouped smaller ones, rising in gradations of beauty with the steps of the platform. The dais was most properly the crowning beauty of the structure, and in a brief description it is impossible to do it justice. Rectangular in form, with a side elevation of two feet, it was without canopy, and beautifully ornamented. The sides were covered with black broad cloth, over which drooped from the top festoons of white merino and tassels of white silk. The end facing the west entrance bore inscribed on a black panel with white border, in silver letters, the word "Lincoln." From the festooning to the top, rose in graceful swell a bed of white roses, immortelles, and orange blossoms, the pure white relieved only by the deep fresh green of the leaves and sprigs accompanying.

The officers, pall-bearers, and committees, after looking upon the remains, retired; and, without delay, the people commenced moving in to look upon the mortal remains of Abraham Lincoln.

First came the various military organizations of the procession—the men formed in four ranks, entering at the west front, moving without noise upon a carpeted way to the catafalque, passing by twos on each side of the coffin, the face and upper part of the body being brought in full view of each individual, and then those on the right passing out at the south, and those on the left turning to the north. Then followed in order the various delegations of the processions, succeeded by the people *en masse*. From half-past nine till four, over fifty thousand viewed the remains.

A platform had been erected immediately in front of the entrance to the Capitol. After appropriate music by military bands, and the singing of a hymn by a choir, under the direction of J. A. Scarritt, a prayer, impressive in thought and earnest in manner and word, was offered by the pastor of the Congregational Church, Rev. Mr. Goodwin. A hymn was then sung, and the Hon. Job E. Stevenson, of Chillicothe, delivered an impressive address.

At six o'clock in the evening, the doors of the Capitol were closed, the bugle sounded the assembly, the soldiers took arms, and the great procession began reforming for the final escort to the depot.

As the body was being brought out to the funeral-car at the west gateway of the Capitol grounds, a national salute was fired. Soon after, the procession moved, and the remains of the President were removed to the funeral-car at the depot of the Great Central Railway.

At Pleasant Valley, great bonfires lit up the country for miles. A large concourse of citizens were assembled around the depot. Two American flags, draped in mourning, were held in hand by two ladies.

At Unionville, O. (9 P. M.), there were about two hundred persons present, most of them sitting in wagons—the people having come in from the country.

At Milford, O. (9.19 P. M.), around bonfires were assembled four hundred or five hundred people, who waved flags and handkerchiefs slowly.

At Woodstock, O. (9.46 P. M.), five hundred people were present, and ladies were permitted to enter the President's car and strew flowers on the coffin. The Woodstock Cornet Band, U. Cushman, leader, played a dirge and hymn. The village bells slowly rang; men stood silent with uncovered heads. The scene was as affecting as it was beautiful.

At Urbana, O. (10.40 P. M.), three thousand people present. There was a large cross on a platform, entwined with circling wreaths of evergreens, which was worked under direction of Mrs. Miles G. Williams, President Ladies' Soldiers' Aid Society. From the top of the cross, and shorter arms, were hung illuminated colored transparencies. On the opposite side of the track was an elevated platform, on which were forty gentlemen and ladies, who sang with pathetic sweetness, the hymn entitled, "Go to Thy Rest." Large bonfires made night as light as day. Minute-guns were fired. Young ladies entered the car and strewed flowers on the martyr's bier.

At Paris, O. (11.24 P. M.), brilliant illuminations, by which might be seen a number of drooped flags. A large assembly stood in silence.

At Westville station crowds were gathered to pay respect to the dead.

At Conover, O. (11.30 P. M.). a long line of people two deep were standing in file; on the right little boys and girls, then young men and women, and on the left elderly people. In the centre, supporting a large American flag, were three young ladies, Miss Eliza Throckmorton, Miss Nora Brecount, and Miss Barnes, who chanted a patriotic religious song with a slow and mournful air.

At Piqua, O., April 30 (12.20 A. M.), not less than ten thousand people were assembled. The Troy band and the Piqua band played appropriate music, after which a delegation from the Methodist churches, under Rev. Granville (Colonel) Moody, sang a hymn.

At Gettysburg, O. (1.10 A. M.), large numbers of people were congregated together around huge bonfires. Drooping flags and other evidences of mourning were seen.

There were like scenes at Richmond Junction and Covington, just passed.

At Greenville, O. (1.36 A. M.), thirty-six young ladies dressed in white, slowly waving the star-spangled banner, greeted the cortege here. Lafayette's Requiem was sung with thrilling effect, by a number of ladies and gentlemen. About five hundred people were congregated on the platform. Company C, 28th Ohio Infantry, was drawn up in line, with fire arms reversed. The depot was tastefully decorated. On either side of the depot were two bonfires, fifteen feet high, which shed most brilliant light all around the train and depot.

At New Paris, O. (2.41 A. M.), great bonfires lit up the skies. A crowd was gathered about with uncovered heads. A beautiful arch of evergreens was formed above the track, under which the train passed. The arch was twenty feet high and thirty feet in circumference.

At Wiley's, New Madison, and Weaver's stations, mourners were congregated to pay respect to the passing dead.

Gov. Morton and suite met the train at Richmond, which was reached at 2 A. M. All the bells of this city rang out their solemn tones to awaken the citizens, and warn them to repair to the depot. Red, white, and blue lamps were suspended from the depot, and the arch spanning the track was lighted with the national colors.

At Cambridge (3.50 A. M.), the bells were tolling and guns firing; thousands of people at the depot. The train passed under an arch, trimmed with evergreens and surmounted by a female figure representing the Goddess of Liberty.

At Dublin, Ind. (April 30), an arch 30 feet high dotted with small Union flags. This place gave Abraham Lincoln its entire vote at the last Presidential election, and nearly 20,000 persons were assembled.

At Louisville, Ind. (April 30), the depot was handsomely trimmed. The people were assembled in large numbers.

At Indianapolis (6 A. M.), all the avenues leading to the depot were closely packed with people. At seven o'clock the funeral train arrived. The military had been drawn up extending from Illinois and Washington streets to the State House door. The corpse was taken charge of by the local guard of soldiers under Col. Symonson, through the open ranks of the soldiers standing at present-arms. The procession took up the line of march to the State House in the falling rain, amid the sound of bells and firing of cannon.

The hearse conveying the remains was 14 feet long, 6 feet wide, and 23 feet high, covered with black velvet. The roof of the car bore 12 white plumes trimmed with black, and on the loops was a beautiful eagle of silver gilt. The panels were studded with large silver stars. The car was drawn by eight white horses. Six of these horses were attached to the carriage in which, four years before, Abraham Lincoln rode through Indianapolis, when on his way to Washington to be inaugurated. In all the intersecting streets were triple arches adorned with evergreens and national flags, arranged in the most tasteful and beautiful manner.

During the performance of a funeral dirge, the tolling of bells and booming of cannon, the coffin was carried to the interior of the State House, and soon after exposed to public view. The Sabbath School children were first admitted, and then ladies and citizens severally passed through the hall from north to south. It was designed to have a grand military and civic procession, with an address by Governor Morton and other exercises, but rain prevented the arrangement. The remains were escorted to the cars at midnight.

OBSEQUIES AT CHICAGO.

At Chicago, May 1, thousands upon thousands of people were congregated at Park Place and its vicinity. From the house-tops, piazzas, windows, steps, and doorways, very many spectators were watching with intense interest the preliminaries of the procession and the surrounding scene.   Minute-guns and the tolling and chiming of bells announced the arrival of the President's remains.   The great multitude stood in profound silence and reverence, and uncovered their heads as the coffin was borne to a tastefully constructed funeral car, between the open ranks of the several officers and civil escort from Washington.   It was carried under the grand arch which extends across Park Place.   The arch was of triple Gothic form, in length spanning a distance of fifty-one feet, and having a depth of sixteen feet.   The height from the ground to the center of the middle or main arch was thirty feet, with a width of twenty-four feet, the side arches being each eight feet wide and twenty feet in height.   The total height of the centre arch and pinnacles was about forty feet.   Each of the arches, all presenting their front elevations towards Michigan Avenue and the lake, was supported by a cluster of hexagonal columns resting on a single base, forming four sets of columns on each front.   The interstices between these columns were fitted up as Gothic windows, and beautifully draped as such in black and white, adding a solemn effect to the general appearance.   At the centre of each arch on the top of the columns of both fronts were large and imposing American shields, from which draped our national ensign, hanging in graceful festoons.   From these flags the mourning drapery entwined about the different portions of the arches, up to the pinnacle in the centre.   The lower portion of the arches was also heavily draped in black and white, beautifully arranged.   Fifty flags in all formed the drapery and surmounted the arches.   On each pediment of the main and centre arches was placed a bust of the lamented dead, and upon each main front, resting upon the pinnacle above the busts, was seen a magnificent eagle.   Underneath the eagle, and above the busts, the drapery took the form of the sun's rays, as if they still hung upon the corpse.

The procession escorting the honored remains, was preceded by a band of music, followed by Major-Generals Hooker and Alfred Sully, and Brig.-Generals Buford and Swett, together with their respective staffs, music, the 8th and 15th Regiments of the veteran Reserve Corps, and the 6th Regiment of United States volunteers.   Then came the funeral-car with the following named gentlemen as pallbearers: Hons. Lyman Trumbull, John Wentworth, F. C. Sherman, E. C. Larned, F. A. Hoffman, J. R. Jones, Thomas Drummond, Wm. Bross, J. B. Rice, S. W. Fuller, T. B. Ryan, J. Y. Scammon. These gentlemen were equally divided on each side of the funeral-car. The guard of honor was mounted as follows: Major-General Hunter, Brevet Major-General Barnard, Brig.-General Ramsey, Brig.-General Caldwell, Brig.-General Eaton, Captain Taylor, U. S. N., Rear Admiral Davis, General McCallum, Brigadier-General Howe, Brig.-General Townsend, Brig.-General Ekin, Major Field, U. S. M. C., Captain Charles Penrose, Commissary, relatives and family friends in carriages, N. W. Edwards, C. M. Smith, Rev. Dr. Gurley, Judge David Davis and son, ten clergymen, the Illinois delegation, the Illinois escort from Washington, consisting of Gov. Oglesby, Jesse K. Dubois, S. M. Cullom, D. L. Phillips, Gen. Haynie, O. M. Hatch, F. E. Leonard and S. H. Melvin, with Col. Brown, of Chicago, as marshal; the Congressional delegation, Sergeant-at-arms Brown, of the U. S. Senate, and N. G. Ordway, Sergeant-at-arms of the U. S. House of Representatives, together with members of the press who accompanied the remains from Washington, the citizens' committee of one hundred, the Mayor and Common Council, judges of the courts and members of the bar, the reverend clergy, officers of the army and navy now in the service or honorably discharged, in full uniform, and bands of music were in various parts of the imposing line.

The second, third, fourth, and fifth divisions comprised among others, Tyler's and Ellsworth's Zouaves, children of the public schools, mounted artillery men, two batteries of Illinois light artillery and several regiments of State infantry, Masons and Odd Fellows, and all other associations and societies, professional, benevolent, and trade. Not a few colored citizens took part in these funeral honors. In the procession was a full regiment of infantry composed of men formerly in the rebel service, and who, taking the oath of allegiance, were recruited at the several prison camps.

The remains of the President were conveyed to the rotunda of the Court House, where they were laid in state. Around the crowning pillars of the rotunda were alternate diagonal wreaths of black and white cambric.

From the entire ceiling drooped festooned rays of black and white muslin. Directly over each of the four chandeliers on the west side of the hall were the words:

"We mourn liberty's great martyr."

and on the east side,

"The altar of freedom has borne no nobler sacrifice."

The walls were draped in black and ornamented with wreaths of white flowers.

Directly beneath the dome was the catafalque. The dais was about three feet in height, and contained an inclined plane as a centre platform. Four upright pillars supported a canopy through which the light of thirty-six stars radiated to the coffin and its surroundings. The roof of the canopy was of ogive form, covered with black velvit, festooned with white silk and silver fringe, and studded with silver stars.

At the head of the coffin stood a velvet pedestal festooned with silver fringe. Surmounting the pedestal was a marble eagle, around which were clustered six flags. On each side of the pedestal rested an Etruscan vase, filled with natural flowers. The sides of the dais incline upward, and were covered with black velvet and festooned with silver stars. The dais was covered with flowers.

The cornice of the canopy was surmounted by eight black plumes. Festoons of white silk were displayed between the plumes, and below the cornice were ornaments of black festoons, silver fringe and tassels. The lamberkin formed the arch between the columns on all sides. The outside was of black velvet, and the inside of white silk.

The entire lamberkin was decorated with silver fringe and stars. The cornice was festooned with white silk, which rested against the lamberkin, making a deep contrast. The columns were draped in white silk. A raised pedestal was placed at the head of the dais, upon which stands the guard of honor.

The Court House opened at six o'clock and remained open the next day. Here, as elsewhere, thousands crowded to view the great President. Meanwhile mournful music added to the solemnity of the occasion.

Every train which entered the city brought hundreds of people from the neighboring cities and towns. Among these were large delegations from Waukegan, Kenosha, Milwaukee, and other cities in Wisconsin. The number of people in the city at the time the procession moved, could not have been less than two hundred and fifty thousand.

At night the coffin was closed and strewn with fresh flowers placed there by virgin hands; the coffin with chant and torch-light was borne to the depot.

Taken all in all, Chicago made a deeper impression upon those who had been with the funeral from the first than any one of the ten cities passed through before had done. It was to be expected that such would be the case, yet, seeing how other cities had honored the funeral, there seemed to be no room for more, and the Eastern members of the *cortège* could not repress surprise when they saw how Chicago and the North-West came, with one accord, with tears and with offer-ings, to help to bury "this Duncan" who had "been so clear in his great office."

Hon. Schuyler Colfax spoke twice—once at Bryan Hall, and in the evening at the second Baptist Church; at the same time Dr. Patten was addressing a crowded audience at Cros-by's Opera House, and Dr. Ryder at St. Paul's Church.

Chicago seemed never to tire hearing the eulogy of Abraham Lincoln.

As the train passed Bridgeport, Summit, Lennox, Joliet, El-wood, Wilmington, Dwight, Lexington, Bloomington, minute-guns fired, and the darkness of night was broken by bonfires and torchlight, revealing arches and funeral decorations.

At Lincoln, a place named after the President, and in the origin of which he had a direct interest, the depot was draped and a funeral arch spanned the road. As the train passed a choir of ladies in white and black raised a chant of sorrow.

VII.

THE RITES AT SPRINGFIELD.

VII.

THE RITES AT SPRINGFIELD.

At last, on the 3d of May, the funeral train, after travelling by a circuitous route about seventeen hundred miles, reached Springfield, the home of the fallen President, where he had been so long personally known and admired.

The remains were received at the Chicago, Alton, and St. Louis Station. A procession formed in the following order:—Brig.-General Cook and staff; military escort; Major-General Hooker and staff; the guard of honor; relatives and friends in carriages; the Illinois delegation from Washington; Senators and Representatives of the Congress of the United States, including their Sergeant-at arms and Speaker Colfax; the Illinois State Legislature; the Governors of different States; delegations from Kentucky; the Chicago Committee of Reception; the Springfield Committee of Reception; the judges of the different courts; the reverend clergy; officers of the army and navy; firemen of the city; citizens generally; colored citizens, etc.

The hearse which carried the coffin was splendidly adorned, and drawn by six black horses. The procession moved through Jefferson, Fifth, Monroe, and Sixth streets, the houses on which all being deeply draped, with appropriate mottoes, and in many cases the portrait of their great townsman.

On reaching the State House the coffin was borne with the usual ceremonies through the north entrance into the Hall of Representatives, a semi-circular colonade of eleven Corinthian columns, supporting a half dome, the straight side being toward the west. At the apex of the dome is a rising sun. On the

15

floor a dais was erected, ascended by three steps. On the dais a hexagon canopy, supported on columns twelve feet high, the shaft covered with black velvet; the capitals wrought in white velvet, with silver bands, and filled the canopy, tent-shaped, rising seven feet in the centre, covered with heavy black broadcloth in radiating slack folds, surmounted at the apex and at each angle with black plumes having white centres. A draped eagle was perched on the middle of each crown mould. The cornice was of Egyptian pattern, corresponding with the capitals covered with black velvet; the bands and mouldings were of silver; the lining of the canopy was white crape in radiating folds over blue, thickly set with stars of silver, and terminating at the cornice in a band of black velvet with silver fillets. Between the columns was a rich valance in folds, with heavy silver fringe, from under which depended velvet curtains extending from each column two-thirds of the distance from the capitals to the centre of the cornice, looped with silver bands. Twelve brilliant jets of gas, burning in ground globes, sprang from the columns, and lighted the interior.

The catafalque was covered with black velvet, trimmed with silver and satin, and adorned with thirty-six burnished silver stars, twelve at the head and twelve on each side, and was built after drawings made by Colonel Schwartz. The floor of the dais was covered with evergreens and white flowers. The steps of the dais were spread with broadcloth banded with silver lace.

The columns of the room were hung with black crape, and the capitals festooned and entwined with the same. The cornice was appropriately draped, and, in large antique letters, on a black ground, were the words of President Lincoln at Independence Hall, Philadelphia, Feb. 22, 1861 : " Sooner than surrender these principles, I would be assassinated on the spot." In front of the gallery were black panels nine feet by two and a half, having silver bands and centres of crossed olive-branches; above the gallery looped curtains of black crape, extending around the semi-circle ; below the gallery white crape curtains overhung with black crape festoons. Each column was ornamented with a beautiful wreath of evergreens and white flowers. On the top of the gallery, extending the entire length was a festoon of evergreens. The Corinthian cornice was festooned on the west at each side, twenty-four feet forward the centre, supported by pilasters of the same order, the space between being surmounted by an arch. At the extreme height, in the upper portion, was placed a blue semi-circle field, sixteen feet across, studded with thirty-six stars, six inches in diameter, and from which radiated the thirteen stripes on the American flag in delicate crape, two feet wide at the circumference of the blue field, increasing to the extreme lower angle, breaking on the dais below and the pilasters on either side, the whole crowned with blue and black crape, and so disposed as to correspond with the blue field, the stars and radiated panels of the ceiling. The central red stripe fell opposite the opening in the curtains at the head of the catafalque. On the cornice, each side of the flag work, were placed two mottoes, corresponding with that on the semicircular frieze, forming together these words: "Washington, the Father, and Lincoln, the Saviour." A life-sized portrait of Washington, the frame draped in blue crape, stood at the head of the dais.

Here, as elsewhere, the citizens of the place, with thousands who came pouring in by every mode of conveyance, sought to gaze on the face of the corpse. All night long the streets of the handsome and generally quiet city, resounded with the tramp of feet. It was estimated that more than seventy-five thousand passed into the hall.

During the morning minute-guns were fired by Battery K, Missouri light artillery. About ten o'clock the coffin was closed forever. Meanwhile a choir of two hundred and fifty voices, and Lebrun's band from St. Louis, sang Pacsello's, "Peace, Troubled Soul," and as the coffin was borne out, Pleyel's Hymn, "Children of the Heavenly King."

After the remains had been placed in the hearse, the procession moved to Oak Ridge Cemetery, under the immediate command of Major-General Joseph Hooker, Marshal-in-Chief. It consisted of eight divisions, three of which preceded the hearse, with its group of eminent men, and included the 24th Michigan, 146th Illinois, 46th Wisconsin, and other veterans of the war. The municipal authorities, sanitary commission, the professions, Masons, Odd Fellows, firemen and citizens, closed the line.

On the arrival of the procession at the Cemetery, the remains were placed in the tomb, after which the choir sang the "Dead march in Saul"—" Unveil thy bosom."

Rev. Albert Hale then delivered an eloquent and appropriate prayer.

At the conclusion of the prayer, the choir sang a dirge, composed for the occasion; music by George F. Root, words by L. M. Dawes. It was sung with much feeling and effect.

FAREWELL FATHER, FRIEND AND GUARDIAN.

All our land is draped in mourning,
  Hearts are bowed and strong men weep ·
For our loved, our noble leader,
  Sleeps his last his dreamless sleep—
Gone forever, gone forever,
  Fallen by a traitor's hand ;
Though preserved his dearest treasure,
  Our redeemed beloved land.
        Rest in peace.

Through our night of bloody struggle
  Ever dauntless, firm and true,
Bravely, gently forth he led us,
  Till the morn burst on our view—
Till he saw the day of triumph,
  Saw the field our heroes won ;
Then his honored life was ended,
  Then his glorious work was done.
        Rest in peace.

When from mountain, hill and valley,
  To their homes our brave boys come,
When with welcome notes we greet them ;
  Song and cheer, and pealing drum ;
When we miss our loved ones fallen,
  When to weep we turn aside ;
Then for him our tears shall mingle,
  He has suffered—he has died.
        Rest in peace.

Honor'd leader, long and fondly
  Shall thy mem'ry cherished be ;
Hearts shall bless thee for their freedom,
  Hearts unborn shall sigh for thee ;
He who gave thee might and wisdom,
  Gave thy spirit sweet release ;
Farewell, father, friend and guardian,
  Rest forever, rest in peace.
        Rest in peace.

A portion of Scripture was then read by Rev. N. W. Miner, after which the choir sang "To Thee, O Lord," from the Oratorio of St. Paul.

The President's last Inaugural was read by Rev. A. C. Hubbard.

After the reading of the Inaugural, the choir sang the dirge, "As when thy Cross was Bleeding," by Otto.

At the conclusion of the singing, Bishop Simpson delivered the following

FUNERAL ORATION.

Fellow-citizens of Illinois, and of many parts of our entire Union—Near the capital of this large and growing State, in the midst of this beautiful grove, and at the mouth of this vault which has just received the remains of our fallen chieftain, we gather to pay a tribute of respect, and to drop the tear of sorrow around the ashes of the mighty dead.

A little more than four years ago, from his plain and quiet home in yonder city, he started, receiving the parting words of the concourse of friends who gathered around him ; and in the midst of the dropping of the gentle shower, he told of the pangs of parting from the place where his children had been born and his home had been made pleasant by early recollections; and as he left he made an earnest request, in the hearing of some who are present at this hour, that as he was about to enter upon responsibilities which he believed to be greater than any which had fallen upon any man since the days of Washington, that the people would offer up prayers that God would aid and sustain him in the work which they had given him to do.

His company left your quiet city, but as it went snares were in waiting for the Chief Magistrate. Scarcely did he escape the dangers of the way or the hands of the assassin, as he neared Washington, and I believe he escaped only through the vigilance of officers and the prayers of his people. So that the blow was suspended for more than four years, which was at last permitted through the providence of God to fall. How different the occasion which witnessed his departure from that which witnessed his return! Doubtless he expected to visit you all again, doubtless you expected to take him by the hand, and to feel the warm grasp which you had felt in other days, and to see the tall form walking among you, which you had delighted to honor in years past. But he was never permitted to return until he came with lips mute and silent, the frame encoffined, and a weeping nation following as his mourners. Such a scene as his return to you was never witnessed among the events of history. There have been great processions of mourners. There was one for the patriarch Jacob, which came up from Egypt, and the Egyptians wondered at the evidences of reverence and filial affection which came up from the hearts of the Israelites.

There was mourning when Moses fell upon the heights of Pisgah, and was hid from human view. There has been mourning in the kingdoms of the earth, when kings and princes have fallen; but never was there in the history of man such mourning as that which has accompanied this funeral procession, and has gathered around the mortal remains of him who was our loved one, and who now sleepeth among us.

If we glance at the procession which followed him, we see how the nation stood aghast, tears filled the eyes of many sunburnt faces—strong men, as they clasped the hands of their friends, were unable to find vent for their grief in words. Women and little children caught up the tidings as they ran through the land, and were melted into tears. The nation stood still. Men left their plows in the fields, and asked what the end should be. The hum of manufactories ceased, and the sound of the hammer was not heard; busy merchants closed their doors, and in the exchange gold passed no more from hand to hand. Though three weeks have passed, the nation has scarcely breathed easily yet. A mournful silence is abroad upon the land. Nor is this mourning confined to any one class or to any district of country. Men of all political parties and of all religious creeds have united in paying this mournful tribute. The Archbishop of the Roman Catholic Church in New York and a Protestant minister walked side by side in the sad procession, and a Jewish Rabbi performed a part of the solemn services. Here are gathered around his tomb the representatives of the army and navy, senators, judges, governors, and officers of all the branches of the Government.

Here, too, are members of civic professions, with men and women, from the humblest as well as the highest occupations. Here and there, too, are tears as sincere and warm as any that drop, which come from the eyes of those whose kindred and whose race have been freed from their chains by him whom they mourn as their deliverer.

Far more eyes have gazed upon the face of the departed than ever looked upon the face of any other departed man. More eyes have looked upon the procession for sixteen hundred miles or more, by night and by day, by sunlight, dawn, twilight, and by torchlight, than ever before watched the progress of a procession.

We ask, why this wonderful mourning—this great procession? I answer, first: A part of the interest has arisen from the times in which we live and in which he that had fallen was a principal actor. It is a principle of our nature that feelings once excited pass readily from the object by which they are excited to some other object which may for the time being take possession of the mind.

Another principle is, that the deepest affections of our hearts gather around some human form, in which are incarnated the living thoughts and ideas of the passing age. If we look, then, at the times we see an age of excitement. For four years the popular heart has been stirred to its utmost depths. War had come upon us, dividing families, separating nearest and dearest friends. A war, the extent and magnitude of which no one could estimate ; a war in which the blood of brethren was shed by a brother's hand. A call was made by this voice, now hushed, and all over this land, from hill and mountain, from plain and prairie, there sprang up hundreds of thousands of bold hearts, ready to go forth and save our National Union. This feeling of excitement was transferred next into a feeling of deep grief, because of the danger in which our country was placed. Many said, is it possible to save the nation? Some in our country, and nearly all the leading men in other countries, declared it to be impossible to maintain the Union, and many an honest and patriotic heart was deeply pained with apprehensions of common ruin, and many in grief and almost in despair anxiously inquired what shall the end of these things be? In addition to this, wives had given their husbands, mothers their sons —the pride and joy of their hearts. They saw them put on the uniform. They saw them take the martial step, and they tried to hide their deep feeling of sadness. Many of these dear ones sleep upon the battle-field never to return again, and there was mourning in every mansion and every cabin of our land. Then came a feeling of deeper sadness as the story came of prisoners tortured to death, or starved through the mandates of those who are called the representatives of the chivalry, or who claim to be the honorable ones of the earth, and as we read the stories of frames attenuated and reduced to mere skeletons, our grief turned partly into horror, and partly into a cry for vengeance.

Then this feeling was changed to one of joy. There came signs of the end of this rebellion. We followed the career of our glorious Generals ; we saw our armies under the command of the brave officer who is guiding this procession, climb up the heights of Lookout Mountain, and drive the rebels from their strongholds. Another brave general swept through Georgia, South and North Carolina, and drove the combined armies of the rebels before him, while the honored Lieutenant-General held Lee and his hosts in a death grasp. Then the tidings came that Richmond was evacuated and that Lee had surrendered. The bells rang merrily all over the land ; booming of cannon was heard ; illuminations and torch-light processions manifested the general joy, and families were looking for the speedy return of their loved ones from the field of battle. Just in the midst of this wildest joy, in one hour, nay, in one moment, the tidings thrilled through our land that Abraham Lincoln, the best of Presidents, had perished by the hand of an assassin, and then all that feeling which had been gathering for four year in forms of grief, horror, and joy, turned in an instant into one wail of woe—a sadness inexpressible, an anguish unutterable.

But it is not the times merely which cause this mourning. The mode of his death must be taken into account. Had he died on a bed of illness, with kind friends around him ; had the sweat of death been wiped from his brow by gentle hands while he was yet conscious ; could he have lived to speak words of affection to his stricken widow, or words of counsel to us, like those we heard in his parting address—that inaugural which shall now be immortal, how it would have softened or assuaged something of the grief. There might at least have been preparation for the event. But no moment of warning was given to him or to us. He was stricken down, too, when his hopes for the end of the rebellion were bright, and the prospects of a joyous life were before him. There was a Cabinet meeting that day, said to have been the most cheerful and happy of any held since the beginning of the rebellion.

After this meeting he talked with his wife—spoke of the four years of tempest—of the storm being over, and of the four years of pleasure and joy now awaiting him, as the weight of care and anguish would be taken from his mind, and he could have happy days with his family again. In the midst of these anticipations he left his home never to return alive. The evening was Good Friday— the saddest day in the whole calendar for the Christian church— henceforth in this country to be made sadder, if possible, by the memory of our nation's loss. And so filled with grief was every Christian heart that even all the joyous hopes of Easter Sunday failed to remove the crushing sorrow under which the true worshipers bowed in the house of God.

But the great cause of this mourning is to be found in the man himself. Mr. Lincoln was no ordinary man, and I believe the conviction has been growing on the nation's mind, as it certainly has been on my own, especially in the last years of his administration. By the hand of God he was especially singled out to guide our government in these troublous times, and it seems to me that the hand of God may be traced in many events connected with his history.

First, then, I recognize this in his physical education, which he received, and which prepared him for enduring herculean labors. In the toils of his boyhood and the labors of his manhood, God was giving him an iron frame. Next to this was his identification with the heart of the great people, understanding their feelings because he was one of them, and connected with them in their movements and life. His education was simple. A few months spent in the school-house gave him the elements of education. He read few books but mastered all. He read Bunyan's Pilgrim's Progress, Æsop's Fables, and the life of Washington, which were his favorites. In these we recognize the works which gave the bias to his character, and which partly moulded his style.

His early life with its varied struggles, joined him indissolubly to the working masses, and no elevation in society diminished his respect for the sons of toil. He knew what it was to fell the tall trees of the forest, and to stem the current of the broad Mississippi. His home was in the glowing West—the heart of the republic—and invigorated by the winds that swept over its prairies, he learned lessons of self-reliance that sustained him in scenes of adversity.

His genius was soon recognized, as true genius always will be, and he was placed in the Legislature of his State. Already acquainted with the principles of law, he devoted his thoughts to matters of public interest, and began to be looked upon as the "coming statesmen." As early as 1839 he presented resolutions to the Legislature, asking for emancipation in the District of Columbia, while, with but rare exceptions, the whole popular mind of his State was opposed to the measure. From that hour he was a steady and uniform friend of humanity, and was preparing for the conflict of later years.

If you ask me on what mental characteristic his greatness rested, I answer, on a quick and ready perception of facts—on a memory unusually tenacious and retentive, and on a logical turn of mind which followed sternly and unwaveringly every link in the chain of thought on any subject which he was called upon to investigate. I think there have been minds more broad in their character, more comprehensive in their sweep, but I doubt whether there has been a mind which could follow step by step with logical power the points which he desired to illustrate. He gained this power by the close study of geometry, and by a determination to perceive the truth in all its relations and simplicity, and when perceived to utter it. It is said of him, that in childhood, when he had any difficulty in listening to a conversation to ascertain what people meant, when he retired to rest, he could not sleep until he tried to understand the precise point intended, and when understood to convey it in a clearer manner to others. Who, that has read his message fails to perceive the directness and the simplicity of his style, and this very trait which was scoffed at and derided by opponents, is now recognized as one of the strong points of that mighty mind, which has so powerfully influenced the destiny of this nation, and which shall for ages to come influence the destiny of humanity!

It was not however chiefly by his mental faculties that he gained such control over mankind. His moral power gave him pre-eminence. The convictions of men that Abraham Lincoln was an honest man, led them to yield to his guidance. As has been said of Cobden, whom he greatly resembled, he made all men feel a kind of sense of himself—a recognized individuality, a self-relying power. They saw in him a man whom they believed would do what was right regardless of all consequences. It was this moral feeling which gave him the greatest hold upon the people and made his utterances almost oracular.

When the nation was angered by the perfidy of foreign nations in allowing privateers to be fitted out, he uttered the significant expression, "one war at a time," and it stilled the national heart. When his own friends were divided as to what steps should be taken as to slavery, that simple utterance, "I will save the Union if I can with slavery, but if not, slavery must perish, for the Union must be saved," that became the rallying word. Men felt the struggle was for the Union, and all other questions must be subsidiary.

But after all, by the acts of a man shall his fame be perpetuated. Where are his acts? Much praise is due to the men who aided him. He called able councillors around him, and able generals into the field, men who have borne the sword as bravely as ever any human arm has done it. He had the aid of prayerful and thoughtful men everywhere, but under his own guiding hands the movements of our land have been conducted.

Turn towards the different departments. We had an unorganized militia, a mere skeleton army, yet under his care that army has been enlarged into a force, which for skill, intelligence, efficiency, and bravery, surpasses any which the world had ever seen. Before its veterans the fame of even the renowned veterans of Napoleon shall pale; and the mothers and sisters on these hillsides, and all over the land, shall take to their arms again, braver men than ever fought in European wars.

The reason is obvious. Money or a desire for fame collected those armies—or they were rallied to sustain favorite thrones or dynasties. But the armies called into being fought for liberty—for the Union, and for the right of self-government, and many of them feel that the battles they won were for humanity everywhere—and for all time—for I believe that God has not suffered this terrible rebellion to come upon our land merely for a chastisement to us or a lesson to our age.

There are moments which involve in themselves eternities. There are instants which seem to contain germs which shall develope and bloom forever. Such a moment came in the tide of time to our land when a question must be settled, affecting all the powers of the earth. The contest was for human freedom. Not for this republic merely. Nor for the Union simply, but to decide whether the people, as a people, in their entire majesty, were destined to be the government, or whether they were to be subject to tyrants or aristocrats, or to class-rule of any kind.

This is the great question for which we have been fighting, and its decision is at hand, and the result of this contest will affect the ages to come. If successful, republics will spread in spite of monarchs all over this earth. I turn from the army to the navy. What was it before the war commenced? Now we have our ships of war at home and abroad, to guard privateers in foreign sympathizing forts, as to care for every port of our own coast. They have taken ports that military men said could not be taken, and a brave admiral, for the first time in the world's history, lashed himself to the mast, there to remain as long as he had a particle of skill or strength to watch over his ship while it engaged in the perilous contest of taking the strong forts of the enemy.

Then again I turn to the Treasury Department. Where should the money come from? Wise men predicted ruin, but our national credit has been maintained, and our currency is safer to-day than it ever was before. Not only so, but through our national bonds, if properly used, we shall have a permanent basis for currency, and an investment so desirable for capitalists of other nations, that, under the law of trade, I believe the centre of exchange will be transferred from England to the United States.

But the great act of the mighty chieftain, on which his fame shall rest long after his frame shall moulder away, is that of giving freedom to a race. We have all been taught to revere the sacred

characters. We have thought of Moses, of his power, and the prominence he gave to the moral law; how it lasts, and how his name
towers high among the names in heaven, and how he delivered those
millions of his kindred out of bondage. And yet we may assert
that Abraham Lincoln, by his proclamation, liberated more enslaved
people than ever Moses set free, and those not of his kindred. God
has seldom given such a power or such an opportunity to man.
When other events shall have been forgotten; when this world shall
have become a network of Republics; when every throne shall be
swept from the face of the earth; when literature shall enlighten all
minds; when the claims of humanity shall be recognized everywhere,
this act shall be conspicuous on the pages of history. And we are
thankful that God gave to Abraham Lincoln the decision and wisdom and grace to issue that proclamation, which stands high above
all other papers which have been penned by uninspired men.

Abraham Lincoln was a good man. He was known as an honest,
temperate, forgiving man; a just man, a man of noble heart in every
way. As to his religious experience, I cannot speak definitely, because I was not privileged to know much of his private sentiments.
My acquaintance with him did not give me the opportunity to hear
him speak on those topics. This I know, however. He read the
Bible frequently—loved it for its great truths and profound teachings, and he tried to be guided by its precepts. He believed in
Christ the saviour of sinners, and I think he was sincerely trying
to bring his life into harmony with the great principles of revealed
religion. Certainly, if ever there was a man who illustrated some
of the principles of pure religion, that man was our departed President. Look over all his speeches, listen to his utterances, he never
spoke unkindly of any man. Even the rebels received no words of
anger from him, and the last days of his life illustrated in a remarkable manner his forgiving disposition. A dispatch was received
that afternoon that Thompson and Tucker were trying to escape
through Maine, and it was proposed to arrest them. Mr. Lincoln,
however, preferred to let them quietly escape. He was seeking to
save the very men who had been plotting his destruction, and this
morning we read a proclamation offering $25,000 for the arrest of
these men, as aiders and abettors of his assassination. So that in
his expiring acts he was saying—Father, forgive them; they know
not what they do. As a ruler, I doubt if any President has ever
showed such trust in God, or in public documents so frequently referred to Divine aid. Often did he remark to friends and delegations
that his hope for our success rested in his conviction that God would
bless our efforts, because we were trying to do right. To the ad-

dress of a large religious body, he replied, "Thanks be unto God, who in our national trials giveth us the churches." To a minister who said "he hoped the Lord was on our side," he replied "that it gave him no concern whether the Lord was on our side or not," for he added, "I know the Lord is always on the side of right;" and with deep feeling added, "But God is my witness that it is my constant anxiety and prayer that both myself and this nation should be on the Lord's side."

In his domestic life he was exceedingly kind and affectionate. He was a devoted husband and father. During his Presidential term he lost his second son, Willie. To an officer of the army he said not long since, "Do you ever find yourself talking with the dead," and added: "Since Willie's death, I catch myself every day involuntarily talking with him, as if he were with me." For his widow, who is unable to be here, I need only invoke the blessing of Almighty God that she be comforted and sustained. For his son, who has witnessed the exercises of this hour, all that I can desire is that the mantle of his father may fall upon him.

Let us pause a moment on the lesson of the hour before we part. This man, though he fell by the hand of the assassin, still fell under the permissive hand of God. He had some wise purpose in allowing him to fall.

What more could he have desired of life for himself? Were not his honors full? There was no office to which he could aspire. The popular heart clung around him as around no other man. The nations of the world had learned to honor our Chief Magistrate. If rumors of a desired alliance with England be true, Napoleon trembled when he heard of the fall of Richmond, and asked what nation would join him to protect him against our government. This had the guidance of such a man. His fame was full, his work was done, and he sealed his glory by being the nation's just martyr for liberty.

He had a strange presentiment, in early political life, that some day he would be President. You see it indicated in 1859, when of the slave power he said: "Broken by it, I, too, may be ; bow to it, I never will. The *probability* that we may fail in the struggle *ought not* to deter us from the support of a cause which I deem to be just; it *shall not* deter me. If ever I feel the soul within me elevate and expand to those dimensions not wholly unworthy of its Almighty Architect, it is when I contemplate the cause of my country, deserted by all the world besides, and I standing up boldly and alone, and hurling defiance at her victorious oppressors. Here, without contemplating consequences, before High Heaven, and in the face of the world, I swear eternal fidelity to the just cause, as I deem it, of the land of my life, my liberty, and my love.

And yet he recently said to more than one, "I never shall live out the four years of my term. When the rebellion is crushed my work is done." So it was. He lived to see the last battle fought and to dictate a dispatch from the home of Jefferson Davis—lived till the power of the rebellion was broken, and then, having done the work for which God sent him, angels, I trust, were sent to shield him from one moment of pain or suffering, and to bear him from this world to that high and glorious realm where the patriot and good shall live forever. His example teaches young men that every position of eminence is open before the diligent and the worthy. To the active men of the country his example urges to trust in God and do right.

To the ambitious there is this fearful lesson: Of the four candidates for Presidential honors in 1860, two of them, Douglas and Lincoln, once competitors—but now sleeping patriots—rest from their labors; Bell perished in poverty and misery, as a traitor might perish, and Breckinridge is a frighted fugitive, with the brand of traitor on his brow.

Standing, as we do to-day, by his coffin and his sepulchre, let us resolve to carry forward the work which he so nobly began. Let us do right to all men. Let us vow in the sight of Heaven to eradicate every vestige of human slavery, to give every human being his true position before God and man, to crush every form of rebellion, and to stand by the flag God has given us. How joyful should we be that it floated over parts of every State before Mr. Linoln's career was ended. How singular that to the fact of the assassin's heel being caught in the folds of the flag we are probably indebted for his capture. The flag and the traitor must ever be enemies.

Traitors will probably suffer by the change of rulers, for one of sterner mould, and one who himself has deeply suffered from the rebellion now wields the sword of justice.

Our country, too, is stronger for the trial. A republic was declared, by monarchists, too weak to endure a civil war, yet we have crushed the most gigantic rebellion in history, and have grown in strength and population every year of the struggle. We have passed through the ordeal of a popular election while swords and bayonets were in the field, and have come out unharmed. And now, in our hour of excitement, with a large minority having proffered another man for President, the bullet of the assassin has laid our President prostrate. Has there been a mutiny? Has any rival proposed his claim? Out of the army of nearly a million, no officer or soldier uttered one note of dissent, and in an hour or two after Mr. Lincoln's death, another, by constitutional power, occupied his chair. If the government moved forward without one single jar, the world will learn that republics are the strongest governments on earth.

And now, my friends, in the words of the departed, "with malice towards none," free from all feeling of personal vengeance, yet believing the sword must not be borne in vain, let us go forward in our painful duty. Let every man who was a Senator and Representative in Congress, and who aided in beginning this rebellion, and thus led to the slaughter of our sons and daughters, be brought to speedy and to certain punishment. Let every officer educated at public expense, and who, having been advanced to position, has perjured himself, and has turned his sword against the vitals of his country, be doomed to a felon's death. This, I believe, is the will of the American people. Men may attempt to compromise and to restore these traitors and murderers to society again, but the American people will rise in their majesty and sweep all such compromises and compromisers away, and shall declare that there shall be no peace to rebels.

But to the deluded masses we shall extend arms of forgiveness. We will take them to our hearts. We will walk with them side by side, as we go forward to work out a glorious destiny. The time will come when, in the beautiful words of him whose lips are now forever sealed, "the mystic cords of memory which stretch from every battlefield and from every patriot's grave shall yield a sweeter music when touched by the angels of our better nature."

The oration was listened to with the most marked attention, and at the conclusion "Over the Valley the Angels Smile," was sang.

At this stage of the proceeding Rev. Dr. P. D. Gurley arose and made a few remarks, and offered the closing prayer. The following hymn and doxology was then sung, and the service closed by benediction, by Rev. Dr. Gurley:

FUNERAL HYMN.

Rest, noble martyr! rest in peace;
Rest with the true and brave,
Who, like thee, fell in Freedom's cause,
The Nation's life to save.

Thy name shall live while time endures,
　　And men shall say of thee,
" He saved his country from its foes,
　　And bade the slave be free."

These deeds shall be thy monument,
　　Better than brass or stone ;
They leave thy fame in glory's light,
　　Unrivalled and alone.

This consecrated spot shall be
　　To Freedom ever dear ;
And Freedom's sons of every race
　　Shall weep and worship here.

O God ! before whom we, in tears,
　　Our fallen Chief deplore ;
Grant that the cause, for which he died,
　　May live forevermore.

DOXOLOGY.

To Father, Son, and Holy Ghost,
　　The God whom we adore,
Be glory as it was, is now,
　　And shall be evermore.

The troops and the fire department then formed into line and marched back to the city.

We have thus followed the remains of President Lincoln from Washington, the scene of his assassination, to Springfield, his former home, and now to be his final resting place. He had been absent from Springfield ever since he left it in February, 1861, for the national capital, to be inaugurated as President of the United States. We have seen him lying in state in the Executive mansion, where the obsequies were attended by numerous mourners, some of them clothed with the highest public honors and responsibilities which our republican institutions can bestow, and by the diplomatic representatives of foreign governments. We have followed the remains from Washington, through Baltimore, Harrisburg, Philadelphia, New York, Albany, Buffalo, Cleveland, Columbus, Indianapolis, and Chicago, to Springfield, a distance in circuit of 1500 or 1,800 miles. On the route five millions of people have appeared to manifest by every means of which they were capable their deep sense of the public loss, and their appreciation of the many virtues which adorned the life of Abraham Lincoln, and one million came in order and sorrow to gaze on his lifeless countenance. All classes, without distinction of politics, spontaneously united in the posthumous honors. All hearts seemed to beat as one at the bereavement; and now funeral processions are ended, our mournful duty of escorting the mortal remains of Abraham Lincoln to Springfield is performed. We have seen them laid in the tomb. The gratitude of his country will rear noble monuments to commemorate his virtues and his services: a more enduring monument is in the hearts of his countrymen.

16

VIII.

THE EFFECT IN EUROPE.

VIII.

EFFECT OF THE DEATH IN EUROPE.

In Europe, the fast crowding events in America had wound public attention to the highest point of tension. The triumph of Sherman, the fall of Richmond, the retreat and surrender of Lee, the complete paralyzation of Johnson, all came in rapid succession. The sudden blow of the murder of Lincoln was as terrible as it was unexpected. The public at large, the press, the civic bodies, the House of Commons, nay, even the House of Lords, and the Queen, all hastened to express their grief, horror, and sympathy.

The London Times says :—

" The intelligence of the assassination of President Lincoln and of the attempt to assassinate Mr. Seward, caused a most extraordinary sensation in the city on Wednesday. Towards noon the news became known, and it spread rapidly from mouth to mouth in all directions. At first, many were incredulous as to the truth of the rumor, and some believed it to have been set afloat for purposes in connection with the stock exchange. The house of Peabody & Co., American bankers, in Broad street, had received early intelligence of the assassination, and from there the news was carried to the Bank of England, whence it quickly radiated in a thousand directions. Meanwhile it was being wafted far and wide by the second editions of the morning papers, and was supplemented later in the day by the publication of additional particulars. Shortly after twelve o'clock it was communicated to the Lord Mayor while he was sitting in the justice-room of the Mansion House, and about the same time the 'star-spangled banner' was hoisted half-mast high over the American consulate, at the corner of Grace-church street. The same flag had but a few days before floated in triumph from the same place on the entry of the Federals into Richmond, and still later on the surrender of Gen. Lee. Between one and two o'clock the third edition of the Times, con-

taining a circumstantial narrative of the affair, made its appearance
in the city, and became immediately in extraordinary demand. A
newsvender in the Royal Exchange was selling it at half-a-crown
a copy, and by half past three o'clock it could not be had for
money. The excitement caused by the intelligence was everywhere manifest, and in the streets, on the rail, on the river, in the
law courts, the terrible event was the theme of conversation. The
revival of the event of the Roadhill murder, which in the earlier
part of the day had created a profound sensation, sank into insignificance in comparison with the interest and astonishment excited
by the news of the tragedy at Washington. A photographer in
Cornhill, 'taking time by the forelock,' exhibited cartes of the
deceased President in his window, inscribed ' the late Mr. Lincoln,'
accompanied by an account of the assassination cut from the
second edition of a contemporary. Throughout the remainder of
the day, the evening papers were sold in unexampled numbers, and
often at double and treble the ordinary price, all evincing the universal interest felt at the astounding intelligence. On the receipt
of the melancholy intelligence in the House of Commons, about
sixty members of all parties immediately assembled, and signed
the following address of sympathy to the American Minister:

" 'We, the undersigned, members of the British House of Commons, have learnt with the deepest horror and regret, that the
President of the United States of America has been deprived of
life by an act of violence, and we desire to express our sympathy
on the sad event with the American Minister, now in London, as
well as to declare our hope and confidence in the future of that
great country, which we trust will continue to be associated with
enlightened freedom and peaceful relations with this and every
other country.

" 'LONDON, April 29, 1865.' "

On Saturday evening, the 29th of April, an immense public
meeting convened, under the auspices of the Emancipation Society,
in St. James's Hall, to express feelings of grief and horror at the
assassination of President Lincoln, and sympathy with the government and people of the United States, and with Mrs. Lincoln, Mr.
Seward and family. The galleries of the hall were draped in black.
Over the end of the gallery hung the American flag. The hall was
crowded with an audience who manifested not merely their warm
admiration of the character and capacity of the late President, and
sincere sympathy with the people of the United States in the loss

sustained, but their hearty approval of the great cause Mr. Lincoln represented.

The platform contained an array of Parliamentary gentlemen, and many leading citizens of the metropolis. Many ladies were present, a majority of whom were in mourning.

Various resolutions were carried, not merely with unanimity, but with an intense feeling rarely seen at public meetings.

The chair was occupied by William Evans, President of the Emancipation Society. Messrs. Forster, Stansfield, Leathern, Taylor, Potter, Baxter, and Baines, members of Parliament, commenced the proceedings with expressions of deep sympathy with the American Government and people, and entire confidence in the Administration of President Johnson.

The Chairman was supported by twenty influential members of Parliament, and a large array of distinguished Presidents, representing every section of the community.

Letters of sympathy were received from Sir Charles Lyell, Lord Houlton, and others.

W. E. Forster, member of Parliament, moved the first resolution, that this meeting desires to give utterance to the feelings of grief and horror with which it has heard of the assassination of President Lincoln and the murderous attack on Mr. Seward, and to convey to Mrs. Lincoln, and the United States Government and the people, the expression of its profound sympathy and heartfelt condolence.

Mr. Forster said this was the time when the tie of blood binding Englishmen to Americans was indeed truly felt. A thrill of grief, horror, and indignation, which has passed through the length and breadth of Europe, and especially possesses the heart of every Englishman as though some painful calamity had fallen on himself. This meeting would send by the ship which left their shores that night, its sympathy with the widows and orphans and country, who had not lost their faith for the future. He was confident in the belief that they had so learnt the lesson of common history that they would prove what strength free and Christian people have to bear up against every blow like this, though it be such a blow as had rarely ever fallen upon any commonwealth. He expressed his convictions that President Johnson would continue President Lincoln's work of restoring peace to the country, and insuring freedom to all who dwell in it.

P. A. Taylor, M.P., seconded the resolution. He expressed deep sympathy with the American nation, which had lost a worthy successor of Washington. Lincoln's great task had been fulfilled.

He had crushed the rebellion of the slaveholder. Time, the destroyer, had not withered one leaf in the chaplet of his glory. He had no fear that the Government of the United States would fall into the career of revengeful retribution. He asked the audience to remember that for years portions of the press and people had heaped every epithet of abuse upon Lincoln, and were now trying to do the same thing by Johnson. He felt confident that the efforts of the new government would be continued in the same direction as Lincoln's, and that it would soon effect the complete restoration of the Union with the complete emancipation of the negro. Lincoln died for that principle, but his death was not the symbol of its defeat, but of its glorious triumph!

Mr. Leathern, M.P., brother-in-law of Mr. Bright, concurred in the hearty tribute paid to the character and services of President Lincoln. They had seen America pass triumphantly through gigantic perils, and they confidently expected that she would come out with equal fortitude and equal dignity from what was perhaps the last and greatest of her triumphs.

Mr. Stansfield, M.P., moved the next resolution, viz:

That this meeting desires to express its entire confidence in the determination and power of the people and Government of the United States to carry out to the fullest extent the policy of which Abraham Lincoln's Presidential career was the embodiment, and establish free institutions throughout the whole American population.

Mr. Stansfield said they had met not only to give an expression of their horror at a deed so foul that history could produce no parallel, but to show our sympathy for a cause which begins by being honorable and great to be righteous, and which by the acts and by the life and death of its Martyr President had now become sacred in their eyes. The South had been fighting for the avowed and deliberate purpose of promoting and perpetuating human slavery. It attempted to found its subsistence upon a national crime, and had met the deserved fate of those who set themselves against the laws of God and man. The North had been fighting for a common country, which they would share, but which they would not allow to be torn asunder. Step by step the North rose to the height of the great and holy argument on which their cause was founded. Each delay, each defeat, seemed but to make their resolve firmer, and higher and purer their policy. When the South finally abolished slavery throughout its States, then victory would finally crown their cause. Throughout all this period, Lincoln guided his country with honor. If anything could strengthen the States in their trial, it would be the deepfelt, spontaneous, and universal sympathy which was now travelling to them from Europe. He was sure all prayed that the government and people might be true to the example of him who was the guide of their cause.

Mr. J. B. Potter, M.P., seconded the motion. He said he now stood in Parliament as successor of Richard Cobden, whose object it was, equally with that of Lincoln, to dignify labor. Lincoln destroyed slavery in America. It should be their wish to destroy serfdom at home. And he trusted the result of the conflict in America would be to give an impetus to the cause of reform in Europe.

Mr. Baxter, M.P., supported the resolution. He expressed hearty concurrence with the eloquent tributes paid to the memory of President Lincoln. All the events of the last four years dwindled into insignificance before the issues involved in the great contest in America. Not only was the great question of slavery involved in the contest, but the question of constitutional government all through the world. He did not believe a great cause depended on a single life, and felt confident that the American people would hurry to a triumphant issue the policy and principles of Abraham Lincoln.

Hon. Lyneph Stanley, second son of Lord Stanley of Aldersley, a member of the cabinet, expressed his admiration for the character of Mr. Lincoln.

Professor Fawcett also supported the resolutions.

Mr. Shaw Lefevre, M.P., said the men who elected Lincoln could not be wrong in the choice of Johnson.

Mr. Caird, M.P., moved that copies of the foregoing resolutions be placed in the hands of Mr. Adams for transmission to the President of the United States, Mrs. Lincoln, and Mr. Seward. He paid a warm compliment to the American Minister, whose moderation and firmness and conciliation had been the best preservation of peace between the two countries. The resolutions were supported by Greefell, Curren, and Ewing, members of Parliament, and Rev. Newman Hall and Mason Jones.

Cyrus W. Field, who was called for, and received with great applause, thanked the chairman and the meeting on behalf of the American people, for their deep sympathy with the thirty millions on the other side of the Atlantic, who were mourning for the death of Abraham Lincoln.

The scene on the Liverpool Exchange was such as will not be forgotten for a long time. At half-past eleven it was announced that Mr. Younghusband, the secretary and treasurer of the Liverpool Exchange News Rooms, was in possession of the news. A terrible rush took place from the 'flags' into the news-room; and after a few minutes it was announced that Mr. Younghusband would read aloud the dispatch from the bar of the news-room. All was now silent; the passage wherein it was stated that President Lincoln had been shot at caused no great dismay; but when the master of the rooms read, 'The President never rallied, and died this morning,' there was a general expression of horror. Certainly there was one dissentient voice, who had the temerity to exclaim 'Hurrah!' His presence in the news-room was of short duration, for, being seized by the collar by as good a Southerner as there is in Liverpool, he was summarily ejected from the room, the gentleman who first seized him exclaiming, 'Be off, you incarnate fiend! you are an assassin at heart.' In the course of the afternoon the flags on the American Consul's house and the Exchange buildings were placed at half-mast; and a deputation, irrespective of American party feelings, proceeded to the Town Hall, in order to consult with the mayor as to the desirability of holding a public meeting for the purpose of sending out an address of condolence to the people of the United States. The mayor being absent, no definite arrangement was arrived at, but the deputy mayor gave orders that the Town Hall flag should be at once hoisted half-mast. The American ships in the river and in the docks, as soon as the news was known, hoisted 'half-high' flags, and in many instances the Union Jack and the Stars and Stripes were bound together with crape or black cloth. The President of the Southern Club convened a meeting of all the members, for the purpose of ascertaining whether it was desirable to take any official action upon the event. The members of the club were unanimous in their expression of abhorrence and reprobation of the foul deed.

On the afternoon of the 27th, a meeting of the merchants was held at St. George's Hall. The Mayor presided; and he and several leading merchants made speeches denouncing the crime and expressing sympathy with the people of the United States in strong terms. A resolution, expressing sorrow and indignation, regardless of all differences of opinion politically, was unanimously adopted, and ordered to be sent to the American Minister at London, to Mrs. Lincoln, and to Mr. Seward.

On the evening of the same day, and at the same place, there was another great meeting of the working classes, at which similar resolutions were adopted. A resolution of a more political character was offered, and led to confusion, amidst which the meeting was adjourned.

(*From the London Star.*)

" For Abraham Lincoln one cry of universal regret will be raised
all over the civilized earth. We do not believe that even the
fiercest partisans of the Confederacy in this country, will entertain
any sentiment at such a time but one of grief and horror. To us,
Abraham Lincoln has already seemed the finest character produced
by the American war on either side of the struggle. He was great,
not merely by the force of genius—and only the word genius will
describe the power of intellect by which he guided himself
and his country through such a crisis—but by the simple, natural
strength and grandeur of his character. Talleyrand once said of
a great American statesman that without experience he ' divined '
his way through any crisis. Mr. Lincoln thus *divined his way*
through the perilous, exhausting, and unprecedented difficulties which
might well have broken the strength and blinded the prescience
of the best trained professional statesmen. He seemed to arrive
by instinct—by the instinct of a noble, unselfish, and manly nature
—at the very ends which the highest of political genius, the
longest of political experience, could have done no more than reach.
He bore himself fearlessly in danger, calmly in difficulty, modestly
in success. The world was at last beginning to know how good,
and, in the best sense, how great a man he was. It had long,
indeed, learned that he was as devoid of vanity as of fear; but it
had only just come to know what magnanimity and mercy the
hour of triumph would prove that he possessed. Reluctant
enemies were just beginning to break into eulogy over his wise and
noble clemency when the dastard hand of a vile murderer destroyed his noble and valuable life. We in England have something
to feel ashamed of when we meditate upon the greatness of the
man so ruthlessly slain. Too many Englishmen lent themselves
to the vulgar and ignoble cry which was raised against him.
English writers degraded themselves to the level of the coarsest
caricaturists when they had to tell of Abraham Lincoln. They
stooped to criticise a foreign patriot as a menial might comment on
the bearing of a hero. They sneered at his manner, as if Cromwell
was a Chesterfield; they accused him of ugliness, as if Mirabeau
was a beauty; they made coarse pleasantry of his figure, as if Peel
was a posture-master; they were facetious about his dress, as if
Cavour was a D'Orsay; they were indignant about his jokes, as if
Palmerston never jested. We do not remember any instance since
the wildest days of British fury against the Corsican " Ogre," in
which a foreign statesman was ever so dealt with in English
writings as Mr. Lincoln. And when we make the comparison we

cannot but remember that while Napoleon was our unscrupulous enemy Lincoln was our steady friend. Assailed by the coarsest attacks on this side of the ocean, tried by the sorest temptations on that, Abraham Lincoln calmly and steadfastly maintained a policy of peace with England, and never did a deed, never wrote or spoke a word which was unjust or unfriendly to the British nation. Had such a man died by the hand of disease in the hour of his triumph, the world must have mourned for his loss. That he has fallen by the coward hand of a vile assassin, exasperates and embitters the grief beyond any power of language to express."

[*From the London Daily News, April* 27.]

" In the hour of his great work done, President Lincoln has fallen. Not, indeed, in the flush of triumph, for no thought of triumph was in that honest and humble heart, nor in the intoxication of applause, for the fruits of victory were not yet gathered in his hand, was the Chief of the American people, the foremost man in the great Christian revolution of our age, struck down. But his task was, nevertheless, accomplished, and the battle of his life was won. So he passes away from the heat and the toil that still have to be endured, full of the honor that belongs to one who has nobly done his part, and carrying in his last thoughts the sense of deep, steadfast thankfulness that he now could see the assured coming of that end for which he had so long striven in faith and hope. * * * In all time to come, not among Americans only, but among all who think of manhood as more than rank, and set worth above display, the name of Abraham Lincoln will be held in reverence. Rising from among the poorest of the people, winning his slow way upward by sheer hard work, preserving in every suc-cessive stage a character unspotted and a name untainted, securing a wider respect as he became better known, never pretending to more than he was, nor being less than he professed himself, he was at length, for very singleness of heart and uprightness of conduct, because all felt that they could trust him utterly, and would desire to be guided by his firmness, courage, and sense, placed in the chair of President at the turning-point of his nation's history. A life so true, rewarded by a dignity so majestic, was defence enough against the petty shafts of malice which party spirit, violent enough to light a civil war, aimed against him. The lowly callings he had first pursued, became his titles to greater respect among those whose respect was worth having; the little external rusticities only showed more brightly, as the rough matrix the golden ore, the true dignity of his nature. Never was any one, set in such high place, and surrounded with so many motives of furious detraction, so little impeached of aught blameworthy. The bitterest enemy could find no more to lay to his charge than that his language was sometimes too homely for a supersensitive taste, or that he conveyed in a jesting phrase what they deemed more suited for a statelier style. But against these specks, what thorough nobility have we not to set? A purity of thought, word, and deed never challenged, a disinterestedness never suspected, an honesty of purpose never impugned, a gentleness and tenderness that never made a private enemy or alienated a friend—these are indeed qualities which may well make a nation mourn. But he had intellect as well as goodness. Cautiously conservative, fearing to pass the limits of established systems, seeking the needful amendments rather from growth than alteration, he proved himself in the crisis the very man best suited for his post. * * * "

The House of Lords—Remarks of Earl Russell.

House of Lords, Monday, May 1 :—My lords, I rise to ask your lordships to address her Majesty, praying that in any communication which her Majesty may make to the government of the United States expressing her abhorrence and regret at the great crime which has been committed in the murder of the President of that country, her Majesty will at the same time express the sorrow and indignation felt by this House at that atrocious deed. In this case I am sure your lordships will feel entire sympathy with her Majesty, who has instructed me already to express to the government of the United States the shock which she felt at the intelligence of the great crime which has been committed. Her Majesty has also been pleased to write a private letter to Mrs. Lincoln, expressive of sympathy with that lady in her misfortune. I think that your lordships will agree with me that in modern times there has hardly been a crime committed so abhorrent to the feelings of every civilized person as the one I am now alluding to. After the first election of Mr. Lincoln as President of the United States, he was re-elected to the same high position by the large majority of the people remaining faithful to the government of the United States, and he was in the discharge of the duties of his office, having borne his faculties meekly, at the moment when an assassin attacked him at the theatre. There are circumstances connected with this crime which, I think, aggravate its atrocity. President Lincoln was a man who, though not conspicuous before his election, had since displayed a character of so much integrity, so much sincerity and straightforwardness, and at the same time of so much kindness, that if any one was able to alleviate the pain and animosities which prevailed during the period of civil war, I believe that Abraham Lincoln was that person. It was remarked of President Lincoln that he always felt disinclined to adopt harsh measures, and I am told that the commanders of his armies often complained that when they had passed a sentence which they thought no more than just, the President was always disposed to temper the severity. Such a man this particular epoch requires. The conduct of the armies of the United States was entrusted to other hands, and on the commanders fell the responsibility of leading the armies in the field to victory. They had been successful against those they had had to contend with, and the moment had come when, undoubtedly, the responsibilities of President Lincoln were greatly increased by their success. But, though it was not for him to lead the armies, it would have been his to temper the pride of victory, to assuage the misfortunes which his adversaries had experienced, and especially to show, as he was well qualified to show, that high respect for valor on the opposite side, which had been so conspicuously displayed. It was to be hoped that by such qualities, when the conflict of arms was over, the task of conciliation might have been begun, and President Lincoln would have an authority which no one else could have had to temper that exasperation which always arises in the course of civil strife. Upon another question the United States and the Confederates will have a most difficult task to perform. I allude to the question of slavery, which some have always maintained to have been the cause of the civil war. At the beginning the House will remember that President Lincoln declared that he had no right by the constitution to interfere with slavery. At a later period he made a communication to the Commander-in-Chief of the United States forces in which he proposed that in certain States the slaves should be entirely free; but at a later period he proposed what he had a constitutional qualification to propose, that there should be an alteration in the constitution of the United States, by which compulsory labor should hereafter be forbidden. I remember that Lord Macaulay once declared that it would have been a great blessing if the penal laws against the Catholics had been abolished from the time of Sir R. Walpole, though Sir R. Walpole would have been mad to propose a measure for that purpose. So the same may be said of slavery, though I believe that the United States were justified in delaying the time when that great alteration of the United States law should take place.

But, whatever we may think on these subjects, we must all

deeply deplore that the death of President Lincoln has deprived the United States of a man, a leader on this subject, who by his temper was qualified to propose such a measure as might have made this great change acceptable to those before opposed to it, and might have preserved the peace of the great republic of America, while undergoing that entire new organization which would be necessary under such circumstances. I think we must all feel both sympathy with the United States in this great affliction, and also a hope that he who is now, according to the American constitution, entrusted with the power of the late President, may be able, both on the one subject and on the other—both in respect to mercy and leniency toward the conquered, and also with regard to the measures to be adopted for the new organization which the abolition of slavery will render requisite—to overcome all difficulties. I had some time ago, at the commencement of this contest, occasion to say that I did not believe that the great republic of America would perish in this war, and the noble lord at the head of the government had lately occasion to disclaim, on the part of the government of this country, any feeling of envy at the greatness and prosperity of the United States. The course which her Majesty's government have had to pursue during this civil war has been one of great anxiety. Difficulties have occurred to us and difficulties have also occurred to the government of the United States in maintaining the peaceful relations between the two countries; but those difficulties have always been treated with temper and moderation, both on this side and the other side of the Atlantic. I trust that that temper and moderation may continue; and I can assure this House that, as we have always been guided by the wish that the American government and the American people should settle for themselves the conflict of arms without any interference of ours, so likewise during the attempt that has to be made to restore peace and tranquillity to America we shall equally refrain from any kind of interference or intervention, though we trust that the efforts to be made for restoring peace will be successful, and that the great republic of America will always flourish and enjoy the freedom it has hitherto enjoyed. I have nothing to say with regard to the successor of Mr. Lincoln. Time must show how far he is able to conduct the difficult matters which will come under his consideration with the requisite wisdom. All I can say is, that in the presence of the great crime which has just been committed, and of the great calamity which has fallen on the American nation, the Crown, the Parliament, and the people of this country do feel the deepest interest for the government and the people of the United States; for, owing to the nature of the relations between the two nations, the misfortunes of the United States affect us more than the misfortunes of any other country on the face of the globe. The noble earl concluded by moving an humble address to her Majesty to express the sorrow and indignation of this House at the assassination of the President of the United States, and to pray her Majesty to communicate these sentiments on the part of this House to the government of the United States.

Remarks of Earl Derby.

My lords, when, upon the last occasion of our meeting, the noble earl opposite announced his intention of bringing forward the motion he has now submitted to the House, I ventured to express my hope that the government had well considered the form of the motion they were going to make, so that there might be nothing in the form which would in the slightest degree interfere with the unanimity desirable on such an occasion. It would have been more satisfactory to me if the noble earl had entered somewhat upon the consideration of the question, and had informed your lordships upon what grounds he proposed so unusual a course—though arising, I admit, out of unusual, if not unprecedented, circumstances—as that of addressing the Crown, and praying her Majesty to convey to a foreign government the sentiments of Parliament with regard to the event which has taken place. For myself, I confess that I am rather of the opinion that the more convenient and—I will not say the more usual, but—the more regular course would have been to have simply moved a resolution of this, in conjunction with the other House of Parliament, expressing those feelings which it is proposed by the motion to place in the form of an address to the Crown. But I am so extremely desirous that there should not appear to be the slightest difference of opinion at this moment, that I cannot hesitate to give my assent to the form proposed by the government, whatever doubt I may entertain that the form is the most convenient which might have been adopted. In joining in this address—that is to say, in expressing our sorrow and indignation at the atrocious crime by which the United States have been deprived of their Chief Magistrate—your lordships will only follow (though the event has been known so short a time) the universal feeling of sympathy which has been expressed from one end of this kingdom to the other. And if there be in the United States any persons who, misled by our having abstained from expressing any opinion as to the conflict now going on, or even from expressing the opinion we may have formed upon the merits of the two great contending parties—if there be any persons who believe that there is a generally unfriendly feeling in this country towards the citizens of the United States, I think they could hardly have had a more complete refutation of that opinion, conveyed in what I hope will be the unanimous declaration of Parliament, following the declarations which her Majesty has been pleased to make both publicly and privately to the American Minister, as well as to the widow of President Lincoln, and again following the voluntary and spontaneous expression of opinion which has already proceeded from almost all the great towns and communities of this country. Whatever other misfortunes may have attended this atrocious crime, I hope that at least one good effect may have resulted from it—namely, that the manner in which the news has been received in this country will satisfy the people of the United States that her Majesty's subjects, one and all, deeply condemn the crime which has been committed, and deeply sympathize with the people of the United States in their feelings of horror at the assassination of their Chief Magistrate. For the crime itself there is no palliation whatever to be offered. There may be a difference of opinion as to the merits of the two parties who are contending, the one for empire, the other for independence, in the United States—I follow the words of the noble earl opposite; but there is, there can be, no difference of opinion upon this point—that the holiest and the purest of all causes is desecrated and disgraced when an attempt is made to promote it by measures so infamous as this. If it were possible to believe that the Confederate authorities encouraged, sympathized with, or even did not express their abhorrence of this crime, I should say they had committed that which was worse than a crime —a gross blunder; because, in the face of the civilized world, a cause which required or submitted to be promoted by the crime of assassination, would lose all sympathy and kindly feeling on the part of those who might otherwise be well disposed towards it. But I am perfectly satisfied—I am as well satisfied as I can be of anything—that this detestable act of assassination is so entirely alien to the whole spirit in which the South has conducted this war—is so alien to the courageous, manly, and at the same time forbearing course which they have adopted in the struggle for everything that is dear to them, that I am convinced that, apart from the error of judgment which would be involved in sanctioning such a crime, they cannot have been guilty of so great a blunder, and cannot fail to express for it their detestation, and to feel

17

at the same time that no step could have been taken which cou'd
have inflicted so great an injury on their own cause. I will not
venture to follow the noble earl even into the slight discussion
which he has originated with regard to the internal politics of the
United States. I will not discuss the difficulty which at the present
moment is felt in the United States—the difficulty caused by
slavery. I will not express any opinion as to the question whether
the late defeats, serious as they are, and apparently·fatal to the
cause of the South, have produced, or are likely to lead to, an
early termination of the war. In whatever way the war may be
terminated, it must be the desire of every friend of humanity that
it should be terminated soon and without further and unnecessary
effusion of blood. But I join entirely with the noble earl in
lamenting the loss of a man who had conducted the affairs of a
great nation, under circumstances of great difficulty, with singular
moderation and prudence, and who, I believe, was bent upon trying to the utmost a system as conciliatory as was consistent with
the prosecution of the war in which the country was engaged.
I agree that the death of such a man, in such a manner, and at
such a time, is a subject not only for deep regret and for abhorrence
of the crime by which he was deprived of life, but that it is also a
serious misfortune in the present condition of affairs, for the State
over which he exercised authority and for the prospects of an
amicable settlement. I can only hope that, notwithstanding some
ominous expressions which have already fallen from him, the successor who has so unexpectedly been elevated to the high position
filled by Mr. Lincoln may be disposed and enabled to follow the
wise and conciliatory course which I believe, in the prospect of
success, Mr. Lincoln had decided upon adopting. I am not insensible to the danger that public exasperation arising out of this
act may force upon the government a less conciliatory and more
violent course than that which Mr. Lincoln seemed to have marked
out for himself; but I am satisfied that the adoption of such a
course can only further protract the horrors of this civil war, adding to the other motives of the South the most powerful of all
motives—the motive of despair—leading the South to fight out
this question to the bitter end; so that while the one side is exas-
perated into a desire to exterminate its opponents, they, in their
despair, will be ready to submit to extermination rather than
accept the unreasonable terms of the North. Thus in the act
itself, in the circumstances under which this crime has been committed, and in the fatal influences which it may exercise upon the
returning prospects of peace in the United States, we must find

reasons for deeply lamenting the occurrence which has taken place; and I am quite sure that, independently of all political motives, but not saying that political motives do not enter into our views, I am expressing the universal feeling of this House and of the country, when I say that we view with horror, with detestation, and with indignation, the atrocious crime by which the life of the President of the United States has been ended.

The House of Commons.—Remarks of Sir G. Grey.

In the House of Commons on the same day, Sir G. Grey said—I very much regret the unavoidable absence of my noble friend at the head of the government, in whose name the notice was given of the motion which it now devolves upon me to ask the House to agree to. I feel, however, that it is comparatively unimportant by whom the motion is proposed, because I am confident that the address to the crown which I am about to ask the House to agree to is one which will meet with the cordial and unanimous assent of all. When the news a few days ago of the assassination of the President of the United States, and the attempted assassination—for I hope that we may now confidently expect that it will not be a successful attempt—of Mr. Seward reached this country, the first impression in the mind of every one was that the intelligence could not be true. It was hoped by every one that persons could not be found capable of committing a crime so atrocious. When the truth was forced upon us, when we could no longer entertain any doubt as to the correctness of the intelligence, the feeling which succeeded was one of universal sorrow, horror, and indignation. It was felt as if some great calamity had befallen ourselves; for in the civil war, the existence and long continuance of which we have so sincerely deplored, it is well known that the government of this country, acting, as I believe, in accordance with the almost unanimous, or perhaps I may say in accordance with the unanimous feeling of this country, had maintained a strict and impartial neutrality. But it is notorious, and it could not in a great country like this be otherwise, that different opinions have been entertained by different persons with regard to the questions at issue between the Northern and Southern States of America; but still I believe that the sympathies of the majority of the people of this country have been with the North. I am desirous on this occasion of avoiding everything which may excite any difference of opinion. I may say, therefore, that in this free country different opinions have been entertained and different sympathies felt, and that in this free country the freest expression has been given, as should be the case, to those differences of opinion. I am sure that I shall raise no controversy when I say in the presence of that great crime which has sent a thrill of horror through every one who heard of it, all differences of opinion, all conflicting sympathies for a moment entirely vanished. I am anxious to say at once, and I desire to proclaim the belief with the strongest confidence, that this atrocious crime was regarded by every man of influence and power in the Southern States with the same degree of horror which it excited in every other part of the world. We may, therefore—and this is all I wish to say upon this subject—whatever our opinions with regard to the past, and whatever our sympathies may have been—we shall all cordially unite in expressing our abhorrence of that crime, and in rendering our sympathy to that nation which is now mourning the loss of its chosen and trustful chief, struck to the ground by the hand of an assassin, and that too at the most critical period of its history. While lamenting that war and the loss of life which it has inevitably occasioned, it is impossible, whatever our opinions or our sympathies may have been, to withhold our admiration from the many gallant deeds performed and acts of heroism displayed by both parties in the contest; and it is a matter for bitter reflection that the page of history, recording such gallant achievements and such heroic deeds by men who so freely shed their blood on the battle-field in a cause which each considered right, should also be stained with the record of a crime such as we are now deploring. At length a new era appeared to be dawning on the contest between the North and South. The time had come when there was every reason to hope that the war would speedily be brought to a close. Victory had crowned the efforts of the statesmen and the armies of the federals, and most of us— all I hope—had turned with a feeling of some relief and some hope for the future from the record of sanguinary conflicts to that correspondence which has but recently passed between the generals commanding the hostile armies. And when we turned to Mr. President Lincoln, I should have been prepared to express a hope, indeed an expectation—and I have reason to believe that that expectation would not have been disappointed—that in the hour of victory and in the use of victory he would have shown a wise forbearance, a generous consideration, which would have added tenfold lustre to the fame and reputation which he has acquired throughout the misfortunes of this war. Unhappily the foul deed which has taken place has deprived Mr. Lincoln of the opportunity of thus adding to his well earned fame and reputation; but let us hope, what indeed we may repeat, that the good sense and right feeling of those upon whom will devolve the most arduous and difficult duties in this conjuncture will lead them to respect the wishes and the memory of him whom we are all mourning; and will lead them to act in the same spirit and to follow the same counsels by which we have good reason to believe the conduct of Mr. Lincoln would have been marked, had he survived to complete the work that was entrusted to him. I am only speaking the general opinion when I say that nothing could give greater satisfaction to this country than by means of forbearance, it may be of temperate conciliation, to see the union of the North and South again accomplished, especially if it can be accomplished by common consent, freed from what hitherto constituted the weakness of that Union—the curse and disgrace of slavery. I wish it were possible for us to convey to the people of the United States an adequate idea of the depth and universality of the feeling which this sad event has occasioned in this country, that from the highest to the lowest there has been but one feeling entertained. Her Majesty's Minister at Washington will, in obedience to the Queen's command, convey to the government of the United States the expression of the feelings of her Majesty and of her government upon the deplorable event; and her Majesty, with that tender consideration which she has always evinced for sorrow and suffering in others, of whatever rank, has with her own hand written a letter to Mrs. Lincoln, conveying the heartfelt sympathy of a widow to a widow suffering under the calamity of having lost one suddenly cut off. From every part of this country, from every class, but one voice has been heard—one of abhorrence for the crime and of sympathy for and interest in the country which has this great loss to mourn. The British residents in the United States, as of course was to be expected, lost not an hour in expressing their sympathy with the government of the United States. The people of our North American colonies are vieing with each other in expressing the same sentiments. And it is not only among men of the same race who are connected with the people of the United States by origin, language, and blood, that these feelings prevail, but I believe that every country in Europe is giving expression to the same sentiments and is sending the message to the government of the United States. I am sure, therefore, that I am not wrong in anticipating that this House will, in the name of the people of England, of Scotland, and of Ireland, be anxious to record their expression of the same sentiment, and to have it conveyed to the government of the United States. Of this I am confident; that this House could never more fully and more adequately represent the feelings of the whole of the inhabitants of the United Kingdom than by agreeing to the address which it is now my duty to move, expressing to her Majesty our sorrow and indignation at the assassination of the President of the United States, and praying her Majesty that, in communicating her own sentiments to the government of that country upon the deplorable event, she will express at the same time, on the part of this House, their abhorrence of the crime and their sympathy with the government and people of the United States in the deep affliction into which they have been thrown.

FRANCE.

In Paris on the very day the terrible news was received M. Drouyn de Lhuys, Minister of Foreign Affairs, despatched a letter to Mr. Bigelow expressive of his sorrow, and immediately upon the return of our Minister from Brest (whither he had gone to participate in the ceremony of the opening of a new line of railway) he was waited upon by an aide-de-camp of the Emperor, who expressed to him the personal regrets of his Majesty at the severe loss to the nation and his horror of the crime. On Mr. Bigelow's return he was overwhelmed with letters of condolence from all parts of Europe. He at once received calls from M. Garnier Pages and several members of the opposition in the Corps Legislatif, as well as from a considerable number of literary men and others who have always sympathized with our cause. A large number also called at the Consulate, and, in accordance with the custom here, subscribed their names in token of condolence.

One of the most remarkable and noteworthy demonstrations was that made by the *Jeunesse d'Ecoles*—the students of the Latin quarter. Nearly a thousand of these young men formed in procession for the purpose of proceeding to the American Minister's to present to him an appropriate address.

Solemn services were also held at the American Episcopal Chapel, which were attended by a large assemblage of French and Americans.

The Princess Murat, who is an American lady, was present, as were also General Franconniere and the Prince Napoleon, M. Berryer, Jules Favre, Ernest Picard, Eugene Pelletan, Prevost Paradol, and a considerable number of literary men.

Henry Martin, the Historian, thus wrote in one of the Parisian journals :

A GREAT MARTYR OF DEMOCRACY.

Slavery, before expiring, has gathered up the remnants of its strength and rage to strike a coward blow at its conqueror.

The Satanic pride of that perverted society could not resign itself to defeat: it did not care to fall with honor, as all causes fall which are destined to rise again; it dies as it has lived, violating all laws, divine and human.

In this we have the spirit and perhaps the work of that famous secret association, "the Golden Circle," which, after preparing the great rebellion for twenty years, and spreading its accomplices throughout the West and North, around the seat of the presidency, gave the signal for this impious war on the day when the public conscience finally snatched from the slaveholders the government of the United States.

The day on which the excellent man whom they have just made a martyr was raised to power they appealed to force, to realize what treason had prepared.

They have failed. They did not succeed in overthrowing Lincoln from power by war; they have done so by assassination.

The plot appears to have been well arranged. By striking down with the President his two principal ministers, one of whom they reached, and the General-in-Chief, who was saved by an accidental occurrence, the murderers expected to disorganize the government of the republic and give fresh life to the rebellion.

Their hopes will be frustrated. These sanguinary fanatics, whose cause has fallen not so much by the material superiority as the moral power of democracy, have become incapable of understanding the effects of the free institutions which their fathers gloriously aided in establishing. A fresh illustration will be seen of what those institutions can produce.

The indignation of the people will not exhaust itself in a momentary outburst; it will concentrate and embody itself in the unanimous, persevering, invincible action of the universal will; whoever may be the agents, the instruments of the work, that work, we may rest assured, will be finished. The event will show that it did not depend upon the life of one man, or of several men.

The work will be completed after Lincoln, as if finished by him; but Lincoln will remain the austere and sacred personification of a great epoch, the most faithful expression of democracy.

This simple and upright man, prudent and strong, elevated step by step from the artisan's bench to the command of a great nation, and always without parade and without effort at the height of his position, executing without precipitation, without flourish and with invincible good sense, the most colossal acts, giving to the world this decisive example of the civil power in a republic, directing a gigantic war without free institutions being for an instant compromised or threatened by military usurpation, dying finally at the moment in which, after conquering, he was intent on pacification—and may God grant that the atrocious madmen who killed him have not killed clemency with him, and determined instead of the peace he wished, pacification by force—this man will stand out in the traditions of his country and the world as an incarnation of the people, and of modern democracy itself.

The great work of emancipation had to be sealed, therefore, with the blood of the just, even as it was inaugurated with the blood of the just. The tragic history of the abolition of slavery which opened with the gibbet of John Brown will close with the assassination of Lincoln.

And now let him rest by the side of Washington, as the second founder of the great republic. European democracy is present in spirit at his funeral, as it voted in its heart for his re-election, and applauded the victory in the midst of which he passes away. It will wish with one accord to associate itself with the monument that America will raise to him upon the capital of prostrate slavery.

In the Corps Legislatif, soon after the opening of that body, M. Rouher, Minister of State, rose and said:

An odious crime has plunged in mourning a people which is our ally and our friend. The report of this crime has produced throughout the civilized world a sentiment of indignation and of horror. Abraham Lincoln had exhibited in the sad struggle which rends his country that calm firmness and indomitable energy which belong to strong minds and are the necessary conditions of the accomplishment of great duties. In the hours of victory he exhibited generosity, moderation, and conciliation. He hastened to put an end to war and to restore peace—America to her splendor and prosperity. The first punishment which God inflicts upon crime is to render it powerless to retard the march of right. The profound emotion and the deep sympathy manifested in Europe will be received by the American people as a consolation and encouragement. The work of peace, commenced by a grand citizen, will be completed by the national will. The government of the Emperor has caused to be sent to Washington the expression of a legitimate homage to the memory of an illustrious statesman, torn from the government of the United States by an execrable assassination. By order of the Emperor, I have the honor to communicate to the Corps Legislatif the despatch sent by the Minister of Foreign Affairs to our representative at Washington. It is conceived as follows:

MINISTRY OF FOREIGN AFFAIRS,
PARIS, *April* 28, 1865.

The news of the crime of which President Lincoln has fallen a victim has caused a profound sentiment of indignation in the imperial government. His Majesty immediately charged one of his aides-de-camp to call upon the Minister of the United States to request him to transmit the expression of this sentiment to Mr. Johnson, now invested with the Presidency. I myself desired by the despatch which I addressed you, under date of yesterday, to acquaint you, without delay, of the painful emotion which we have experienced; and it becomes my duty to-day, in conformity with the views of the Emperor, to render a merited homage to the great citizen whose loss the United States now deplore.

Elevated to the Chief Magistracy of the republic by the suffrage of his country, Abraham Lincoln exhibited in the exercise of the power placed in his hands the most substantial qualities. In him firmness of character was allied with elevation of principle, and his vigorous soul never wavered before the redoubtable trials reserved for his government. At the moment when an atrocious crime removed him from the mission which he fulfilled with a religious sentiment of duty, he was convinced that the triumph of his policy was definitely assured. His recent proclamations are stamped with the sentiments of moderation with which he was inspired in resolutely proceeding to the task of reorganizing the Union and consolidating peace. The supreme satisfaction of accomplishing this work has not been accorded him; but in reviewing these last testimonies to his exalted wisdom, as well as the examples of good sense, of courage, and of patriotism which he has given, history will not hesitate to place him in the rank of citizens who have the most honored their country. By order of the Emperor, I transmit this despatch to the Minister of State, who is charged to communicate it to the Senate and the Corps Legislatif. France will unanimously associate itself with the sentiment of his Majesty.

    Receive, &c., &c.,   DROUYN DE LHUYS,
M. DE GEOFRY, Chargé d'Affaires de France à Washington.

After the reading of the despatch, which was received with unanimous marks of approbation, M. Rouher continued:

This despatch needs no commentary. The Emperor, all France, are unanimous in their sentiments of condemnation of a detestable crime, in their respect for a grand political character, now a victim of the worst criminal passions, in their ardent wishes for the re-establishment of harmony and concord in the grand and patriotic American nation.

M. Schneider, President of the Corps Legislatif, said :

GENTLEMEN—I desire to be the interpreter of your sentiments in publicly expressing the sorrow and true indignation which we have all felt at the news of the bloody death of President Lincoln. This execrable crime has revolted all that was noble in the heart of France. Nowhere has the emotion been more profound and universal than in our country. We also desire unqualifiedly to unite our sentiments with the sympathies which have been mani-fested by the government. Called to the direction of affairs in an ever memorable crisis, Abraham Lincoln showed himself equal to his difficult mission. After displaying unshaken firmness in the struggle, it seemed that he would, by the wisdom of his language and his views, soon bring about a happy and durable reconciliation among the people of the country. His last acts are the crowning ones of the life of an honest man and good citizen. Let us hope that his wishes and his sentiments will survive him and inspire the American people with pacific and generous resolutions. France has herself trembled at these bloody struggles which have afflicted humanity and civilization. She ardently desires the re-establish-ment of peace in the midst of that great nation, her ally and her friend. May our prayers be heard, and may Providence put an end to these sad trials. The Corps Legislatif will acknowledge to the government the receipt of the communication which it has just made it, and will ask that an extract of the *procès-verbal* of this session shall be officially addressed to the Minister of State.

No further remarks were made upon the communication.

In the Senate the same communication was presented, and the following remarks made by the President :—

GENTLEMEN—In receiving this communication from the Minister, I ask the Senate to permit me to express, in its name, a sentiment which, by its unanimity and its energy, will be received by every heart. The Senate has experienced a profound emotion at the re-port of the crime committed upon the illustrious chief of a friendly nation. Mr. Lincoln, placed since 1861 at the head of the Ameri-can nation, had passed through the saddest trial which a govern-ment founded upon liberty could have encountered. It was at the moment when victory offered itself to him—not as a sign of conquest, but as a time for reconciliation—when a crime, still obscure in its causes, has destroyed the existence of this citizen elected to so high a position by the choice of his fellow-countrymen. Mr. Lincoln fell when he thought he had reached the end of the evils through which his country had passed, and while nourishing the patriotic hope of soon seeing it reconstituted and flourishing. The Senate, which has always deplored this civil war, detests with stronger reason those implacable hatreds which are its fruit, and which produce a bloody policy of assassination. There is in this body but one voice to unite itself with the sentiment expressed by order of the Emperor, in the name of a policy generous and humane."

ITALY.

The Italian Chamber of Deputies was draped in black on the 27th, and continued so for the three following days, in mourning for Abraham Lincoln. The Minister of Finance moved, and the Chamber agreed, to send this address to the American Congress expressing the grief of the country and the House at Mr. Lincoln's assassination.

To the President of the Congress of Representatives of the United States of America:

Hon. Sir:—The intelligence of the assassination of President Lincoln has moved and profoundly grieved the deputies of the Italian Parliament. From all the political factions of which this Chamber is composed one unanimous cry has arisen denouncing the detestable crime that has been committed, and conveying the expression of deep regret and sympathy for the illustrious victim and the free people whose worthy ruler he was. This Chamber has unanimously resolved to cover its flag with crape for the space of three days, in token of mourning, and has charged me to notify you in a special message its grief, which is also that of Italy, and of all friends of liberty and civilization. The news of the attempt made to assassinate Mr. Seward has inspired the Chamber with like sentiments. In readily, though sadly, fulfilling the mission with which I have been charged, I beg you will accept, Hon. Sir, the assurance of my sympathy and consideration.   CASSINIS,
President of the Chamber of Deputies.

BELGIUM.

The King of the Belgians charged one of his aides-de-camp to visit Mr. Sanford, and express the feelings his Majesty experienced at the attacks made upon the President and Minister for Foreign Affairs of the United States. The Count of Flanders also sent one of his orderly officers to the American Minister for the same purpose. The Minister for Foreign Affairs and the other members of the Cabinet have also lost no time in paying their respects to Mr. Sanford, and instructions have been forwarded to the Belgian Legation at Washington to express to the American Government the sentiments of regret and reprobation excited by such disgraceful acts. At Saturday's sitting of the Chamber of Deputies M. le Hardy de Beaulieu stated, in the most sympathizing terms, the emotion produced in Belgium by the news of the tragic event, and recalled all the claims of President Lincoln to general consideration. M. de Haerne spoke in the same sense with much feeling. The Minister for Foreign Affairs said that the government fully agreed with the sentiments which had just been expressed, and that it had already conveyed its opinion to the government of the United States and their representatives at Brussels. He added his sincerest good wishes for the recovery of Mr. Seward, whose life he considered highly important for the definitive pacification of the country so long desolated by the war, and whose prosperity was earnestly desired by all the friends of liberty.

PRUSSIA.

The death of Mr. Lincoln was received with great concern in this country, and Herr Loewe, himself an old American, and now one of the most active and influential members of the Lower House, rose at the first sitting to devote a few solemn and admiring words to the memory of the deceased republican statesman:

"Gentlemen," he said, "permit me to request your attention to a subject which, though not coming within the limits of our immediate task, is yet one of the gravest interest to us, and, indeed, the world at large. Many of the honorable members have felt it a duty, on the occasion of the untimely death of Mr. Lincoln, to give expression to their sincere sympathy with the nation who now mourn his loss. Abraham Lincoln has been taken away in the hour of triumph. I trust that the task he so faithfully conducted in the service of a great and glorious people will be completed by his successor; and while I cannot but congratulate myself on the earnest and most effective support he received from so many of our countrymen on the other side of the ocean, I wish to assure the German Americans, as well as the Americans generally, that we glory in their glories and sorrow in their sorrows. It was the banner of freedom he carried aloft; and if, while transacting vic-

toriously the most important business of one of the greatest nations
of the earth, he remained a simple, modest, and unpretending man,
nevertheless he will be all the dearer to the German heart for performing his duty without pomp or ceremony, and relying on that
dignity of his inner self alone, which is far above rank, orders, and
titles.   I have drawn up an address expressive of these sentiments,
which will be presented to Mr. Judd, the American Minister at
this capital.   As it might be contrary to rules to move for the
House entering into communication with a foreign diplomatist, I
invite such of you as are disposed to share in our condolences to
send in your signatures privately, and pay your respect to the
deceased, who was a faithful servant no less of his commonwealth
than of civilization, of freedom and humanity."

At the close of the speech the House rose in token of respectful
assent.   The conservatives alone and a few ultramontanes kept
their seats: but these, too, declared, through the mouths of some
of their leaders, that they shared the horror and indignation of
the other parties, and that they would have supported the preceding speaker in giving utterance to a feeling which was a common
one all over the civilized world, had not his condolence been mixed
up with politics.

The address to Mr. Judd, which was signed by a vast majority
of members, runs to the following effect:—

"Sir—We, the undersigned, members of the Prussian House of
Deputies, pray your acceptance of our heartfelt condolence on the
heavy loss the government and people of the United States have
suffered by the death of the late President Lincoln.   We turn in
horror from the crime to which he has fallen a victim, and we are
the more deeply moved by this public affliction, inasmuch as it has
occurred at a moment when we were rejoicing at the triumph of
the United States, and as it was accompanied by an attempt upon
the life of Mr. Seward, the faithful associate of his labors, who,
with so much wisdom and resolve, aided Mr. Lincoln in the ful-
filment of his arduous task.   By the simultaneous death of these
great and good men, the people of the United States were to be
deprived of the fruits of their protracted struggle and patriotic
devotion at the very moment when the triumph of right and law
promised to bring back the blessings of a long desired peace.

"Sir, you have been staying among us a living witness of the
deep and earnest sympathy which the people of Germany, during
a long and serious war, have entertained for the United States.
You are aware that Germany has looked with feelings of pride

and joy at the thousands of her sons so resolutely aiding with law and right in this your war. You have seen our joy on receiving good tidings from the United States, and know the confidence with which we ever looked forward to the victory of your cause, and the reconstruction of the Union in all its ancient might and splendor. The grand work of reconstruction will, we trust, be not delayed by this terrible crime. The blood of the great and wise chieftain will only serve to cement the Union for which he died. To us this is guaranteed by the respect of the law and the love of liberty which the people of the United States evinced in the very midst of this tremendous contest.

" 'We request your good offices for giving expression to our condolences and our sympathies with the people and government of the United States, and communicating this address to the Cabinet you represent.

" Receive, &c.,

"THE MEMBERS OF THE HOUSE OF DEPUTIES.

"BERLIN, April 28, 1865."

The address was immediately signed by deputies of the House.

A solemn service, in the German and English languages, was performed on May 2, in the Dorothea church, Berlin, in memory of President Lincoln. Numerous deputations were present. Herr Von Bismark attended, and the King was represented by his aides-de-camp. The church was crowded.

IX.

POEMS.

IX.

POEMS.

ABRAHAM LINCOLN—AN HORATIAN ODE.

BY RICHARD HENRY STODDARD.

Not as when some great Captain falls
In battle, where his Country calls,
    Beyond the struggling lines
    That push his dread designs

To doom, by some stray ball struck dead:
Or, in the last charge, at the head
    Of his determined men,
    Who *must* be victors then!

Nor as when sink the civic Great,
The safer pillars of the State,
    Whose calm, mature, wise words
    Suppress the need of swords!—

With no such tears as e'er were shed
Above the noblest of our Dead
    Do we to-day deplore
    The Man that is no more!

Our sorrow hath a wider scope,
Too strange for fear, too vast for hope,—
    A Wonder, blind and dumb,
    That waits—what is to come!

Not more astounded had we been
If Madness, that dark night, unseen,
    Had in our chambers crept,
    And murdered while we slept!

We woke to find a mourning Earth—
Our Lares shivered on the hearth,—
    The roof-tree fallen,—all
    That could affright, appall!

18

Such thunderbolts, in other lands,
Have smitten the rod from royal hands,
    But spared, with us, till now,
    Each laurelled Cesar's brow!

No Cesar he, whom we lament,
A Man without a precedent,
    Sent, it would seem, to do
    His work—and perish too!

Not by the weary cares of State,
The endless tasks, which will not wait,
    Which, often done in vain,
    Must yet be done again:

Not in the dark, wild tide of War,
Which rose so high, and rolled so far,
    Sweeping from sea to sea
    In awful anarchy :—

Four fateful years of mortal strife,
Which slowly drained the Nation's life,
    (Yet, for each drop that ran
    There sprang an armed man!)

Not then;—but when by measures meet,--
By victory, and by defeat—
    By courage, patience, skill,
    The People's fixed " *We will!* "

Had pierced, had crushed Rebellion dead,—
Without a Hand, without a Head;—
    At last, when all was well,
    He fell—O, *how* he fell!

The time,—the place,—the stealing Shape,—
The coward shot,—the swift escape,—
    The wife—the widow's scream,—
    It is a hideous Dream!

A Dream?—what means this pageant, then?
These multitudes of solemn men,
    Who speak not when they meet,
    But throng the silent street?

The flags half-mast, that late so high
Flaunted at each new victory?
 (The stars no brightness shed,
 But bloody looks the red!)

The black festoons that stretch for miles,
And turn the streets to funeral aisles?
 (No house too poor to show
 The Nation's badge of woe!)

The cannon's sudden, sullen boom,—
The bells that toll of death and doom,—
 The rolling of the drums,—
 The dreadful Car that comes?

Cursed be the hand that fired the shot!
The frenzied brain that hatched the plot:
 Thy Country's Father slain
 By thee, thou worse than Cain!

Tyrants have fallen by such as thou,
And Good hath followed—May it now!
 (God lets bad instruments
 Produce the best events.)

But he, the Man we mourn to-day,
No tyrant was; so mild a sway
 In one such weight who bore
 Was never known before!

Cool should he be, of balanced powers,
The Ruler of a Race like ours,
 Impatient, headstrong, wild,—
 The Man to guide the Child!

And this *he* was, who most unfit
(So hard the sense of God to hit!)
 Did seem to fill his Place.
 With such a homely face,—

Such rustic manners—speech uncouth—
(That somehow blundered out the Truth!)
 Untried, untrained to bear,
 The more than kingly Care?

Ay!　And his genius put to scorn
The proudest in the purple born,
　　Whose wisdom never grew
　　To what, untaught, he knew—

The People, of whom he was one.
No gentleman like Washington,—
　　(Whose bones, methinks, make room,
　　To have him in their tomb!)

A laboring man, with horny hands,
Who swung the axe, who tilled his lands,
　　Who shrank from nothing new,
　　But did as poor men do!

One of the People!　Born to be
Their curious Epitome;
　　To share, yet rise above
　　Their shifting hate and love.

Common his mind (it seemed so then),
His thoughts the thoughts of other men;
　　Plain were his words, and poor—
　　But now they will endure!

No hasty fool, of stubborn will,
But prudent, cautious, pliant, still;
　　Who, since his work was good,
　　Would do it, as he could.

Doubting, was not ashamed to doubt,
And, lacking prescience, went without;
　　Often appeared to halt,
　　And was, of course, at fault:

Heard all opinions, nothing loth,
And loving both sides, angered both:
　　Was—*not* like Justice, blind,
　　But watchful, clement, kind.

No hero, this, of Roman mould;
Nor like our stately sires of old;
　　Perhaps he was not Great—
　　But he preserved the State!

O honest face, which all men knew!
O tender heart, but known to few!
   O Wonder of the Age,
   Cut off by tragic Rage!

Peace! Let the long procession come,
For hark!—the mournful, muffled drum—
   The trumpet's wail afar,—
   And see! the awful Car!

Peace! Let the sad procession go,
While cannon boom, and bells toll slow;
   And go, thou sacred Car,
   Bearing our Woe afar!

Go, darkly borne, from State to State,
Whose loyal, sorrowing Cities wait
   To honor all they can
   The dust of that Good Man!

Go, grandly borne, with such a train
As greatest kings might die to gain:
   The Just, the Wise, the Brave
   Attend thee to the grave!

And you, the soldiers of our wars,
Bronzed veterans, grim with noble scars,
   Salute him once again,
   Your late Commander—slain!

Yes, let your tears, indignant, fall,
But leave your muskets on the wall;
   Your Country needs you now
   Beside the forge, the plough!

(When Justice shall unsheathe her brand—
If Mercy may not stay her hand,
   Nor would we have it so—
   She must direct the blow!)

And you, amid the Master-Race
Who seem so strangely out of place,
   Know ye who cometh? He
   Who hath declared ye Free!

Bow while the Body passes—Nay,
Fall on your knees, and weep, and pray.
   Weep, weep—I would ye might—
   Your poor, black faces white!

And, Children, you must come in bands,
With garlands in your little hands,
   Of blue, and white, and red,
   To strew before the Dead!

So sweetly, sadly, sternly goes
The Fallen to his last repose;
   Beneath no mighty dome,
   But in his modest Home;

The churchyard where his children rest,
The quiet spot that suits him best;
   There shall his grave be made,
   And there his bones be laid!

And there his countrymen shall come,
With memory proud, with pity dumb,
   And strangers far and near,
   For many and many a year!

For many a year, and many an Age,
While History on her ample page
   The virtues shall enroll
   Of that Paternal Soul!

ABRAHAM LINCOLN.

FOULLY ASSASSINATED, APRIL 14, 1865.

(From the London Punch.)

You lay a wreath on murdered Lincoln's bier,
　You, who with mocking pencil wont to trace,
Broad for the self-complacent British sneer,
　His length of shambling limb, his furrowed face,

His gaunt, gnarled hands, his unkempt, bristling hair,
　His garb uncouth, his bearing ill at ease,
His lack of all we prize as debonair,
　Of power or will to shine, of art to please.

You, whose smart pen backed up the pencil's laugh,
　Judging each step, as though the way were plain;
Reckless, so it could point its paragraph,
　Of chief's perplexity, or people's pain.

Beside this corpse, that bears for winding-sheet
　The stars and stripes he lived to rear anew,
Between the mourners at his head and feet,
　Say, scurrile jester, is there room for you?

Yes, he had lived to shame me from my sneer,
　To lame my pencil, and confute my pen—
To make me own this hind of princes peer,
　This rail-splitter a true-born king of men.

My shallow judgment I had learnt to rue,
　Noting how to occasion's height he rose,
How his quaint wit made home-truth seem more true,
　How, iron-like, his temper grew by blows.

How humble, yet how hopeful he could be:
　How in good fortune and in ill the same:
Nor bitter in success, nor boastful he,
　Thirsty for gold, nor feverish for fame.

He went about his work—such work as few
　Ever had laid on head and heart and hand—
As one who knows, where there's a task to do,
　Man's honest will must Heaven's good grace command;

Who trusts the strength will with the burden grow,
   That God makes instruments to work his will,
If but that will we can arrive to know,
   Nor temper with the weights of good and ill.

So he went forth to battle, on the side
   That he felt clear was Liberty's and Right's,
As in his peasant boyhood he had plied
   His warfare with rude Nature's thwarting mights—

The uncleared forest, the unbroken soil,
   The iron bark that turns the lumberer's axe,
The rapid, that o'erbears the boatman's toil,
   The prairie, hiding the mazed wanderer's tracks,

The ambushed Indian, and the prowling bear—
   Such were the needs that helped his youth to train:
Rough culture—but such trees large fruit may bear,
   If but their stocks be of right girth and grain.

So he grew up, a destined work to do,
   And lived to do it: four long-suffering years,
Ill-fate, ill-feeling, ill-report, lived through,
   And then he heard the hisses changed to cheers,

The taunts to tribute, the abuse to praise,
   And took both with the same unwavering mood:
Till, as he came on light, from darkling days,
   And seemed to touch the goal from where he stood,

A felon had, between the goal and him,
   Reached from behind his back, a trigger prest—
And those perplexed and patient eyes were dim,
   Those gaunt, long-laboring limbs were laid to rest!

The words of mercy were upon his lips,
   Forgiveness in his heart and on his pen,
When this vile murderer brought swift eclipse
   To thoughts of peace on earth, good-will to men.

The Old World and the New, from sea to sea,
   Utter one voice of sympathy and shame!
Sore heart, so stopped when it at last beat high;
   Sad life, cut short just as its triumph came.

X.

THE ASSASSIN AND HIS END.

X.

THE ASSASSIN AND HIS FATE.

BOOTH, after escaping from the theatre, galloped away so rapidly, yet quietly, that his accomplice, Harold, stationed there did not at first notice it, and was consequently unable to overtake him for a considerable time. Their flight had, however, been well planned; their confederates, who had regularly called out to each other the time in front of the theatre, had, as the blow was struck, cut the telegraph wires. Booth and Harold's destination was Surrattville, the tavern of Mrs. Surratt, one of the conspirators. Here carbines and whiskey were in readiness for them, she herself going that very day for the second time to prevent mistake or delay. Although Booth, in his leap to the stage, had broken the smaller bone of his leg, this did not prevent his flight, and galloping past the Patent Office, over Capital Hill, and crossing the Eastern branch at Uniontown, Booth gave his name to the officer in charge, who having no tidings of the crime, and seeing nothing suspicious, allowed him and Harold to proceed, but detained a third.

Having passed this first obstacle, Booth pushed on, and at midnight the two reached Surrattville. Harold immediately roused Lloyd, the landlord, and got from him the carbines, whiskey, and field-glass which Mrs. Surratt had directed him to give them. They took but one carbine, Harold saying that Booth had broken his leg and could not carry it. The other carbine remained in the hall and was found by the officers.

Just as they were about leaving, Booth said, "I will tell you some news, if you want to hear it." Lloyd says that he replied: "I am not particular; use your own choice about telling news." "Well," said Booth, "I am pretty certain that we have assassinated the President and Secretary Seward."

Thus proclaiming his crime, Booth and his comrade dashed

away across Prince George's county. His wound was now painful, and although he seems to have wished to get the surgical aid of Dr. Stewart, he stopped on Saturday morning, before sunrise, at the house of Dr. Samuel A. Mudd, three miles from Bryantown. Mudd was brought to trial with Mrs. Surratt, Harold, Payne, and others, and is shown to have known Booth, and had private business with him a short time before. At all events he now cut off Booth's riding boot and hastily set his leg, extemporizing splints, and ordering a hired man to make him a pair of crutches. Dr. Mudd knew that there was need of haste, and used all expedition. He sheltered them all day, but towards evening they slipped their horses from the stable and rode away in the direction of Allen's Fresh.

Below Bryantown run certain deep and slimy swamps; along the belt of these Booth and Harold picked up a negro named Swan, who volunteered to show them the road for two dollars; they gave him five more to show them the route to Allen's Fresh, but really wished, as their actions intimated, to gain the house of one Sam. Coxe, a notorious rebel, and probably well advised of the plot. They reached the house at midnight. It is a fine dwelling, one of the best in Maryland. And after hallooing for some time, Coxe came down to the door himself. As soon as he opened it and beheld who the strangers were, he instantly blew out a candle he held in his hand, and without a word pulled them into the house, the negro remaining in the yard. The confederates remained in Coxe's house till 4 A. M., during which time the negro saw them drink and eat heartily; but when they appeared they spoke in a loud tone, so that Swan could hear them, against the hospitality of Coxe. All this was meant to influence the negro; but their motives were as apparent as their words. He conducted them three miles further on, when they told him that now they knew the way, and giving him five dollars more—making twelve in all—told him to go back.

But when the negro, in the dusk of the morning, looked after them as he receded, he saw that both horses' heads were turned once more toward Coxe's, and it was this man, doubtless, who harbored the fugitives from Sunday to Thursday, aided, possibly, by such neighbors as the Wilsons and Adamses.

At the point where Booth crossed the Potomac the shores are very shallow, and one must wade out some distance to where a boat will float. A white man came up here with a canoe on Friday, and tied it by a stone anchor. Between seven and eight o'clock it disappeared, and in the afternoon some men at work on Methxy creek, in Virginia, saw Booth and Harold land, tie the boat's rope to a stone, and fling it ashore, and strike at once across a ploughed field for King George Court House. They thence reached the Rappahannock at Port Conway, and crossing, were aided on their route by a party of rebel cavalrymen on their way to their homes. By their help they reached the house of one Garrett, near Bowling Green, the court-house town of Caroline County, a small scattered place.

Meanwhile the authorities at Washington had been scouring the country in vain, till the regular detectives of Baker's force were set at work. A negro was soon found who declared that he had seen Booth and another man cross the Potomac in a fishing boat. The point of crossing led Colonel Baker to conclude that he would attempt to pass Port Royal as the only feasible point. A party of twenty-five cavalry, under Lieutenant Dougherty, was accordingly despatched, the expedition being under the command of Lieut.-Col. E. J. Conger, of Ohio. At Port Royal they got the first certain traces of the assassins; pushing on they surprised, in bed, at Bowling Green, Jett the rebel captain, on whose horse Booth had ridden. He soon revealed all he knew. The party then taking him as a guide retraced their steps, and by two o'clock on the morning of the 25th of April they halted at Garrett's gate. Rousing up the proprietor, they demanded where the men were. Garrett at first declared that they had gone, and the women of the family, whose rooms were searched, corroborated this statement. But Garrett's son acknowledged that the fugitives were in the barn. This was at once surrounded; but instead of bursting in at different points, they began to parley. Lieutenant Baker hailed:

"To the persons in this barn. I have a proposal to make; we are about to send into you the son of the man in whose custody you are found. Either surrender to him your arms and then give yourselves up, or we'll set fire to the place. We mean to take you both, or to have a bonfire and a shooting match."

No answer came to this of any kind. The lad, John M.

Garrett, who was in deadly fear, was here pushed through the door by a sudden opening of it, and immediately Lieutenant Baker locked the door on the outside. The boy was heard to state his appeal in an under tone. Booth replied: "Damn you. Get out of here. You have betrayed me," and apparently attempted to kill the lad, who escaped in terror. Baker then said:

"You must surrender inside there. Give up your arms and appear. There is no chance for escape. We give you five minutes to make up your mind."

"Who are you, and what do you want with us?"

Baker again urged: "We want you to deliver up your arms and become our prisoners."

"But who are you?" hallooed the same voice.

Baker.—"That makes no difference. We know who you are, and we want you. We have here fifty men, armed with carbines and pistols. You cannot escape."

There was a long pause, and then Booth said: "Captain, this is a hard case, I swear. Perhaps I am being taken by my own friends." No reply by the detective.

Booth.—"Well, give us a little time to consider."

Baker.—"Very well. Take time."

Here ensued a long and eventful pause. What thronging memories it brought to Booth, we can only guess. In this little interval he made the resolve to die. But he was cool and steady to the end. Baker, after a lapse, hailed for the last time.

"Well, we have waited long enough; surrender your arms and come out, or we'll fire the barn."

Booth answered thus: "I am but a cripple, a one-legged man. Withdraw your forces one hundred yards from the door, and I will come. Give me a chance for my life, captain. I will never be taken alive."

Baker.—"We did not come here to fight, but to capture you. I say again, appear, or the barn shall be fired."

Then with a long breath, which could be heard outside, Booth cried in sudden calmness, still invisible, as were to him his enemies:—

"Well, then, my brave boys, prepare a stretcher for me."

There was a pause repeated, broken by low discussions within, between Booth and his associate, the former saying, as if in answer to some remonstrance or appeal, "Get away from me. You are a damned coward, and mean to leave me in my distress; but go, go. I don't want you to stay. I won't have you stay." Then he shouted aloud :—

"There's a man inside who wants to surrender."

Baker.—"Let him come, if he will bring his arms."

Here Harold, rattling at the door, said: "Let me out; open the door ; I want to surrender."

Baker.—"Hand out your arms, then."

Harold.—"I have not got any."

Baker.—"You are the man who carried the carbine yester-day; bring it out."

Harold.—"I haven't got any."

This was said in a whining tone. Booth cried aloud at this hesitation : "He hasn't got any arms; they are mine, and I have kept them."

Baker.—"Well, he carried the carbine, and must bring it out."

Booth.—"On the word and honor of a gentleman, he has no arms with him. They are mine, and I have got them."

At this time Harold was quite up to the door, within whisper-ing distance of Baker. The latter told him to put out his hands to be handcuffed, at the same time drawing open the door a little distance. Harold thrust forth his hands, when Baker seizing him jerked him into the night, and straightway delivered him over to a deputation of cavalrymen. The fellow began to talk of his innocence and pleaded so noisily that Conger threatened to gag him unless he ceased. Then Booth made his last appeal in the same clear, unbroken voice :—

"Captain, give me a chance. Draw off your men and I will fight them singly. I could have killed you six times to-night, but I believe you to be a brave man, and would not murder you. Give a lame man a show."

Ere he ceased speaking, Colonel Conger slipping around to the rear, drew some loose straws through a crack, and lit a match upon them. They were dry and blazed up in an instant. Booth was now at bay. Unable from the light to detect any one of those outside, he at last, carbine in poise, pushed to the door, evidently resolved to sell his life dearly, but before he reached it, Boston Corbet, a sergeant, eyeing him through a crack, fired.   The ball entered Booth's head, and he fell. Conger and two sergeants then entered, and carrying him out of the flames laid him on the grass.   He appeared to be insensible, but in a few minutes partially revived, and made efforts to speak.   By placing his ear close to Booth's mouth, Colonel Conger heard him say, "Tell my mother I die for my country."

He was then carried to the porch of Garrett's house.   Colonel Conger sent to Port Royal for a physician, who, on his arrival, found Booth dying.   Before the moment of final dissolution he repeated, "Tell mother I died for my country.   I did what I thought was for the best."

When an effort was made to revive him by bathing his face and hands in cold water, he uttered the words "Useless—useless." He was shot at about fifteen minutes past three A. M., and died a little after seven A. M., on Wednesday.

When it was ascertained that he was dead, the body was placed upon a cart—the only conveyance that could be procured —and brought to Belle Plain, where it was placed upon the steamer, and conveyed to the navy yard at Washington.   After it was deposited there it was identified by Dr. May, who had on one occasion cut a tumor from Booth's neck, and recognised the scar thus made.   It was also identified by some thirty others, who were familiar with Booth during his lifetime, as well as by his initials on his arm.   The body was somewhat bruised on the back and shoulders by the ride in the cart from Garrett's farm to Belle Plain, but the features were intact, and perfectly recognisable.

After the identification, by order of the War Department, the body was privately buried, in the clothing which was upon it at the time Booth was shot.

Thus closed the career of Booth, who is to be regarded either as one of that silly weak-minded class in the Border States, who have outheroded Herod in their attempts to gain the good opinions of the South Carolinians, or perhaps more likely as a mere cut-throat, lured by a bribe to commit treason in its most concentrated shape, the assassination of the head of the government, the base-born son of a mad actor, the fitting tool for the last crime of Slavery.